# NORTHMAN PART 1

THE EARLS OF MERCIA
BOOK THREE

MJ PORTER

MJ PUBLISHING

Cover design by MJ Porter
Cover image by
36359112
© Mr1805
Dreamstime.com

ISBN:9781914332029 (ebook)
ISBN:9781500579937 (paperback)

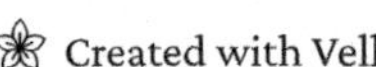

*For my cousin Sam, and his beautiful wife, Heather, on their wedding day*
*31st July 2014*

*All my love for a happy and bright future together*

# CONTENTS

# THE STORY SO FAR...

Leofwine is the ealdorman of the Hwicce in eleventh century England.

Wounded in an attack led by king Swein of Denmark in Shetland a decade ago, Leofwine has no vision in his left eye, and uses a hound to guide his steps. Leofwine's wife, a prominent member of the Hwiccan nobility, gives legitimacy to his governance, and he's the father of four sons and a daughter.

King Æthelred, initially sceptical of Leofwine's abilities, has come to rely on his ealdorman, and took his advice in waging war on the kingdom of Strathclyde in AD1000 as a step to preventing further Viking Raider attacks on England.

The offensive was a success. But the king returned to England and was plunged into deep grief by the death of his wife, more Viking Raider attacks, the treasonous actions of Ealdorman Pallig, king Swein's brother-in-law, and then the death of his long domineering mother, Lady Elfrida.

Leofwine has been promoted to the ealdordom of the whole of Mercia, having saved the king's mother and his children from a deadly attack by Thorkell the Tall and Erik, allies of king Swein. And the king has remarried, to Emma of Normandy, a much younger woman than the king, the result of an alliance with Normandy to prevent them assisting the Viking Raiders in attacking England.

Following yet another attack on England by king Swein of Denmark in AD1005, which Leofwine repelled, only for Swein to reappear, king Æthelred has decided to punish Leofwine by restricting his area of governance back to only the Hwicce, while Eadric, an upstart from Northern Mercia gains favour with the king.

Although Leofwine has now beaten Swein in battle once more, and driven him from England in the midst of winter storms, that information has yet to reach the king, and Northman Part 1 begins as news of Leofwine's disfavour with the king becomes a reality.

# 1

# MIDWINTER AD1006, NORTHMAN

He pulled his cloak tighter around his shaking body, to ward off the chill air and streaming rain that was hitting him directly in the face and pooling down his frozen cheekbones. His eyes were steely and fixed in place, the only thought in his mind that he must reach his father as soon as possible.

His mother had come to him and told him that they were to leave the house in Lichfield with all haste and that he'd need to assist her in getting his brothers and sister ready for the journey. He hadn't questioned her words, completely out of character for him, but then, he'd never heard such seriousness in his mother's voice. It was the first time in his ten years that he'd heard fear in her shaky voice.

He wondered if he'd have leapt to his duties quite as promptly if he'd not overheard the archbishop's message delivered by one of his household troops. He shrugged the thought aside. It was irrelevant. He had heard the message, and he knew of his father's, if not disgrace, then dressing down. Rage burned within him, bright and pure. His father was a good man. The best. Even he knew that. He was respected and feared in equal measure. He was fair and honest, always taking the time to discuss issues with both sides of the party. Men vied to have his support at the shire courts, and quaked in fear when he refused to give it.

To know what the king had done to his father filled his heart with hatred. He knew he shouldn't think so, but while the thoughts were his own, they could bubble happily through his mind, in time to the pounding of his horse's hooves on the hard frozen ground they traversed.

Beside him, Leofric sat miserable atop his horse. He was a little more forthcoming with his anger, his slender shoulders rigid where they held the reins of his horse and every so often, he muttered something foul that he'd learnt from a member of his father's household troop. Northman wanted to chastise him, but as he agreed with his every word, he was letting him alone. Time would come soon enough when they'd be forced to guard against everything they thought, let alone said. This time alone, in the sheeting rain was theirs and theirs alone.

For now, all he wanted was to see his father, and the same determination had coloured his mother's every move that day. Brisk and to the point, she'd ruthlessly rushed through their home packing, scrupulously only what was theirs to take, her face white and set with suppressed anger.

And then there'd been old Wulfstan. His hair all but white, he'd trembled at the news, as he had when Eadric had made his unexpected visit earlier in the year demanding to foster Northman. That time his father had miraculously appeared and headed the situation off. This time, he'd not, despite Wulfstan's longing glances at the doorway that Northman had watched with sadness. Northman had felt pity for the man, as close to his grandfather as he'd ever had, and he'd gone to him and helped him pack his possessions, mindful to keep him out of the way of his mother's bustling and efficient servants. His slow movements would have occasioned much muttering and frustration, for all that they'd not have meant it. No one in the household did not respect the ageing man. No one.

With the help of Leofric, they'd taken the old man outside, almost speechless with shock, and they'd saddled his just as old but sturdier horse, and wrapping him in two thick wolf pelts and cloaks, had assisted him into the saddle. Only then had Northman run back inside what had once been his home, and gathered his small collections of possessions and stuffed them into a handy sack that he wore strapped to his back. An old and much loved wooden sword, a board and wooden pieces and most importantly, a tiny shield Wulfstan had gifted to him when he could barely walk.

He now purposefully rode beside Wulfstan, and while the old man didn't speak, his more sociable horse was clearly pleased to have the company. Between the mutterings of Leofric, and the silence from Wulfstan, Northman sat hunched and miserable, but braver than he'd ever felt before. His mother had, by her acceptance of his actions, made him responsible for his brother and his father's closest confidant on the way back to Deerhurst. It filled him with pride.

Irritably he wiped the bitter tears that fled down his face. His responsibility came as a bitter tonic when it was thrust upon him at such a time of crisis. Beside him, Wulfstan glanced at him and coughed drily,

"Come, lad, no need for that. Your father will be hale no matter what the king does to him. He's a wise man, more than aware of the king's sometimes contrary nature."

Northman glanced at the steadiness in the man's voice in shock. The state of him earlier, he'd not expected such stoicism.

"But, none of it makes sense."

"Nothing about court politics will make sense to a ten-year-old." Wulfstan chuckled, not unkindly. He wiped angrily at the rain that drizzled into his face. "The king has his favourites, and he has his men who he can rely on to do what needs to be done. Sadly, on occasion, he confuses the two. He'll come to his senses soon enough, or he won't, and your father will recover his position anyway. In the eyes of all who know him, he loses nothing. If anything, the king loses more because he shows how little regard he has for those who are his genuine, loyal followers. The respect most men and women hold your father in should be obvious to you. The hasty actions of the king won't devalue him in anyone's eyes. And certainly, shouldn't in yours."

Northman looked away to consider the words and realised with a start that Wulfstan too was according to him more respect than before. He was speaking to him as if he was a man grown.

"Thank you for your words," Northman uttered, incredulity colouring his voice, "I'll think about them further."

"I know you will, lad, and that's why I've spoken them to you. And you have my deepest thanks for your assistance earlier. You'll be as wise and just as your father with a few more years under your belt."

Northman felt his cheek flush with embarrassment at the compliment from the man who he'd always held in high regard.

"And just remember who taught you everything you know," Leofric interjected into the conversation, his voice boyishly high with delight at undermining Wulfstan's words of endorsement. Northman cast him a barely veiled look of annoyance, but was greeted with an enormous cheeky grin on Leofric's face, and he heard Wulfstan chuckle. Huffing quietly to himself, he turned back to his thoughts. Younger brothers were well and good, most of the time.

At his horse's feet, his hound ran swiftly beside him, and he peered into the slowly descending gloom. Mid-winter; not a time to be on the road. He was looking frantically for the abbey where they'd find shelter for the night, but he feared they wouldn't reach it before full dark fell. With a quiet word to Leofric to stay beside Wulfstan, he rode to his mother's side.

Her face was white and pinched; blue tinged with cold, and a shot of fear pierced Northman's heart. She'd not long since had his baby brother, and this rushed journey was the last thing she needed in the black of winter. A smile touched her face as she saw her oldest son.

"Mother, are we far from the abbey? Only it's growing dark. Should we light brands?"

She peered into the gloom as she considered his question.

"It shouldn't be far now, but perhaps you should check with Lyfing. He'll know better where we are."

With a tight smile for his mother and a poke of his tongue at his younger sister who sat beside her and had been doing the same to him throughout their conversation, he turned his horse and cantered back towards the front of their tightly formed line. Sisters, or at least his only sister, never seemed to see the severity in any situation. She even appeared to be enjoying this furtive canter through the winter landscape.

The majority of his father's men had travelled with him first to the Witan in Shropshire, and then to do battle with Swein, but enough remained that they were adequately protected as they cantered through the cold day. In total ten men rode with the small party of children and servants and the veritable herd of hounds who, only by the intervention of God, managed to avoid the horse's hooves.

Lyfing was taking his duties seriously, and when Northman called to the man, he pulled his horse up short and waited for his Lord's oldest son to catch him.

"What is it Northman?" he queried, "Does your mother have some new command for me?"

"No, just my question Lyfing. Should we light brands or are we nearly at the Abbey."

Lyfing, as Northman had done moments before, peered into the gloom and then gave a cry of delight.

"Over there my young Lord. I can see lights, as I was expecting. Now come, I need a warm fire and some food in my belly."

Lyfing, calling attention to the faintly glowing lights of welcome, and the occasional waft of smoky air, directed their party to the abbey.

Northman felt himself relax a little at the news. Not home yet, but more home than not. He'd see his father, soon, and then he could assess the value of Wulfstan's words for himself.

They found a warm welcome within the abbey where concerned monks assisted his mother and sister and old Wulfstan, settling them around the huge roaring fire and feeding them a warming soup. There had been exclamations of surprise when they'd first arrived but in no time at all, everyone had been settled, the horses stabled out of the rain, and a strange calmness had settled around the great hall. Northman, counting himself amongst the men, had slept within the hall, wrapped in his cloak, exhaustion and outrage warring with each other only briefly before he'd fallen asleep.

When he woke in the morning it was to a day dark and gloomy, the sun still some time away from fully rising. He'd glanced around in confusion, before recognising the men who milled around the hall. His father's men. Jumping to his feet, he'd wound his way to Oscetel, talking quietly to an alert looking Lyfing.

"Your father's not here Northman, but I've come with another ten men to escort you all home."

Nodding to show he understood, he turned away to rouse his mother and sister. He liked Oscetel; he was always to the point and didn't hold with the view that it was acceptable to keep young boys waiting for answers. But, he wasn't his father, and he couldn't help wishing that he'd come too. Turning back abruptly he thought to ask,

"Is father well?"

A grimace fleetingly crossed Oscetel's face.

"He's well. A little sick of heart when I left him, but he's not injured. We had an excellent time with Swein. Now hurry, and then you can see for yourself."

Relieved his father wasn't missing due to an injury, he quickly set about rousing his mother, and then went to find Wulfstan. The old man slept deeply, and for a moment he worried that his stillness alluded to something a little more sinister, but with a few shakes and nudges, Wulfstan woke. Confusion creased his face as he looked from his young Lord to his surroundings, but it cleared quickly enough.

"Oscetel is here with more men to escort us home."

"Good, I'll let my guard down a little today then," Wulfstan, quipped, and Northman smiled at the attempted humour.

"Perhaps I will too," he retorted, hunting around for Wulfstan's boots and cloaks.

Wulfstan laughed dryly at him and once dressed, rubbed his hair affectionately as he walked from the small cubicle he'd slept within.

"You're a good lad, don't forget that."

A hasty breakfast of hardened bread and cheese saw them mounted and on their way. The day was clearer than the day before, but the dampness chilled even inside huge cloaks, and it was a miserable day of perseverance. Even having Oscetel and the other men recounting tales of their newest encounter with Swein and his men couldn't lift Northman's spirits, and he almost cried when the familiar sight of his birth home came into view, smoke puffing in welcome through the thatch.

This was his home and his birthright, so different to the house in Lichfield. Here, he could be himself, let his guard down a little, play with his brothers and sister without fear of who might see or comment on what he was doing.

Sitting straighter on his horse, he wiped his listing hair from his eyes, setting his face in a bright smile while beside him Leofric kicked his horse to a tired gallop, desperate to see their father. His attempts at acting the young Lord abandoned, he too kicked his horse onwards, the beast as eager as him to be near home. He just wanted to see his father. Nothing else mattered.

The wind rushing around his clammy face, his eyes focused on the door of his house; he shouted with joy when his father ambled through the front door, his hand shielding his eye so that he could see who approached his house.

All attempts at maturity beyond his years evaporated as he flung himself into his father's waiting arms, and he sobbed with relief. His father. He was here, as immovable as stone, as unchanging as Heaven.

# 2

# EARLY AD1007, NORTHMAN

THEY'D ONLY JUST MADE IT HOME IN TIME. AS THE HORSES AND PEOPLE HAD been settled within the suddenly, a little too crowded, house near Deerhurst, the faint whispers of snow had begun to fall and by the time the short day was over, the land was coated in the snow that reached high up the legs of the hounds.

And it didn't stop there either. A full week of snow followed, sometimes soft and gentle, at times tumultuous in its ferocity and always settling to the ground, the layers increasing daily. Those who were forced to venture outside grumbled at the severe cold and the wet, while those indoors complained at the opening of the door that presaged a sharp blast of harsh wind. Tempers did not flare because the mood within the house was sombre anyway. The realisation of what had happened to Leofwine slowly being accepted by all.

Amongst the sea of sullen faces, Northman found himself seeking the comfort of Wulfstan's steady presence. Remarkably, of them all, he appeared the one most able to shrug the dishonour accorded to Leofwine aside. He was angry and shared his Lord's outrage, and yet, he did not raise his voice or, when the mead flowed too freely, stand and shout curses at the king or Eadric.

And Northman was not alone in his preference for the older man's company. His father was often sat with him, polishing his sword or sanding his shield. He too calmed when Wulfstan was near and in those few days of fire and cold, heat and chill, Northman gained an insight into the power that Wulfstan held over men.

His words were never hurried, his tone rarely angry and yet, all listened when he spoke. Initially, Horic had roared and screeched with his rage, earning himself some sideways glances from Æthelflæd and his wife that he'd ignored at his peril. Only when he'd been struck down by a monumental headache brought on by the vast quantities, he'd drunk had he subsided to calmness. He too had gravitated towards Wulfstan, where Oscetel and the men of the war band had been slowly gathering.

None plotted treason or revenge. Their stoicism in the face of such treatment after they'd faced Swein of Denmark for their king and beaten him into retreat amazed Northman.

One night, as the fire in the centre of the hall, had crackled and roared with the huge amount of wood heaped upon it, Wulfstan had leant towards Northman.

"What do you think lad?"

"About what?" Northman had uttered, stunned to realize these were the first words he'd spoken all day.

"Of your father's men? Do you understand their acceptance of what's happened, or like your brother, are you angry that the men do not shout for justice?"

Northman took a moment to consider his reply. Wulfstan was right in what he said. Leofric was angry and unmanageable. His high-pitched voice could often be heard angrily berating his younger brother and sister, and more than once, their father had been forced to intervene, carrying a sobbing Leofric to his private quarters so that they could talk about his behaviour. Northman understood the rage that coursed through his brother's blood but couldn't bring himself to mirror that rage.

"I think they wouldn't be so high in my father's esteem if they didn't think as he did."

Wulfstan chuckled at the reply.

"As I said boy, you're growing wise with your years. Remember that."

Northman nodded to show he understood the lesson.

"Do you think the king will act further against my father?" the words were forced past the lump in his throat that formed whenever he considered that possibility. They felt more harshly rung than any sentence he'd ever yet had to speak.

"No lad, I don't. The king has no cause to drive your father further from his counsels. He needs men who are compliant and do as they're told. And we all know that they're in short supply around this king. But no, the king will let matters settle now. Eadric has what he wants, and mayhap, he too will let the dust settle before he asks for anything further from the king."

Again, Northman nodded to show he understood.

Before him, Finn was leading the huge array of children in a fair imitation of a learning rhyme, and for the first time in years, Northman was almost tempted to add his voice to the song of his early years. Leofric was sat with his sister, his face, for once, free from the scowl that had graced it for the last week. Near the fire, his mother sat quietly nursing the baby, a smile of contentment on her face, free from lines of worry for the time being. His father was embroiled in a lively debate with Horic about the virtues, or not, of the axe as both a fighting weapon and a weapon of the farm.

It all felt very normal, and Northman relaxed, his small shoulders un-tensing, his eyes half-closing as he leant against Wulfstan. Normal felt good.

The songs of the children swirled around his head, like the stray smoke from the fire, and he slept where he sat, not even stirring when he felt the strong arms of his father carrying him to his bed, warmed by his already sleeping hound.

# 3
# EARLY AD1007, LEOFWINE

THE LAD WEIGHED AS NOTHING IN HIS ARMS AND FOR A MOMENT HE HAD A flashback to the first time he'd held his tiny son in his arms. Many years might well have passed since then, but still, he couldn't shake the feeling that actually little had changed. The years had allowed the boy to grow and thrive, but still, he was his first-born son, as light as a feather in his battle-weary arms.

Placing him on his bed beside his faithful hound, Leofwine stilled in thought. To think his worry when he'd returned from the Outer Isles was that he'd not be able to fight again. He felt as though he'd done little since but call his fyrd together, and ride against their enemies. And now, now he wasn't sure where to look for his enemies.

In one stroke, Swein had released him from their blood feud while his king seemed to have placed him under one. Shaking his head angrily, he walked quietly back to where Wulfstan sat quietly, staring at the blazing fire. Everyone else sleeping the night away.

His wife had long since sought her bed, the new babe and the sudden turn of events wiping much of her strength. She smiled, and she played the dutiful wife, as she always had done, but every so often, he caught sight of her with gentle tears rolling down her face. He didn't know if she cried for him, for herself or their children, and neither did he ask her. He could only offer so many words of assurance, and even they were starting to ring a little hollow in his ears.

Wulfstan spoke first,

"He's an exceptional boy. A credit to you and Æthelflæd."

Nodding in agreement, Leofwine sat beside his oldest friend and counsellor, while Hammer sidled up to him for some much-needed affection. He, like his master, suddenly found himself master of an extended household. The hounds of his Lord's children were mostly well behaved, but Hammer was exhausting himself keeping peace amongst the slightly snappy beasts as frustrated as everyone else to find themselves housebound following the snowstorm.

"He'll be worthy of the task when it's demanded of him," Wulfstan added ominously, and Leofwine shuddered at the thought.

"He's just a boy and my son at that."

"Yes, he is. With your resourcefulness and resilience."

"It's too much to ask for."

"Yes, but Eadric will demand it and if you refuse the king will enforce his will."

"Æthelflæd won't forgive me."

"Perhaps not, but don't let that stop you preparing Northman for what will come. Let him be useful to you when it comes. Teach him what he needs to know, how he should act."

"How should I know what to teach him?" Leofwine countered, his voice rising a little harshly in frustration.

"Teach him what you would do if the situation were reversed." Wulfstan offered with assurance and Leofwine looked at him afresh. He'd clearly been thinking about this, whereas Leofwine had refused to let the thoughts enter his mind since his family had returned to him.

"What would you do?" Leofwine asked, intrigued despite the distasteful topic.

Wulfstan glanced from the fire to look at Leofwine intently,

"He needs to know to watch, to listen. To take in every piece of information no matter how irrelevant and how little he might understand it. He needs to know to fight for his own corner when he trains, to make friends with those he can, and to trust as few as he can. He needs to be subservient, but not too submissive. He needs to show some unhappiness at what's happened to him. Otherwise, Eadric won't be convinced, and he needs to allow himself to be won over by the kindness that Eadric will show to him. The man wants to take something else of yours and either take it from you or turn it against you. Don't let him. Northman is no blunt weapon to hammer away at you. He can be sharp as steel and twice as deadly. Let him be these things."

Anger blossomed deep within him at the words of Wulfstan, but he let it blow itself out quickly. Wulfstan was, as ever, right. Northman, his first born son, was quick and athletic, good with his sword and shield, gaining from his instructions under both Leofwine's household troop and Horic's more rugged boys who fought as their father did. He was intelligent too. His thinking was sound and logical. Leofwine was proud of him and grateful for the love and care his wife had lavished on all their children. But to let him go to Eadric of all people was almost too hard to countenance.

A warm hand on his shoulder and Leofwine attempted to smile away his worries.

"I didn't say it'd be bloody easy," Wulfstan offered by way of an apology. "Whatever hold Eadric has over our king, it's total, and it is still not complete. Use your son as a weapon. But caution him. Eadric must think that he has him completely under his power or it'll be a worthless exercise."

Leofwine sighed deeply at the images flashing through his mind. He wouldn't want to be under the power of Eadric and could think of nothing less appealing for his oldest boy. At least his son would have some advantages to him. He was beguiling to all he met. It would be a man far more hard-hearted than Eadric who'd manage not to fall under his spell. And it needn't be forever. Fostering normally started at an earlier age than ten, but there was no need that it should be for many years. Two years, maybe three, and he could legitimately call his son home, as he'd be required to learn more specifics about the governance of the Hwiccan lands.

"And Leofric."

"What of Leofric?" Leofwine asked, distractedly.

"You should see to him being fostered to your advantage as well."

Leofwine looked at his friend incredulously.

"I can't deprive Æthelflæd of both boys."

"It's high time that the boys were sent out to learn the ways of another household. Not that he need go far," Wulfstan, cautioned apologetically. "I was thinking of perhaps Horic's home, although you may have other ideas. And stop looking at me like that. You know that it's standard practice, it's not as if I'm telling you to send them to the raiding bastards to be fostered."

"No, you're not, but still, this isn't the most salubrious of conversations we've ever had."

"I didn't say it would be. Why do you think I've waited until the household sleeps to speak of this with you?"

"Horic?"

"Yes Horic, he's a good man and he has the advantage that his household is run more along the lines of his homeland. Leofric will learn much about the ways of the Raiders. I don't think the harrying of our lands is over, not by a long shot, and he would be well to be educated by one of their own. Anyway, Horic's wife keeps order there. It's her who'll be responsible for much of his education, as Æthelflæd is here. You already have some of their sons in the household troop. I'm sure they'd be amenable to returning the honour."

"How long have you been thinking about this?" Leofwine asked grudgingly.

"A while."

"Anything else you've decided upon?" he queried in aggravation.

"Oh yes, but I'm not telling you all my plans now."

Before Leofwine could ask for more details, Horic's wife, Agata, came and planted herself beside them. Leofwine hadn't realised she was still awake.

"My Lord," she began, only for Leofwine to shake his head at her.

"Come on. You know better than that," he interrupted her.

"I do, but when I have a favour to ask, I thought I should use the correct address."

"Ask away, and don't call me my Lord, especially when everyone else is happily sleeping."

"As you will Leofwine," she stumbled with a hesitation and a small smile. "The house is a little crowded," she began. "And Horic is bad tempered."

"Isn't he always?" Wulfstan interjected.

"Not quite this bad, Wulfstan," she offered.

"And you wish to travel home?" Leofwine asked, guessing already what she wanted.

"I think it would be for the best."

"I'm sorry that we've descended so abruptly on your home here."

"It's your home. I was always only its custodian in your absence."

"And you've done an excellent job. I don't want you to think that you have to leave on my account."

"I don't. I just believe that with your growing family, and my growing boys, that there are too many of us in too small a space."

"Then, of course, you have my permission to travel home. But please, come back when the weather improves. I may have to build an addition to this house. As you say, my family is growing, and if this is to be our more permanent home, it will not be adequate to my needs. And, I may yet have another favour to ask of you, but first, I must discuss it with Æthelflæd."

"As you will Leofwine, and my thanks for your understanding. The inclement weather makes him crotchety and feel his slowly advancing years. And, Leofwine, if what you wish to ask is what I think you want to ask, Æthelflæd is already well aware of the necessity, and it would be my honour."

She stood abruptly and walked away then, and Leofwine watched her go with narrowed eyes.

"Anything else going on in 'my' household of which I'm not aware?" he asked moodily.

"I would have thought so. You've been much distracted of late, and women will talk, and young men will fall in love."

"Who?" Leofwine asked all ears for any interesting titbits of information.

"You'll need to work that out for yourself, my Lord," Wulfstan muttered, with a small bow of his head, and a chuckle-raising his shoulders. "Now go to bed and keep your wife warm," he admonished, and slowly Leofwine stood, every muscle in his body aching from exhaustion and inactivity.

"And what plans have you made for yourself?" Leofwine stopped and asked, not looking at Wulfstan as he spoke, fearing to see the confirmation of his fears.

"Not what you think," Wulfstan countered defiantly. "Now, bed."

Taking care not to step on the sleeping shapes lying on the floor of his congested home, Leofwine made his way to his private room, his mind whirling with his fears for the future. A moment of whim from his king, and suddenly everything was changing, and much of it was outside his control. It was unsettling, and he thought he'd not sleep, but curled around his wife's warm and soft body, sleep settled over him quickly and for the night at least, he didn't have to consider anything further.

# 4
# EARLY AD1007, LEOFWINE

He woke slowly the next morning, more content on waking than he had been all week long. Reaching lazily for Æthelflæd he found only a warm spot in their bed, and gradually opening his eyes he found her sitting with her back to him, having her luxurious hair plaited by her maid. He could hear the energetic sucking of his youngest child, and he smiled to himself for a moment forgetting the circumstances that had brought his wife home in the middle of winter.

Tugging the furs higher, he rolled back over to sleep a little longer, but he had his ambitions thwarted.

"Leofwine, we must talk about the future," his wife spoke softly, but with iron in her voice. She'd evidently decided that he'd had long enough to consider his next actions. Groaning softly to himself he asked,

"Which part of the future?"

Turning towards him, her eyes flashing a little dangerously in the candlelight, he was taken aback by the anger there.

"Apologies, I didn't mean to belittle your question," he quickly interjected before she could berate him. Her face instantly softened, and she shooed the maid away, handing her the fat little bundle of his youngest child. Reaching down she pulled her dress closed over her exposed breast but not before a thrill of pleasure coursed through his sleep contended body.

Still sitting on her chair, she spoke quietly but urgently, undoubtedly aware of the bodies moving around in the great hall who might, or might not, be able to hear their conversation.

"What do you plan to do now?"

Sitting upright in his bed, so as to be more on a level with her he replied,

"What I've always done. See to the courts, attend the shire meetings, and ensure the fyrd is provisioned, as they should be. Serve the king as I am commanded."

"And what else?" she asked, her brow furrowing in thought as she weighed up his words.

"Prepare our sons for what must now happen."

Her sharp eyes penetrated his face,

"And what would that be?"

"Fosterage."

"With who?" she replied, her voice dangerously low.

"Ah, Æthelflæd don't make this any harder than it already is. You know whom, at least for Northman, even Wulfstan knows. There is little sense in putting off the inevitable."

"I would not give my prized sow to that bastard," she commented harshly, shocking Leofwine with the venom in her voice.

"I know my love, and our prized firstborn son is worth far more than the bloody pig. But Eadric is so high in the king's estimations at the moment that we must use every weapon we have to ensure the survival of our family for our boys and our daughter."

"Weapon!" she shrieked. "He's just a boy."

"And a fine boy at that. But Wulfstan spoke to me of this last night, and he has some excellent ideas of how we can turn this situation to our advantage."

"I do not want my son to be a weapon," she interjected before he could continue.

"I appreciate that, more than you, but neither do I wish to send him off to Eadric with no protection."

Sighing deeply, she looked away from Leofwine, acceptance already showing in her slightly deflated stance.

"And how does Wulfstan plan for our boy to be a weapon?"

"He thinks that Northman is quick witted enough to play Eadric and win his confidence and his trust, and he'll then be able to use what he learns to benefit our family."

"And you will teach him this?" she asked incredulously, "the precious only son of a man who wouldn't let you out of his sight? Who died in your stead at Maldon?" In an instant, her anger had returned full blown, and Leofwine was taken aback by her hastily flung words. Never before had she alluded to his father's death or the circumstances surrounding it. Even after all these years, the knowledge of what his father had done still caused his heart to stutter and grief to overwhelm him. He felt his anger ignite, but before it flared, he felt his wife wrapping her arms around him, as tears flowed freely down her face.

"My apologies my Lord. That was beneath you and me. I hope you know that I don't think like that. My rage simply got the better of me."

Wrapping his arms tightly around her and burying his face in the gentle warmth of her breasts he allowed himself to be comforted briefly, before he turned to kiss her, lovingly on her pliant lips.

Gently pulling away from her, he held her loosely and looked at her for the first time in a long time. She'd aged in their time together, but her beauty hadn't diminished. He still desired her and would have much rather coaxed her to their bed for something other than this conversation.

"It's nothing, don't worry about it. I know it's fear for your boys that cause you to lash out. And you are correct to say what you did. My father pampered me. I never spent more than a few nights away from home until I was much older than the boys and he sent me to the king's court, which then was ruled with steadiness by the king's mother, a wise woman for all the rumours that have circulated since her death. This, this is completely different, but I think we shouldn't underestimate the boy. Wulfstan has given it much thought."

"I thought he might. He's had a shifty look in his eyes ever since we came here. For all that he is a little slow in his movements, his mind is sharper than your blade."

"I think he hones his mind instead of his sword," Leofwine joked, pleased to have left the subject of his father behind.

"You must speak to Northman then, prepare him for what will come, but we'll not let him go without a fight." She nodded as she spoke, her eyes far distant and Leofwine wondered what she thought of.

"No, we'll wait until it's a command from the king before we act, and Northman must go as a sulky youth, not as a boy keen to do his duty for his family."

Nodding again, she slipped her arms from his shoulders.

"But you said, boys? What other plans do you have?"

"Wulfstan suggested that perhaps Leofric should be fostered too."

"Did he now?" she stood abruptly pacing the room. "Next thing he'll be sending Eadwine to be fostered."

"Don't be ridiculous, Æthelflæd," he countered calmly, secretly enjoying watching his wife work herself into a state. She looked truly beautiful with her hair tied back and her dress coming open at the front to expose her full breasts as she marched from one side of their bedroom to the other.

"And where is Leofric to go?" she almost shouted, only remembering the thin walls when she heard an abrupt cease in the noise coming from the hall. Guiltily she looked from Leofwine to where she imagined her son was standing with his ears pressed against the wooden wall.

"With Horic," Leofwine answered succinctly, wondering how she'd react to that news. Instantly she quietened, her agitation forgotten for the moment, and her furrowed brow lifting.

"Well if you'd said that first, I'd not have been so angry would I? Horic's a fine choice. He's a good man, and his wife an even better woman."

Hiding his smile of amusement at the abrupt change in emotions, he pulled his fur covers aside and stood up. A quirked eyebrow from Æthelflæd at his apparent interest in her, and she was in his arms, kissing him passionately. Only then she pulled away from him and turned aside.

In concern, he reached and pulled her face level with his own so that he could see the set of her face. She laughed a little nervously as she retied her dress with fumbling fingers. He looked at her quizzically.

"I think, that for all Wulfstan's sage advice it's time you finally learnt the truth about what passed between him and your father fifteen years ago."

His arousal forgotten, he sucked in a sharp breath.

Reaching forwards to run her hands over his face, she looked away again, and then gently planted a soft kiss on his lips. Holding his head still with her hands, she spoke to him urgently.

"He is ageing Leofwine. It can't be denied any longer. You both owe it to your father to know what happened. Otherwise, you'll not be able to instruct your sons."

Shaking his head roughly, he pulled away from her embrace and turned his own back on her.

"You know I'm right Leofwine," she added softly.

He growled his response,

"It doesn't mean I have to bloody like it, does it." Shrugging his tunic over his head, and his trousers up over his long and well-muscled legs, Leofwine strode from his bedroom, while a deep sigh escaped Æthelflæd's mouth at his unhappiness. He chose to ignore it for now.

Hammer rushed from his place near to the fire, to escort his master, and feeling a little mollified by the show of absolute devotion, he scratched his hound between his upturned ears and made his way carefully through the press of snoring bodies that littered his floor.

At the fire, he came across a grumpy looking Leofric, sat with his shoulders hunched in defiance on the wooden bench he'd shared with Wulfstan last night.

"Morning son," he offered and received a glance from a filthy tear-stained face in response.

"What've you been doing now?" he asked calmly, as he picked up and added more wood to the fire.

"Nothing," sullenly burst from his lips.

"So why you crying then?"

With a loud sniff, Leofric launched into a complicated account of how he hadn't tormented his sister by tying her hair to the bedpost. Suppressing an amused sigh at the discord in his own house, he spoke again.

"So, if you didn't do it, then who did?"

"I don't know," came the outraged reply and Leofwine worked hard to keep his face straight at the blatant lie.

"You know, sometimes it's easier just to say sorry when you're in the wrong."

Leofric sucked in a deep breath of denial, but then let it out quickly again.

"S'pose so," he muttered and shuffled his way forwards from the wooden bench to go and find his sister, who likewise, was sobbing in pain on the other side of the fire. The maid, who'd so painstakingly plaited his wife's hair, was now offering words of comfort and shushing the distraught little girl, who seemed to have a rather large area of her head now devoid of hair. Leofwine flinched at the imagined pain of waking abruptly and finding himself unable to move thrusting his head forward and leaving much of his hair behind.

Before her, Leofric was apologising, and with haughty eyes, his sister was sobbing softly and refusing to listen to her older brother, until he stepped forward and held something out to her, by way of an apology. Leofwine couldn't see what his son gave his daughter, but noted the delighted grin that spread across her face. It was almost sure to be something she wasn't supposed to have. Having two older brothers had made his pretty daughter crave wooden swords and wooden shields. His wife didn't approve, but Leofwine knew that her brothers, when they weren't fighting, often shared their toys with her.

Moving to where his second son and only daughter were now engaged in a fierce conversation about their plans for her new trophy, Leofwine spied the outline of a small wooden dagger under her long dress. Ignoring the contraband, for now, he decided he'd let Æthelflæd deal with that little issue. Personally, he was happy for his daughter to be able to defend herself.

He strode to his front door, finding his cloak near the doorway, and throwing it over his shoulders. Regardless of the cold, he needed some time outside with his thoughts.

Opening the door only a thin slither so that the cold air didn't permeate the room, he and Hammer slid from the warm hall and were instantly assaulted by a cold and icy blast of wind. A rueful glance from Hammer, as if questioning the sanity of the idea, and Leofwine was strolling towards the stables. His horse was in as much need of a bit of exercise as he was. Behind him, the door opened and closed, and when he entered the animal barn, Horic caught him up.

"A ride my Lord?" he queried, his voice rough from sleep.

"Yes, now that the snow's stopped falling. Are you joining me?"

"Yes, I've been banished from my bed," he grumbled, arousing a laugh from Leofwine.

"I know the feeling."

"These long nights and short days are starting to test me," Horic continued.

"Not long now and the days will begin to lengthen."

"Not before time."

Amongst the tidy barn, more sleeping bodies were curled up tight against the cold, and Leofwine good-naturedly kicked a few of his men to wake them. Loud grumbles greeted his noisy movements, but before too long, he had a respectable looking contingent of men to accompany their Lord on an early morning canter across his lands.

At the last moment, Northman snuck inside the barn and looked towards his father. With a faint nod of approval, his son mounted his own smaller horse and joined the men milling at the shut gate.

"Now men," Leofwine called when everyone was as ready as they were going to be. "Remember, we've been housebound for over a week, and the animals are only just rested up. No silly behaviour. Just a sedate canter to check that the snow's not causing too much damage to the roads and hedges."

Hostile nods greeted his words, causing Horic to lean over and whisper conspiratorially,

"Fat chance of that my Lord."

With a cry of delight, Leofwine led his men through the now open door, catching sight of a small battle taking place between Leofric and Ealdgyth in the shadow of the house. Her face was ferociously determined as she attacked her brother with her new toy. They'd probably be bruises and a bit of blood before she'd finished with him.

They rode for some time in the crisp day, surveying the snow-coated land as they went.

"Horic, I have a favour to ask of you," Leofwine finally said, turning to his commended man as they rode side by side at a gentle trot.

"Anything my Lord, you know that."

"I do, yes," Leofwine smiled, feeling his cold face crack against the unexpected movement.

"It's about Leofric."

"Ah, my Lord, he's a good lad at heart. He's just still a bit too young to deal with his temper and his anger."

Leofwine suppressed his amusement at hearing his burly friend speak so of his own son when he'd not have tolerated such behaviour amongst his herd of strapping lads and strong willed girls.

"There's no need to make excuses for him. I know he'll grow and learn to control his emotions better. But, I'd still like you to help him with that."

"Help him how?" Horic queried, his eyes confused and a little unfocused.

"Will you foster him for me, when you go home?"

Recognition flashed across the grizzled face, and Horic answered with a booming laugh,

"It'd be my pleasure and Agata's too. She's too old now for more babes, but she'd enjoy the pleasure of adding another to her household. But can I ask, what of Northman? Should he not be fostered first?"

Leofwine swallowed against the bile in his throat. It was one thing to talk to Wulfstan and his wife about such things, but to mention it to Horic would make it more real.

"He's to be fostered too," he finally spat out, and Horic turned quickly to glance at him.

"Ah my Lord, not to that bastard Eadric?"

"I'm afraid so. Wulfstan and I are confident that the king will demand it and so we must prepare him for the inevitable and accept it for what it is."

Horic's face had flushed an angry red, emphasised by the white landscape that surrounded them. But he didn't speak, considering something first.

"Then my Lord, if you will, I demand you let my youngest go with him."

Startled, it was Leofwine's turn to study his friend's face.

"Really?"

"Yes, Northman will need someone to watch his back for him, and the two are good friends."

"Shouldn't you check with Agata first?" Leofwine re-joined.

"Contrary to what everyone thinks, I'm able to make my own decisions about my family. Anyway, she'll probably suggest it before I get the chance when I speak to her of Leofric. She's a quick-witted woman, and more honourable than I," he added ruefully.

Leofwine laughed at his friend's contrite expression.

"Then, yes, I think Northman would like that very much. But for now, let's not talk of this to the boys. I need to break the news to Northman in the right way, and this isn't it."

"As you will, my Lord. And Leofwine," he turned to where Horic was plodding along slowly beside him, fiddling with his horse's harness as an excuse not to look at his Lord, whom he never referred to by his first name. "You have my thanks for your trust and for all you've ever done for my family."

Leofwine was aghast with surprise, to hear such words from his friend, a man he'd thought capable of taking nothing seriously, ever.

"You saved my life. Never forget that."

And before the conversation could take any more of an uncomfortable turn, Leofwine spurred his horse onto a fast canter. Sod the snow and the ice, he needed to feel the speed of his mount beneath him and just run away from his problems for the time being.

# 5
# EARLY AD1007, NORTHMAN

THE FIRE WAS BLAZING HOT, WARMING HIS WIND-REDDENED CHEEKS ALMOST painfully but he didn't want to move. Once again, he found himself sat beside Wulfstan, seeking comfort from the old man's steady presence. He knew the older members of his family and their entourage were discussing something about him, and he feared he knew what it was. Shaking his head, he noted his father walking towards him, and his stomach turned icy with dread.

"Wulfstan, Northman," his father greeted as he sat before them, having brought a small wooden stool with him.

Wulfstan turned his face to glance at Leofwine and a half-cracked smile towards Northman.

"Um, my lad. This isn't good when your father seeks out both of us so nonchalantly. I think one of us, or maybe both of us, might be in trouble."

Leofwine's countenance creased with dry humour at the words.

"I'm afraid it might be you alone that doesn't appreciate this conversation."

"Well then, my Lord, that can mean only one thing, and I'd first like to thank you for not asking the question before today."

Northman glanced between the two men wondering what they spoke of. And then Wulfstan began to talk, and it all became clear.

"It all started well enough, but then, all battles do, until someone is the victor and someone the loser. Your father and your grandfather Northman," Wulfstan nodded at him as he was included in the conversation, "was in good spirits that day. Brythnoth had roused us all to battle with fine words, and an excellent strategy. We had high hopes that a few slashes of our swords, a few thrusts of our axes and the enemy would be the ones making a meal for the scavengers, and turning to dust under the harsh sun's rays. We were wrong, but only because Brythnoth was a man of his word, an honourable man, and a pleasure to be commanded by."

Wulfstan paused then, his eyes far away, and Northman looked at his father. His face was keen to know and yet a little hooded at the same time. He was aware from discussions within the household that Wulfstan had never before recounted the tale of Maldon because Leofwine had never before asked him to. Northman wondered what had changed his father's mind now, and why he was being included in such a profoundly private matter.

"He spoke beautiful words that to this day I recall as if it were yesterday,

'Do you hear, sea-wanderer, what this nation says? They will give you spears as tribute, the poison-tipped javelin and ancient swords, those warlike trappings which will profit you nothing in battle.'

And we screamed and shouted our support of him." Wulfstan's face had smoothed as he spoke, and Northman had the strange idea that the old man suddenly thought himself as young as he was on the day he was talking about.

"The sun rose higher and higher, and the Raiders took advantage of Brythnoth's generosity in letting them cross the marsh land so that they fought on an equal footing. They sent one of their men, or maybe more, to slay him where he stood, and when they succeeded the men who only that morning had shouted their acclamations, melted away, leaving behind only those men honourable enough to fight and die by their Lord's side, as was right."

Tears wetted Wulfstan's eyes, and Northman held his breath in wonder at tales of a battle fought before his birth.

"Your father, who was a principled man, would not stand aside, he would not run as the others did, but I saw the conflict in his wary eyes. I saw him stop and think while the battle raged around him. while men and swords and axes beat their way to his side, he stood, and he looked longingly towards home, the spectre of his son dancing before his eyes. I saw it all, and I pitied him but knew his resolve, and his honour would find him making the decision he would be able to live with, even if only for a few short lengths of time longer."

"What I didn't factor in, was his need to ensure the safety and survival of his son but neither could I ignore his request. I, who had far less to live for than my Lord, was tasked by him to return home; to tell his son of those final moments, and to speak to him of all that his father had hoped and prayed for him. I didn't want to leave him there, to die without me, but he left me little choice. He bid me speak to you of old conversations and yet I've never done so, for you've never wanted to hear, and I'm grateful for that. Now an old man, I want to reminisce, to look back on a life I've lived well. He chose wisely that day when he told me to live."

"You were honoured by the king for his bravery and yet, in every word and conversation we've ever had, I've heard him telling me his thoughts, and guiding you as he would have done had he still been here. He was far wiser and far more honourable than even I understood at the time. And that blood flows through both of you. You should be proud of him and what he did for you, and you should take that knowledge and use it to temper your every action."

Northman listened attentively to Wulfstan's words, privileged to hear them.

"And my father? Who killed him?" Leofwine asked in a voice

barely above a whisper. He earned himself a sharp stare from Wulfstan, denial evident in his face.

"I don't believe, for even a moment, that you left without knowing that he was actually dead," Leofwine added cajolingly.

"No, my Lord, I didn't. I saw the warrior who cut your father down in the prime of his life, but I think you already know who it was."

"Olaf," Leofwine spoke decisively, the confirmation of a half-formed idea on his lips.

"Yes, Lord Leofwine, it was Olaf. You're one-time ally and the man who led you to danger and then ensured your survival."

"I don't deny that, and I even think he felt some remorse for his actions, otherwise why gift me back my father's cross."

From a wrapped piece of cloth that Northman hadn't even realised his father was holding, he pulled forth a spectacular massive golden cross, so heavy it caused the veins on his father's hands to strain with effort. The blood red rubies flashed tantalisingly in the glow from the fire, and unintentionally Northman reached out to run his hands over the cross.

"You should honour your father by restoring that to the Church," Wulfstan commented without rancour.

"I know, but until today, I wasn't ready to hear the words that would confirm its provenance."

"Olaf was an exceptional enemy, and an even more praiseworthy friend," Wulfstan offered as confirmation of their conversation.

"And that's the king's problem. He's used to enemies who become honourable friends. What he can't understand are the fine enemies who persist in staying enemies."

Wulfstan chuckled at the summing up of the king's woes as Leofwine placed the cross within his son's outstretched hands with a shrug of encouragement. The cross was monumentally heavy, and Northman was amazed by the great weight of gold that must have gone into its construction.

"No, and neither can he understand that friends are not always honourable."

"There's a lesson to be learnt, lad," Wulfstan offered, turning towards Northman.

"And what is that lesson?" he asked, only listening with half an ear to the reminiscing of his father and the old man.

"When you tell me, you let me know," Wulfstan retorted while Leofwine rolled his eyes a little at the irrelevant answer.

"I think son, that Wulfstan is warning you that it's not always easy to differentiate between your enemies and your friends. A wolf can wear sheep's clothing. Never forget that. Olaf killed my father, and yet, he saved my life and remembered what had gone before, gifting back to me something of great value that Finn more than likely had to steal to return to me. He made Finn take a huge risk, but his intentions were honourable."

"I'd be a little more succinct than that if I had to be. Our friends might be our enemies, and our enemies our friends. It's a hard lesson to learn." Wulfstan commented sourly.

"And why should I learn it?" Northman asked, a little defiantly, a little fearfully. Suddenly he knew what his father was going to say to him.

"I think that Eadric will demand that you be fostered by him, as some bargaining counter for my good behaviour."

"And you want me to go?" Northman screeched in fear, standing abruptly, and only just catching the golden cross before it tumbled to the floor.

"No, not at all. I don't want you to go. I'll fight for you to stay here if you will it. You know that son. But no, I trust you to go, as my son, and as the grandson of my father. You've honour within you, and you'll want to do this." His father's voice was sad, resigned to the words he spoke, and before Northman could deny it; jump up and down with anger at his father's abandonment of him to the man who'd usurped his position in the Mercian lands, Northman realised that his father was right. He would want to do this. He would want to be honourable and act in a way to counter anything that Eadric would ever do.

Nodding in acceptance, he handed the cross reverentially to his father and sat back down.

"And before I go, you'll make me your commended man. In secret."

Wulfstan gasped at the words, and Leofwine's face scrunched in grief, but he answered levelly enough.

"I will, son. But, I'll hold you to that oath, and you better remember that."

Satisfied that his father, a man of his word, and Wulfstan, a man of his oath, would do as he demanded, he went to sit amongst the group of children one last time. He felt himself suddenly inducted to the world of men, but for now, and while the sky was dark, and the snow fell, he could think himself a child again, even if only for a short space of time.

He wasn't to know that behind him, his father shook with pride and grief, his mother with anguish and joy, and old Wulfstan, with memories of another young lad, so many years ago, who'd understood honour even before he'd learned to raise a wooden sword.

# 6

## AD1007, NORTHMAN

THE PRIDE HE'D FELT IN HIS FATHER'S WORDS TO HIM CARRIED HIM THROUGH the next few days so that he gave no thought to how he'd actually fare in Eadric's household. Clearly, Wulfstan and his father were entrusting him with a great honour but eventually, his fear won through, and he found himself seeking out his mother.

She was busy in discussions with Agata, about Leofric's fosterage, but she took one look at his face and turned her full attention to him. Agata melted away with a sympathetic look on her face, and for the first time, Northman felt traitor tears form in his eyes.

The snowstorm had continued in vengeance after their brief trip, and snow liberally covered the ground in all directions preventing any from leaving the house. Horic had managed to curb his frustration at being cooped up inside but only by becoming embroiled in a ferocious debate with Oscetel about the best fighting techniques to employ against the Raiders from the North. Late into each night, they could be heard discussing tactics and each morning Horic woke and continued where they'd left off.

"Northman, what is it?" his mother asked calmly, beckoning him to pull a stool closer to her.

"I ... I don't know really."

She smiled at his hopeless shrug and leant forward towards him.

"You know that your father wouldn't ask this of you if he didn't think you were capable. I know that might not bring you much comfort now, and your fear is well justified, but you should be aware that Eadric will treat you respectfully and as he would his own children."

Northman felt himself shrug a little hopelessly at his mother's words.

"But, he doesn't have any children," eventually burst forth from his mouth and his mother nodded in understanding.

"And you're worried that he'll have you to practise on and then learn from his mistakes?"

"No, I'm afraid he'll have no idea how to raise children and that he'll just expect me to act as a man should and allow no mistakes."

This time, his mother considered her words before she responded.

"I imagine that he'll be married before he requests you again, and as he hopes to wed one of the king's own daughters, I would suggest that he'll be kind in his treatment of you. After all, he may well have the ear of the king, but the girls are strong women, determined and set in their ways. They had their grandmother as an example of how royal women should live, and Elfrida, no matter what's whispered about her now, was a wise and just woman."

Northman stared at his mother as he processed her words. They made sense to him, and he suddenly realised that he would be answerable to more than just Eadric, even if he were his to foster. As within their own household, there would be household troops and commended men, maids and cooks, farmers and metal workers. He'd be able to find allies wherever he needed them.

"Does that make you feel a little more confident?" she queried into his silence.

"Yes, I'd not considered anyone other than Eadric when I

thought about it. But you're right. There will be others who I'll be able to turn to."

"And Northman," his mother added, as he stood to walk away. "Remember that you'll still be our son, and our own followers, whenever they cross paths with Eadric's household, will be looking to ensure you're cared for and treated as you should be. It's not as if you'll disappear behind the closed doors of his household."

# 7
# EARLY SUMMER AD1007, LEOFWINE

THE WINTER WAS LONG AND SLOW, PROVIDING ADEQUATE TIME FOR Leofwine to spend time with his oldest son, and teach him the skills he'd need to survive in the household of Eadric. As much as he'd usually welcomed the thaw and the return of the lighter days, this year, he found himself pleased when the weather stayed viciously cold, and the lambs began to arrive in the midst of a ferocious snowstorm.

Eventually, though, and despite his hopes that the warmer weather would never come, a week of pleasant weather arrived along with the Easter festival, and deciding, out of mere spite more than anything else, to leave Northman at home, he travelled to meet the king at his Easter Witan. His heart grew heavier with each step of his horse's hooves, but he was in for a surprise. For when he arrived at Winchester, Eadric was nowhere to be seen.

Neither did he appear during the three-day duration of the Witan meeting, nor the Easter masses that seemed to be a requisite for each morning and evening. The quiet questioning of Athelstan revealed the news that Eadric had been unable to attend the summons of the king. There was some half-hearted attempt at an excuse but to all intents and purposes, it appeared as though Eadric had refused his king. For the remainder of the early summer, Leofwine smirked with joy whenever he considered his king's angry and twisted face and had almost forgotten about the plans Eadric had for Northman when he attended upon the king again at the height of the summer.

Sadly, Eadric was dancing his attendance upon the king and proudly showing off his soon to be wife. Leofwine tasted bile from the moment he spied out Eadric and his pleasure at now being one of only a few ealdormen his king relied on was quickly diluted when it became apparent that Eadric's opinions were once more swaying the king.

Biting back his anger, Leofwine settled back to watch Eadric work. He couldn't shake the feeling that Eadric had absented himself from the Easter Witan with the express intention of not being asked to deliver the geld he'd convinced the king to pay Swein and his men. Instead, that task had gone to Leofwine, so that after the Easter Witan he'd returned home only to collect together his share of the tax that was due before repeating his journey towards the coast of the Isle of Wight.

Along the way, he'd been met by representatives from Ælfric of Hampshire and by Athelstan and his brother, Edmund. They were to act as the king's representatives when they met with Swein.

Leofwine was unsure how he'd felt about meeting him again. He'd hoped on their last meeting when Swein had released him from the blood feud, and he'd sent him running with his tail between his legs back to his ships, that he'd never see the man again. The king's decision to buy him off sat uneasily with him. He couldn't shake the feeling that by giving him geld now they were sending out the wrong message. Once again, it was as if everything he did for the king ended up running counter to the prevailing wind.

The weather had been beautiful on their journey, making it far more pleasant than their mad dash to the coast in the middle of winter and their slower ride home with the first snowfall. The company had been reasonable as well, and when they'd met Swein at the prearranged location of Southampton, a contingent of the king's household troops had already arrived.

Swein was his usual swaggering self, and Leofwine knew a moment of premonition. Yes, he might have decided that he'd leave England's shores on receipt of his geld, but Leofwine knew that this would not be the last they saw of him.

Too confident in his demeanour, he'd been to the point when he'd noticed Leofwine amongst the dignitaries who'd come to ensure he left as agreed.

"My Lord Leofwine, we meet again I see."

"King Swein," Leofwine had offered, his head a little bowed, but not enough to take his eye from Swein's contemptuous face.

"I think that your king is, perhaps, not quite as dedicated as you in driving me from your lands. His methods certainly make a return here quite tempting." His voice was smug with delight and Leofwine worked hard to let the words pass him by without penetrating his resolve.

"As with your one-time ally, Olaf of Norway, I'm here to ensure that you know that England will not pay any more geld to you. Our coffers are near to empty and our land, still not yet recovered from the famine that last time caused you to flee the land so promptly."

"There was little need for me to starve along with your slaves and holy men," he'd countered quickly, his accent a little twisted as he spoke in ire. Leofwine noted that it seemed a bit too easy to break through his smug deportment.

"But perhaps a little less weight on your stomach and you'd have had more success in the battle against me at the turning of the year." Leofwine had shocked himself with his petty outburst, but Swein had surprised him by laughing at the jibe.

"You made an excellent adversary Leofwine. Your sword was always as sharp as your tongue. And now I'd like to introduce you to my son, Cnut."

From amongst the large delegation of men who'd accompanied

Swein to this meeting, a slight youth stepped forwards. He was no more than sixteen years of age, and yet already, he sported a fine collection of armrings on both arms. He nodded smartly to Leofwine and Athelstan before standing at his father's side.

"He's an exceptional warrior for all that his years are few," Swein spoke, the pride in his son clear to hear.

"He fought with you when we last met?" Leofwine queried, seeking confirmation of his hazy recollection of the battle.

"Yes, he did. Perhaps, after all, your eyesight is not such an impediment as you would believe," Swein offered by way of confirmation.

"I'm sure I'd see better with two eyes, but that is irrelevant now. As you say, I've adjusted and grown used to my injury."

Swein nodded absentmindedly as Leofwine spoke, and he belatedly realised that his attention was taken up with someone behind him. Turning, he looked to see who held the Danish king's attention and his eyes alighted on Northman and a smirk of pride tugged at his lips.

"And this my Lord, is my son, Northman."

Northman stepped forwards confidently, his face a careful mask of indifference, just as Wulfstan had taught him, even though his introduction to the Danish king was an impromptu action. Swein eyed him carefully before he spoke.

"He has your looks that's for sure. And perhaps your cockiness as well. But his name, that's an interesting choice."

Leofwine smiled wide then, enjoying what was about to come.

"I was away when he was born, Swein, after the altercation on Shetland. I'm sure you recall. My wife named him in my absence, and she chose a name to mark him so that he would seek vengeance for my death. You're perhaps lucky that I returned alive."

Swein eyes lit with fire at the reminder of their skirmish, and he fixed Leofwine with a penetrating stare.

"A son's vengeance for his father is always far keener than a man's revenge for himself. As you say, I think the old Gods and the new bless me that you returned alive. I would not fancy my chances in a few years time against your son."

"I'm glad too that he doesn't have to spend his adult life seeking you out. Vengeance is not the best way to spend your time."

At his father's side, Cnut was also watching Northman intently. There were a handful of years separating the two, Cnut just bordering on manhood, while Northman stood a little ways back from it. As the two boys stared at each other, Leofwine felt a crushing moment of premonition on what the future might hold for the two, but he swept it aside angrily. His king was strong and would remain so, and after him, he had skilled sons to govern in his stead. There was no need for Northman and Cnut even to meet again, past this day. Provided Swein left and never returned.

"And now to other business, I think," Swein spoke, although his eyes never left Northman's face. Leofwine wondered what he looked for there. Northman held his place well, never flinching from the gaze and finally Swein's face broke into a broad smile.

"I like him Leofwine. Would you allow me to gift him with something to remember me by? Not something too incendiary. Perhaps a small knife or ring, as settlement of our debt?"

Secretly amused by the Danish king's response to the physical appearance of the boy who could very easily have spent his adult life hunting him to his death, he nodded to show he accepted the man's offer. In a bizarre exchange, he watched his son receive a small knife from the man who was even then receiving an almost endless array of chests heaped high with the geld his king had agreed to pay him to leave the lands of the English.

Swein crossed the invisible boundary, which until then, had been separating them, and in all seriousness spoke quietly to Northman and handed him his trophy.

Swein's son, Cnut, stood idly by, watching his father, an unfathomable expression on his face, compelling Leofwine to speak.

"Cnut, I too would like to settle any debt that may have arisen from the animosity between your father and I. Would you also accept a small gift from me."

Cnut turned in surprise to look at Leofwine, and for the first time in a long time, Leofwine felt the white-hot pressure of having someone examine his face in detail, noting the scar tissue and the blood shot remains of his useless eye.

"Your injury, it came at my father's hand?" the lad spoke carefully. His English was excellent, with only the hint that it was not his usual language.

"Well not at his hand, but by his command. I was keeping company with Olaf and your father didn't approve."

"Ah, I remember the story. Olaf was a slithery bastard," Cnut commented his speech easy to understand, his disdain for Olaf even clearer to hear. Leofwine was impressed that the youth had taken the time to learn the language of the land they raided and attacked, even if he didn't share in his dislike for Olaf.

"I only knew him for a brief period, so can't really comment."

"No, but I understand he thought highly of you."

"He remembered me upon his death. That's certainly true."

"And why was that?" Cnut asked, his eyes narrowing. Leofwine had the distinct impression that Cnut knew exactly why, but he honoured his question with a quiet answer.

"He killed my father at the Battle of Maldon." Even now, that admission cost him dear and at his side, both Oscetel and Horic stilled in readiness for what might come next.

Beside Cnut, a tall warrior stepped forwards, his eyes carefully watching Swein's every move and yet seeming to be completely aware of the situation developing between his Lord's son and Leofwine. He whispered something to Cnut and with a visible start Cnut swept the assembled men a brief look.

"Apologies my Lord Leofwine. I spoke without thought for your loss. Yes, I would be honoured, as your son has been, to receive a small token from you."

Pleased that someone had interrupted their unpleasant conversation, Leofwine turned to speak quickly to Horic. Horic, who was himself carefully watching the taller raider, nodded in agreement to his Lord's command and shouldered his way through the dense throng of men to where the horses were being minded by some of the squires. He returned quickly and handed a small cross to Leofwine. Leofwine looked at the cross carefully. He'd been planning on adding it to the geld, but had changed his mind at the last moment, thinking that he didn't want to let another family heirloom fall into the hands of the Raiders. But now he felt a little differently.

"This is a replica of the cross that Olaf returned to me upon his death. I had it made to remind me of my father's greatest treasure. And now I give it to you, and I hope it will work as a token of our friendship, as it once did with Olaf."

Surprised by the nature of the gift, Cnut didn't immediately step forward to take the pro-offered gift, and Leofwine suddenly wondered if he'd miscalculated. Abruptly, with a flicker of fire in his eyes, Cnut reached out to take the cross, the jewels that embellished it flashing in the bright sunlight.

"An elegant gift Lord Leofwine, and I echo the sentiment behind it. You may not realise, but my father is a convert to the Christian faith, and I follow him, for all that it is sometimes a little too easy to slip to the older doctrine of many Gods. But I will treasure this, and count it as a personal gift from you."

Bemused, Swein watched his son at work, again, the pride in his son clear to behold.

"We've done a good job here today," Swein said into the sudden silence that fell as everyone watched the exchange between Leofwine and Cnut. "Let's hope that our past differences are now all healed and we can look forward to long and prosperous lives."

Amongst the men, a drinking horn began to circulate, and when Athelstan and Edmund had both taken their fill, they passed it to Swein who gulped greedily, letting the fluid splash down his full beard.

"Taking gold this way is thirsty business," he offered by way of an apology before offering the beautifully carved horn to Leofwine. Leofwine reacted as he knew he should, raising the horn to toast Swein's success before handing the cup back to Cnut. They might well have done excellent work that day, but Swein was still the winner in the contest and his king the poor loser. He could only hope that they'd either never see Swein again, or that his king would agree to a much more robust defence of their lands.

And now at the Witan, Leofwine sat amongst the select band of ealdormen, aware that in all likelihood he was being held responsible for the geld that had been paid. He'd physically transported the payment and met with Swein no matter that he'd also fought him twice the previous year and sent him back to the Isle of Wight. If the king hadn't already agreed to the geld, Leofwine thought it most likely that Swein would have returned home with nothing. After all, he had another kingdom to govern. If no payment had been forthcoming from the English king, he'd have earned nothing for his troubles, and dissent amongst the men would have, in all likelihood, forced him to seek plunder elsewhere or an agreement to pay them from his treasury at home.

Eadric was smirking slightly where he sat, deep in conversation with Ulfcytel of the East Angles and Uhtred of Northumbria. Leofwine didn't want to get close enough to the select band of men to discover what they spoke of.

In many ways he was now the odd man out, Ulfcytel was married to the king's daughter, and Eadric had made no pretence of his intention to do the same. It was also believed that the king had given permission for Uhtred to marry his remaining daughter, when she was old enough. Although that would be many years in the future. For now Uhtred had another wife, and sons already. Leofwine wondered whether the poor woman was aware that her marriage would not last forever.

Amongst them all, there was only he who wasn't related to their king, or likely to be soon. There was only him who was expendable. Although, Leofwine reconsidered, being related to the king had not always proved to be key to a long and secure tenure of ealdorman. Not many years had passed since the king's father-in-law had been swept from his position as Ealdorman of Northumbria following his failure to prevent the invasions of the Raiders.

Feeling a little mollified by the thought, Leofwine surveyed the rest of the assembled Witan. The king's sons were in full attendance, with even his first born by Emma, Edward, now taking his seat beside Athelstan, small and blond, a picture of innocence.

Leofwine admired Athelstan's resolve for not flinching when the small boy was seated in a preferential position to himself. The king had far too many sons vying for a position. He really needed more daughters, not more sons with his young wife.

Emma too was attending the Witan. She'd grown into her position as England's queen but she still often sought out Leofwine's attention within the crowded witan, a mark of his favour with her that Eadric did not share.

Emma was regal in her bearing, and she'd survived many storms at the hands of some of the English who still didn't fully accept her as their queen. Only the previous year she'd been accused of colluding with Swein and his Raider ships.

Leofwine knew it was a ludicrous sentiment. She'd never forgive Swein for chasing them across the sea when she first came to England. She'd told Leofwine in no uncertain terms that she wasn't happy that he and Swein were now more friends than enemies.

It hadn't been an easy conversation the previous day when she'd sought him out upon his arrival at the palace. He'd apologised to her for any upset he'd caused, and she'd immediately forgiven him, but still, she'd not been best pleased. He was relieved that their private conversation appeared to have had no impact on their public appearances. He enjoyed having the ear of the queen, especially when his king could be so changeable in his attitudes towards him.

The king seemed cheerful, a fact Leofwine didn't approve of. He'd just forced his people to raise a massive tax, admittedly one they could afford, to clear the land of a menace that had already been defeated. He didn't seem concerned by that knowledge, and Leofwine wondered what would happen if the population as a whole ever learned the truth. While he'd defeated Swein, Eadric had demanded the king raise a geld to pay the self-same Raiders off, and it was the geld that won the battle. Leofwine knew such a chain of events would outrage the men and women who worked the land. And yet the king had apparently not considered it.

He wondered if the king would be so content if he weren't related to the vast majority of the ealdormen. It was an intriguing thought and one that filled him with even more apprehension. Of them all, he was the odd one out. Perhaps, when Northman was fostered by Eadric, that would assure the king even more of his loyalty.

Still, he chafed to be constrained. The king had acted rashly and without due consideration of all the facts. No matter how Wulfstan tried to push that blame onto the men who counselled the king, Leofwine knew in his heart that the king was at fault, and it was an uncomfortable realisation.

From his place amongst the men of the cloth, Wulfstan, the man who'd warned him of the king's intentions before the New Year and who'd sent word to his wife of the king's actions, met his eye with a sedated nod of his head. Leofwine looked around expectantly wondering who else had noted the exchange and found the pulsing glare of Eadric fixated on him. Leofwine raised his eyebrows in a query as he met the man's gaze, and was pleased when it was Eadric who looked away first.

During the dark winter months, he'd given much thought to Eadric. And then had decided to act decisively and made the decision to send Finn to discover all he could about the man. He'd hardly disguised himself to do so, but neither had they been entirely truthful.

Finn had found for himself a position within Eadric's house, acting as a scribe for the man. Only when the weather had improved had Finn made his excuses and left to return to his real Lord with tales of Eadric. Leofwine had not been pleased with what he'd learnt, but neither had he despaired for his son.

Eadric was just one of many brothers, albeit the most successful by far. Brihtric, Ælfric, Goda, Æthelwine, Æthelweard and Æthelmær had all made themselves comfortable in their brother's home, and along with their father, Æthelric, they'd spent the winter months conniving and deciding how best to profit from their close association with the king. The first thing they'd decided was that Eadric was not to be associated with the geld and its delivery. Jokingly, they'd decided it was best if Leofwine was the one tainted with that task.

Finn had barely been able to contain his anger when he'd reported to Leofwine. His words had rushed from his mouth as his face had grown angrier and angrier. Only the calming words of Wulfstan had settled Finn, and only firm words from Leofwine had convinced Finn that he shouldn't give vent to his anger in front of Northman.

For all that, it had transpired that Eadric was not a harsh man for his people to deal with. While he wasn't as conscientious in his new duties as Leofwine had been, he still appreciated that people would only seek him as their lord if he proved himself able in the matters of justice and tax collection. Indeed, he'd been a little lax in his efforts, using it an excuse to further blacken Leofwine's good name by putting it about that he'd been overzealous in his duties.

Without ever saying anything to the effect, or at least not in Finn's hearing, Eadric had managed to convey the idea that he was a far better man than Leofwine had ever been. And that knowledge had been worth sharing with Northman. He needed to know that there would be many within the household who'd seek to blacken his father's name in his hearing, and Northman would need to learn to take the intended slights with good grace, even if it burned him inside to hear such slanderous words.

Finn had also determined that Eadric and his brothers intended to infiltrate the king's court in anyway they could. Already their father Ælfric had acted as one of the king's thegns. His sons now strove to do the same. Eadric had high hopes that he'd soon have a faction at court who'd support him, even if, and when, that meant going up against the king. Leofwine had not liked that item of information.

With feigned disinterest, Leofwine glanced to the seating area of the king's thegns. He wondered who amongst the men were Eadric's brothers, and then he had to think no more for he could clearly see the resemblance in the bearing of five men, one of them older and the other four much of an age with Eadric. He wondered how he'd not noticed before that so many of the men were alike. And then he dismissed the thought. It wasn't that rare for one family to have multiple representatives amongst the king's thegns. Indeed, many of the men looked similar, and Leofwine smirked as he pondered just how many of them were related to each other.

Certainly, it wasn't rare for the ealdormen to intermarry, one marrying another's daughter, or even for the king to marry one of the ealdormen's daughters. He needed to stop looking for a conspiracy where none existed.

The king quickly brought the summer witan to order, his mind focused on the future, although strangely devoid of any thoughts of how the land should be defended from the Raiders. Leofwine felt his anger mounting. The king had once again decided that with the payment of the geld there'd be no more Raiders, instead focusing on his daughter, Edith's, marriage to Eadric, and matters of law and precedence amongst his sons.

Luckily sense prevailed, and Edward was accorded no greater priority than any of the other sons when it came time to witness the charters. But Leofwine could already sense an undercurrent of unease amongst the older sons. For the first time in his life, he was pleased he was an only son.

It was when the work of the day was done that the king called Leofwine to him, and the smirk on Eadric's face as he approached his king was all he needed to know. It was going to be the conversation he didn't want to have.

"Leofwine," the king began, his face intent as he watched the milling around of the rest of the Witan, "I wanted to thank you for your handling of the arrangements with Swein."

Taken aback by the start of the conversation Leofwine nodded in deference,

"It was my honour to act as your representative. Athelstan was a credit to you as well."

Æthelred turned his attention to Athelstan then, watching as he spoke to some young men similar to him in age, clearly re-enacting either a battle they'd fought or some training they'd participated in.

"Yes, he's a good son, handy with his sword, and friendly with the men of the household troop he commands. He is, I think, more warlike than I."

"With the relationship with Swein and the other Raiders as it is, it's good to have bred warrior sons."

Æthelred glanced sharply at Leofwine then, his face easy to read, but Leofwine had meant no rebuke by his words.

"And your son," the king began, "he is good with a sword?"

"Yes, he grows into his strength well. The men of my household troop are pleased with his progression."

"Yet you've chosen not to foster him with another family?"

Leofwine paused for a beat to compose himself,

"No, not yet. My wife and I share a special bond with him, born as he was when I was missing, presumed dead."

The king waved aside the reminder of those events as if they were unimportant and Leofwine fought his flaring anger.

"But all boys should be fostered with someone who will see to their well-being if the worst should happen to their parents."

"I'd generally agree, my king, but the boy is happy and content with us, and with the men of my household troop he doesn't lack for supporters or comradeship."

"I'm sure he doesn't, but I think it's time he was fostered, and if you don't arrange it yourself, then I'm afraid that I must insist upon it. Eadric is a good man, send the boy to him. He'll benefit from being raised in a household over which my daughter rules."

Hating himself for the words he was forced to say, he pushed them through his clenched teeth,

"You honour my family with your thoughtfulness."

"I know I do, but see that it's done, and soon at that. And Leofwine, you're not the only one in the room to realise that I have no blood ties to you. Remember that in your dealings with your people and with Eadric in particular. A man could not ask for a finer son in law."

Bowing his head as words were beyond him, Leofwine stepped away from the king and walked directly into Eadric who'd been closely hovering. Hammer, unaware that his master had started walking only to stop again, carried onwards only turning when he reached Oscetel.

"I'll expect the boy by the summer," Eadric spoke abruptly, "and don't be filling his head with anything but the best of thoughts about me."

"My thanks Eadric for your kind honour."

"You should have arranged it when I first asked," Eadric mouthed angrily and softly. "You shouldn't have made me make this a matter for the king. He doesn't like to be concerned with small issues such as this."

"Then you should not have made it a matter of concern for him," Leofwine responded, just as angrily and just as quietly. "He's my oldest boy, and if any harm should befall him, I will have your head, your father's, your brothers and anyone else I can think of."

# 8

# SUMMER AD1007, NORTHMAN

HIS FATHER HAD DEMANDED THAT THE BEST OF HIS MEN ESCORT NORTHMAN to the hall of Eadric, but that didn't stop the cold dread that curled in his stomach with each breath. For the hundredth time that day he wished himself Leofric, sent to be fostered by Horic and his wife, not Northman, oldest and unluckiest son in the lands.

Wulfstan had bid him goodbye with a cheerful comment, but he saw the haunted look in his eyes and knew he feared that he'd not see him again. Wulfstan aged almost daily now, carrying his years with care. Belatedly everyone in the household had realised that Wulfstan's time was growing shorter and slowly, but surely, he'd been asked to do less and helped more to do the things he wanted to do.

Northman smiled around the hard lump in his chest. When they'd set out earlier that day, Wulfstan had been in his usual spot inside the training grounds. A stout wooden stick in his hand and a small chair behind him for when it all became too much, shouting commands in his firm voice and berating or complimenting the work of the young squires. Until yesterday they'd been Northman's training partners, but they were now the lucky ones who got to stay behind and see Wulfstan in his final days.

Northman wondered if when he'd gone, Wulfstan had crumbled to his chair, as if content to have watched his Lord's son on his way and know that his work for the day was done. It was a thought that made Northman appreciate the old man's stubbornness and respect.

His mother had reacted in an equally perverse way when he'd been leaving. She'd not allowed herself to show her fears or her grief, but had stood, fiercely proud and fiery in her demands of the household troop. Northman had watched with fascination as she'd stepped forwards and spoken her commands to Oscetel while giving her own son barely a look.

His father had told him to expect no less from her, and so it'd come as no surprise that she'd not let her emotions show at all. It had been his sister that he'd had to turn to for tears and wailing. She was deeply unhappy that her two oldest playmates had been denied her. Her tantrum had echoed through their house on both Leofric's departure, and now on Northman's own.

As a parting gift, he'd given her his wooden training shield and sword. She'd grinned with joy at her new trophies, and he'd held his reservations in place. She was old enough and intelligent enough to look after herself. And he'd be far enough away that his mother's wrath wouldn't reach him.

His father had spoken to him the night before, not to issue any last moment commands, but rather to assure him of his support and love. Northman knew that he'd been trying to tell him something but without actually using the words, but he hadn't yet deciphered the hidden meaning of their conversation. His father had smiled sadly at his evident confusion and then offered him both an embrace and also the opportunity to make himself his father's commended man.

Northman had been relieved that his father had remembered his desire, and he'd spoken the words with pride as the men of the household troop had looked on, his mother with pleasure on her face, and his sister with a petulant look on her own. He wondered how his father would deal with her when it was time for her to marry for surely she'd rather be her father's commended woman than anyone's wife.

The words had burst with gratification through his chest, and he'd known then what it was to be an adult. He knew he'd not regret his choice. His family would always come first, no matter what the bloody king or Eadric tried to impose on him. After all, he'd been recognised by another king only recently, Swein of Denmark, and an imposing man. His gift he carried with him now about his belt, and he was looking forward to explaining to the other boys and Eadric himself where he'd obtained such an excellent treasure.

Beside him, Horic's son rode with him, a broad smile on his face. Olaf, named after his father's one-time war leader, was almost Northman's twin, born when his father had been escorting Leofwine home from the Outer Isles. He'd grown up with Northman, and the two could be best friends or best enemies, as brothers should be, and that was how Northman regarded him. He was ecstatic that his father had arranged that he not go alone.

Eadric greeted their small party close to his home, early the same evening. He'd been hunting with his men, and a dizzying array of similar looking men all milled around Northman as though he was a prized pig to be examined.

Northman, trained by his father to endure such scrutiny, didn't let it upset his carefully fortified façade. He was courteous, although with a slight veneer of anger. His father had told him that Eadric would probably look upon him as some project, to be broken and torn away from his father's loyalty. Northman wished the man well and realised, now that the nerves in his stomach had quietened, that contrary to what he'd thought, he might hold the upper hand in the situation.

Eadric was desperate to make him his friend, his son and his viper in the nest for the man he thought of as his enemy, Leofwine. Northman had no such agenda at play, although he had a sneaking idea that he might develop one soon enough, and that meant that he could act as naturally as he chose to, or not, as the mood took him.

The inspection over, and an almost bewildering mass of introductions later, Northman and Olaf were escorted to what would be their new home for at least the next two to three years.

It was a well-maintained hall, a little smaller than his father's, but not by much. It was well cared for and showed the markings of recent repair work to the roof and the walls. Northman supposed that if the king's daughter were soon to live here, she'd need to be accommodated in suitable surroundings. And that was why his father had not brought him here.

In only seven days time, Eadric was to marry Edith, in right royal splendour. By rights, Northman should have travelled to the wedding with his father and then been handed over to Eadric's care, but Eadric had made so much fuss because he was marrying into royalty that Leofwine had agreed to the boy going a few days earlier. That way, Eadric had decided, he'd be able to make Northman welcome in his household before his royal wife arrived.

He jumped to the ground with some elasticity. It had been a long day's riding to get here. Beside him, Olaf too jumped from his horse, and the two beasts were led away to be cared for.

Oscetel milled around on his horse, not having been offered hospitality by Eadric, and for an awkward moment, Northman worried that he wouldn't be. Only with a loud cry of exclamation, Eadric finally mouthed the words of welcome required, and ordered a drinking horn be passed around.

Olaf rolled his eyes at the attempt at circumventing the regular duties of hospitality, and Northman giggled with unease as he stood, a little uncertainly, unsure what to do next. It wasn't the most auspicious start to his fostering.

"You've grown boy," Eadric mouthed from where he stood directly in front of Northman, sizing him up.

"So my mother says," Northman offered, meeting Eadric's eyes for the first time. He was a younger man than his father, but not by much, and when he spoke wrinkles formed around his mouth.

He had brown eyes, and auburn hair, hanging low down his back, but it was his clothes that drew Northman's attention. They were fine, very fine, for a man who'd been out hunting, as the dead carcases of the animals now being lifted from the back of at least five different horses attested.

A small spot of blood marred his face, and down his soft blue tunic, more splatters of blood could be seen. Northman couldn't help but hear his mother's voice chastising him in his head if he'd acted so rashly.

"She struggles to keep me adequately clothed, but she's sent many new clothes with me so that I might grow into them."

"Your mother is a thoughtful woman, but if she thinks that you're finely dressed now, then she's mistaken. For the wedding, you must have far more elaborate garb. I'll ask my servants to begin work on something immediately."

Eadric turned aside then to start a conversation with his steward and Northman, still unsure what to do with himself, stood in the dusty courtyard. Beside him, Olaf shuffled from one foot to another in impatience, and he caught a sympathetic glance from Oscetel as Eadric busied himself giving directions on how his kills were to be treated as if Northman wasn't there at all.

He felt annoyance war with amusement, and for the first time began to appreciate the pettiness and meanness of Eadric. He wondered how his father had ever tolerated his small slights, intended only to annoy.

"My Lord Eadric," Oscetel broke into his conversation, and Eadric flashed him a look of annoyance. "I'm sure your people know how to butcher the deer, should you not welcome your new foster son into your house and make him comfortable? It's been a long day for the lad."

Oscetel spoke blandly, his voice showing neither annoyance or petulance. The same couldn't be said for Eadric, his face creasing into a scowl as he looked at Northman with a little contempt.

"Go, inside boy, make yourself at home. Surely you don't need a nursemaid to assist you."

"Come, my Lord, that's no way to speak to the boy. He's here at your request after all."

"Not my request, Oscetel, the king's, as you well know. I've only agreed to the arrangement because the king demanded it."

Oscetel smirked then,

"Ah my Lord Eadric, if that were the case then you wouldn't have approached the lad last year. Now, stop with your delays and distractions. We're all hungry and thirsty and need excellent hospitality. Clearly, you can provide it after such a good day's hunting." Oscetel nodded to where the fourth deer carcas was being lifted down from the backend of one of the horses.

Annoyance once more flashed across Eadric's face,

"You may speak to your own Lord in such a way, but not in my household will the hired help talk so openly." His words were heated, his face flushing to be reminded so publicly, and Northman's fear returned as Oscetel visibly bristled at the phrase, but then Eadric continued.

"But, you may have a point. I've not been the most welcoming of hosts. Come, lads, bring your things and I'll show you where you'll be sleeping. And you, Oscetel, you may take your horses to the barn and see to them yourselves. I'll ensure a meal is prepared for you."

Without further thought, Eadric strode inside his house, and Northman followed unwillingly, his thoughts too confused to voice.

The interior of the house, like the exterior, showed recent signs of having been repaired and in its centre a massive fire roared and above it, one of the deer was already being slowly roasted. The smell was tantalising to hungry stomachs, but it wouldn't be ready until late in the evening. Olaf, realising this, groaned a little at the delay. Northman caught a smirk on Eadric's face and realised that this too had all been planned.

The hall had been recently cleaned and refreshed. From the rafters, crowds of fresh smelling herbs hung, and discoloured wood marred the far end of the hall, showed that the hall had recently been either repaired or extended slightly. Looking up, Northman saw a small second floor and reasoned that this was the new addition. He assumed it was probably a new room for the use of the king's daughter.

At the other end of the hallway was a rickety looking ladder, extending into a darker and dustier looking space and it was that way that Eadric now walked.

"This is a house for men, not families, well not yet anyway. For the time being, you can bed down up there," Eadric pointed up the ladder, "and hopefully in time, I'll have the space refurbished like the other end of the hall. If you're unhappy, you can always bed down on the hall floor with the men."

There was some contempt in Eadric's voice that Northman shrugged aside. Clearly, he had little good to say about the young. Climbing the ladder when Eadric beckoned him to, Northman was pleased to encounter a clean area, although quite full with equipment and sacks of cloth. He wondered where he and Olaf would find space to sleep.

Noting the lack of rails to the raised platform, Northman strode as far forwards as he could, before he was forced to bend because of the sloping roof. Looking around intently, he noticed neither mouse droppings nor pools of water and decided that here was as good as anywhere. He even found some hooks around the rafters from which he could hang his possessions.

Olaf followed him to the same spot, and dumped his bag of belongings onto the floor, causing the space to vibrate a little. From below them a cry of outrage rang out from whoever had just been covered in age-old dust and filth. Northman tried and failed not to giggle at the strange situation and Olaf joined him. Then they heard heavy footsteps on the ladder and a dusty head appeared over its top.

"It's not funny boys. You two had better be careful," it growled before disappearing again, and the boys giggled soundlessly at the strange apparition. When they'd controlled themselves, they set to work unpacking their few belongings, hanging their tunics from the rafters and leaning their weapons against the roof.

Northman looked around for some furs or bedding but didn't find anything. Shrugging to himself he looked at Olaf and found him busily pulling a huge fur from his bag.

"What's that for?" he whispered in query.

"My mother warned me that Eadric wouldn't be the sort of man who'd think about our comfort. She made me bring this with me."

"I wish my mother had thought the same," Northman muttered darkly, eyeing the creaking floor with disdain. He was used to a warm and comfortable bed, not the unyielding floor.

"We'll share, don't worry about it. We'll get sorted eventually."

A shout from below for Northman had him scampering back down the ladder where he found Oscetel standing carrying a huge sack stuffed with something.

"You've forgotten this boy," Oscetel commented, handing the load to Northman with a twinkle in his eye, and Northman thought a little more kindly of his mother. Clearly, she had thought of everything.

"Thanks, Oscetel," he replied in delight and turned to throw the sack towards where Olaf was hanging over the ledge in a precarious position. His eyes were dancing, Olaf caught the bag and then, making sure it wouldn't fall, made his way down the ladder.

"You sleeping up there?" Oscetel asked quietly, his eyes busily taking in all there was to see in the hall.

"Yep."

"Any bed?"

"No," he responded sourly, and Oscetel smirked in sympathy.

"It'll make you more manly," he quipped, while Northman glared at him.

"Not you as well."

"What d'you mean, not me as well?"

"Eadric says this isn't a house for boys."

"Eadric's an arse," Oscetel muttered under his breath. "Make friends with the servants and his wife when she gets here and try to ignore the fool. You'll be fine."

Momentarily tears clouded his eyes, and Northman shook his head angrily. Now was not the time. Maybe later when he slept, he could give into his despair and grief. Not now, though. Now, he had his father's work to do.

# 9
# SUMMER AD1007, NORTHMAN

In discomfort, he rolled his shoulders and tried to flex his arms, but the embroidery on his tunic was simply too stiff. No matter that the item he wore had been made to fit him by his mother and her women, the work of Eadric's seamstress, as beautiful as it was, was simply too much. The cloth was pulled too tightly in places and barely let him breathe.

Beside him, Olaf was no less uncomfortable as he too shuffled in his seat.

The two boys were sat within the great Church waiting for the wedding to be over and done with so that they could escape the watchful eye of Eadric and more importantly, as they'd soon learnt, his cantankerous father. While he allowed his sons to run wild within the household, acting more like children than the men they were, every little thing that Northman and Olaf did was carefully scrutinised and if he could find fault, he'd lay a hand on them both soon enough.

The number of sharp slaps across the backside that they'd both endured during the last week had quickly become too great to keep a record off. Now he sat in his own beautifully embroidered tunic, which Northman noted sourly fitted him perfectly, and glared at the two boys. Northman decided he'd rather endure the scrutiny of the king over his new foster grandfather. Not that he dared to call him that. He'd done it once, and his legs had smarted all day long. For an old man, he had a wicked strength about him, and Northman didn't doubt that he'd prove lethal if they ever had to fight him.

Now Northman sat as still as he could, and tried not to make it too obvious as to how keen he was to see his father, mother and sister. She'd been deemed old enough to attend the coming royal wedding, and while their mother had fretted about what to dress her in, she'd scowled and poked her tongue out at Northman. She was more likely to be found in a tunic and trousers than a fine dress, and Northman was looking forward to seeing her look as unhappy as he did.

At his side Olaf fidgeted again in the hush of the interior of the Church and even Northman was annoyed by him.

"Keep still. The old man's watching us."

"I know he is, but I can barely breathe. My chest feels tight."

"Take smaller breaths and take them more often."

Olaf quieted beside him, and Northman attempted to take a deep breath himself. He was starting to feel a little dizzy and could only hope that the wedding would soon get under way so that he could stand. It was easier to tolerate the tight clothing when he stood.

A hushed silence greeted the arrival of the king and his wife, both finely dressed, although Northman doubted that as much embroidery had gone into the king's outfit as his own. Only as the king took his seat did he see his father and mother. Unbidden a tear came to his eye, and he swept it away with annoyance. It was good to see his parents, that was a certainty, but there was no need for him to be quite so emotional about the whole thing.

The ceremony was over quickly, and Eadric, in his elaborate clothes and mass of armrings flashing in the candlelight, beamed with triumph at everyone assembled before them.

Northman took a moment to eye his foster father's new wife. She was a well-measured girl, perhaps a little too tall for Northman's liking, but her hair was beautifully plaited with trailing ribbons. She didn't exude satisfaction, as Eadric did, but neither did she look unhappy at the match her father had made for her. Again he had a flash of his sister's future wedding, and he took the decision that she must be married under his father's directions. He'd not be held responsible for making her a match she was less than pleased with.

The prayers and the sermon over and done with, Northman filed out of the Church behind his foster father, and for the first time managed to catch his father's eye. Leofwine smiled with real joy at him, and Northman felt himself relax a little. Well, at least until he heard the angry hissing of Eadric's father behind him, asking him to hurry up. He'd not even realised that he'd stopped where he stood.

The king's palace was decked in summer greenery to celebrate the union, and many tables groaned under the weight of food. Both doors were flung wide open, and a pleasant breeze flowed through the confined space.

He sat with Eadric's family, his foster-father's brothers arrayed all around him, and it was there that Hammer found him. The hound had been groomed for the occasion and Northman shared the thought with him that they were both beasts trussed up waiting to be cooked.

And then he felt his father's hand on his back and he turned with pleasure to see his mother and young sister. She smiled brightly at him, twirling her bound hair between her fingers, but his mother was the one who looked truly beautiful. An older woman she might be, but apart from the queen, she outshone everyone in the room. Even the king's other daughters.

"You're well son?" his father queried, having nodded in greeting to Eadric's father and brothers.

"Yes thank you, my Lord," he offered as an after-thought.

"Your tunic is beautifully decorated," his father continued, and Northman hazarded a guess that he knew just how uncomfortable it truly was to wear.

"Yes, a week of solid embroidery has gone into this."

"It befits your foster-father," his mother offered demurely, a smile playing around her lips. She too knew how uncomfortable he would be.

"Your brother fares well with Horic, I've had a report from him in the last few days, and your parents send their best wishes," Leofwine said, looking at Olaf as he spoke.

"Thank you, my Lord. Please let my mother know that I'm well and enjoying my time within Eadric's fine household."

Under the table, Northman pushed against Olaf's leg. He didn't need to overplay the part too much.

And then Eadric was amongst their midst and the conversation turned a little tenser.

"My Lord Leofwine, might I introduce you to my new wife, the king's daughter, Edith."

Leofwine turned to face Eadric with a pensive expression on his face that quickly morphed into a smile of joy.

"My Lord, my Lady, my congratulations. I wish you a fruitful life together."

Eadric's superior stance was sickening to see, his outgoing clothing a stark contrast to the more demure appearance of his parents.

Edith glanced between the two men a little uncertainly, but Æthelflæd spared her from any discomfort, by bobbing her head in deference and then exclaiming that they must speak about Northman in more detail, and away from the men. Eadric watched the pair of them walk away, back towards where a large group of royal women had converged with a predatory look on his face.

"Your boy needs some work," he thundered so that all along the table could hear. Leofwine's face stilled at the words of criticism.

"My apologies if he is still a little too young to be of use in your household. I'll happily take him back until he is more acceptable to you." His words were smooth and well placed. Northman felt a tiny flicker of hope that Eadric quickly doused.

"It's nothing that I can't resolve with the help of my father and royal wife."

"As you will my Lord, but if you would like to speak to me in more private surroundings of what exactly the problem is, I'll have a discussion with my boy."

Eadric smirked with half his face, his eyes still on his wife, where she stood to converse with Æthelflæd, watching events play out between Eadric and Leofwine. Northman had the uncomfortable feeling that the pair spoke about him, and he wondered what his mother was saying.

"It's of little concern to you my Lord Leofwine. I'll mould the lad to my ways soon enough. Certainly, he's good with a weapon, although a little stupid with his mouth."

Mortified, Northman looked at his shoes, and it was Olaf's turn to nudge him in support.

"He's young. He'll learn to hold his thoughts in check soon enough."

"He better," Eadric muttered, as he walked away, his eyes never leaving his wife.

Eadric's brother stood then, Brihtric and took his place.

"Apologies my Lord, but my brother has other things on his mind today than your son and his well-being."

"I'm sure he does, but he must learn that he's responsible for something far more valuable to me than almost anything else in the world. A man's son and heir are to be cherished by all who care for him."

Brihtric conceded the point while glaring at his father. Northman had already discovered that not all the brothers accorded their father the respect he deserved. He'd been shocked at first, but had since realised that this was another way he could attempt to survive in the strange household of his foster father.

"Still, it's also the role of the father to ensure a child is correctly taught."

Leofwine snuck a quick glance at Northman then but quickly

realised that the conversation he was involved in wasn't really for him at all.

"If you don't mind, I think I'll speak with my son," Leofwine intervened before anything else could be said, and Brihtric nodding absent-mindedly. He was torn between his scowls at his brother's good fortune in marrying into the royal family, and at his father, who'd clearly done him some ill as a child.

Relieved to get away from the suddenly tense situation, Northman felt his father's arm around his shoulder, and looking on the other side, saw Olaf was there too. Taking advantage of the open doorway close to them, Leofwine escorted them outside, Hammer faithfully at his father's side.

Outside, the sun was blazing hot, and irritably Northman tugged on his tunic.

"Just take it off lads, no one will care now that the ceremony is done. Do you have other tunics with you to change into?"

"No, we travelled in this, and tonight, we'll be travelling back in them," Olaf groaned, tugging in vain to get the offending garment over his head.

"Then you have my sympathies," Leofwine offered, helping the two boys in their struggles.

Oscetel had followed his father outside, and he looked bemused by the semi-naked lads.

"That bad aye?" he asked a chuckle in his voice. Neither boy answered verbally, preferring instead to cast looks of loathing his way.

Around them, servants and guests dashed to and fro, providing more food and drink when it was needed. Men of the king's household troops lounged about in the sun, their swords holstered, sweating through their padded tunics. Not that anyone was expecting any trouble.

Indicating that they should walk towards the stream curling along the king's lands, Northman began to speak,

"It's not been too bad with Eadric. It's his father who's the menace. How's Wulfstan?" he asked quickly, remembering his concern for the old man when he'd left.

Leofwine shrugged as he replied,

"The same as when you left. A little too old and a bit too grey, but his mind is clear."

"You will tell me, if, or should, or when he ails?" Northman asked, realising just how worried he'd been about him.

"Of course I will never fear. But now, to you. How are you faring? Is it bearable?"

"It's not home, that's for sure," Olaf spoke so darkly that Leofwine glanced a little swiftly at him, and mistimed his next step. Luckily Hammer was on hand to steady him over the uneven surface, and Olaf offered a muted apology.

"I'll tell your mother you miss her rages and your father, his beatings."

"I'd rather take both of those things than Eadric's snide remarks and the sniggering from amongst his household troops. And his father, as Northman says, is a nasty piece of work."

"But they're kind to you?"

"They're not unkind, but neither are they kind. They've decided to tolerate us, I think," Northman said.

"And there's been no attempts to have you speak against me?"

"Oh yes, all the time. He's always dropping little asides into his conversations with us, but mostly, we train with the men, and we have little to do with Eadric. For all that his father is clearly a warrior, as are his brother's, he much prefers pampering himself and having others do his work for him."

Leofwine listened intently,

"Do you think you'll survive the winter there?"

"Of course we will, all we need to do is avoid the old man, and I'm sure Eadric will be too busy making little Eadric's to care much for me."

The implied slight in his voice made Oscetel snicker behind him, and Northman turned in surprise,

"I'm sure that it'll only be a few more years, and you'll be thinking the same," Oscetel remarked with a raised eyebrow.

Northman felt himself blush at the change in conversation. Apart from his mother and sister, he'd never paid the slightest bit of attention to what a woman looked like, and he had no intention of starting now. Olaf shared his embarrassment, as the two older men laughed in mirth, they both ran on, mindful that just for a little bit, they could be boys and not men in the making.

# 10

## EASTER AD1008, NORTHMAN

THE HORSES BLEW HOT AIR IN THE CHILL EARLY SUMMER AIR. HE'D WOKEN early from his disturbed sleep within the hastily erected tent of last night, and not wishing to disturb the others he shared the space with, he'd slunk out of the tent and pulled his riding tunic over his head. He'd shivered in the chill, but he was looking forward to some time alone with his thoughts and decided the cold could be borne for a few moments.

The men on guard during the night nodded in greeting but left him alone with his thoughts.

It's been a hard few months within Eadric's household. The arrival of the royal wife had not made it any easier, and contrary to his hopes, Eadric had been far from besotted with her. He was courteous to her and mindful of her needs, but Northman had quickly discovered that Eadric had another woman he found more to his liking, and it was to her that he went after he'd fulfilled his marriage vows to his wife. As soon as Edith had been with child, Eadric had avoided her as much as he could.

Edith had initially reacted with dismay but quickly had formed a new faction within the household, made up of those servants she'd brought with her, and also two of Eadric's brothers and more of the servants and household troops. The conversations at night could get quite heated, and Northman had quickly learned that if he wanted any peace he needed to coast between the two parties.

Edith had stayed behind on this trip to the king's Witan. The child she carried was due any day now, and she'd eagerly shooed both Eadric and his mistress from her home. Northman harboured the hope that she might not let Eadric back into his home when he returned.

He'd not seen his father since the wedding in the summer, although he'd had the occasional message from him, via one of the messengers who plied Eadric with information about the king's court. The ones who were not adverse to taking the extra coin to let Northman know that his father and mother were well and that Wulfstan still lived.

Still, he was apprehensive about seeing his father again. He was aware that the last few seasons had changed him. He was a boy no more. He knew things he didn't want to, and he'd seen things he wished he hadn't. Eadric could be cruel when he wanted to be, not above making spectacles of unfortunates who crossed him. More than once he'd seen a whipping or an amputation. Every time he thought of the suffering of those people, he felt physically sick.

Not that Eadric wasn't above taking payment instead of punishment. In fact, he was a little too keen to do so, and it was only the poor who suffered so harshly at his hands. Almost anyone else could save themselves if they could pay enough of a fine.

Eadric had decided to take a keen interest in Northman. He often had him eat with him, and demanded he hunt with him. Initially, the special favour had rankled, because he'd not held any illusions that it was out of the desire for his company. Instead, it just allowed Eadric the opportunity to plant more seeds of doubt into his head about how well, or not, his father had once governed the Mercian lands, and how, he Eadric, was so much better at it.

Sometimes, he wasn't always sure he could see the truth for

what it was anymore. He felt disillusioned with his father and equally disappointed with Eadric. Eadric had quickly taught Northman that Leofwine was too keen to listen, to talk and to make arrangements with the men who looked to him. Eadric was too quick to lash out, and make pitiful attempts at reconciliation later. He was too sharp with his judgements and too blinkered to look for any solution other than the one he'd devised himself.

He was also devious in his dealings with the king. Northman knew how much tax the king should be due, but Eadric bemoaned the whole process of collecting it and delivering it and then complained until the king allowed him to keep more of it than he should. And yet with those who owed him service, he was harsh and exacting, his steward a tough man to encounter with any sort of lack.

And now he was officially part of Eadric's household troop. He'd not yet been called upon to swear an oath to him, thankfully, as he couldn't, he was his father's commended man. He must fight for Eadric, and see to his safety, when really, he wanted nothing more than to never see the two faced malicious man again.

In the early morning quiet, he heard the unmistakable sounds of Eadric on his mistress and bile filled his mouth. The thought of the opposite sex didn't stir him, not as much as holding an elegant sword in his hand, and although Olaf had happily experimented with the servant women, and told tales to Northman, he still didn't feel the urge.

At his feet, his hound wove in and out of his legs, and his horse's, as he bent down to stroke the intelligent eyes he saw there. The hound was his one true friend, and he was pleased that Eadric took it as a given that wherever he went, his hound must follow. Clearly, his father had made the men of the court oblivious to the animal that provided him with an extra eye.

There'd been no reports of Raiders during the winter months, and Northman knew that the king was congratulating himself on finally seeing the back of them. His father, however, was planning something else entirely. Long missives between the king and Eadric had included discussions on whether the English should finally be pro-active, and raise a ship-army to defend itself. The king was unsure of the value of the project. Leofwine was adamant that it should be done immediately, and Eadric didn't seem to care, provided he didn't have to spend his money on it, or his efforts on organising it.

Northman thought the idea was a good one, but he wasn't saying so to Eadric. Instead, he'd learnt to make as many little comments and remarks as he could in any conversation, leaving his company on many occasions, knowing that Eadric was pensively thinking about what he'd said. Had his foster son agreed with him as he thought he had or had he flatly rebuked his ideas?

Northman found him a strange man. He had a magnificent sword, a beautifully crafted shield, and a war axe topped with precious jewels. He never practised his sword craft, unlike his brother Brihtric, and the gems made the weapons almost worthless, the soft gold used to mount them weakening the integrity of the weapons. No wonder he never wanted to fight the Raiders for his king. Soon enough they'd have injured him and cost him a fortune, at the same time.

Behind him, the camp began to wake quickly, and in no time at all, they were all mounted and resuming their journey towards Enham. Northman had never visited Enham before, but he'd been told it was little different to any of the king's other palaces. And at least, once he was there, he might be able to spend some time apart from Eadric.

As they journeyed that day, Eadric called Northman to his side. He didn't speak to him, just had him ride there all day and not until they reached Enham did Northman realise why. When they crossed paths with his father, he knew that Leofwine noted the honour being done to his son, and he cursed himself for a fool. He should have somehow realised that Eadric was up to his tricks again.

Leofwine watched his son ride past him without any rancour, but it burned Northman. He was constrained by his fosterage with

Eadric, and it didn't sit well with him. At that moment he craved being a man in their world, able to make his own decisions and act as he knew he should. His father had, despite Eadric's denials, taught him what he needed to know to rule men well, and he was aware that he'd be better at it than Eadric ever would.

Briefly, he saw his father that night as they ate within the king's hall. Sadly there were too many people to make it possible for them to speak in private, and so instead, he contended himself with the presence of Hammer, and a small conversation with Oscetel, who sent his mother's love and Wulfstan's best wishes. It had been a cold winter, long and dark, but Wulfstan had settled himself before the fire and seemed to have moved as little as possible during that time. Not that his mouth had been still, Oscetel assured him. Between Finn and Wulfstan, Leofwine was being written an excellent piece of history about his own rule as ealdorman and his time in the Outer Islands. Northman could visualise the scene only too well, and he felt a pang that he'd missed it.

On this occasion, Horic had also allowed Leofric to attend upon his father, and Northman felt jealously swamp him as he saw his younger brother allowed to sit amongst the men, for all that his voice was still high, and he had the physique of a boy, not a man.

The talk swirling around the hall was of the king's intentions. It was no secret that discussions had taken place about mounting a ship-army, and Northman noted, as he sat quietly amongst Eadric's rough men that everyone there seemed to have their own opinion about what should happen when it should happen and how it should occur.

The following day, the discussions reached their height, Leofwine arguing passionately that, as eight years earlier, it was time for the king to act decisively. Eadric decried the expense, while Uhtred of Northumbria and Ulfcytel of East Anglia appeared to agree with the king, who either diplomatically, or realistically, could see the benefits of Leofwine's suggestions.

Northman watched the king carefully. He fancied himself

becoming an expert on how to read men. His father was perhaps too caught up in the idea of Æthelred as his king and failed to see the man behind the title. Northman thought he was beginning to understand him. He appeared to be a strong man, but a weak king, a strange juxtaposition that he couldn't quite reconcile.

He gave the matter much thought. At his age, all of twelve, Æthelred had already been king in name for a few years. He'd grown up knowing who he had to be, and he'd reached maturity under the watchful eye of his mother and his father's older ealdormen.

Northman thought he wouldn't have much liked that himself. Until he'd come to Eadric's house he'd been allowed to be his own person. His parents had tried to allow him to become himself, to show him right from wrong, to imbibe him with the correct amount of respect for his parents, his Church and his brothers, sisters and other children. They'd not pushed him one-way or the other. Not like in Eadric's household.

In the home of Eadric, he'd quickly learnt that others expected to control him, almost as though he was an extension of their own person. It made him think even less highly of Eadric, while at the same time appreciating the logic of having your household think and act as you would. He'd once tried to stand up to Eadric when he disagreed with him on a matter of justice, but he'd learned very quickly that his opinions mattered for nothing. He wondered if that was how Æthelred had been raised; to think as he was told and never utter a word against it. It was an interesting thought. But if that was what had happened, why would he have grown into a strong man, but a weak king? No, he decided, something else must have happened to make him as he was.

The king was not much older than his father, and yet he seemed a little greyed now, a little sunken and his eyes were no longer quite as quick to flash with humour or annoyance as they once had been. Northman wondered if the king had finally learned to hide his thoughts, or whether he was just tired of his bickering ealdormen with their conflicting advice.

"Do you know how much it would cost to build ships and arm the men?" the king asked into a semi-silence that had fallen as Eadric appeared to have finally run out of things to say against the idea.

"As a rough idea, it's been discussed that every three hundred and ten hides provide for a ship and from every eight a helmet and byrnie."

The king fixed his father with a keen eye.

"You've given this much thought," a statement, not a question.

"Not just me my Lord, the archbishop has assisted me, and some of his clerics have produced those figures."

The king's eyes swept from where his father was talking earnestly to his king from his place at the front of the Witan, to where Wulfstan was keeping his own place amongst the churchmen. Northman wondered if the king looked a little angry, but quickly decided he was more intrigued than anything.

"Eadric, this doesn't seem like a huge burden for the people. What are you wittering on about?"

"My Lord, and father," Eadric began, his face blotching with colour as he felt the eyes of everyone in the room on him.

"I hadn't realised it would be so little. I'd thought it'd take far more taxes to build so many ships and outfit the men. Your figures are correct?" he asked acidly, his eyes on Leofwine although it was Wulfstan who answered.

"As they can be my Lord and my king. They're taken from as many accounts as could be found of modern shipbuilding."

Eadric turned to glance at Wulfstan, his stance immediately a little more deferential for all that Northman knew he hated the interfering archbishop.

"So you're arguing against something without all the facts, and trying to cite our family relationship as a way of enforcing your opinion?" the king asked Eadric coolly. "And my daughter, why is she not here?"

Eadric bowed low to the ground, and Northman suppressed a sigh of irritation at the honeyed words, oiled with insincerity.

"She grows near her time of delivery, and decided it wasn't safe to travel. She is of course well, and looking forward to providing you with another grandchild."

The king didn't seem at all impressed by the words, almost as if the notion that he would become a grandfather was distasteful to him, a reminder of his age, Northman thought, and an unwelcome one at that.

Brushing aside his son by marriage, Æthelred looked at the assembled men and women before him. There was a hush over the entire room, no sound stirred, not even the squawk of a chicken or the lowing of a cow from outside where daily life continued as normal. It was as if the world waited on the answer the king might give.

"And where would we station our ships, and how many ships would this give us, and how many men could we outfit, and where would they all come from?"

Northman watched his father's back with interest. Did he have all the answers to these questions? The king liked answers.

"More than a hundred my Lord," Leofwine spoke calmly and matter of factly, consulting a piece of parchment in his hand. "Each ship would have roughly forty men so we would need four thousand of them, and they would need to be trained in basic seamanship."

The king turned sharply to Leofwine at the mention of so many men, in ships, facing the Raiders.

"So many! That should more than double any force that has yet come against us," his voice sounded calm but excited, and Northman knew there and then that the king had already decided that the answer would be yes. He wanted a fleet of ships. He wanted that force. He already imagined the damage it would inflict. Northman felt the excitement stir within him. Here was something that would make a man out of him.

"It's a clever idea my Lord, but where would we get so many men to command the ships?"

"Eadric, you're annoying me," the king said without preamble. "This is an excellent idea and one I am almost minded to agree to immediately without asking for further thoughts, but you, you seem determined to knock down this attempt. Why is that?" he asked harshly, his voice angry for all that his face stayed calm.

"No, my Lord, of course, I'm not trying to deter you. I just think ... we need to give the matter more thought."

"I disagree with you, but I'll discuss my thoughts with you at a more convenient time. For now, I would like to hear more about how the ship army would be built and where we would house it."

Wulfstan had now taken to his feet. His head bowed towards the king.

"My clerics have drawn up a lengthy document detailing many of these things. It would please me to make more of the details known."

"Excellent, come on then."

And so the room returned to almost silence, only the voice of Wulfstan rising and falling as he spoke of where the wood could be found for the ships. And further, of the men who could build the ships and the pros and cons of stationing the ships at Sandwich as a fleet, or dotted around the coastal regions, and where the men should come from and who should command the ships.

Northman was amazed. He could only imagine that the entire winter months had been spent gathering the intelligence that Wulfstan, and apparently his own father, had at their fingertips.

They knew of ship builders in all the main ports, and many had already said they would happily put aside all other work for the next year and build for their king, and their safety.

Infected with enthusiasm for the project, those of the king's thegns who fancied themselves as more ships commanders than tax collectors, spoke amongst themselves of how they could manage the men.

As it went on, Eadric's lips curled unhappily as he switched his angry gaze from the serene back of Leofwine to the austere and well dressed archbishop Wulfstan. Somehow, and Northman wasn't entirely sure how Eadric needed to gain the upper-hand here. Northman found it unsettling to realise that he had no difficulty in believing that Eadric would manage to bring about a complete reversal of opinion. He thought it would do him a lot of good to keep watching the many faces of Eadric. He'd learn yet another way of deceiving those who trusted if he watched closely enough.

And then a thegn Northman didn't know or recognise, stood and waited for the king to call the rest of the Witan together. He waited patiently, not seeming concerned that the king was so slow in noticing him. Slowly silence began to fall amongst those who spoke, and it wasn't at the king's request, but more out of respect for the man.

Northman watched him with interest. He seemed a self-assured sort of man, not as old as his own father, but apparently confident enough that he was prepared to put himself so much on display and face being completely ignored by the king. By rights he should have been ignored, only the rest of the Witan hadn't been so keen to hear what he had to say.

"Yes good thegn," the king finally asked, his gaze settling on the man, his eyes a little narrowed but his stance easy for all that. He was just as intrigued as the other men.

"My king, I'm Wulfnoth, and I have my own ships, four of them all told." He shrugged in a self-depreciating manner at his admission, aware that he spoke of his wealth with pride but that others might mock him for its meanness. "And I have shipmen, and I know of other shipmen, and I know of other thegns who would be able to crew and command the ships that the king intends to build. I would be pleased to oversee as many of these ships as the king thinks I should."

A low murmur ran round the room, and Northman watched Eadric's face darken further. Not for the first time, Northman wondered why the idea so infuriated his foster-father. Surely he didn't think that he could arrange to protect the land solely on his own.

Now Æthelred was intrigued,

"And your shipmen. What do they do in your ships?"

"We trade, we fish, we sail, and we get to know the lay of the coast. And when the winter comes, we stay at our homes, and we repair our sails or make new ones. My king," he added hastily.

"And how do you support these ships and your men?"

Wulfnoth looked thoughtful now,

"The men are my commended men, just as on the land, only the commanders owe me for their ships and only some small piece of land. The shipmen and warriors are sometimes my commended men, and sometimes they are just bound to me. Some, I confess, are slaves."

"And these others you speak of, are they the same as you? Men of land and also ships?"

"Yes, my Lord king. We build our homes and then we build our ships, or maintain ships passed down to us."

"It's interesting to know how your ships are managed. And you have my thanks for speaking out. When my ships are built, I will ensure that you are made commander over some of them. Again, my thanks."

Realising he'd been dismissed, Wulfnoth sat down, his face a little flushed. The king had done him a great honour, although he didn't seem to realise that it had been his words that had further swayed the king to the idea of building the ship army.

"Members of the Witan, I think, as I'm sure you agree, that this idea is the best chance we have of defending our shores. If we can stop the Raiders before they make landfall, then they will be able to do us no harm. Those who have spoken of this, and especially my archbishop Wulfstan and Ealdorman Leofwine, you have my thanks for your time and consideration. I will have the scribes draw up details of how much tax must be collected and where the ships should be built, and where we should then muster. For now, I think that we should discuss matters of law."

And that was the end of any debate. The king had spoken, the ships would be built, and Northman felt a flutter of excitement. Like king Swein and his son Cnut, he would very much like to go to sea, to understand the way the ships sliced through the water. His father's ship, moored with the few others of the king's sometimes standing ship army, had long been far away from home and he'd not been in it since he was a small boy. Hopefully, that would all change now.

His father turned and winked at Northman as if hearing his very thoughts, and he grinned widely back at him, before Olaf nudged him in warning. Eadric was glaring at him, and he looked very much less than pleased.

Amongst the row of thegns close to Wulfnoth, Northman could clearly see Eadric's brothers and father bickering amongst themselves. Unable to stop himself, his eyes rolled in aggravation at the men, and when Olaf stood firmly on his foot in warning, he looked away, avoiding Eadric's eyes and focusing instead on the king's many sons.

Athelstan was sitting quietly, his eyes downcast. His brothers did the same and Northman admired their resolve all over again. They were circumspect in their every movement, and word spoken within the Witan. Northman knew for a fact that, no matter how thorough his father's training had been, he'd never have been able to sit quietly by while his father made decisions without reference to them. He relied on his ealdormen and his thegns and his ecclesiastics but never consulted his sons. He happily sent them to war, or to do his bidding within the lands he controlled, but he never asked them what they thought on a matter of law. Even Northman realised that he denied his sons a thorough grounding in statesmanship. Not that it seemed to be stopping them from building their own power bases.

Northman knew that his father thought highly of Athelstan and his next oldest brother, Edmund. He'd also grieved when Ecgberht had died of contagion. He'd been young, and his death made

Northman feel a little cold. It just showed that there was no guarantee of reaching manhood. Even in times of peace.

The king spoke at some length then, about the laws he wished to change or make but Northman wasn't listening, his mind focused on the future glory he envisaged. Him, with some of Horic's countrymen at his command, manning the most mobile and responsive ship in the king's soon to be fleet, earning the king's undying respect and land and riches beyond his wildest dreams.

The time passed quickly, and then, finally, he was able to slink away from Eadric's still furious face, and spend time with his father and his father's men. In the company of the other men, Northman did something he hadn't done since entering Eadric's household, he relaxed and laughed and smiled, listening with joys to the tales of misfortune that had occurred to his younger brothers and sister in his absence. It was only with a heavy heart that he turned his back on his father's men and retired when Eadric bid him to his bed. Being with the others had made him remember how much he was missing out on. He hoped that soon he'd be allowed home.

# 11

# EARLY WINTER AD1008, NORTHMAN

THE FIRST FAINT STIRRINGS OF WINTER WERE WRAPPING THEMSELVES AROUND the land, and atop his horse, he pulled his cloak a little tighter and tugged his gloves on a bit more snuggly. He was cold with his breath steaming in front of him, but he knew that Eadric had no intention of seeking shelter anytime soon and so resolved himself to overcoming his discomfort.

At the king's command, Eadric had been sent to inspect the shipbuilding taking place at London. The waterfront and dock area was awash with noise and a sea of men, busy about their business, purposeful in their every movement. Northman felt out of place beside Eadric, who was doing his very best to show off his total ignorance at all things ship related. Northman realised that he knew far more about the process than Eadric for all that he'd not been on a ship since he'd been a small boy.

The ship builder trying to oversee the building of the fifty ships that had been ordered was quickly losing his patience with the officious ealdorman and Eadric was too blind to see it. Not for the first time, Northman wondered how the man, who was so often quick witted when dealing with those he didn't like, could be so slow and bumbling in situations that he should have been able to control and dominate. There was no point in denying that by the end of the week, news of Ealdorman Eadric's complete ignorance would be known around the entire shipyard and probably far further afield as well. Northman wondered why he'd not researched how the men would build the ships before coming here. He knew his father would have done so.

Beside Eadric, his brother, Brihtric, was transfixed by what he was seeing. Ever since the Witan at Enham he'd been keen to see the ships being constructed and to know who would be commanding them. Northman found it unfair that Brihtric was apparently angling for a ship's command, even though he was completely unsuitable for it, while he was offered nothing. Neither his father or Eadric had asked if he'd like to be trained as a shipman and he felt deeply annoyed at their oversight.

He sighed deeply, and Olaf leant over to nudge him.

"Keep your temper under wraps. I don't think he's forgiven you yet for the incident with the dog."

Northman jumped at the nudge and sighed at the reminder. Eadric and his hound didn't get on, and sometimes Northman felt as though Eadric went out of his way to ensure that the hound was tempted to snarl or snap at him. For no one else did the dog show even the smallest bit of temper. Eadric was his sole source of strife and Eadric knew it and exploited it as a means of infuriating Northman.

The latest incident had occurred when they'd been out hunting, and the hound had unwittingly caused Eadric to miss a large deer, simply by being in the wrong place at the wrong time. Days later Eadric was still to be heard decrying his lack of venison that evening and his mood was black whenever Northman was brought to his attention.

He'd been surprised when Eadric had commanded that he join him on this journey. He'd fully expected to be left at his home, keeping his wife and new child company. And Eadric's grumpy father. He was pleased that he hadn't been, or at least he had been. Now he wasn't too sure. Better to have stayed home than witness this.

The master ship builder was from the lands of the Five Boroughs, a proud man and evidently well skilled in managing his people, and building ships. A massive stockpile of beautiful Mercian Oaks was piled on the dry land, and everywhere Northman looked men were preparing the wood for the ships. The sound of axes on wood echoed encouragingly in the small space. Some men sang as they worked, others muttered to themselves and yet more laughed and joked above the carcases of the ships they were constructing.

Northman watched in fascination as the men used a series of wedges delicately tapped into the sides of the logs to split them into only three or four long planks of wood. One of the men, seeing his questioning look, stood from his labour and wondered over to where he sat atop his horse.

"You must be Ealdorman Leofwine's son. You look just like him." Northman nodded and smiled at the same time. He was more often than not recognised, especially in the Mercian lands, where his father had been a constant presence.

"And who might this tall fellow beside you be?"

"This is Horic's son, Olaf." The man's face split even wider in a toothy grin,

"Aye, you've the look of that old rogue as well. Have you come to inspect the shipbuilding? Your father was only here one day last week. But come, if you want to see how we work, you'll have to hop down from your mighty steed and come and see."

Pleased with the invitation, Olaf and Northman were both on their feet immediately, as a young lad came forward to lead the horses away.

"I'm Halfdan by the way, and that's my smallest son, Bjorn. He's good with the animals. Far more than I am. I prefer the fish and the slap of the waves against a well-made keel. I think he'll not follow in my footsteps. He has no joy in the building of the ships, and the little blighter vomits whenever I put him on a ship. I think a productive piece of land will have to be found for him."

Northman watched the young lad with interest for a long moment, until his curiosity got the better of him and he was away with the ship builder, wandering through the selection of half finished, or barely begun vessels. Everywhere there was the smell of freshly chopped wood, mixed with an unpleasant smell of hot animal hair. He wrinkled his nose briefly until he remembered who he was.

Halfdan had been busily working on a half-finished ship, its keel and the stern and aft clear to see, but little in between. Beside the carcass of the ship, men, boys and women laboured as they worked in the chill air, many casting aside all cloaks as they sweated despite the cold air.

Northman ran his hands along the smooth surface of the wood, while Halfdan picked up his axe.

"Come, I'll show you how to split the logs precisely."

Without pausing for breath, he picked up some small wooden wedges, almost pegs, and began selecting places on the nearby log, mounted on what looked like three half finished tables, where he could gently tap them into place. Intrigued Northman stepped ever closer, trying to see what it was that made the man pick those spots.

"It's just something you learn when you work with wood," he finally offered by way of an explanation when Northman found himself scratching his head in puzzlement.

"The wood has certain soft spots where you know you can hammer home a wedge and know that the wood will split straight. I can't explain it any better than that, and nor can the rest of the men. It's just something you learn along with your craft as a youngster."

Satisfied that the wedges were in place, Halfdan handed both Northman and Olaf a small hammer each.

"Go and stand down there," Halfdan pointed to the far end of the log, "and you, Olaf, you stand at the other end. I'll stay here in the middle, and when I say hammer, we'll all hammer together and get ourselves a nice straight plank of wood."

Feeling a little nervous, Northman tapped away hesitantly on the wedge when he was commanded to do so by Halfdan, but the older man laughed at his feeble efforts.

"You need to use all your strength boy or it'll never work. The time for delicacy is over."

And so having flung aside his cloak, Northman did as he was advised, hammering roughly on the wedges that were near to him. Some of the other men, who'd been assisting Halfdan before they'd arrived, stood quietly by, muttering amongst themselves and offering the stray word of encouragement. And then a sharp crack as the wood gave all the way along its length on one side.

"Good lads, now, the other side as well."

They repeated their actions and in a much shorter span of time, another sharp crack echoed around the shipyard and Northman gave a little cry of delight to see the wood almost pop itself free from the long trunk.

Halfdan was beaming with joy at their success,

"Well, if either of you ever decides that staying on the land is no fun, I'll happily have you in the shipyard. You listen well, and you're strong, and now this plank of wood can be used in this ship here. But now, you'd best be off and let the rest of us get back to work. We've still another two or three planks to prize from this little beauty."

The man ran his hands covetously down the length of the now disturbed log, and Northman took a moment to appreciate the craftsmanship that went into building the beautiful ships, even the cutting of the planks of wood was a delicate matter.

"My thanks for showing us how you keep the planks so straight."

"My pleasure, and Northman, your father was speaking very highly of you last week, and I think he has the right of it. You're a pleasant and beguiling young man, for all that you must spend time with Eadric," he offered in an undertone.

Northman smiled tightly at the unexpected praise and clasped the arm of the man in friendship. This wasn't the first time he'd experienced a situation where people unfriendly towards Eadric took the time and effort to mention his father to him. It reinforced what his mother had told him when he first learned of his fosterage. He might well be in the home of Eadric, but everywhere he went, others had an eye out for his interests and well-being.

Walking back towards where Eadric was busily arguing with the master ship builder, Northman listened to what Eadric was actually saying.

"But it's a waste. These trees take decades to grow and look, all you do is extract three of four planks of wood from them. Surely you could double that amount if you used a different method of splitting the wood."

The mastership builder's face was almost puce with anger as he glanced from Eadric to his brother.

"But my Lords, the strength of the planks is vital to the strength of the ship, and the way we split the wood takes advantage of the wood's natural properties. The trees were massive when they stood on the ground, supporting a weight even I can hardly comprehend. It's imperative that we find that strength."

"But it costs more, and we must ensure that the king doesn't spend all the people's tax heedlessly."

"My Lord, forgive me, but it's not heedlessly. Watch the men who split the wood. They're skilled and grizzled sea captains, men who have their own ships or who command ships. They understand the way the sea will use the wood, and the way the wood will use the sea. That sort of skill is a hard-won thing, not a waste at all. My Lord Leofwine was pleased with our work."

He ended on a plaintive tone as if despairing of a way to make Eadric understand and Northman stepped forwards.

"Foster father," he began, ignoring Olaf's in-drawn breath at his timidity, and Eadric's anger at the mention of Leofwine "come, let Halfdan show you the skill of splitting the trunks. It's fascinating."

Eadric fixed him with a hard stare that he ignored, purposefully.

He felt no loyalty to Eadric, but he wanted the ship builders to be rewarded for their pains and care. There was little point in building ships that would not be sea-worthy and Eadric needed to understand that sometimes, money just had to be spent even when he begrudged it. He'd not be creaming the top of this latest tax, no matter how much he wanted to.

Opening his mouth to speak, and then shutting it again, Eadric jumped free from his horse, his feelings difficult to read from his posture.

"Come, boy, show me this Halfdan. If I appreciate his skills, then I can report back to the king that the building proceeds well and is not wasteful." As he spoke, he cast a dark look towards the master ship builder, and Northman suppressed a sigh. All threats and implied threats, would Eadric never learn that men thrived on respect, not fear? Compliment on a job well done and they were more likely to work on it even more diligently next time. Bitch and moan and they were liable to skimp and produce shoddy workmanship, for what was the point in making it perfect if it wasn't to be recognised as such?

Halfdan had been watching the exchange so that when Northman arrived and made his request, he was ready and prepared.

"Now my Lord Eadric, as I was showing the boys, the trunk has to be split in a certain way, but a master woodworker will just 'know' where the divisions should be made, and will work to tease the wood free from the log. Now, if you'll allow me just a few moments, I'll finish placing these small wedges where the wood is at its weakest, and will give the strongest planks of wood."

Eadric, for once, stood attentively, watching the man through narrowed eyes. He shuffled a little impatiently, but Northman and Halfdan ignored him, while the master-shipman spoke to Brihtric about what exactly Halfdan was doing. Brihtric was as intrigued as Northman had been and Northman felt himself easing a little towards him. Yes, he was jealous that he might get to command a ship or ships, but really, was the king going to allow a twelve-year-old boy the honour? Not likely, unless he was his son. And that was not the case.

Halfdan, with courteousness, finally showed Eadric and his brother to the same positions that Northman and Olaf had occupied the first time round, and with the same instructions they set to work relieving the log of its plank of wood.

Eadric was even more hesitant than Northman had been, and he stepped forwards and mentioned it, in a quiet voice that no others could hear, not looking at Eadric as he did so. It was better not to make eye contact with him.

He prided himself on the tact he'd learnt in Eadric's household, not that it didn't chaff at him. Why should a twelve-year-old have to be so discreet? He imagined that in any other home he'd have been allowed to be as grumpy and self-obsessed as he wanted to be. But not here.

His eyes narrowing at the commands from Northman, Eadric did at the least, follow his instructions, and soon a loud crack rang out, and the wood came loose on one side. Eadric smirked at his success in creating such a straight edge to the plank of wood, running his hands along the smooth wood.

As he was doing so, Halfdan copied his exercise with the wedges on the other side of the log, and this time, Eadric didn't flinch away from the force needed to prize the plank loose. Another loud crack and the wood sprang free from its home, and two men stepped forwards to take the plank away. Eadric watched it on its way towards a ship that was even less built than the one beside them.

"But there is much waste," he said, pointing at the discarded elements of the once mighty tree.

"They're not wasted. Those parts can be used for other bits of the ship. We can make smaller planks of wood with them, which will be fitted to less vital parts of the ships. And the branches of the tree are used too, sometimes as small staves at the points of the ship where they join, and other times to make oars. It all depends on the size of the tree."

Still not convinced Eadric smacked the remainders of the wood where they rested on stands along the busy shipyard.

"And this is the way that the Raiders build their ships?"

"Oh yes, my Lord. My skills have been passed onto me from forebears who were original settlers, back in Halfdan's day, when he made his treaty with Alfred. This is the traditional way and the only way to build these types of ships." Halfdan was talking excitedly now, pointing to the ships in their various stages of construction.

"See, this ship here," and he pointed to an almost finished vessel, being caulked by a selection of youths about Northman's age, "has been fitted with a false bottom. It stops the ships being damaged so much when they're run up the beach. And this one here, this one has an extra high mast so that it can make use of even the slightest breeze. These are all tricks that the Raiders know off and make use off. We'll not be beaten in a test of our knowledge and skills."

Evidently impressed by Halfdan's knowledge, Eadric indicated that he should continue to show him around the yard. Northman noted the look that passed between Halfdan and the master ship builder at Eadric's far more pleasant demeanour towards Halfdan and allowed them to walk on before turning to him.

He extended his hand to the irate man,

"I'm Northman, son of Leofwine of the Hwicce, and foster son to Eadric."

"I know who you are," the man growled in an unfriendly manner, but Northman pressed on.

"My apologies for my foster father's annoyance. The king's very keen for this part of his defensive strategy to work. He's also aware that he mustn't tax the people too much."

"I know all that you young upstart, but that doesn't mean that Ealdorman Eadric can come stomping in here with his demands when he doesn't know anything about shipbuilding." The man was so angry he could barely string his words together in a coherent manner.

"I entirely agree. You're doing good work here, and if I have the opportunity, I'll ensure my father and the king are made aware. Will you work all winter?"

The man growled then and finally tore his eyes away from the retreating figures of Eadric, Brihtric and Halfdan.

"We must if the king is to have his ships, but it'll be hard work to have them ready and seaworthy by the Easter festival next year. I could do with more men and more supplies, and more cover for the workers."

Northman had already noted that they worked outside, with only a small wooden shed to shield them from the worst of the weather.

"Can you commission another barn?" he asked, wondering if that would solve the problem, and how many ships could be kept inside it.

"Well yes, but it'd take the men away from their work, and that'll push the schedule even further back. Typically we build four, maybe five ships a year here. That's all, not twenty-five."

Nodding in sympathy, Northman turned to watch Eadric. He was more animated now, enjoying learning about shipbuilding, and for once, not thinking of the coin he'd spent, or his king had spent, or that he'd have to spend to complete the project. Sometimes he knew that Eadric forgot the simple fact that it was the king's money he collected from the men of the shires, not his own.

"I'll try to put in a good word with Eadric for you. Didn't you mention this to my father last week?"

"No, the weather was still clear, and I confess I didn't. But now that winter has cast its first few cold mornings, the workers have complained, and I could curse myself for a fool for not considering it sooner."

"If I can, I'll get word to him then. There must be some men on the farms who'd be able to help now that the harvest is collected. That way you wouldn't lose your ship builders."

The ship builder looked at Northman with interest,

"You're a wise one for your lack of years."

"I learnt from a true master, Wulfstan, my father's commended man and oldest advisor."

The man chuckled at his slightly rueful tone, "Old people are full of lessons that must be learned and sometimes they forget what it is to be young. Still, they're wise, and most of their lessons are valuable in later life."

"I'm starting to realise that," Northman countered. "Your ships are truly magnificent beasts. Are they to be crowned with a ships head?"

"Oh yes, I have a real wood sculptor who's working on the mastheads. He's a strange fellow but come. I'll let you meet him."

Walking across the raised wooden dock back towards the covered barn, the ship builder took Northman to a corner of the room where a fire burnt brightly in a covered fire pit, the heat almost unbearable. But the man sitting beside the fire, accompanied by a young lad and a woman, was uncaring of the heat. Sweat beaded his face and dripped from his nose onto the floor as he worked and chipped away at the wood, a selection of tools littered untidily around his feet. Wood chippings surrounded him and the smell of sawdust hung in the air, probably masking the smell emanating from the man, and he chanted as he worked.

"Northman this is Erik. Don't speak to him, he won't respond. But he is our carver. See what he's made so far."

Three finished mastheads leant against the side of the barn, far higher than Northman's head. They looked so life-like, the open mouth of the dragon with its vicious teeth almost glinting for all that they hadn't yet been decorated. Beside it was another fiery head of a beast that Northman didn't recognise and next to it was a bird head, raven-like with a sharply hooked beak. Northman shivered with dread when he saw it. It was more nightmarish than the dragon.

"Designed to give everyone nightmares, lad, I wouldn't worry about it," the shipbuilder offered.

Beside him, Olaf was studying the mastheads with enthusiasm, while his hound had his nose close to where the carver worked. Erik looked up briefly, his eyes slightly glazed, eyeing the dog with interest.

"What's he working on now?" Northman asked, watching the exchange between his hound and the strange man with amusement.

'Gods alone know," the shipbuilder responded, and then grimaced at his open admission to the old faith. "It's good to keep your peace with the old Gods on the seas. I think they hold more sway than the one true God,' he offered by way of an explanation. Northman nodded in understanding. It was common to find people following a strange mixture of the old and the new God and with the time he'd spent with Horic and his own shipmen, he knew both religions to have benefits to those who worked in certain trades. Unlike his father, he never let a man's religion concern him. That was for every man, woman and child to decide. Provided they could make their peace with their God, that was all right with Northman.

He stood for some time, just watching the carver at work before Olaf nudged him and reminded him that Eadric was probably waiting for them.

Making small talk with the master-shipman, he walked back to his horse and mounted him absent-mindedly. He was too intrigued by everything he saw about him, and Olaf was as awe-struck until Eadric reappeared. He walked briskly, already dismissing the shipyard from his thoughts, without speaking to his men, he turned his horse back towards the roadway, and they were off.

Turning one last time, Northman waved goodbye to Halfdan and nodded towards the master-shipman. Now he just needed to get a message to his father, before Eadric made his report to the king.

# 12

# SANDWICH, AD1009, NORTHMAN

NORTHMAN WAS GRINNING WITH DELIGHT, AND HE KNEW IT AND COULDN'T stop himself, no matter if he looked like a little child given his first wooden sword.

The view was both stunning and amazing. The entire fleet arrayed before him. To have been involved in the discussions that had made this incredible accomplishment happen was as nothing compared to actually seeing the ships, sea ready, and filled with their full complement of men.

His jealousy had evaporated in the face of the splendour. Not that he wouldn't have given almost anything to be on one of the ships, but he couldn't let his own disappointment detract from the joy the men who were lucky enough to be on one of the ships were enjoying.

There was a festival feel to the air. It might well only be just past Easter but the air was warm, the breeze gentle and the sun welcoming. The sea was calm, reflecting back a pure blue and the waves were a counterpart to the cries of the excited men as they showed their skills to their king and his Witan.

The king seemed as awestruck as Northman, his gaze switching from the ealdorman or churchman he was supposed to be talking to, to the grand vista as though he couldn't stop himself.

The king had ordered the construction of a small tented village for the inauguration of his ship's fleet, but with the weather so fair, no one was sitting within the carefully constructed structures, and the doors flapped a little desolately in the mild breeze. Not even the queen and her young children could be contained within the tents. She sat in her royal chair, next to her husband, her children cared for by nursemaids and men of the household troop, but all of them looked seawards.

This was a great day for England. A great accomplishment. Northman knew there, and then that Æthelred would go down in the pages of the Anglo-Saxon Chronicle as the most significant ship-building king their country had ever had. He would defend his people and his land by making use of the sea. Northman was proud to be English that day. Proud to be a part of the fantastic event.

Athelstan sought Northman out on the grassy slope they all stood upon.

"Northman, you're well?" he began.

Northman was taken aback by his special notice and hastily swallowed his annoyed response at being disturbed from his contemplation of the fleet.

"Yes, my Lord. Thank you for asking. And you, my Lord? You're well?"

Athelstan grinned in delight at his flustered words.

"Northman I haven't come to spoil your day. There's no need to be so formal with me. I thought you knew that by now."

"With thanks, Athelstan," Northman choked again, rolling his eyes at his inaptitude before the atheling.

Athelstan was accompanied by his brother, Edmund and Northman looked from the one to the other with a feeling of unease, despite Athelstan's assuring words.

"We were wondering if we could speak to you about our sister, and about Eadric."

Slightly taken aback, Northman nodded enthusiastically.

"Of course, what do you want to know?"

"Is he kind to her? Is he a good Lord?"

Narrowing his eyes a little he realised where this friendly conversation was going and at the same time made a decision. He'd not lie about his foster father, but neither would he offer platitudes.

"He can be mostly kind to her but since the birth of your nephew, she has been a little preoccupied and I don't think that Eadric enjoys being ignored."

Athelstan glanced at his brother. Clearly, this wasn't news to them.

"And his people, he's good to them?"

Northman shrugged, while Olaf shuffled on his feet beside him.

"In truth, he can be, sometimes and if it fits with him. On other occasions, he can be challenging and belligerent."

"And the shipbuilding and the tax collection, he was happy with that?"

Northman barked a short laugh then, for no, Eadric had not been happy about anything to do with the shipbuilding. Even now, he worked to turn the king aside from his plans, even though the ships were all built and it seemed a ludicrous endeavour.

"I don't think that Eadric enjoys being on a ship, and sadly, that, and the money paid for the ships means that he's not a close adherent of the project."

Athelstan raised his eyebrows at him then, and a smile touched the corner of his mouth.

"Your tact is worthy of sainthood," he offered by way of an explanation and beside him Olaf laughed bitterly.

"His father's best trait," he interjected, and for a brief moment, the four of them smiled in mirth at the difficult situations Leofwine had managed so well over the years.

"Why do you ask?" Northman queried when silence had fallen.

"We hear rumours at the Witan that Eadric is unhappy with the ship army, unhappy with the king, and unhappy with his wife. While our father brushed the problems aside, we feel, Edmund and I, I mean, that more attention should be paid to these rumours. We don't want the work of our father to be compromised by Eadric."

"I've heard nothing that worries me," Olaf muttered.

"And would you hear it, if there was something to hear?" Edmund asked pointedly.

"Eadric rarely lets us out of his sight, so I imagine we would, yes. But then, he has many brothers who could act for him and we don't know what they think of the shipbuilding. Other than Brihtric. He's keen to get involved and he's been made a commander and has ships at his disposal now."

Athelstan glanced back towards the ships gently bobbing in the calm waves as Northman spoke. He looked concerned and a little irate. Northman wondered just what they'd heard.

"If you tell me more, I can think about it. Tell me what you suspect and I'll let you know if I've listened to anything that might relate to it."

The two brothers shared a look that Northman didn't understand. Then Athelstan spoke,

"It's just concern for Edith and the baby. Father thinks little of her but we worry about her, as we do Wulfhilda and Ulfcytel. He tries to make his hold on the country stronger through these marriages, but we're not so convinced that it works. We think we should be the ealdormen."

Northman stilled at the bold statement from the brothers. He'd not considered it before but could see their viewpoint. How would he feel if his father asked the man his sister married to control some of the lands of the Hwicce and overlooked him entirely? He'd not be pleased.

"And you're looking for a way to discredit Eadric?" Olaf quizzed, the interest in his voice clear to hear.

"Not discredit as such, but some action that the king will find difficult to overlook."

"Eadric seems to be firmly in the king's pocket, so I wish you luck with your endeavours."

"Um, we know," Edmund's face turned down as he spoke.

"But we can hope," Athelstan countered, his outlook on the future a little brighter.

"But Northman, don't speak to Eadric of this. We wouldn't want the king to find out that we're asking questions about him. I'd rather not be censored by my father."

"Of course, I wouldn't speak of it anyway, and neither will Olaf." Olaf was nodding vigorously at Northman's words.

The two athelings walked away then, and Northman quickly dismissed them from his thoughts. Eadric was far too close to the king now for anything the king's older sons said to make any difference. He knew that but wondered how long it'd take Athelstan and Edmund to realise.

Olaf wasn't so quick to dismiss their conversation, and later when they'd found a space to bed down in for the night, he whispered,

"Do you think they stand a chance?"

"Who?" Northman asked sleepily. He'd forgotten the conversation already.

"The athelings, against Eadric?" Olaf reminded him with frustration.

"Doubt it. The king does everything Eadric says."

"Not where these ships were concerned," Olaf countered darkly, as Northman's eyes snapped open. Olaf was correct. The king had overruled Eadric on the building of the ship army. Perhaps, after all, the king was not quite so much in awe of Eadric as Northman had thought.

# 13
# THE KING'S WITAN, AD1009, LEOFWINE

ÆTHELRED WAS INCENSED. HE MARCHED AROUND HIS SMALL CHAMBER without pause for breath, constantly talking loudly and angrily. Leofwine was struggling to keep up with his thought processes but dared not interrupt him.

A messenger had woken him in the middle of the night, rudely demanding that the king needed to see him, as soon as possible and that sleep and night-time should not stop him from leaving immediately. Concerned and annoyed in equal measure, Leofwine had dressed and called half of his household troops to him, to serve as guard duty, and had left a sleepy Æthelflæd with a kiss and gentle caress.

The messenger had known little of the king's immediate need. Although Leofwine had pressed him at the start of their journey, all he'd been able to offer was the news that three messengers had arrived, one after another, early the previous evening, and that he'd then been sent to find Leofwine.

The king was at Oxford, waiting for his ealdorman, and so intrigued, Leofwine had ridden as fast as he dared through the early summer night. And now, arrived, and in the presence of the king, he still wasn't sure what the rush was about.

The king was clearly in a rage, striding backwards and forwards across the wooden floor, but until he stopped and informed Leofwine of what the problem was, there was little that Leofwine could do but watch his king.

He seemed to have lost his flush of pleasure so evident when the ship-army had been launched, and now his face was drained of all colour, and he looked as though he'd not slept for a week.

"What do you say Leofwine?" Æthelred finally asked, but Leofwine could give him no answer.

"My Lord, I don't yet know what's happened here? Your messenger didn't tell me."

Æthelred cast a look of annoyance at the closed door through which he must have imagined the messenger waited.

"Why didn't you say anything? All this time you've been stood there like a mute!"

The king was vexed and infuriated. But, he stopped his pacing and sat in his chair, throwing his cloak around himself as he did so. There was a small brazier burning, but the room was filled with the chill of an early summer's day.

"Last night I had three reports about the ship-army."

"We're not under attack already are we?" Leofwine interjected, before realising that he'd interrupted the king.

"No, no, nothing like that. Well, sort of. We're not being attacked by the Northmen, but instead, the ship army seems to have turned on itself."

"I don't understand," Leofwine uttered, "how could it turn on itself?"

"The commanders have argued and, according to the messengers, some of the ships have separated themselves from the remainder of the fleet."

"Under whose command?" Leofwine asked, hoping against hope that it was no one he'd recommended for the role.

"Eadric's brother, Brihtric."

"Why?"

"Eadric came to me at Sandwich with rumours that the thegn who spoke up during the Witan when we decided to build the ship army had accused him of things he shouldn't have done. Hoarding the tax for himself, being ignorant of ship building, being cruel to my daughter – you must know of what I speak. I placated him and thought nothing more of it. Wulfnoth seemed to me a good man. He has had his own ships refitted to the specifications we decreed, at cost to himself, and brought them to the inauguration at Sandwich. I just assumed that Eadric was still harbouring a grudge against him because it was he who spoke up against him. Eadric's made no secret of his hatred for this project of ours."

Leofwine listened without interrupting, almost fearing to know where this was going.

"I thought the matter resolved, I told Eadric to leave it alone. Wulfnoth is a good captain. He was gifted with another fifteen ships from the fleet, and everyone was happy to serve under him. I'd not even considered the problem since Easter. But Eadric's brother has been more active in trying to seek an end to the strife. He openly accused Wulfnoth before all the other commanders of lying and trying to have his brother removed from his office. Wulfnoth did not .. react well to the accusations, levelled as they were amongst men he thinks of as his friends and family."

Leofwine closed his eye and grimaced. He had a feeling he knew what the king would say next.

"That night he took his twenty ships and left the fleet. Just abandoned it like that, and turned his back on the lands of his people. Even now, he's been caught raiding as far north as the Humber."

"Raiding his own people?" Leofwine gasped in shock, "but why, they're not even Eadric's lands."

"No they're not, but he's disguised himself as a raider and as such has been going wherever he wants."

"And this news you kept to yourself?" Leofwine asked, annoyed at the king for trying to hush up something that involved his favourite ealdorman.

"No Leofwine, not at all," the king almost pleaded, "I learnt all this from my messengers last night. Eadric seems to have been aware of what was happening, but it took a message from Uhtred of Northumbria for me to be made aware of it. I've sent messengers to you and Eadric and Ælfric in the hope that we can decide what to do next and piece together all the events."

"Do you think that Eadric planned this?" Leofwine asked, not believing the words himself but realising that this was the conclusion the king had reached.

"I can think of no other reason for Brihtric to have made such a scene. And now, he's taken eighty of the ships and is trying to chase Wulfnoth down."

"On whose authority?" Leofwine demanded, standing in annoyance and frustration. This couldn't be happening. Not now. Not when the king was desperate to take some action against the Raiders and the pretensions of the Danish king. His own anger built with every piece of new information he had.

"His own, but no doubt Eadric will attempt to portray it as his decision. What are we to do?" Æthelred asked plaintively, and for once, Leofwine had no ready answer. This was a disaster. Only a month ago the people of England had felt safe knowing that they'd worked hard to outfit a ship army to protect themselves during the summer season, and now that army seemed to have turned on its own people.

Wiping his hand over his face, Leofwine slumped forwards in his chair, so that he held his head in his hands while his elbows rested on his knee. He felt unable to stand any longer. His legs turned to fluid as he listened to the latest disaster to befall the king.

"We must recall them both. Get the ships back. It will be damaging morale every moment that it continues."

"But how are we to get them back?"

"Did Uhtred not say anything further in his message? Does he not have people out looking for Wulfnoth?"

"Yes, yes he does," the king exclaimed loudly, shuffling the three offending messages on the table before him as he spoke.

"Then you must send word of what is to happen if he should capture Wulfnoth."

"But what should happen to him?"

"He'll need to come to the Witan. Offer an explanation for his actions or stand trial. If he has risen against your people using the ship army, then he can be tried for treason and banished."

"And if his actions were justified?" Æthelred countered by asking, his eyes lightening a little with delight at being able to voice his fears and thoughts.

"We won't know until we have all the facts before us," Leofwine commented unhappily. "And Brihtric, we'll need to take action against him as well."

"I know, and Eadric too. I almost hope he doesn't come here today. I don't want to see his smug face as he tries to talk himself out of another situation that should never have arisen."

Leofwine's eyebrows raised at the king's criticism of Eadric. He'd never heard the king utter a word against him. He'd thought that whatever hold Eadric had over the king was immovable but clearly it wasn't.

"We need to hope that the rest of the fleet stays alert for Raiders. I can't help feeling that this year more will come."

Now it was Æthelred's turn to look sharply at Leofwine,

"I'd feared the same myself. We must act so that the ship-army knows they have my full support, despite this .. unfortunate turn of events."

"Perhaps another visit to Sandwich?" Leofwine mused aloud, "Or maybe send Athelstan or even the queen."

"No," Æthelred stated categorically "I'll go. These are my men, manning my ships, with money raised from my people. I'll go and show the people that the work they do is valued and needed."

With that, Æthelred made a motion with his hand, and Leofwine felt a rush of air pass him as food and drink were brought into the small room. A loud grumble erupted from his stomach at the tempting smell of pottage and Æthelred smiled tiredly.

"Leofwine, I've been remiss. You were up half the night and not a morsel to eat when you arrived. Now please, eat and we'll wait and see what replies we get from the messengers."

"I'll be staying a few days then my Lord?"

"Yes, I'll have need of you. Send to your family to let them know. I'd not want your wife worrying unnecessarily."

Leofwine spent much of the day contemplating this strange turn of events. Most importantly he wondered at the motives behind the attack on Wulfnoth. Leofwine knew little about the man, other than that he'd come forward and said he agreed with the king's decision to build a ship-army and had said the costs could be acceptable. Other than that all Leofwine knew was that he was some distant scion of the once powerful family of Athelstan, known as Half-King, a very powerful ealdorman during the reign of Edgar, over sixty years ago. The family had fallen from power and their position, but still, he'd been so successful that even now, the use of his name wasn't without power.

He wondered if somehow, Eadric's rule in Mercia had brought him into conflict with other members of the family.

And then he pondered the idea that Eadric was merely trying to sabotage the king's plans. That thought burnt the brightest and the truest and with a heavy heart, he acknowledged that to be the most likely reason. He pitied the king when he found out and then realised that the king probably already had an inkling of the truth.

A little bolt of excitement leapt through his body. Perhaps Eadric would be tainted by this mini-rebellion, and he'd lose his position and then his son could come home to him. He hoped so but knew in his dark moments that the king would accept any excuse Eadric gave him and that he'd never lose his position, not while the king lived.

Messengers reached them early the next morning, by which time the older athelings had also congregated at the king's Witan. Leofwine had sent a messenger home with Frakki, one of Horic's sons and another three men. No doubt Æthelflæd would be worried, but he hoped that his message would ally her fears of having her husband woken in the middle of the night, and rushed away from her.

With the messengers came Eadric, aggressive and outraged. Without thought of precedence, he stamped his way into the king's private room, only to be forcefully restrained at the last moment by the king's household troops. Leofwine was amazed at the man's timidity and watched with satisfaction as Æthelred's face hardened at the upset.

The news from the messengers was the worst that could be expected. A freak summer storm had blown up and scattered the ships at Sandwich so that they now had to work hard to regroup and find each other. Further north, Wulfnoth still harried the coastal areas, and it had been confirmed that Brihtric had formally taken eighty ships and set off in pursuit of the runaway.

Leofwine wondered what effect the storm would have had on the pursuit but stilled his tongue. Right now he was more interested in Eadric's petty excuses.

Finally, the king allowed Eadric into his private room, and surrounded by his older sons, Leofwine and the men who made up the king's intimate acquaintances, demanded answers from Eadric. He offered Eadric no chair and had him stand before everyone as though he were already facing trial for his treason.

"My Lord king," he began beseechingly, clearly having decided that the angry approach wasn't going to work. "Why have you commanded me to come here and not allowed me to speak directly and in private with you?"

"The crimes of your brother make it impossible for me to talk to you in private. You must be accountable for his crimes, and in allowing this argument with Wulfnoth to continue you have imperilled the entire ship-army, the whole country."

"I didn't my Lord. I told my brother that I'd not pursue Wulfnoth, although he spread lies about me. You have my word, my Lord. I wouldn't go against your wishes. Any actions that he's now taken can only be because he believes he's acting in your best interests."

"Bah," the king spat. "How can it be in my best interests if half my ship army is off either attacking my land or attacking my own ships. Explain to me Eadric how that can be for the good of my country?"

"My Lord," he sputtered, "my brother has a hot head, we all know that. Everyone in this room knows that. What he does, I can't always be accountable for."

"Yes, you can, as I'm responsible for the actions of my sons and as you make Ealdorman Leofwine responsible for the action of his son, who you foster, and demanded to foster. Your excuses mean nothing to me, and simply show how little you respect the kingship, the kingdom and the effort that has gone into mounting the ship-army."

The king paused for breath then, and Leofwine held his breath to see what his next words would be.

"I'm going to Sandwich, with my witan, to reinvigorate what remains of my ship-army. You need to find your brother and have him bring my ships back to me at Sandwich. You have seven days, no longer, and then, and only then, will I make a decision as to your future."

"My Lord king," Eadric said shakily, "I'm your son by marriage."

"If you were my own child, I'd still punish you for this, as my sons know only too well. Now go. I only wish to see you when you have my 100 ships back, in full working order, and have put your dispute with Wulfnoth behind you. Do this Eadric, or you will lose everything, and I mean everything."

Bowing, although his eyes flashed angrily, Eadric swept from the room and could be heard shouting commands outside. Through the open doorway, Leofwine caught a glimpse of Northman, his eyes a little frightened although he held himself well. Looking to the king for permission, he went towards his son and spoke quickly to him.

"Watch him Northman. See that he does as the king has commanded and report back to me, secretly, when we next meet. The king will welcome your help in this."

Northman, eyes as downcast as his foster-father's nodded in understanding and went to walk away. Leofwine grabbed him then, a quick hug and no need for words, hopefully, unseen by Eadric.

"Be well son," he whispered, as Northman gave him a cheeky grin,

"As always father," he said, and was gone, in a swirl of his own cloak.

Behind him, he felt a scuffle and was surprised when the king's voice permeated his thoughts,

"A good man, your oldest son?"

"Yes, my Lord. The best. Although I'd rather, he was with me and not Eadric."

"Fostering is a difficult concept for parents to accept, but he'll grow from his experience. Although, if Eadric can't control his brother, I think you might get your boy back sooner than you thought."

Pleased that the king hadn't forgotten his part in his son's fostering, Leofwine smiled a little. Northman had been gone for nearly two years now, and that was too long. His son had grown tall, developed his muscles well and clearly still had his sense of duty and humour. Now, he needed to come home.

# 14

# AD1009, NORTHMAN

The rage sweeping from Eadric was a physical force, so powerful that it kept all his men of the household troop away from him, as he raced through the summer's day. Northman was unsure where they were going, but assumed that it had to be north, to where he might find his brother.

Northman was reminded of the conversation with the athelings only a month ago when they'd asked if Eadric had anything planned. He'd answered honestly then, and he'd not known that Eadric and his brother had arranged for such a devastating attack on the ship-army. It was so counter-productive to the future of the country that Northman could almost believe that it was all a mistake, a misunderstanding. But then he looked at Eadric and knew with certainty that this was exactly the sort of thing that Eadric was capable of.

As usual, Olaf accompanied Northman everywhere he went, and so the two of them, and Eadric's guard of twenty men, raced towards the east coast, no words exchanged between any of them.

Northman wondered how Eadric thought he could find Brihtric when the coast was so vast, but received his answer two days later when the men met at what must have been a pre-ordained position, not quite at the Humber, but not far from it either.

With dismay, Northman noticed that Brihtric was on land, surrounded by only a few of the original fleet. Where were the others?

Without preamble Eadric greeted Brihtric,

"You bloody fool," he shouted, not heeding any around him, "what have you done with all the king's ships?"

"There was a storm," his brother answered defiantly, his smile of welcome dropping from his face. "A massive storm that blew half the ships one way and half the other. There are many casualties. I'm lucky to be alive," he finished, but Northman doubted that Eadric felt the same.

"Better you'd died, you fool. The king is threatening me with treason, and half his ships are gone. Where's Wulfnoth? Please tell me that you managed to capture him?"

Brihtric looked pained now,

"I only wish I could, but he's gone. I don't know where."

Eadric stepped close to his brother now, and for a moment Northman thought he would hug his brother, but instead he punched him, hard on the nose.

A cry of outrage from Brihtric as his nose erupted in a sea of bright red blood, and the two men attacked each other, cries of outrage erupting from both of them.

The men of the household troop and those shipmen who were on dry land looked at each other uncertainty, and for once, Northman felt no remorse in not intervening. This altercation was a matter of brotherly concern and needed resolution as such.

Eadric held his brother in a headlock, pounding on his face over and over again, only for Brihtric to tackle his legs and bring them both crashing down in an untidy heap, but one that he could exploit. He kicked Eadric over, where he lay sprawled on the wet sand, and when that only earned a mild groan of dismay, he picked his face up by the fabric at Eadric's neck and beat him savagely with the other hand. And then he started to fumble for something at his belt, and Northman felt that now was the time to intervene. Before they killed each other.

He shouted for the shipmen to do something, knowing that they wouldn't owe their allegiance to Eadric and wouldn't be punished for their intervention, and when they refused to do anything, he stepped forward ignoring the household troops. They'd never yet stopped a brawl their Lord was involved in and were unlikely to now.

"Eadric," he shouted, trying to work out where his foster-father's face was.

"Go away boy," he growled, but Northman ignored him.

"Your brother is getting his knife," he shouted instead, and Eadric took a moment to look at what his brother was doing. Wiping blood and spit from his face, he followed Brihtric's arm to where it still fumbled for the knife, or so Northman imagined.

"Don't be such a bloody fool," Eadric hollered at his brother. "If you kill me, our father will kill you."

"I don't care, you bastard. I did what you wanted and you come here and berate me. You've probably already betrayed me to the king. I'd rather you were dead and then your mouth can't be put to any more ill use."

Eadric was trying to force Brihtric off him, unbalance him so that he couldn't get at his knife, but he was having no luck. Aggrieved at the sight of the two men fighting in such an unruly manner, Northman stuck his foot out, and tripped Brihtric, who fell to the sandy floor with a growl of annoyance.

Quick to react, Eadric was back on his feet, but Northman held him back from further attack, and Olaf now ran to help Brihtric to his feet as well.

Both men were covered in a combination of wet sand, blood and mucus. And then, unbidden, Eadric started to laugh. Northman looked at him in surprise, how could he smile now? When Brihtric began to laugh as well, Northman walked away in disgust. He'd never understand these two men, no matter how long he knew them they always surprised him.

As the men of the household troop made themselves a small campsite above the wash of the waves, Northman slumped to the floor and looked out at the depleted fleet. He no longer felt proud of his king's achievements. No, he felt cheated. And by Eadric. Again.

# 15
# SANDWICH, AD1009, NORTHMAN

THEY ARRIVED AT SANDWICH ON THE EVENING OF THE KING'S SEVENTH NIGHT. Purposefully. Reinvigorated with the knowledge that he'd just about thwarted the king's plans, Eadric had lingered on the eastern coast, talking with his brother, plotting further, and being ignorant of the need of his king and his people.

Northman had held his aggravation in check as much as he could but, he was furious with Eadric. What made him think he could overpower the king's wishes, bring them crashing down around everyone? What made him think he could make such decisions when the whole of England had been behind the scheme? The arrogance of the man shocked Northman, and he hoped, and he prayed a little, that this time, the king would take substantive action against his unruly ealdorman.

He stayed closed to Eadric for all that, watching his every move, listening to every conversation. At night, he and Olaf would find a quiet spot, unheard by any others or seen by anyone, and they'd share stories about what they'd learnt.

The most damning evidence they had were still the words Brihtric and Eadric had initially flung at each other when they'd met. The shipmen had been gossiping amongst themselves, along with the ship's captains, and Northman knew that the shearing of the king's fleet had been pre-planned. The allegations against Wulfnoth were false, but everyone who knew him, knew that he was quick to take offence and so attacking him on spurious grounds had been sure to elicit a response. They'd not quite expected one quite so fast or huge, but it had all gone according to the half-hatched plans of Eadric and Brihtric.

The ships that his brother had taken to find Wulfnoth had not only failed in their quest but had also managed to get themselves tangled in the large freak summer storm. Forty-six of the ships had been lost. Either they'd been sunk, or the ship men and their vessels had been scattered so far north that they'd not yet made it back to their original mustering point.

Northman had said prayers each night for the shipmen who'd lost their lives at the whim of their God, and more importantly, an ealdorman who should have known better.

He felt sickened every time he thought about those families who'd lost husbands, fathers and sons. To die at the hands of the Danish and other North men was bad enough. To die for nothing but a petty grudge was a waste of a good life.

Eadric had said not one word about those who'd perished, and Olaf had overheard many disgruntled comments from the shipmen who remained. They thought that Eadric acted on the king's orders and that by process of elimination, Brihtric did as well. Northman knew that the king would have to take firm action against Eadric, public action if he was to restore the faith of the men he had left to him. Every night that the ship docked on dry land, more and more of the men slunk away in the night, and Eadric ignored what was happening.

Not that Northman blamed the men. No, he knew who was responsible.

Sandwich was gloomy on that summer's evening, the pageant of Easter long forgotten. The ships, commanded by Brihtric had arrived before Eadric, but only just. Still, there'd been long enough before him for the king and his advisors to number the ships and know that they were now over fifty less than they had been. Unless of course, Wulfnoth had reappeared with his ships.

The rest of the fleet was in place, as it had been at Easter. With squinting eyes, Northman noted that many of these ships had taken a battering in the storm as well, and some were beached on the ship, upended as a swarm of craftsmen refitted or fixed problems. He wondered if Halfdan was out there somewhere, repairing the ships he'd built with such pride, or whether he was as yet ignorant of the events that had befallen the ship army.

Eadric and his men were escorted to where the king had taken shelter in the house of the local portreeve. The hall was a stunning example of craftsmanship, mounted with small touches that Northman would more commonly expect on a ship, but which made him realise just how much life on the land here revolved around the sea.

At the doorway, Eadric dismissed his men and went inside to seek his king. Northman watched him pensively as the cries of the master craftsmen drifted from the harbour. And that was how his father found him.

He smiled grimly at his son but reached out to embrace him, as he did every time they met. Those brief reminders of his life before fosterage were always a little painful, reminding him of what he missed out on, while at the same time, reinforcing his belief that what he was doing was for the good of his family.

"Son," Leofwine asked, "You're well?"

"Of course father. I'd like to say I was a little frayed from riding up and down the east coast at great speed, but regrettably, that's not the case."

They moved away from the busy comings and goings at the king's doorway and didn't speak again until they walked upon the sandy shore of the beach, the gentle breeze carrying the cries of the men at work towards them, and making them mindful that they should be quiet in their conversations.

Olaf joined them, as always, and Leofwine's greeting for his friend's son was almost as warm as that for Leofwine. Behind them, Oscetel and Wighard kept pace with them, ever vigilant.

"Father, this was all planned by Eadric. He wanted to jeopardise the king's endeavour. He's made no secret of it, and the men who're left on the ships are disgruntled, and many are sneaking away at night. It's a total cock-up."

Leofwine nodded sadly at the confirmation of his fears.

"The king has reached the same conclusion and is saddened by Wulfnoth's implications in the scheme. But, I don't know what the king plans to do about it. He's spoken to me a little of his annoyance with Eadric but nothing more."

Northman looked out along the sea front, feeling the stirrings of joy at so many ships, ready and waiting for the attack that he hoped would never come.

"I find him intolerable to be around," Northman finally uttered, the recognition of the truth in his words showed by the violence with which the words fell out of his mouth.

Leofwine's eye closed in grief,

"The king has hinted that he might allow you home if Eadric is found guilty of treason."

Northman's face darkened,

"We all know that's as likely as snow in the summer father. Whatever Eadric is to the king, he'll hold his place. Even after all this."

"You've a wise head on your shoulders," Leofwine commented sourly, and Northman stopped in his tracks. His father sounded so sad, so aggrieved and so out of sorts. Northman realised at that moment the strain his father laboured under. Every single day he worked for his king, and every single day his king undermined his work and took the advice of those who were fools.

"I know I do, Wulfstan always told me so, and so have others I've met on my journey's around the Mercian lands. How do you do it father?" he asked with curiosity.

"Do what?" Leofwine asked, although he clearly knew what his son meant.

"Tolerate all this, Eadric, the king, the slights to your character. There's not a single place that I've visited within the Mercian lands, or even in the Five Boroughs, when Eadric deems it time to show his face there, that doesn't speak highly of you. Craftsmen, Reeves, even the bloody moneyers, they all take a moment to tell me how much they respect you, and by inclination don't respect Eadric. How do you manage to continue each day when Eadric and the king only work to blacken your name and cause disquiet within the kingdom?"

Instead of brushing Northman off with a belittling comment, Leofwine took a moment to study his son, his bright flashing eyes and mobile face, the first inklings of a beard forming on his chin.

"I have a positive inner core, an absolute belief in myself that what I do and have done, is recognised by someone, by the people that matter. The king, Eadric, even myself, we're merely figureheads for our society. At its core, it works well. Yes, there are some issues that need fixing, law and order and justice, adherence to the Christian faith, but at our heart, all of us respect each other. We want to live well, and in peace. The king, he's trying to accomplish that. Eadric is just trying to have the cream for himself. The king doesn't realise that."

He paused for breath, and Northman didn't interrupt. He was fascinated to hear his father's innermost thoughts.

"As Wulfstan has said, and I know he's spoken to you of it as well. The king's not an evil man, but he doesn't like criticism, and I think he struggles to find fault with others unless it's thrust in his face. He sees good in everyone he surrounds himself with, and that makes him weak and susceptible to those who mean him harm."

"And Eadric means him harm?"

"Yes, I think of all the ealdormen Æthelred has ever had, Eadric does indeed mean him harm. Eadric only wishes to please himself, to put bread and food on his table, and wood on his fire. The other ealdormen, especially old Ælfric, they're just a bit incompetent. He has his strengths, don't get me wrong, and in times of peace, he'd have been a good man. But in these troubled times, he's not the right man for the job, and now his age goes against him."

"The king needs men who speak their mind, who support him regardless, but who will if and when the need is apparent, tell him no."

"So how do you cope with it all?"

"As I said, I believe that I'm working for the good of everyone. I think that the king thinks he does too, and so I overlook his slights, and his pettiness when he does attempt to exert his power. I like my role in our society. I enjoy being the ealdorman. I like having men come to me, swear their oaths to me, but I don't abuse that power. I wouldn't ask them to do something I didn't believe in. I hope the king sees things the same way."

"And Eadric, what of him?"

"I don't know. The king is too much under his sway. It's almost as if the king is desperate to win his favour, and it should be the other way round. I have my misgivings that the king will ever be strong enough in himself to push him away. Eadric is taking Ælfric's place. Swiftly. Another who could be good at his role if only we weren't under constant attack."

"So you think Uhtred and Ulfcytel are better ealdormen?"

"I believe that they're ealdormen who can face down the enemy. They have no qualms about fighting and killing and defending their lands. They would rather shed blood than money. And at this moment in time, that's what the king needs."

They resumed walking along the beach then, both thinking about what had been said.

Finally, Northman broke the comfortable silence,

"The things I've witnessed Eadric do, they'll not change the king's mind?"

"No, they won't. He'll need to see for himself, but all the same, it's good that you watch and listen and hopefully learn how not to be an ealdorman, husband and Lord."

"Oh believe me," Northman said with a mirthless chuckle, "I'm learning that in good measure."

"Your mother misses you," Leofwine said, changing the subject to something more pleasant. "And your sister is a hell fire with that sword you gave her."

Northman felt his face flush a little with guilt at that, but Leofwine surprised him by laughing.

"I think it a good thing that she learns to protect herself. This country isn't finished with the Northmen, and she may yet need to call on her skills to defend herself. And old Wulfstan agrees. He has her training with the younger boys."

Northman was incredulous at the news,

"And mother allows it?"

"She has little choice," Leofwine smirked, "Ealdgyth has your brother's way with words and your way with stubbornness."

"How does Leofric fair?" Northman asked all of a sudden remembering his brother.

"Excellent. Leofric thrives in Horic's household. I think, and you'll have to excuse me here Olaf for speaking so of your mother and father, that they are more demanding of Leofric than your mother, and I were, but, I think he needs so many rules and regulations."

Olaf spluttered with amusement then, evidently recalling life with his parents.

"I would say, my Lord Leofwine, that they could be harsh on occasions, and exacting at times. In fact, as much as I dislike Eadric as a person, life in his household is far less ... controlling."

Leofwine cast an appraising look at Olaf for his words and nodded in agreement.

"Well put, even you, I fear, might be learning tact."

Ruffling his son's foster-brother's hair, the small gathering rapidly deteriorated into a more friendly crowd, and not minding their dignity, they rolled in the sand, enjoying laughing without fear of being overheard or reprimanded for not being about their duties.

And that was where any enjoyment of being at the hastily convened Witan evaporated. Rumours were flying when they returned to the king's hall and Eadric was nowhere to be seen. With a hasty goodbye, Northman and Olaf set off to find their foster-father, while Leofwine, now sombre again, entered the king's hall to learn the truth of what had arisen.

They found Eadric fuming on the beach, with his remiss brother, and another of his brothers, Æthelwine. His face was sour with disapproval, and he'd been sent from their father. The crotchety old man was fuming from his fireside seat, or so Æthelwine informed his older brother, not without glee, only adding to Eadric's anger. Clearly, things had not gone as well with the king as he'd hoped and assumed they would.

Luckily for the two boys, they sneaked back into the general humdrum of people without their absence being noted by anyone other than a member of the household troop, Ceolmund, who was almost their age and sympathetic to their plight. Ambling towards them, the large youth sat beside them and filled them in on all they'd missed.

"The king was angrier than I've ever seen him, and Eadric was just about as obnoxious as it's possible to be. For every question the king had, Eadric reacted with a dismissive answer, and when he was tasked with single-handedly demolishing the ship-army, he reacted so violently that many thought he'd strike the king. He's made it clear that he denies any wrong-doing, he blames his brother, but more than that, he blames Wulfnoth and has again listed his grievances against the man, as though that somehow makes his actions acceptable."

"The king was just about puce by the end of the interview, and if Eadric had mentioned one more time that he was the king's son by marriage, I think Æthelred would have had the marriage annulled there and then."

"What was the outcome?"

"The king dismissed him and said he'd consult with the other ealdormen, and would have him back for a decision early tomorrow morning. What amazes me is that he didn't even try to defend his brother's actions. He thinks they were right and correct, and blames Almighty God for the summer storm. He even alluded to the king's new coins, telling him that in issuing something so overtly religious, he'd insulted God and he was now taking his revenge."

Olaf sucked in a sharp breath at Ceolmund's words and Northman was shaking his head in shock. He, like Ceolmund, couldn't believe Eadric's reactions.

The king's new coinage, arranged at the time that the tax was being collected for the ship army, had been a change from anything anyone had ever known. Northman knew all about it because the first moneyer he'd visited with Eadric had exclaimed at the design in shock. Never before had any image so overtly religious been used on the king's coinage; the Lamb of God on the one side and the Dove, a symbol of peace on the other. The king's intentions had been clear. He'd just about removed himself entirely from the coinage of his people, calling for divine intervention and more importantly, for peace.

While at the same time the recall and restriking of coins had allowed the king to exact even more tax from his people by allowing for a slightly slimmer design to the previous coins, it had also been a genuine attempt at benefitting his people and his land. Northman was almost as proud of it as if he'd had the idea himself.

Lapsing into silence, the lads watched Eadric and his brothers in furious conversation. Northman wasn't looking forward to the next day, not at all. No matter what the king's outcome was, he'd be travelling home with a furious Eadric, and that was not a pleasant sounding proposition.

# 16

# SANDWICH, AD1009, LEOFWINE

THE KING CALLED LEOFWINE TO HIM AS SOON AS HE WALKED OUT OF THE bright evening sunshine and into the darker hall, cooling pleasantly as the day drew to a close.

He was more composed than Leofwine had expected, at least until he'd heard the news from Northman. Then the king seemed to slump in on himself, and he dismissed Leofwine with one of his usual brusque motions that always stung, no matter how often they happened.

With Hammer at his heels, Leofwine quickly stepped outside again, finding Oscetel waiting for him. They didn't speak; there was little need. Not until the following day would they know any more than they already did.

That night, stretched out in his tent, Leofwine thought longingly of his wife, warm and soft in his arms, until sleep finally claimed him, and when he woke the next morning, he was disappointed to find he wasn't at home. Heavy-hearted, he rose and dressed for the day. The summer should be the time of year he loved most, but instead, he dreaded it, knowing that with the warmer weather the

Raiders would come, and they were clearly not the only threat to his lands.

He found the king calm and composed and refrained from asking what his plans were, instead taking his seat on a wooden bench dragged into use around the king. It was a little damp, and Leofwine wondered where it'd come from as the water slowly seeped into his trousers making him grimace in discomfort. He thought the weather had been dry for weeks, but then he remembered the storm out at sea that had scrambled the ship army, sending half of it one way, and half of it the other. It must have struck land at Sandwich as well.

There was a reasonable turnout of attendees for the Witan. Uhtred and Ulfcytel were busy conferring in a corner, and Leofwine watched the few churchmen who were there with interest. What must they think of this state of affairs? They preached for their king and had already mentioned that to compliment the new coinage the people of the land should perform a series of penances. The king had refrained from that action, for now, hoping to unite a little profit with a little godliness. Leofwine wondered if he was pleased with the results, or cursing himself for linking profit to the scheme. Perhaps, after all, he had angered his God one time too many.

Quickly, the witan came together, Eadric striding through the door just as the king was about to speak, as though he had not a care in the world. Leofwine suppressed a grimace, Hammer nudging him on the leg at the same time. Northman had entered the room, his hound with him, and Hammer, as ever aware of the pups he'd once helped raise, was asking permission to seek the other dog out. Leofwine let him go. It was going to be a long session, he could tell. The dog would get bored at about the same time he did, but he imagined the wrangling and recriminations would continue for far longer than that.

So resolved, he shuffled his damp behind and turned to his king. Behind him, he felt a similar movement affect everyone in the room. There was a suppressed excitement, everyone who'd ever fallen foul of Eadric hoping that this time, this time, the king would banish him from their lands. It was a futile hope, but still, it was hope all the same.

The king opened the witan, his voice heavy with the responsibility to what must be done that day.

"Eadric,"

"My Lord king," he bobbed to his feet and bowed to his master.

"You have done as I requested, I see, well almost. Where are the rest of my ships?"

"As I mentioned to you yesterday, the ship-army was devastated by the summer storm that blew up. The men," and here he shrugged, "were too inexperienced to master their ships during the storm. If you ask around, you will see that those who have long been shipmen have survived, while those, more inexperienced men have perished."

A gasp of outrage flooded the hall. Many had lost someone they knew, if not a family member. But before anyone could voice their anger the king held his hand up for silence.

"And this is the best excuse for what's happened that you can bring before me?" he asked, his voice dangerously low and threatening.

"I can only give you the truth," Eadric responded, "ask the men, call forth the captains and commanders and ask them their opinion."

"I have Eadric, I've spoken to the brave men who command my ship army," and here he laid emphasis on the 'my', "and they have to some extent offered an agreement of what you say. However, they have also made it clear to me that the ships should not have been away from the harbour, that they warned your brother of the storm brewing, and advised him, because they could not command the Earl of Mercia's brother, to stay his hand for the time being."

Eadric glanced to where his brother sat amongst the thegns at the back of the hall. This was clearly news to him, and he looked murderously at his brother. Leofwine suppressed a sigh of frustration, once more pleased that he had no brothers to call his own.

"I was unaware of that, my king. Perhaps we should call Brihtric forwards and have him offer a recounting of events?"

"No, we will not," the king intoned. "However, you can provide an explanation as to your petty feud with Wulfnoth. I'm intrigued to know more of the basis for the initial disagreement that led your brother to act against him."

Eadric's eyes narrowed dangerously. Clearly, he'd not been expecting to be quizzed on that element of events.

"It was little and nothing," he tried to dismiss the question, but the king was above diverting from his questioning.

"I am curious as to how you two came into conflict. He's a man of the southern lands, my lands in Wessex, and yours are in Mercia. What have you cause to complain off?" he insisted. "How do you even know each other?"

"My Lord," Eadric swallowed around the words. "It is an old family dispute."

"They always are, and still, I would like to know more, as would everyone in this room."

Seeing that there was no way out of the king's questioning, Eadric began to speak; his voice purposefully kept low so that the entire assembled crowd was forced to silence and to bend forward if they wanted to hear what he said.

"As you know my Lord, Wulfnoth is a distant descendant of Athelstan, Half king, the ealdorman who once ruled East Anglia, and who was a great favourite of your ancestors."

"Yes, I know of that. Now."

"Because of that, he has land inherited from his forebears close to my own."

"But your lands are on the border with the Britons, how can they be anywhere near the lands of the Five Borough's?"

"I perhaps used the incorrect word, my Lord. The lands are close to those that I hold directly from you, in my role as ealdorman."

"Ah, now that makes more sense to me, as I'm sure it does to the rest of the men in the room."

"And Wulfnoth, he incurred my displeasure, on your behalf of course, by altering the boundaries without consulting me, and by placing some of ... your land, my Lord, in the hands of the local monastery."

"And ..."

"Well, my Lord, I did come to you with my concerns."

"Yes you did, you came to me with some muddled words about a man I didn't know much about who'd gifted land to a monastery that I already support."

"Yes my Lord I did, and you didn't ask me to take any action, but I couldn't let him get away with it." Eadric finished in a rush.

"So you complain about a man who gifts his own, or my land, to a monastery that I support anyway. When I advise against taking action, for what does it matter to me whose land it is as long as I'm happy with the gifting of it, you and your brother use this as an excuse to antagonise the man. You drive him from my expensive and newly built ship army, and then your brother takes nearly a third of my ships and chases him to ... somewhere. I lose my twenty ships, on top of those that perished in the summer storm, and you somehow think that this is an acceptable price to pay for this tiny piece of land?"

The king's summing up of the matter appeared to be accurate, and Leofwine smirked a little at Eadric's unease. To say he'd allowed his personal enmity for the man to grow out of all proportion was an understatement so huge that Leofwine struggled to comprehend it. 'Rash' just didn't cover it.

"It was your land, my Lord," Eadric squeaked into the silence.

Æthelred ran his hand over his bearded face as he contemplated Eadric. His face was bland, but his eyes danced with anger and flashed violently in the reflected glow from the fire. Leofwine shuffled forwards on his bench, forgetting the dampness permeating his clothing.

"My land to do with as I please?" only it wasn't a question. "Did you have the claims on the estate examined before you acted?"

"No, my Lord, I know they're your lands."

"And how do you 'know' that?" the king queried perilously softly.

"Because they fall within the boundaries of your demesne."

"And you've just told me that Wulfnoth is a descendant of a man who was once close to the royal family. Did it not cross your mind that the lands may well have been a gift made by one of the kings that Athelstan Half-King served and that they would, therefore, be close to royal lands?"

Silence greeted the words. It was evident that Eadric had given the matter no thought.

"Did you seek the view of the monks?"

"Yes, my Lord, but they told me the land was theirs now and so it didn't matter who it had belonged to."

"And did you listen to their words?"

Another silence,

"No, my Lord, I didn't. As with all things I was acting in your best interests," he said, looking directly at the king with the strength returning to his voice. Always, the king was more tolerant if those accused of wrongdoing could make their case to his benefit. This time, Leofwine didn't think it was going to work. And certainly hoped it wasn't.

"My best interests were in keeping my ship army together, as you well know, not in having it dispersed in some irrelevant argument about who owns what, when I own everything anyway and wouldn't have objected to the transfer, even if it was my land, which it isn't." The king's voice had fallen to a harsh whisper as he spoke, and Eadric, caught under his king's harsh glare had begun to fidget like a child being chastised by his parent.

"My Lord, you have my sincere apologies for any ... error that may have occurred."

The king barked at that understating of events, continuing to glare at Eadric.

Long moments passed, the sense of expectation built and not

one person in that room dared breath. This was it, the moment they'd all been waiting for. Eadric would triumph, and if he did, Leofwine knew that his ambitions would never be contained again. Either that or he would be exiled from the king's presence. Banished, if he was lucky. Executed if he was not.

Eadric took a deep breath as if to speak but Æthelred glared at him so he subsided back into silence. And then the king spoke, his voice thick and heavy with emotion.

"You've disappointed me Eadric. Of all my men, I had hopes that you shared my thoughts and hopes for my people and my land. You, as you say, are my son by marriage, father of my grandson and you should be striving to make this kingdom free from terror. For the boy's future, if not your own. And yet you don't. You work against me, and I can't tolerate that."

A murmur of approval swept the room, but Leofwine knew that the king was about to qualify his statement.

"Yet, your work as ealdorman is efficient, sometimes too much so. And I'll not disturb my people again by removing you from your post."

The whispers grew in volume as everyone realised that the king wasn't about to dismiss Eadric altogether.

"But, I'd rather have you in my sights, than not, so that I can keep a firm watch on what you're doing. You're now detained at my pleasure. You'll have my daughter brought to my hall at Winchester, and for the next, say half a year, you will stand in daily attendance upon me. You will do all I ask, and in your absence, the reeves will govern Mercia for me."

Leofwine approved of the king's sanctions, for all that he was dismayed that Eadric had not been charged with treason there and then and banished. But then, the banishment of Leofsige and his subsequent alliance with Swein had soured the king from that punishment. Far better to have him where he could be seen.

"And your brother, he will rebuild my ships, at his cost. All thirty-six of them that were damaged and are now missing in the summer storm. You'll rebuild my other twenty that Wulfnoth took. This is my decision. Do you accept it?"

Eadric was like a man drowning at sea, weighed down by his shield and sword, the colour drained from his face. Any moment now he looked as though he might tumble to the floor.

As he tried to compose himself, he seemed incapable of speech and the king looked at him expectantly, waiting for his agreement.

Surely Eadric would give it, Leofwine thought. Surely he wouldn't make a further mockery of the king.

"My thanks my Lord," he finally uttered, his voice lifeless, all defiance fled, and Leofwine knew what it was to experience the granting of all his wishes, only to be sickened by how he felt now. To see the man so deflated was demeaning, and so damaging to his future, and yet, what else could the king have done. Eadric had defied him. His motives had been purely malicious. He's worked to undermine everything that the king had been working towards for over a year.

A murmur of approval rang through the hall, and Æthelred looked straight at Leofwine. He stood stiffly in response. His king had need of him now.

"My Lord, I think your mercy is evident in your decision, and I congratulate and endorse it," he said into the slowly building swell of conversation. Eadric didn't even turn to look at him. He knew who spoke. There was no need to acknowledge him.

Quickly Ulfcytel and Uhtred uttered similar words and the king, while not looking pleased with the outcome, gracefully accepted their consensus.

Leofwine wondered how Eadric was to finance the ships that needed rebuilding, how Brihtric was? But they were not his concerns. Instead, he sought out his oldest son and saw him sitting with Olaf and the two hounds. The heads of the four of them were bowed close together, and Leofwine couldn't see how he'd reacted to the news.

At his side, Ulfcytel and Uhtred spoke in low voices to each other, but he ignored them, watching Eadric carefully. No longer under the king's scrutiny, Eadric sank to his bench, lifeless, bereft. Leofwine wondered sardonically just how long this blow to his pretensions would cripple him. He didn't think it would be long.

# 17
# WINCHESTER, AD1009, NORTHMAN

Being at the king's hall at Winchester was a holiday compared to his time with Eadric in Shropshire. Eadric was quiet and contained in his ways. His every action angled to regain the king's trust. Northman knew it wasn't working anywhere near as well as Eadric had hoped, and that was good. While Eadric cowered and simpered before the king, struggling to raise the funds to rebuild the king's lost ships, Northman was free to join in with the training of the king's household troops. His long weeks of training were making him stronger, fitter, and lethal with a sword or a war hammer.

Olaf trained as hard as he did, both happily falling into their sleeping sacks at night exhausted but a pleasant exhaustion from physical exertion, not from having to watch what they said and whom they said it to.

Northman felt happy and content. This sort of fostering was much more to his liking.

And in his time at the king's hall, he'd come into daily contact with the king's oldest sons, Athelstan and Edmund. They trained their own men with the king's and while there were rumblings of discord between the king and his oldest sons, the men of all the household troops didn't let it have any impact on their training. When the Raiders next struck, they knew they needed to fight as a cohesive force, no matter that Athelstan thought his father too lenient, and Æthelred thought his son too harsh, while Edmund watched Eadric like a hawk.

He'd not seen his father since the meeting at Sandwich, but he was a step closer to home in Winchester, and he knew that if he'd asked Eadric he'd have let him journey home. He just didn't want to. Not right now. There was a feeling every morning that the news would come of attackers that day, and Northman wanted to be in the troops sent to rout them, the final barrier if the Raiders ships managed to make their way through the king's reconstituted ship army, still depleted but whole other than that.

He could almost taste the need for battle when he ate. He was ready, and he was willing.

Olaf shared his lust for battle glory. They'd been training their whole lives for this, and they were as prepared as they could be. Even Athelstan had complimented their fighting techniques and praise from him was rare and to be treasured. All the men said the same.

The days were hot and sweaty, the nights cooled by a gentle breeze, and it was that breeze that finally brought the Raiders to their shores. A vast fleet. A fleet so huge that none could count it. And heading that fleet was the man Northman had glimpsed when he met Swein, Thorkell the Tall or at least the hot and sweaty messenger said it was him.

News of the arrival of the ships at London was greeted with a fierce dismay. Where was the ship-army? What had happened?

Roused from their beds early one late summer's day, Northman felt a surge of excitement, fear and trepidation. Eadric, as the king had commanded, was forced to remain with him, but his men were not so constrained, lead as they were by Athelstan and Edmund in his disgrace. Collecting their supplies, they mounted their horses and began to ride to where they understood Thorkell to be attacking, London.

The men were orderly, calm, and keen even to face this new threat. No news had yet reached them of how the ship-army had managed, all they knew for certain was that a new threat had struck at Sandwich and had then rapidly turned to attack London. Most had interpreted that as a good sign, hoping that the ship-army had prevented this new pretender to their land from making landfall.

Olaf was happily optimistic as the priest offered blessings before they rode away from the king's hall. Northman swallowed his fear, the acceptance of what was happening not passing him by quite as easily as Olaf. The untested ship army, against a raiding fleet? He lacked conviction that they'd be effective first time round. Not that he didn't hope they would be. But still, he wasn't convinced.

The household troops, swelled by the ranks of Athelstan and Edmund's men numbered in their hundreds. A sizeable force. But no one knew just how many Raiders there were. Not this time.

They found Thorkell long before they reached London, stumbling upon him at Oxford, having ridden the mighty Thames all the way inland.

Thankfully, outriders had returned with the news that a vast fleet of ships moored at Oxford, and they'd prevented the army from stumbling upon Thorkell unawares. Athelstan called together a hasty conference. They knew this land well. How could they best hem Thorkell in or drive him out?

The church bells at Oxford were ringing, signalling the attack, but by the time the discussion was done with, an ominous silence had fallen, causing everyone to wonder what had happened. Athelstan called for calm, sending out yet more outriders to try and determine what had happened, although the smell of burning flesh in the air was all some of them needed to know that an attack had already occurred.

A messenger appeared, the news was not good.

"My Lord Athelstan", he gasped, sweat from his quick return running freely down his face in the hot weather.

"Oxford has been attacked, overrun. As we speak, Thorkell and his men are turning the town's defences against us."

Athelstan looked grim at the news, Northman having managed to work his way through the press of men so that he could listen first hand to decisions being made about his future. Olaf had attempted to sneak through the press of men with him but had become trapped between the imposing figures of two of Athelstan's greatest warriors. He'd cast a look of despair at Northman when he'd turned to look for him, and Northman had pressed on without him. Better one of them knew what was happening than none of them.

"How many do they number?" Edmund asked as though reckoning the number of enemies was an everyday occurrence.

"I'd say at least five full ships have come this far, and possibly others have come on land. There are a significant number of horses inside the fortifications."

"And how big are the ships?"

"As big as those that our ship-men have constructed. I'd say at least sixty men to each ship. So a start of three hundred men, before any reinforcements are factored in."

"That's a larger number than I was expecting," Athelstan pondered, and yet, Northman couldn't help noticing, the news didn't seem to phase him.

The English household troops and even the fyrds were the most prepared they'd ever been, and the commanders had confidence in them. Northman wondered if the discussion would be quite so calm if they numbered merely thirty with rusty old weapons and no hope of raising more troops.

"There are some dead, my Lord, but not as many as I'd have feared, and they seem to be getting a Christian burial."

"Then, what is that smell of burning?" Edmund queried.

"Well, they're burning their own casualties, as is their way."

Silence fell amongst those assembled, and a grumble worked its way to the back of the crowd. Those who knew the king's sons well were shrugging free of their packs, and dumping them on the ground. Northman wasn't sure whether that implied that they were attacking immediately, or preparing to stay put for the night.

Athelstan and Edmund glanced at each other and turned to their most trusted and battle hardened warrior, a man called Sired. He nodded at some unspoken words, and Athelstan turned to the men who surrounded him.

"Pull back, before we make camp. We need to assess the situation. I need to know which gate they've breached before we act further. The king will be most unhappy if Thorkell attacks his mint but I imagine that was why they came to Oxford. Rumours of its high status must have been much discussed, not to mention the recent founding of the two new Churches. We need to know what's happened at London and Sandwich."

Edmund nodded in agreement, and the men found themselves remounting and retracing their steps.

This wasn't what Northman had expected. He'd hoped to come riding in and attack. The thought of delaying the attack made him nervous. He'd need to steel his resolve all over again.

The brothers arranged for outriders to ride as far and as fast as they could before nightfall and return with as much detail as they could. Another set of riders raced to the king, Sandwich and of course London. For now, they had only one thing in their favour. Thorkell seemed to be unaware of their lightning quick response.

Northman occupied his mind for the rest of that day with the routine of camp life. No fires were lit, as they didn't want to alert Thorkell to their presence, so instead they ate provisions from the king's kitchen – the bread baked overnight and meats that had been cooked and allowed to cool. It was a good meal, but he hoped that the next day they'd either move on or attack. His nerves knotted his stomach.

Early the next morning, Northman woke to a gentle sun on his face, and the quiet conversation of serious men. Glancing from where he lay on the soft grass to where the king's son had spent the night, in their tent, he noticed a group of men milling around. They could only be the returned outriders.

Waking abruptly, he strode to the athelings tent, intent on listening to the news.

"My Lord," a dishevelled youth spoke first, "I made it as far as London, and travelled all night to get back. The news is bad, my Lords. The ship army is vast, almost beyond counting. This small force is just that, a small force. More ships are moving along the Thames. They don't hold London, but they're amassed there in huge numbers, with some of the ships choosing to risk passing the closed gates, with most succeeding."

Another outrider spoke then,

"I didn't make it as far as London, but I followed the Thames as closely as I could. I came across four separate groupings of men upon the shore. I'd say another ten ships are already on their way to Oxford and might arrive at any time."

"And our ship army?" Athelstan queried, "is there news yet of where they are?"

"No, my Lord, although ... and I hesitate to mention this. I did come across some other camps, but they were filled with English men. I fear they may have begun to disperse from the ship-army, after all, their time will be done by now if they were only members of the fyrd."

Edmund shot the messenger a veiled glare at the words,

"I hadn't considered that," he said, far more blandly than Northman would have expected from his look. But perhaps, after all, Edmund was enough of a man not to blame those who brought him the unpleasant news.

"Did you come across just the one camp of English men?"

"No, my Lord, at least two. I was unsure if I should approach them, and so I didn't. I suppose it's just as possible that the men are on the way to Sandwich, to fulfil their obligations to the fyrd, but the season is late, and everyone is thinking of the harvest after all the good weather we've enjoyed. "

Nodding as he thought, Athelstan looked a little bleakly to where small wisps of smoke could be seen rising in the predawn light.

"Do you think it hopeless to attack them?" he asked aloud, to no one in particular.

Edmund didn't respond, and the commander spoke gravely,

"It seems as though we're greatly outnumbered, but that shouldn't stop us. If we can take advantage of them while they're separated, we could do some serious damage."

A faint smile began to tug on Northman's face. The commander was a cunning man. Perhaps he would infuse the athelings with enthusiasm for the hard task ahead.

"Then we should attack Oxford and drive them out?" Edmund queried.

"We must yes. But first, we should try a little bit of diplomacy. Tempt this Thorkell to show his face. I'm not unaware of him, and I know young Northman here," Northman jumped a little at the mention of his name, thinking his presence had been un-noted, "also knows of the man. Perhaps we'll first determine how many other commanders make up their army, and what their plans are."

Athelstan looked from his commander to Northman, thinking of what he'd been told, trying to reconcile it with what he knew his men were capable of.

"I agree. We'll treat with the man. Sadly, it means he'll know that his movements are not unknown. That might panic him when he thinks he's here all unmarked. Northman, you'll accompany me and point out Thorkell to me, although, I understand his by-name, 'Tall' is not unwarranted."

Northman glowed with pride at being so recognised by the atheling, and, mindful that he would need to know all the plans the three men were now making, stayed within the tent of the royal brothers, feeling now that he should be there after all.

During the morning, as the men argued and planned, more and more messengers arrived. There was still no word from Sandwich, but an outrider from the king shared his dismay that the Raiders were at Oxford. The king didn't command his sons to attack, only to act in the best interests of their countrymen and their king.

And then finally, and only after a messenger had already approached the closed gates of Oxford, and demanded to speak with Thorkell to arrange the meeting, did news arrive from Sandwich. The outrider sent the night before had intercepted another messenger flying through the moonlit night on his way to the king.

The news was terrible. The ship-army had disbanded. The messenger knew nothing of the arrival of the Raiders. So late in the season, the commanders had taken the decision to send the men home to their farms.

Immediately Athelstan acted, calling the outriders back to him, and asking them to seek out those they'd encountered on their night time travels and command them to return to their ships at Sandwich. He sent another messenger to his father to let him know of this blow to their plans.

And then, composing himself, he motioned for five of his household troops to mount up and escort them to their arranged meeting with Thorkell. Edmund, he left behind to control the rest of the force should Thorkell play them false.

Accompanying them was Athelstan's commander and the priest who'd journeyed with the force. He'd be able to provide the king with an accurate accounting of the words that passed between his son and Thorkell, and could also send more private messages in writing, illegible to many of the warriors.

Breaking free from the cover of the trees, they made their way carefully through the carefully planted fields, swaying with their crop that was in need of harvesting, and alighted on the road that ran to, and then through, Oxford.

Their intelligence told them that Thorkell had entered through the western gate, and they approached the southern one. It was further from the ships that were moored near to the western gate and would be a test of how much of Oxford Thorkell held.

The gate opened as they approached, and a similar sized group of men came forth. For the briefest moment, Northman caught the haunted faces of those inside Oxford, now captive at the hands of the Raiders. They looked scared and defiant all at the same time. Abruptly the gates slammed shut on the inhabitants, and Northman was facing Thorkell.

Nudging his horse forwards, he muttered softly to Athelstan of who the mighty warrior was, but it was clear that Athelstan had already made the connection.

He was a huge man, worthy of his name, and somehow he'd found the largest horse that Northman had ever seen. He was imposing and confident, flanked by a man who shared his stature, and another, slightly smaller, but still well muscled. The three were evidently warriors in more than just name.

Athelstan spoke first,

"I'm Athelstan, eldest son of the king of this land, Æthelred, and I've come to demand that you leave this place, return to your ships and leave our land."

Thorkell didn't react to the words, instead turning to glare at his brother. He walked his horse forwards so that he could speak more easily to his brother.

"My brother, Thorkell, is not as skilled in your language as he'd like. I am his brother, Hemming, and this is Eglaf," he indicated the other man, "and the rest of the men are our warriors and you need not know their names. Not yet."

Northman watched Hemming closely. He was dressed well, but a splatter of a darker fluid darkened the front of his byrnie. Northman quelled at the sight of so much blood casually worn. He quickly spoke to his brother in his native tongue, and Thorkell gave a small half-bow from his saddle.

"We decline to leave this land quite as soon as we've taken it. We have our own demands that you will hear?" Hemming queried.

'We will hear them, but I will have to relay them to my father, the king."

"And as you do so, we will stay here. This place, Oxford, is wealthy and comfortable. And now to our demands."

Northman listened in fascination as the huge Norseman reeled through a list of demands.

"We will leave if we have enough gold to pay each man in our service. We calculate that we will need £30000 of silver." He smiled then, a brief grunt of laughter. "We are not kings, and so we are a little cheaper than king Swein but no less lethal. We think you're getting a good deal."

Again, he spoke to his brother and the other men, relaying his joke as they all chuckled aloud. Athelstan stiffened on his own horse, and Northman could almost feel his dismay at the mockery they made of his proud father.

"As well, we will need feeding while we're on your lands, and the exchange of hostages is a given. We'll take you if the king allows it."

Northman's horse shifted under his weight, and he squeezed his legs tightly to still the beast, but the slight movement was enough for Thorkell to notice him. Walking his horse forward he sidled up to Northman, examining him keenly all the time. He spoke in a rush, and his brother translated just as quickly,

"You're the son of Leofwine, the man half-blinded by Swein in the Outer Isles?"

It was less a question than a statement, but Northman answered all the same.

"I am, my Lord. I'm surprised you remember me."

Another swirl of words,

"I'm no Lord boy, but my thanks for your respectfulness. Is your father here? I'd much rather speak with him than the king's son."

A little flustered, Northman was unsure how to respond, other than truthfully.

"No my Lord, Thorkell. My father isn't here. He's busy governing his lands."

A thoughtful look crossed Thorkell's face. But he didn't speak as it appeared his brother knew his mind too well.

"We'd like one of the hostages to be a member of Leofwine's family. He's an honourable man and if we hold his son, and one of the king's sons, I know that we'll resolve our little disagreement amicably."

"And in the meantime, you'll harm no more people of Oxford?" Athelstan demanded, "Or reinforce your position here, or send for more men from London."

The words were abruptly translated as Thorkell turned his horse and returned to his brother's side. Northman was pleased he was no longer under such scrutiny.

"I see you're well appraised of our movements, and yet we've met no resistance yet, other than from the people of London and the people of Oxford."

Ignoring the barbed comment Athelstan watched Thorkell intently, although it was Hemming who spoke the words.

"We have an intricate network of intelligence. Never think that you're movements are undetected."

The man laughed at the implied threat and Athelstan stiffened at the apparent disrespect.

"And don't forget that we, likewise, have our own network of intelligence, and I think, much of it unknown about by your king. But for now, we agree with your terms. We will await instructions from your king as you act in his name but not for him. We'll go back inside, and we will stay there. We give you seven days to return with your hostages."

Arrogantly, he turned his back on his horse, speaking quickly to the others as he did so. Only one horse didn't immediately turn, and Northman felt a start of recognition. Cnut. The Danish king's son was with Thorkell, and he understood English as well as Hemming, if not better.

Without thinking, he called to the young warrior, sat proudly on a dun coloured horse.

"Cnut, I bid you hello." He ignored the glare from Athelstan for speaking and watched a variety of emotions flit across Cnut's face.

"Northman," he eventually replied, making it unclear whether he'd not remembered him, or had been deciding whether he should acknowledge the hello.

"You've grown," Cnut continued, speaking like an old man who'd just met his grandchildren after some time apart.

Northman smirked as the image of Cnut as an old man raced through his mind, but responded warmly all the same.

"You haven't, thankfully. I'd feared you would tower above Thorkell before you stopped growing."

Around them, the men of both parties were listening to the young men exchange pleasantries, neither party calling their errant member to task.

"It's been good to see you again," Cnut said, starting to turn his horse away.

Thinking how best he could gain from this strange little exchange, Northman hastily spoke,

"Send my good wishes to your father as well, king Swein."

Cnut turned a strange look his way, his eyes slightly unfocused.

"I will not be able to do that anytime soon, as he remains in Denmark, but I will let him know all the same when I do see him. And Northman, please extend the same courtesy to your own father from me."

Then he turned aside and guided his horse back through the gates that opened as soon as he came close enough to him. Beside him, Hemming paused a moment and took a long look at Northman. He didn't flinch from the scrutiny, but he little enjoyed it either. Thorkell used his distraction to walk his own horse towards Northman, pausing when they would have drawn level if he'd not been such a massive giant of a man.

"Northman," he said thickly, working hard to form the sound, while his mouth turned upwards in appreciation, "Northman. A good name."

Then he too turned away, and Northman was left reeling from their exchange. Whether he'd helped the atheling or not, he wasn't sure, but he knew he'd been marked by these Raiders as surely as anything.

Back at their campsite later, Athelstan called Northman to him. Northman entered his tent nervously. He couldn't help feeling that he'd acted incorrectly. He shouldn't have spoken. He should have kept the knowledge to himself and told Athelstan later. Now Thorkell, Hemming and Cnut all knew, that he knew, that Cnut was amongst them. Cnut was a rich prize provided they could catch, and the enemy would be even more on their guard now that the English knew Cnut was with them.

"Northman," Athelstan began from his small wooden camp chair, positioned to catch the warmth of the evening sun. "I wanted to thank you for your bravery earlier. It was brave of you to point out the Danish king's son."

"My thanks my Lord, I'd feared that I'd erred in my judgement."

"Not at all. You gave us a little advantage when we needed one. These Raiders are arrogant, and it's that which will cost them most dearly. It would have been well and good to know that Thorkell was the Danish king's commander but to know he has the king's son with him is priceless. It means that their actions here have the blessing of their king. That'll goad my father to action more than anything else. He'll not wish to pay more money to the man. Only two years ago he was sent from our shores with £36000. The king will pay no more. And we also know that your father and his men can defeat Swein and his. That's worth knowing."

"I'm pleased I was of some assistance."

Edmund glanced up from polishing his sword to glance at Northman.

"Your name is also known to Thorkell?"

"I think news of my father's injury at the hands of Swein was spread far and wide by both Olaf Tryggvason, and then Swein himself. It's no secret that my mother named me so that I'd avenge my father's death."

"Is that the reasoning for the name?"

"Oh yes, my Lord. My mother was adamant; my father's told me the story, and he didn't try to deter her. After all, my name was my name by then."

"So you've been marked from birth as someone who would avenge themselves against these Raiders."

"I suppose you could look at it that way. But other men carry the name as well. I can't see that they were all named for the same reason."

Edmund smiled at his positive response, "I think you'd be surprised. While many are named for their ancestors, and by family tradition, these Raiders have caused untold distress to many families. I imagine that many sons would like to exact revenge for their father's untimely death."

Soberly Northman considered that. He'd been lucky. His father had returned alive if damaged.

"I wouldn't like to think that my naming and the circumstances of my birth have marked the course of my life."

"No, but it's more than likely so. Take Athelstan and I. The king's sons both, but not the right sons for our father. Still, we were born as athelings, and we'll remain as such until we die, no matter what the king and the current queen try to do about it. We're just as marked by our births as you."

Athelstan grunted in agreement and then beckoned Northman closer.

"Come, sit with us. I'd like you to tell me more of your father. I know him, of course, in fact, there was a time I thought we were close allies, but then Eadric appeared, and your father lost much of his power base. I believe he grows ascendant now, and I'd like to know more of him."

Honoured to be asked to stay with the athelings, Northman spent the night being plied with ale and questions, finally sleeping where he sat, his head curled on his arms on the table before them. The morning would bring his headache.

# 18

# WINCHESTER, AD1009, LEOFWINE

AGITATION WAS EVIDENT IN HIS EVERY STEP. HIS LIMP, ONCE SO PRONOUNCED but almost missing for the last five years, was back with a vengeance, unbalancing him in his anger.

The bloody king! His plans to counter the new menace of Thorkell and the Danish king's son included his own son, and he was outraged once more. Why not, in all good conscious, send that snake Eadric as their hostage? It wasn't as if he was any use whatsoever at the king's hall. And all knew of just how important he was to the king, his continuing attendance upon the king a sign of his favour.

Angrily, he stamped the thought from his mind. What could be worse than sending bloody Eadric to be Thorkell's hostage? The idea of the devastation he could cause snapped Leofwine back from his angry rampage. Eadric sulked and skulked his way around the king's hall at Winchester, unrepentant and determined to have his say with anyone who would ask him about it.

But his son, his second born son, as another victim of the king's plans, was untenable, unthinkable, and yet, he knew it would happen.

With Northman still fostered by Eadric, despite his disgrace and

Northman now being with the king's son at their encampment outside Oxford, the king had need of another from Leofwine's family, and he had decided on his second eldest son. At all of eleven years old, Leofric had been fostered by Horic until the king's latest missive. Never far from home, both he and Æthelflæd had often spent time with him, and every summer so far he'd returned to his parent's home for an extended stay, but this time he was to go as a guarantee of the king's good intentions in reaching an agreement with Thorkell.

Leofwine could barely breathe at the prospect.

His king could be so flippant with him and so neglectful of him when it was not in his interests, and he knew that his precious second son would not be the king's primary concern. No, the man who had almost enough sons to form his own household troop, who struggled to placate his queen and her desires for her children with those of his own full-grown children, would think nothing of leaving Leofric where he was, and of having him suffer the consequences if he displeased Thorkell.

Leofwine could only hope that Thorkell, the foster-father of Cnut, would have more parental concerns for the boy. The treasonous thought swept through his mind unbidden, but with it, he began to relax. He knew there was truth in that idea. Thorkell, the warrior who they now understood to be a part of king Swein's elite fighters, was rumoured to be an excellent foster-father to Cnut. He was kind, caring and mindful of the honour done to him in being chosen as his foster-father, and yet he was also prepared to let the boy grow under his care, and become the man he'd need to be if he was to succeed to his father's throne.

Within their small room at Winchester, Oscetel and Horic watched Leofwine carefully. The pair were as outraged as their Lord but had realised even before the typically practical Leofwine, that there was never a choice in the matter. They'd taken some time to debate how long it would take for Leofwine to reach the same decision, and Horic was trying his hardest to hide his grin of delight for he had foreseen this and had won a small but beautiful dagger from Oscetel. One he'd long coveted.

Only four days had passed since the messenger from Athelstan, and the king had received Edmund. In that time he'd acted swiftly to have Leofwine sent for, and his son. The more permanent members of the king's inner circle had spent the intervening time debating the demands of Thorkell and trying to determine whether they should firstly send the hostages as required, and secondly, what the implication was of Thorkell coming with such a massive fleet.

At the same time, greater intelligence was gathered. The number of ships in the combined fleet had been counted as fully one hundred, and the fleet at Sandwich had been fully stood down. The men who'd formed the ship-army were not to blame for their disbursement, but while they harvested the land they farmed, their neighbours would be called up for the land fyrd in the heartlands of the king's old Wessex kingdom.

Those shipmen who made up the core of the king's far smaller fleet hadn't abandoned their posts when the fyrd ship-army had returned home, but they'd been too small to stop such a vast fleet. Instead, they'd chased Thorkell's men to London, and now effectively barricaded them in, guarding the exit from the town. Again, no one had yet decided whether this was good tactics or not, but for now, it meant that every single member of the raiding army was contained in only one of three places. It was a good start.

A knock at the wooden door flung hastily open by Leofwine himself, found him facing one of the queen's ladies on the other side. She was shocked to see him answering the door and took a moment to recover her wits.

"My Lord Leofwine," she stumbled prettily, "the queen wonders if you might have a moment to visit with her."

Not used to a royal summons from the queen, Leofwine immediately agreed and followed the girl from the room. Behind him, Oscetel strained to see what was happening while Horic leapt to his feet to escort his Lord, but Leofwine pulled the door closed, not unkindly, but right now, his curiosity about the queen was something he didn't want to share.

Emma, as he still always called her in his mind and in private, was pacing within her own suite of rooms, and he smirked at the similarity of their state of minds.

"My queen," he spoke, dropping to his knee before her.

"Oh stand up Leofwine," she sharply demanded, and he did so with elasticity. "By now you must know better."

"Of course I do Emma, but I must still show you the respect you deserve. And you know I should."

She waved her hand briskly to dismiss his words, but he knew he'd acted correctly, even if she was unhappy.

"My mind is awash with unease," she said into the companionable silence. "Æthelred is too quick to agree to this Thorkell's demands, and I fear that in letting him get his own way, especially in respect of your own son, that firstly the king does you no honour and secondly that he shows Thorkell greater recognition. It is wrong, and I want you to know that."

She stopped her pacing before him and grabbed his hands within her own.

"You did much for me when I first came to this land, and I know that although you're friendly with the king's elder sons you look upon my own children as just as eligible for the throne should the worst befall the king. You and your wife are good people. Neither of you should be punished further. You must act. I must act, but I don't know what to do."

Seeing the queen's distress was a balm to Leofwine's tortured soul. To hear her say that the king was treating him unfairly soothed his own anger.

"Emma, I'm more pleased than you can imagine hearing you speak so. I thought that my own anger was born directly of selfishness. But, and I stress this, I don't think there's anything we can do to dissuade the king. We know that he always looks for the simplest solution to any problem and he sees this as that."

"But it's not right," she cried, dropping his hands and resuming her pacing.

"I've tried to speak to him about it, but he dismisses me and tells me I know nothing about the stresses he's under. As if I could be his queen without knowing what distresses him."

Her anger was magnificent to behold and once more he thought the king, a lucky man to have her as his bedfellow. By rights, she should have been with Athelstan, and there was not one person in the kingdom who didn't know that.

"Your sons are precious to you. I do all I can for Northman here, and I know that Athelstan does the same. But Leofric, he can't go to Thorkell. He's a thug, a warrior without thought or care past his own profit and his own needs."

"You know him by reputation?"

"Yes and no. I know of who he was from my youth in Normandy. He was one of those names that were uttered in hushed whispers. No one wished to say his name out loud for fear he would physically manifest once given voice."

"And yet Swein of Denmark trusts him with his son."

"Of course he does. What king wouldn't want his son to learn to be as ruthless as his most revered commander? Cnut's reputation will grow by his association with Thorkell."

"And so might Leofric's," Leofwine couldn't quite believe that he was counter-arguing for his son to go to Thorkell, but it felt good to have a new voice to reason with. Perhaps this discussion with Emma would help him put the matter into the correct perspective.

"How old is your son?" Emma snapped.

"He's just turned eleven," he answered.

"Eleven," she all but squeaked.

"My lady, boys grow quickly once they're out of childhood. I know you look to your own boys and make comparisons, but really, Edward is only a baby still at five years. Think how far he's come in five years, and think how far he'll come when he's added that same amount of time to his age."

Unconvinced, Emma strode to where her two boys and baby daughter were being cared for in the corner of her rooms. Her baby daughter lay squirming on thick furs, naked before the fire. Her boys were sitting quietly, as one of the maids regaled them with stories of royal saints.

"Look at them," she said pointing needlessly to them. "They are babies, to be cherished and cared for and nurtured. Not to be sent out as hostages to some strange warrior who lays claim to land unlawfully."

Not wishing to infuriate her further, but unable to resist stating the obvious, Leofwine spoke almost abruptly,

"Then be grateful he does not demand your children."

She cast him a disdainful look as she swept passed him again to resume her aggravated walking.

"And your wife allows you to say such things?" she spat in exacerbation.

"Of course not, my Lady, and in all honesty, I am merely answering your valid arguments the way that the king will if I raise them with him. I don't agree. Not at all. My sons should be home and safe, either with their foster parents, or with us well Leofric should be, not Northman. Not with a warrior I've only met once or twice."

"Good, at least you have some sense," she spoke, a little mollified, and finally met his eyes again.

"What will we do?" she asked desperately, but he shook his head slowly.

"We can't do anything. We'll have to do as the king commands. We can't be divisive, not when the country is threatened again."

She stepped forward and looked him in the eye,

"Do you think you can do that?" she whispered. "Again."

It was his turn to look away, his fears rapidly resurfacing as the reality of the situation made itself evident.

"I have no choice."

She didn't deny his words. They'd been friends a long time, and she knew what the king had done to him in that time. She knew their shared history as well.

"Then you have my pity."

"And can I have your word that you will continue to badger the king to have my son returned to me."

"Of course Leofwine. If he allows your second son to go, I will plague him at every possible opportunity. When he sees his boys, I will mention Leofric. When he sees his grandchild, I will mention Leofric. I will do all I can."

"That is all I ask of you, Emma, and you have my sincerest thanks for all you do on my family's behalf."

"It's too little, and it frustrates me, but I hope you know that I do what I can, and always will. Leofwine, you're the most loyal man within the Witan, you and Wulfstan the archbishop. You work tirelessly for the king," and here a note of pleading entered her voice, "please don't stop."

Her look was steady, her hand on his arm wasn't. It was just as hard for her to stay loyal to her husband as it was for him. It was a burden they shared and rarely spoke about, but it always hovered between them.

Bowing his head, he excused himself and wandered back to his rooms, a little consolidated and a little saddened at the same time. If only the king could see his actions more clearly.

# 19
# OUTSIDE OXFORD, AD1009, NORTHMAN

He felt a little sick inside, with more than just nerves. Today was the day, seven days since Thorkell had given his demands, and as yet there was no news from the king about how they should proceed.

Fear for his younger brother had prevented him from sleeping for much of the last six nights. Fear for his brother, and fear for himself and his father, and whichever of the king's sons was chosen as a hostage for the good behaviour of the English while Thorkell and his mighty fleet bedevilled their coasts and waterways.

True to their word, Thorkell and his men had not ventured out of Oxford and neither had more ships made the now perilous journey towards their commanders. All was quiet, but an uneasy calm that made the hair on the back of his neck stick up and made him grumpy and short-tempered.

And he wasn't alone. All the men camped near Oxford were similarly afflicted.

Rising from his sleepless night, he wondered over to the tent of the king's sons. Since his help a week ago, he'd often been admitted to their counsel, so much so that he no longer thought it strange to be served by the squires when normally he would have been doing the serving.

The brothers were as awake as he was, Athelstan having just returned from a walk along the ridge of the valley, vainly looking towards Winchester where the king was in residence. He was shaking his head to show that there was still no sign of a messenger. Yesterday evening they'd sent yet another messenger, but he'd not returned although the journey could easily have been accomplished provided he'd not stopped long when reaching Winchester.

"Nothing?" Edmund questioned, resignation in his voice.

"Nothing. He better send one soon, or we'll be thought of as even bigger fools by Thorkell and his men."

Edmund grunted in agreement,

"You're not wrong, brother. But father will act. He has no choice."

"I wish he'd get on with it. My patience is frayed and so is everyone else's. And I bet that within the walls of Oxford, the inhabitants are feeling abandoned, and goodness only knows how the ship-men are keeping themselves amused."

Although they'd routinely sent a small foraging party towards Oxford, they'd seen no sign of any Raiders nor any fleeing inhabitants. Oxford was locked up tight. Those inside were not getting out, no matter what.

They'd seen to the burial of the bodies of those who'd fought at the Western Gate and lost their lives there, but other than that, all surveillance had been covert.

Silence fell between them, broken only by the crackling of their small fire set in the brazier, and the shuffling of the animals and men who worked quietly around the campsite.

The sun had risen long ago, the summer heat was gently building, and in the abandoned fields around Oxford, crops waited to be harvested. But no one was coming.

"If they stay inside Oxford, or if father doesn't agree, they'll have to arrange for the harvest to be brought in."

"No, they won't. They can just as easily demand that the king feeds them," Edmund responded slowly, as though he thought as he spoke.

"But that's a waste."

"Yes, but so is murdering the people of Oxford."

"Yes, but they needed to get inside, and if they stood in their way, then they needed to be removed."

"Huh, I suppose you're right," Athelstan concurred and with the conversation done, for the time being, they fell back to silence.

The day passed interminably slowly. Northman watched the sun work its way around the cloudless sky with a mounting sense of panic. Surely the king would act.

Finally, when the late afternoon sun was starting to lose its heat, a cry from the men on guard duty alerted them to the arrival of someone. Tempted to rush from the tent but knowing he shouldn't look too keen, Northman walked towards the noise. Who had the king sent? What decision had been reached?

Squinting into the sunlight, Northman felt a jolt of recognition and a cry of joy burst from his mouth. His father had come.

He raced towards his father and his men, forgetting the implications of his father's arrival until his eyes alighted on his younger brother, with whitened face and fear-crazed eyes. Oh no, anything but this.

Stopping abruptly, Olaf almost knocked him flying where he'd been running behind him. He only just managed to avoid falling forward on his face because Olaf grabbed him roughly and kept him upright. Realisation struck Olaf at the same time and sedately, they walked towards his father, a crazy smile for his brother because he'd not seen him for nearly a year and it was a surprise to see him grown so much.

"Northman," his father greeted warmly, his eyes kindly and resigned towards his oldest child.

"Father," Northman answered, "it's good to see you. And Leofric, you as well." He grabbed his younger brother in a hug, not caring that he'd never shown so much affection to him in the past.

His brother's slender body trembled in his arms, and although he tried to impart some of his strength to him, just using a simple hug, he knew he'd never be able to give his brother the strength he needed, not on his own.

Then his father wrapped his arms around both of his sons, pulling Olaf to him as well, and they stood like that until the atheling caught up with them.

"My Lord Leofwine," Athelstan spoke courteously, and Northman felt himself being released by his father.

"My apologies My Lord, for not coming to you straight away," Leofwine said, emotion heavy in his voice.

Smiling Athelstan brushed the comment aside,

"I'd not expect it, Leofwine. Not in the circumstances. I take it from your son's presence that the king has agreed to their demands."

Leofwine's face darkened slightly, but he spoke clearly,

"He has but with some provisions. Thorkell isn't to get everything his way."

"Excellent, but come, we must speak more privately."

Northman thought they might be left where they were, but his father pulled them both beside him, so stumbling back towards the campsite, he followed his brother. They didn't speak as they walked, but Northman noted the faces of those who he'd trained with at the king's hall in Winchester. They clearly saw him, and his brother, who looked similar to him and who had his father's features, and a murmur of understanding spread through the camp.

By the time they reached the tent of the athelings, Edmund had been appraised of the situation. Edmund grinned at Leofric, and welcomed Leofwine and the others who'd him.

The king had sent a number of his advisors with Leofwine, including Archbishop Wulfstan. With no time for pleasantries, Archbishop Wulfstan spoke first,

"The king has agreed to the exchange of hostages, Leofric here, and also one of his sons. Edmund, your father has decreed you must go as his hostage."

The archbishop spoke succinctly, and surprisingly Edmund shrugged aside the news,

"I'd thought he would. Athelstan has been saying that father wouldn't agree to one of his sons, but I know him better. He has many sons, and although he loves us all, I think he'd do anything to keep our kingdom safe. Please tell him I understand his reasoning and accept his decision."

Northman was dismayed and overjoyed at the same time. Edmund was honourable and courageous. He would keep Leofric safe in Thorkell's camp.

"He's also decided that the other ealdormen in the kingdom should send hostages to Thorkell. That's why we were delayed. We understood that Eadric's youngest brother was to join us, but sadly, he didn't arrive in time. It's hoped that tomorrow Uhtred of Northumbria's oldest son, Ealdred, will come, and so too will Ælfric's son. Ulfcytel has agreed to send one of his older brother's."

"And what of the demand for food and payment?" Athelstan asked, speaking to the archbishop but looking at his brother as he spoke.

"Food can be organised. The king has arranged for people from nearby to harvest these fields. The food will then be gifted to Thorkell. As to the payment, the king refuses. He's offered £5000 instead, provided they leave within seven days and never return."

Shocked eyes looked at the archbishop, but he looked undaunted.

"It wouldn't be prudent to bow to their demands immediately. It's to be hoped that we can reach an agreement somewhere between the two amounts. Remember, the English have already been heavily taxed to build the ship army. It's not possible to ask for more."

"And I am to pass these details to Thorkell?" Edmund asked.

"No, well, not alone. It's also been decided to send a man of God in the hope that he can convert these pagans from their Gods."

Here a pale man stepped forward; his fingers ink-stained, his clothes the brown of a monk.

"My name is Cynwulf, and I'm one of the archbishop's monks from Worcester. I'll come with you, give you all the word of God as you need, and hopefully, practise some of my conversion skills on the men."

Cynwulf had small beady eyes that flickered nervously, but for all that, Northman instantly liked the monk. Cynwulf seemed honest. He thought that Archbishop Wulfstan had made the right choice.

"And now, and if you're ready Leofric and Edmund, I believe that we should approach Oxford and arrange the exchange of hostages. I wonder who Thorkell will send as a hostage for his behaviour."

Leofwine looked suddenly shrunken at the thought of handing Leofric over to Thorkell, and he commented sourly,

"Let us hope it's not the Danish king's son. I'm sure that King Æthelred would find much to gloat about if Cnut is the hostage."

But Leofwine's words proved to be accurate. While Northman went with the rest of the armed force, Leofwine, Leofric, Edmund and Archbishop Wulfstan, rode to their rendezvous at the gates of Oxford.

No sooner had they arrived than the gates opened, almost as if they'd either been waiting for them or had known of their imminent arrival.

It was Hemming who came first, followed by Thorkell and Cnut, but no others.

Northman was not close enough this time to hear the exchange between the men, but he watched his brother with a lump in his throat and narrowed eyes, as his father lifted him down from his horse and then up beside Thorkell. Thorkell sat astride his great horse. His father lingered for some moments, and Northman considered whether he was using his Danish to entreat the man to look after Leofric.

Edmund also dismounted and walked towards the small party, while the monk accompanied them. All the time Archbishop Wulfstan and Hemming spoke. And then Northman watched as Cnut walked towards his father, and mounted the horse that Edmund had dismounted.

There was a small delay as Archbishop Wulfstan and Hemming finished their conversation. Only then were the horses turned, and Leofwine was on his way back towards the safety of the armed men. Northman watched him carefully, amazed at his father's resolve when he didn't look back towards the closed gates.

The men whispered about Cnut and who he was, but Northman was unable to enlighten them. His throat seemed to have gone completely dry, and fear had sucked all his strength from his legs. Would he see Leofric again?

Back at the camp, a swirl of activity greeted the arrival of Cnut, and it was only much, much later that his father came to find him. He'd not been sleeping, but had moodily been throwing bits of pulled grass onto the fire that burned before him. Around him, men snored, and he wondered how they could sleep at a time like this.

A touch on his shoulder and Northman followed his father to where they could talk without waking the other men.

"I'm to return to Winchester with Cnut tomorrow. I have permission from the king to take you, but appreciate you might want to close to your brother. The choice is yours, Northman. I'll not make it for you. I understand that here you're away from Eadric."

Northman thought for barely a breath before he nodded, his decision made.

"I'll stay. I wouldn't want to abandon Leofric."

"My thanks, son, your mother would be proud of you."

"How could you let the king?" Northman whispered urgently, fear making his voice wobble.

"I had little choice, but I also reasoned that if Thorkell is good enough for the Danish king's son, then he's also good enough for my own. No harm will come to Leofric. Thorkell isn't so inclined, and neither are his men."

"Are you sure of that father?" Northman asked, hating himself for doubting his father.

"Yes," Leofwine said quietly, not elaborating further.

"Who'll care for Cnut?" Northman asked, realising his father didn't want to talk about Leofric anymore.

"I imagine he'll stay with the king, but I'll use the opportunity to get to know him better. I'll do my best to remain at the king's court. Cnut at least knows who I am, and I should use that to our advantage. Now, son, you must sleep. We'll leave early in the morning. If you're sleeping, I'll not wake you. Any problems with Leofric, any at all, send for me, or send Olaf to his father. He'll know what to do. And Northman."

"Yes, father?"

"My thanks for being such an honourable man."

As his father walked away from him, Northman glowed with the unlooked for praise. His father was a kind man, a strong man, and a loyal man. Yet for all that Leofric clearly loved Northman and his brother, he didn't always tell them so. Being called a man now was a real sign of respect from his father.

During the next three days, the other hostages arrived, and for every person who entered Oxford, one of Thorkell's men was sent outside. The exchanged hostages were to stay with the forces camped close to Oxford. No one were as important as Cnut and so they stayed with Athelstan.

A sense of uncertainty hung over the camp, for Thorkell made no decision regarding the geld offered by the king. The fields around Oxford were rapidly harvested and the grain stacked outside the gates of Oxford each evening. Even from the distance of their camp, the gates could be heard creaking open in the predawn light. When daylight stole over the land, the food was gone each day.

But that was it. No word came from the king, and none from Thorkell.

Northman grew uneasy, as did Athelstan and the men in the camp. It was all taking far too long to resolve.

And then, more than a week after the last hostage had been exchanged, the gates opened and a lone man rode from Oxfrod, and then stopped. Athelstan, who'd been waiting for this very event, rode his way down to the gates that had been resealed.

The household warriors were alert as they watched the solitary exchange. Northman willed the gates of Oxford to open and the Raiders to ride to battle so that the king's warriors could slaughter them all, driving them from the safety of the gates.

But there no such luck. A brief conversation took place before Athelstan made his way back to the camp. Athelstan's glowered, and Northman dreaded to know what Hemming had said to him.

A flurry of activity and a messenger was on the way to the king. The message he carried was that the price had increased to £35000.

# 20
# LATE SUMMER AD1009, LEOFWINE

### Winchester

LEOFWINE WAS SO UNDECIDED AS TO WHAT TO DO FOR THE BEST THAT HIS inaction had kept him at the king's court for the last seven days. For once, he appreciated how the king must surely sometimes feel; overawed by the magnitude of a decision he didn't want to make and attacked on all sides because of that indecision.

How should he proceed for the best? Should he have stayed with his sons at Oxford, return to his wife, or stay by the king's side so that he could work for his son's returns.

Leofwine had split his men, sending half to augment the troops at Oxford, a third of those who remained staying with him at Winchester. The rest he'd sent home to protect Æthelflæd. The people were uneasy, the news of Thorkell's attack spreading with the advance of the harvest northwards and Leofwine shared that unease.

News from the north had been sparse since Wulfnoth's incursions, and that filled Leofwine with foreboding. What was to stop another raiding army attacking in the North? What if Thorkell's fleet had split before they'd come to London and Oxford?

Cnut was a sullen hostage. He was treated well by all, and Leofwine went out of his way to speak to him each day, but nothing could detract from the knowledge that the household troops watched his every move.

The king too was curious about Cnut and spoke to him as often as he could. It was clear that the king wanted to learn as much as he could about Swein, the reasons for Thorkell's attack and Cnut held nothing back.

He wasn't exactly arrogant, but neither was he as docile as a fawn. Cnut knew a great deal, and he realised how valuable that information was. Still, he dispersed it as freely as seeds in the wind.

"My Lord Æthelred," he began on only his first night at Winchester, "your hall is magnificent, your food excellent and your household troops strong and daunting. I hear nothing of where you train your men, how you train your people and how the strongest are chosen for the duty of protecting the kingdom."

Unsure what response Cnut was looking for, Æthelred had not spoken from his place at the table. It had been one of his other son's, Eadwig, who'd asked what they were all thinking.

"And how do those things get accomplished in your land."

Cnut had smirked then, and leant back in his chair, waiting for all around him to focus on him and listen to his words. When they came, they were devastating in their effect upon the morale of the men.

"My father has had built or is in the process of creating, four special villages geared only for the warriors in his armies. I will tell you the names of the villages for they will mean nothing to you: Trelleborg, Fyrkat, Nonnebakken and Aggersborg. There the men and boys are trained and selected. Only the most skilled earn their places in the standing army, the rest can stay and train and learn, but they are not the ones who the king will call on first to defend his lands."

"And how many men are within each village?"

"At least one thousand men in each one, allowing him to call upon a force of four thousand at any one time."

Leofwine had stilled at that huge number of men, seemingly ready at the will of his king, and a hush had fallen within the large room.

"And these men are here with Thorkell?" Leofwine queried, knowing that the king wouldn't ask the question, although he wanted to know the answer, his posture tense as he pretended he wasn't listening to the conversation.

Cnut smirked at him, pleased with the reception his words were having.

"No my lord not all of them. Those are the king's men, and although Thorkell has been allowed to bring a small proportion of the men, these warriors are mostly Thorkell and Hemming's men. I would say they're no less well trained, but they look to those men and not to my father."

"Your father's well-trained troops are no great threat to us then," Leofwine opined, "but it's good to hear the king makes excellent use of the geld paid to him a few years ago."

Cnut shot Leofwine an appraising look, and then as the conversation in the room returned to its normal level, Eadric joined the conversation, and things took a turn for the worst.

For some reason, Cnut took an instant dislike to Eadric, and not that Leofwine didn't understand his antipathy for the man, but it certainly made Cnut's stay with the king a lively thing.

"Thorkell thinks highly of you to send you as his hostage?" Eadric asked lightly, contempt dripping from his voice as he picked at his food before him, pretending disinterest.

"No my Lord, Eadric, is it not? Thorkell knows that your king will not harm the son of the Danish king when they've only recently made terms, and he has an army of four thousand men ready to seek revenge if anything should befall me." His tone was matter of fact, his interest elsewhere in the crowded room, and he showed no respect for the Mercian earl. Leofwine harboured a belief that somehow Cnut knew that Eadric was in disgrace with his king.

Eadric spluttered at the response,

"So your father will approve of you being used as a hostage?"

"My father believes that Thorkell is the best man to be my foster father. If he can't raise me himself, then he believes his great friend and commander should fulfil that role. Whether he approves or not is irrelevant. It is not his choice to make, and anyway, I offered to come."

It was Leofwine's turn to look at Cnut with interest now. When they'd met briefly with Swein, he'd known that there was something about the boy. That was why he'd made the effort to make friendly overtures to him. Now he realised that he'd probably been right. The youth was intelligent.

"To partake of the king's hospitality?" Eadric pressed.

"No, to see who the king respects and who he does not."

Leofwine suppressed a smirk at the outrageous statement and the furious look on Eadric's. He somehow felt he could like Cnut far more than he ever had Eadric. His bluntness reminded him of Olaf, and he felt a little pang of regret at the sudden flash of memory for the man he'd known for only a matter of weeks but who'd affected the course of his life ever since.

Undaunted Eadric pressed for more information,

"And what have you found so far?" he baited the young prince of Denmark.

"That some of the men are bags of wind and others are men of action. I don't think you would like me to make my views common knowledge, but if you ask anymore, I'll have no choice." Boredom, forced or not, infected his speech, in stark contrast to the effect his words were having on Eadric.

Moodily returning to his food, Eadric cast dark glances Cnut's way. Cnut ignored them, his focus on the women of the court.

"Thorkell, he is a good foster-father?" Leofwine asked into the lull.

"Yes, the best. He'll care for your son, as he would his own, don't fear for him. Provided your king is honourable, Swein will be just as noble."

Somewhat mollified, Leofwine lapsed into silence. The food the king served to his hostage and the hall at large was exquisitely cooked, and yet it tasted like nothing to Leofwine.

His thoughts were with his sons, his wife, and his other children, and also the men of his household troop, almost as much family as his marriage family. He hoped the king would find a quick solution to the problem of Thorkell, but he doubted it.

And his fears were well founded. When the messenger came back from Oxford that the geld demanded had now increased to £35000 the king's rage was monumental. In a rare moment of decision, Æthelred had Cnut packed and on his way back to Oxford before the ink on the parchment that accompanied him, had dried.

The king's offer was simple, £5000 would be paid if the Raiders left. If they didn't leave, Thorkell could take Cnut back, and the king would have his hostages back. The war of attrition would continue.

There were shocked murmurs around the court when the king's decision was known, but Leofwine approved of his stance, and not just because it meant his son would be freed. He didn't dare contemplate Thorkell reacting angrily and killing his son. Thorkell didn't seem the sort to take his revenge on innocent children

The court became of swirl of activity. The king suspected that Thorkell would refuse the offer and wanted to be ready for any retreat from Oxford. Messengers raced to Mercia, Northumbria and the lands of the East Angles, demanding that the fyrd be gathered and put on high alert. King Æthelred wanted to be ready to face the Raiders in battle.

Sadly, the king's distraction with the Raiders worked in Eadric's favour, and after another interview with the king, that Leofwine had the misfortune to witness, Eadric won his opportunity to redeem himself and leave the king's side. Eadric raced to Mercia to gather his fyrd. Leofwine watched him go, confident that they'd not see him anytime soon and grateful that in his rush, Eadric had forgotten all about his foster child.

Into the maelstrom of activity, Archbishop Wulfstan stepped calmly, and Leofwine listened to his new ideas with interest. He'd planned long and hard and actually believed that if the king wanted victory and peace he needed to do more that just issue a coinage embodying peace. Archbishop Wulfstan wanted Æthelred to call for a nationwide reaction to the raids. The archbishop believed the king should call for a penance from all, before Michaelmas, for three days. Archbishop Wulfstan believed that a fast, a church service and a geld raised during the penance would go a long way to ensuring that the English had God on their side for any coming battle.

Leofwine approved of the archbishop's beliefs and King Æthelred grasped the idea firmly. Perhaps, Leofwine considered, he now regretted the hasty decision to send Cnut from court and refusal to pay the geld.

Archbishop Wulfstan presented an excellent way to counter the attacks, one not considered before. It would be a complete penance. Even slaves would be freed from their duties for three days to pray for the good of the country.

In fact, the entire court readily accepted the idea, and a commotion commenced as messengers were sent fleeing across the land. The king produced an official code of conduct to be read aloud so that the English would understand how important their actions would now be. Surely, if the entire country united in faith, their God would drive back the wicked Raiders?

A day passed, and then two, and finally a small troop arrived, with Leofric amongst them, and all knew that Thorkell had refused the king's reduced geld, and was determined to hold onto Oxford. But Thorkell had made no move to leave Oxford and had called for more of his shipmen to join him there.

Leofric and the king's son had been well treated by the Raiders. Leofric said that the people of Oxford, those who'd survived the initial attack, were under no threat from their new masters, for what point was there in being a lord, even if only temporarily, of people too dead to work for you? Instead, Thorkell allowed everyone to go on as they had before, they only change being that they couldn't leave Oxford, and any who did were immediately executed.

Leofwine greeted Leofric with joy, and the king, Edmund the same. Then Leofric and Edmund were debriefed, every little nuance of information extracted from them.

Leofric looked haunted by his experience, but in a matter of two days was back to his usual self. Northman had refused to leave the encampment, and Leofwine knew a moment of combined pride and grief. What if his oldest boy came to harm?

With permission from the king, Leofwine withdrew from Bath, where the king had temporarily relocated, because it was so far from Oxford. The king wasn't running away from the threat, but he was showing more wisdom than he had for many years.

From Bath, King Æthelred issued more details about the country-wide penance and held out hope that Thorkell would over-winter at Oxford. If the Raiders were in just one place, it would make it easier to keep track of their movements.

Returning to Deerhurst, Leofwine stopped by the turning that would have taken him to Oxford, and spent a moment pondering the wisdom of retrieving his son and taking him home with him. Realising that Northman would react violently to such a restriction on his attempts to grow up, Leofwine travelled with a heavy heart. His son had his blessing, but he'd rather have him in easy sight.

Beside him, Leofric talked almost none stop about Swein, Hemming and Eglaf and Leofwine realised that his son was more than a little smitten with the fierce warriors invading their lands. It would serve him well. Respect for their enemies would ensure that if the Raiders still plagued the England when he was a man, he'd never underestimate their abilities. Leofwine prayed to his God that they wouldn't, but he could see no end in sight.

If only the penance worked.

If only.

# 21

## NEAR OXFORD, AD1009, NORTHMAN

Rain fell heavily all throughout the night, daylight bringing little change to the conditions. Sat within his tent, Northman felt a little miserable. He was cold and felt like he had been for the last three days. He had every layer of clothing he could find wrapped around his body, but it didn't alleviate the chill. The fire smouldered outside the tent, fighting the rain and the damp wood, and the spirit of the camp was muted.

They'd been in position now for almost two months, and nothing had happened. Not one thing. There was no prospect of actually making battle with Thorkell, and every day, more and more of the ships and men of Thorkell's army arrived to overflow the gates of Oxford. Small tents now propped up the outer defences in the area furthest away from where the English encamped and Northman was just as aware as everyone else that the quantity of tents increased each day.

The reports from yesterday had even hinted that some of the shelters might be being made more permanent. The sound of axes on wood had reached the ears of the scouting party, and almost everyone was ready to accept that the Raiders were preparing themselves for the winter months. It was nearly Michaelmas. The weather was turning chilly, the morning damp, and this persistent rain was churning the hard packed earth to mud and covering everything in a layer of filth.

The king's sons were as sullen as the rest of the encampment. Edmund had been reunited with his brother following his captivity with Thorkell. Northman was at a loss as to what would happen next. Would the king allow them to break camp and return to warmer winter quarters, or would they stay here, all winter long, ensuring that Thorkell and his men didn't ride out from Oxford?

His father had paid a brief visit to the camp only seven days ago. He'd brought with him details of the king's countrywide penance, and the request that they all take part. The men's morale had risen a little at the thought that the king was still thinking of a way to defeat the Raiders. But news from further down the Thames was showing that Thorkell's rougher men were making lightning quick raids into England and people were in danger if they left the safety of their homes and fortified farms.

The harvest was collected, the gates of all the burhs had been closed and were only opened when a representative from the king arrived. An expectancy infected the land. Just about accepting that Thorkell wouldn't attack, no one was quite willing to drop all arms and hold firm against the coming winter storms. There was the possibility that the month after Michaelmas would be fair, and if it was, Thorkell could escape or attack.

The fyrds had gathered in the separate ealdordoms, but soon even their service would come to an end. Then everywhere would be unprotected unless the reeves and royal officials kept their personal household troops on high alert.

Beside him, Olaf snorted in his sleep, and a grim smile spread across Northman's face. His friend had taken to the enforced inactivity by sleeping for much of each day. Northman had been teasing him for his bear-like qualities, but Olaf wasn't concerned. He was a growing boy and the day passed far quicker if he slept through most of it. Then he could stay up late playing small games with the other men. Northman wished, not for the first time, that he could sleep.

Later that day a messenger arrived from the king and a whisper of interest lifted the spirits in the camp. The king had decided that the small army camped at Oxford should be replaced. The men had cheered with some joy at the thought of warm beds and warm food, but Athelstan looked sour when Northman went to seek him out later that evening.

"Northman," he spoke dully, as he entered the tent.

"Athelstan, what ails you?" Northman responded.

"Bloody Eadric."

"What's he done now? Northman asked, his heart sinking. He'd almost managed to forget all about his foster father.

"Somehow, he's managed to convince the king that his men should come and take our place here. What tricks does he have planned now?" Athelstan moaned, annoyed and dismayed in equal measure.

"Surely he's just trying to win the trust of the king?"

"Ah Northman, I wish I could share your positive spin on things. I can't help thinking that if we let Eadric anywhere near these Raiders, he'll cause harm. Again. I've not forgotten, although my father seems to have done so, that it was Eadric's brother who depleted our ships only a few months ago."

"If not for him, our men wouldn't have been so disillusioned that they dispersed home as soon as they could. If the ship-army fyrd had just stayed on alert for a day or two more, they would have stopped Thorkell and we wouldn't have spent two months scratching our arses, watching him eat our food."

Northman couldn't deny the logic of the æthelings reasoning, and yet, his thoughts had turned inwards to himself. What would he do if Eadric demanded him back? He'd become used to being one of the household troop. He looked to Athelstan and Edmund as his lords, and knew that he'd earned his father's respect for his acceptance of his impending manhood. He was needed for greater things than listening to Eadric's half-cooked schemes.

Belatedly, Northman realised that Athelstan was looking at him,

"Apologies, My Lord, I was thinking of Eadric. What did you ask?"

Athelstan gave him a look of understanding.

"I was asking what you'd do when we return to the king, now that Eadric is no longer under house arrest."

"I was thinking the same, and honestly, I'm not sure. I'd prefer to stay amongst your men."

"I'm sure you would, but whether that'll be possible or not I'm unsure. I suggest you come with us, provided we don't hear from either your father or Eadric in the meantime. Bed down with us for the winter. I'll be returning to my hall. You can train with us and we'll see what the new year brings."

Grateful to the ætheling for being as concerned with his future as he was, Northman returned to find Olaf waking from another daylong sleep. He was grinning and full of joy to be leaving, but Northman was uneasy. Now that Athelstan had pointed out to him the probable intent behind Eadric's actions, he shared the same unease. And with that discomfort came the belief that, if he was to truly be his father's son and a loyal man to the king, he should offer to remain here with Eadric. The thought made his gut clench, and bile choke him.

# 22
# WANTAGE, NEAR OXFORD, AD1009, NORTHMAN

As it transpired, Eadric had no more forgotten about his foster-son, than Northman could forget his father was Leofwine, the famous half-blind Ealdorman of the Hwicce, the one-time personal enemy of the mighty king of Denmark and now almost friend. Even before they'd packed up their camp, causing a flurry of activity at Oxford itself, where Thorkell's men watched them with the beady eyes of hawks, a small force arrived at the campsite with instructions from Eadric.

Feeling deflated, and also pleased that the decision had been taken from him and that he must keep an eye on Eadric, Northman sought out Athelstan. The atheling was apologetic, but Northman had no time for that.

"My Lord, I'll do my best to learn all that Eadric has planned. We're to go to the king's palace at Wantage and ride out each day to check on Thorkell and his men. If you arrange for men loyal to yourself to cross my path, I'll pass on what knowledge I can."

Athelstan's eyes blazed with fire at the thought of his spy within Eadric's camp, and quickly he called five of his most trusted warriors to him. He explained what would happen, and the household troops gave Northman admiring glances.

"We'll attempt to cross paths with you at least once a week," the leader of the small group advised him. "There's a small farm not far from here, and they'll happily rent us their barn and a place to sleep for the winter if we pay them handsomely enough. Not to mention, they'll welcome having their war band with them. But, we'll try not to compromise you at all. Once Eadric spies one of us, another will take their place. If we exhaust our small band, we'll send for others."

A little bounce in his step, Northman hastily said his goodbyes to Athelstan and Edmund. He was sad he'd not see them anytime soon, but pleased to have thought his way out of his self-inflicted predicament.

Eadric hadn't sent just anyone to get him, but his youngest brother, Æthelweard. Northman didn't have any feelings of love or loathing for the man, but knew he shared many of his older brothers characteristics; a little mean, a little belittling, and more than a lot of attitude and self-belief. His time as a hostage with Thorkell had not improved him at all.

Olaf had groaned at the news, but once Northman had whispered of their intentions, he too cheered, and greeted the band of ten men amicably enough. And to their credit, they waited until they were out of sight of Athelstan and his men before they began chiding and berating the boys for abandoning their Lord and foster-father. As the reality of what was happening sank in, Northman felt his anger and grief at his casual handing over as a virtual hostage for his father's good behaviour surge through his body. He held the rage deep and close to his chest. He was going to need it if he was to survive another winter with the scheming Eadric.

Wantage was one of the king's finest halls and a mark of utmost respect and concern that he now let Eadric take control over it. Eadric only marked Northman's arrival by a small rise of his head from where he ate at the top of the king's hall. The bruises and rapidly swelling eye that marred his face were clear indications that his brother had carried out his wishes as he'd hoped.

Spitting blood and anger, Northman found himself a small space to call his own and cursed his inability to fight off ten men at once. Olaf was unscarred; clearly, he didn't share Eadric's anger, for which he apologised so often that Northman grew short-tempered with him and demanded he be left alone.

Hungry, but warm for the first time in days, and with the stable structure of the wooden hall around his head, Northman slept deeply and soundly until he was rudely woken by a kick to the face in the morning. Waking in pain and hunger, Northman leapt from his bed, grabbing the chest of the man who woke him so.

Not caring when he recognised Eadric's brother, Brihtric, he growled,

"Leave me alone you piece of shit, or I'll have no choice but to pay you back for my face. A little more respect in future."

At his feet, Olaf had gasped with fear and shock, rudely awoken by the altercation. But Brihtric only laughed in his face when Northman gradually reduced his hold on his tunic.

"You and who?" he asked mockingly. "You're a little child, no more than that, and we'll treat you as such. Now get dressed. You're on the first recon."

Northman let his anger cool, and turned away from Brihtric without apologising. It was about time they started to treat him as more than a child, and for all the arrogant words that had burst from Brihtric's mouth, Northman had felt him shake a little in fear at his violent response, and he knew that Brihtric knew it as well. Smirking, and ignoring his pounding head, Northman dressed and strode outside into the early morning. Tomorrow the countrywide penance would begin, but he doubted he'd be allowed to join in. Just another petty way that Eadric, who'd not even spoken to him yet, would punish him.

A small team of twenty men milled around outside, and Northman noticed that Eadric was intent on leading this foray himself. His heart sank at the idea. Clearly, he did have greater things on his mind than just watching Thorkell, for why else would he lead something as insignificant as a reconnaissance trip?

"Northman," he called arrogantly, "you'll ride with me. You know this land well, and I'd welcome your advice."

Cursing his bad luck, Northman mounted his waiting horse and walked him over to Eadric. He sat smugly atop his horse, his disgrace with the king a thing of the past, just as Eadric had forgiven Brihtric.

"You've grown boy," he said without preamble, and Northman felt his resolve falter again. How in just three words had the man offended so much?

"It's been many months since I last saw you," Northman responded, clinging to the truth to stay civil. "I've been training with the household troops on a more than daily basis, and my physique has improved significantly."

"Hum," Eadric responded vaguely. He was evidently disappointed that Northman had reacted so calmly. "And now you'll make use of your knowledge to assist me in keeping a careful watch on Thorkell."

"Gladly, my Lord. We were making daily forays around Oxford. We will be doing the same?"

"It's doubtful. I don't have the resources at my disposal that the king does. But once a week should be enough once the weather turns."

Biting back his horror that Thorkell was to be allowed so much leeway, he wondered why Eadric had agreed to babysit Thorkell if he had so few men. Concentrating on ensuring his horse's tack was correctly fitted, he didn't give Eadric the satisfaction of knowing how dismayed he was. If Thorkell watched Eadric carefully enough, he'd know how often they were checked on, and when the best time was to make good his escape. In effect, he'd be able to gain nearly a week's worth of grace without any trouble. He and his men could get almost anywhere in England with a week between their escape and it being noticed.

"And of course, once the weather turns, you'll be able to make the forays on your own, with some of my men, of course. So pay attention and look well, boy."

So dismissed, Northman ambled back towards where Olaf was grumbling into his saddle. He did little more than roll his eyes in annoyance but Olaf understood all too well. The constraints of being back with Eadric were onerous.

The return journey to Oxford was accomplished more quickly than the day before. They arrived to discover the embers of the fires of the encampment barely cold. Northman took some consolation in the knowledge that Swein wouldn't yet have had time to do anything but note the withdrawal of the troops. He'd now need to bide his time and discover what the English king had in store for him. He glanced into the distance where he knew Athelstan's men would have made their winter hideaway, but he saw nothing to suggest anyone was remotely close; no smoke from a fire marred the skyline.

The flames from Oxford itself smouldered spasmodically in the damp day, as they neared it, Eadric deciding on the route, despite his words to Northman to the contrary. Sitting on a small rise, he glanced out at Oxford, with a strained expression on his face. Northman wondered what he thought about but received his answer in an unexpected way.

With a grin of delight, Eadric kicked his horse into action and tore across the land towards the gates of Oxford. Beside him, ten of his men followed him and Northman realised that this had been pre-planned. But what did he hope to achieve?

More sedately, and with concern, the rest of the small force followed their Lord towards the gates of Oxford, Northman not once taking his eye from the firmly closed gates. He had a terrible feeling that he knew what was going to happen next.

Before they caught up with Eadric, the gates of Oxford came fully open, and an answering force of no more than twenty men erupted forth. They were mounted on beautiful horses, and

Northman recognised Thorkell, Cnut and Hemming amongst their number.

Incautious now, he raced to catch Eadric. He wanted to hear every single word of this exchange so that he could work out if it had been planned or if Eadric was just trying to make his mark.

He arrived to angry exchanges between Thorkell and Eadric aided by Hemming. He didn't know what they argued about, but Cnut was smirking, his contempt for Eadric written into his very stance.

"...gone, and we will be here, watching you instead. My men will make more mobile camps, a little smaller, but no less threatening."

Thorkell waited for the words to be translated, even though he seemed to understand many of them anyway, his eyes rising to where he knew the camp had lain before that day.

"And is this just a courtesy call?" Hemming inquired when he'd finished speaking to Thorkell.

"An opportunity to get to meet you that is all." Eadric simpered, "I've heard much about you from Cnut."

Cnut spluttered with amusement at the lie Eadric spoke, but made no other move to deny it.

Thorkell took the time to look at Cnut, who shrugged the comment aside but something made a little more sense to Thorkell then, and he moved towards Eadric with a more menacing stance.

Eadric backed his horse off a little when Thorkell came too close to him, and spoke to Hemming, while his eyes remained on the mighty warrior. From his position, Northman couldn't see Eadric's face, but he imagined it sheened in sweat.

And then something happened, only Northman again didn't see what, and a grin spread across Thorkell's face, and he quickly turned his horse and headed back inside Oxford. Confused, Northman tried to replay the events in his head, but could discern nothing that Eadric had done to cause that reaction.

A smile on his face, Eadric turned away from the closed gates and proceeded to circuit Oxford. The whole time, Northman wondered what had happened and what import it might have. But he didn't receive any answers.

They returned to Wantage, and daily life resumed as it had done before the disaster with the ship-army. As Eadric had advised him, a weekly foray out to Oxford, even when the snows came, was all that was required of him. That, and enduring the daily verbal beatings from Eadric and his men.

Despite his fears, he was able to partake in the king's penance, when as if for three days, the kingdom came to a standstill. The words of prayer were the only ones that passed most lips, and only the barest of foods. Northman prayed earnestly for those few days hopeful that this tactic would work, fearful that it wouldn't. As with many of the men, he realised that he'd not know if it had been successful or not until the beginning of the summer season.

As winter advanced he kept a close eye on Eadric, and sent word when he could to Athelstan's men, but other than that first meeting with Thorkell, Eadric never again left the hall, or at least, not as far as Northman knew. He did have a niggling fear that on the days he went to Oxford Eadric was himself going elsewhere, but he never gained any proof, not until the weather turned for the better and he realised what a fool he'd been not to understand his intent and send word via Athelstan's men near Oxford. And then, it was all too little, too late.

# 23
## EARLY SUMMER, AD1010, NORTHMAN

A FLURRY OF ACTIVITY WOKE HIM EARLY AS THE FIRST FAINT STIRRINGS OF better weather enveloped the land, and made him cast aside his heaviest fur covering. Coupled with the warmth, a commotion inside the king's hall alerted him that there were visitors.

Crawling to a spot where he could see who'd disturbed his rest, he was dismayed to recognise the man speaking with Eadric. Hemming. What was he doing here?

The men were not exactly comfortable with each other, but there was an intimacy that Northman wouldn't have expected after their last encounter. Words were exchanged, and then Hemming hastily left the room, the sound of his horse being ridden away reached Northman's ears. He'd not been alone either.

Eadric was quickly joined by his brother Brihtric and then spoke quietly and swiftly before Brihtric himself went outside and rode off as well.

Northman's unease grew.

What was happening?

What was with all the secrecy and why was Hemming within the king's hall, speaking to Eadric on what appeared to be friendly terms?

When nothing else happened, Northman returned just as quietly to his bed, but he didn't sleep again, his mind whirling with implications.

The next day was his usual day to ride out to Oxford, only on this occasion, Eadric announced that he'd come too. Annoyed, Northman rode in an ill humour that worsened the closer he came to Oxford. He had a feeling that Thorkell and his men would no longer be there, and he was proved right.

Cursing aloud, he first noticed that the gates were flung wide open, and then he noticed the lack of ships that had until last week, been drawn up tight to the Western gates. And thirdly, he saw the tide of figures limping through the open gates, the smell of smoke drifting in the warming day.

Spurring his horse on, with no heed for Eadric lagging behind him, he was amongst the refugees in no time at all. He dropped from his horse and walked amongst them.

"What's happened?" he asked, "Where are the Raiders?"

An older man, his eyes dulled with hunger, came staggering towards him,

"They've gone. This morning. Hemming, he came with supplies and riches, and then they all left. They told us we could have our lives, but they've taken all our food and animals. We have nothing left."

Nodding in understanding, Northman looked about for Eadric, and glimpsed in the distance, a lone horseman who he hoped was one of Athelstan's men. No doubt, they would get word to the king.

"Were they good to you?"

"Some of the time," came the reply, "until the food and the wood for burning ran small, and then they were not so good to us."

"Thank you for your answers. Here," and Northman fiddled with the saddle bag on his horse, "take what food I have, but please, share it as best you can."

The man grabbed the food readily enough, but stilled himself,

"My thanks, young Lord. Your generosity is welcome."

Belittled by the man's gratitude, Northman continued his ride into Oxford. His curiosity was thoroughly aroused. What would he find within?

Inside, the privations of a long winter could be clearly seen. Some of the buildings nearest to the wall had been torn down, no doubt for fuel. The roadway was worn thin, but still glowed with the traces of the metals that ran through it, and the defences had not been repaired at all. The debris of too many people had been tidily swept to one side, nearest the wall, and would soon be crawling with flies, when the weather turned much warmer.

But it was the people he cared most about, they streamed out of Oxford, with anything they could carry. They were thin and bedraggled, but alive. He wondered how many hadn't been so lucky. He didn't find the cause of the smoke and hoped that if fires had been deliberately started, they'd been quickly brought under control.

He came across the Church closest to the Western gate and noticed disturbances in the ground. Those were the poor wretches who'd died with the winter. And then he found someone of note, the head of the Church. He was a gaunt man, made thinner by the winter shortages, but his face was creased with a smile, and joy shone from within him. He hummed as he worked, tidying the small graveyard, and Northman called softly to him.

"Priest, you are well?"

With glowing eyes, the man turned to look at him,

"Yes thank you, young Lord. Fairly well."

"The Raiders are gone?"

"Completely, and they've vowed not to come back again. They've had all they can from the men and women of Oxford."

"Where have they gone?" Northman pressed. By now the others of Eadric's reconnaissance trip had arrived, and Olaf was close beside him.

"To the east," the priest sang, still in his singsong voice. Olaf raised his eyebrows at Northman and mouthed, "Is he not quite right in the head?" but Northman didn't yet know.

"Why did they leave and travel to the East?"

"They received something this morning, and they were content and joked about it. And now they've gone to the East, as they'd been told to."

Frustration creased Northman's forehead,

"Who told them to?"

"Whoever sent them the box of coins," the priest responded blithely, and Northman felt his anger building. Surely Eadric had not paid the Raiders to attack their people in the East? Surely not? These must just be the strange ramblings of a man apparently pushed too far by the months he'd been a captive of Thorkell and his men.

"Have you had any visitors at all during the winter?" Northman continued to ask, desperate for some denial to his dark thoughts.

"No, but often the Raiders have ridden out, to the north, or so they say, but never very far for they could make the journey in a day. They often came back laughing and joking."

Olaf was quick to catch on to Northman's thoughts, and his face clouded. This time, he whispered, "Eadric?" and Northman found himself nodding while looking for the man they discussed. He suddenly felt fearful for the Priest. If Eadric overheard him talking so freely, he'd be sure to silence him.

Just then more monks rushed from the Church, calling the name of the Priest. They stopped abruptly when they saw Northman, but he beckoned them on.

"Take him from here. Keep him away from the Lord Eadric. And try to stop his ramblings."

The two monks nodded in understanding and began to lead the man away. A third stayed where he was, looking from Northman to the open gateway.

"Does he speak the truth?" Northman asked impatiently, "about the Raiders leaving here once a week?"

"Yes he does, but we've been told not to mention it or face death.

But yes, someone has bribed Thorkell and Hemming, and they've taken the bribe right enough. They're heading to the East to steal land and coin and kill the men who pledge allegiance to the king's son by marriage. It's a shameful thing."

"My thanks," Northman said, mindful that he not put the monks in any further danger or harm. Hastily, he pulled forth his small amount of coin from inside his money sack and pressed it into the hand of the monk.

"Take it. Use it to repair the church or buy food. I'll try and get word to my father of your need."

Just then a commotion at the gate alerted Northman to the arrival of Eadric, and he all but leapt back into his saddle, as the monk scurried away. Olaf had moved his horse so that it blocked any view from the gate, but still, Northman was unsure if he'd been spotted speaking to the monk.

"Northman," Eadric bellowed, "get out of there. No doubt there's disease and contagion inside the place."

"But my Lord, we must check for any remaining Raiders. They might have left their sick and dying to fend for themselves."

"They might, yes, but it's not our place to discover them."

"But they might know where they've gone."

"They've gone, that's all that matters. Now come. We must travel home, and then get word to the king."

"Would it not be best to seek the king directly?"

"No, it wouldn't. Now come, and be quick about it."

Without further conversation, Eadric turned his horse around, shooting out the gate in a swirl of mud and muck, unaware of those who staggered around him at his passing. Northman winced for the man who fell under the horse's hooves, rushing to help him to his feet. The man was aggravated but welcomed the support and the coin that Olaf pressed into his hand.

"Where will you go?" Northman asked.

"To the outlying farms. They'll help us and feed us and then we can come back to Oxford and rebuild our lives. The Reeve says he'll stay, and his men will guard our homes and businesses."

"There are some of the king's men near to the South," Northman muttered under his breath, "If you see them will you please let them know that the Raiders have gone to the East, to the lands of Ulfcytel."

Surprised eyebrows greeted his words, but the man nodded in understanding.

Northman clambered back onto his horse and rode more sedately out of the gate. Eadric was already almost out of sight, and once clear of the refugees, he spurred his horse to catch his foster-father, never having wanted to do anything less in his life. The man was a traitor. He worked actively against the king and had been doing so all winter, even leading him astray. Anger and anguish warred within him, but it was a calm vengeance that filled him. He would make Eadric pay for this. Somehow.

# 24
# THE KING'S WITAN, AD1010, LEOFWINE

THE WINTER HAD BEEN AS PRODUCTIVE AS MOST. THE WEATHER HAD BEEN grim, the snows deep preventing any messengers from reaching him from either the king or his son. But now, the coming summer brought an impetus to everyone. Leofwine, deciding that the lack of news was a worry had sought the king at the earliest opportunity and found him at Enham. He arrived at the same time as a small and ragged collection of mounted men did, and Leofwine knew that something monumental had happened.

The leader of the men greeted Leofwine abruptly, his rush to see the king evident, and so instead of stopping the men; he rode quickly to keep up, dismounting at the same time as them.

Forgetting he was grimy from the road, he followed the leader inside and gained admittance to the king at the same time.

Æthelred was eating his dinner to muted conversation, but the king's son Athelstan stood on seeing the man and the colour drained from his face.

"Burghed, what news is there?"

"My king, my Lord and my Lady," he began noticing, as Leofwine hadn't, that the queen accompanied the king,

"Thorkell and his men have left Oxford. They've gone East, to the lands of Ulfcytel."

Dismayed gasps greeted the words, and Æthelred stood at the unexpected news, before sitting again, a little surprised by his actions.

"How do you know this?" Athelstan asked, signalling that his man should be served with food and mead, both of which were gratefully accepted.

"We've seen it with our own eyes, and we also saw the refugees leaving Oxford. They're all but starved and will need to seek bounty from their neighbours and yourself."

Nodding in agreement, the king gestured that he should go on.

"And as to where they're going, one of the refugees told me. But, there was another development which I think should be shared in more private surroundings."

Æthelred shot once more to his feet, indicating that Athelstan should also come with him, as should Leofwine, who he'd now noticed, and a select few from his permanent household. Once inside one of the smaller rooms, Æthelred turned to Burghed.

"My Lord, it pains me to inform you so, but I saw Lord Eadric and his men in Oxford. They arrived within moments of Thorkell leaving, did nothing to help the fleeing men and women and promptly rode back to Wantage. Your son, my Lord Leofwine, arranged for the messenger to seek me out with the news that they were going to the East. I know nothing more, but I suspect much."

"What do you suspect?" the king queried, although his flat voice made all aware that he knew what the man would say next.

Swallowing around the news and with a nod of encouragement from Athelstan, Burghed spoke,

"I think Eadric has paid Thorkell to raid the Eastern lands. A small party of men was absent during the night, but returned at cock crow, weighed down with something that was small enough to be concealed on their body."

Æthelred's paced as he heard the words,

"You're sure of this?" he asked, his teeth clenched, his words forced past those teeth.

"As sure as I can be. There have been comings and going all winter long. Whenever Northman and the men rode to Oxford to check on the Raiders, a small party would already have left Oxford. They'd return once Northman was gone."

"And where did they go?"

"We didn't have the men to follow them, but we suspected it had to be somewhere close."

Athelstan was incensed,

"We must do something father. Call out the fyrd to assist Ulfcytel and banish Eadric once and for all."

"We must call out the fyrd, yes, but we have no proof that he paid Thorkell to attack Ulfcytel. Bring me the proof and I will act. For now could you please take your household troops to the East and try and track down Thorkell. Send word so that we know where to attack."

Athelstan wanted to argue. That much was clear, but for once, the king was giving him the opportunity to act independently and on behalf of his people. His joy at that warred with his frustration, and it was his desire to serve his nation that won. With a hasty word of goodbye, he sped from the room. Outside Edmund had loitered, waiting for his brother, and he quickly joined up with him and strode from the hall.

Into the thunderous silence, no one spoke or coughed, or breathed. Leofwine watched his king with interest. How would he react to this new treason when he'd not yet fully forgiven the last one?

Anguished eyes turned his way, and Leofwine felt for the man who was the only master he'd ever known. Who could he call his friend when everyone worked for his or her own ends? Not for the first time, Leofwine acknowledged the loneliness of power.

"My Lord," he began quietly, and Æthelred nodded to show he should continue, although his eyes stayed firmly on his feet. "We should act on the news of Thorkell's movements. Athelstan will travel fast and well and inform us as soon as he can. But we must get word to Ulfcytel. He needs to be aware of what is coming his way."

"Of course Leofwine, we must inform my son by marriage. Can you arrange that for me? I don't think they'll be able to travel directly to the East. Not as a few lone men. God only knows what they might encounter."

The king's dismay rang loudly when he blasphemed, but Leofwine didn't react, and neither did his household priest. Treacherous times, when, for want of a better explanation, God did seem to have abandoned his people, called for harsh words.

"I would suggest sending the men via the sea, but I don't think that would aid us at all. If Thorkell is at loose near the Eastern coast, our messengers will surely be spotted. No, I'll send a few small parties with the news. And my lord king?"

"Yes, Leofwine?"

"Would you like my men to bring your daughter home?"

Visibly gulping at the reminder of his daughter's precarious position, Æthelred met Leofwine's eye.

"If it's possible, yes. If not, have your men stay and offer more protection. I know Ulfcytel will not let any danger befall her, but still, I'd feel reassured."

Bowing and excusing himself from the king's presence, Leofwine rushed from the room, or as much as he could with his leg stiff from riding, and his hound weaving between his legs.

In the hall, the queen was eating sedately, her efforts at calm working wonders on the women of the king's hall. While men shot hither and wither, collecting supplies and clothing and food, the women of the court went about calmly, handing our packages of food to Athelstan and his warriors, while healing herbs were carefully placed within the horse packs of the healer who would accompany Athelstan.

Just for the briefest moment, Leofwine stopped and watched all the people at work. Who would still be here within a week, a month, and a year? The vagaries of time would alter the makeup of this hall, and it saddened him to know that he could no sooner say goodbye to those who would die than he could predict who they'd be.

Beside him, Horic came into view, and Leofwine waved him outside. He wanted this conversation in private.

Horic had heard much of the news, and the men who'd only just ridden in were making ready to leave again. Leofwine looked at his men. Who should he send on this perilous journey? Not Horic, and not Oscetel and not Horic's sons. But who then? He could ask for volunteers, but it would be Horic and Oscetel who shouted the loudest for the honour. He didn't want to lose his men for all that they'd walk through the fires of Hell for him.

"I need three groups of men, four in each cluster. You're to travel East, and avoid Thorkell and his Raiders, and find Ulfcytel. He needs to know that Thorkell is coming to him next."

A grin split Horic's face. He'd grasped the subterfuge needed instantly, but he didn't speak. Instead, he turned to Oscetel and spoke,

"Shall we go together or apart?" he queried, a playful tone in his voice. The chance of a battle, any battle, drove other thoughts from his mind.

Oscetel raised his eyebrow and looked a challenge,

"I say you shouldn't go at all. Send your boys old man."

Horic smirked at the transparent attempt to rile him.

"My Lord Leofwine," he said, turning towards Leofwine with a cocky stance, "I volunteer. I'll take my oldest son, and also two other men who'd like to come with me. We'll ride like the wind and get to Ulfcytel first."

Heavy hearted, Leofwine accepted his friend's wishes, watching the men of the war-band vie for the honour of being with Horic. Immediately afterwards Oscetel spoke the same words, and again, men competed to go with him.

That just left the third group. If Northman had been here, he'd perhaps have let him lead the third party, but he was not, and although Leofric was frantically trying to catch his eye, Leofwine knew he was too young to understand the word discreet.

Instead, he looked at Brithelm's son. In the ten years since his father's death, the lad had never once spoken of his death in the Battle of Chester, but he carried the wound with him, and Leofwine couldn't deny him the opportunity to seek some redress from any who dared to attack this land.

Brithnoth's eyes lit with fire, and three of his closest comrades agreed to go with them. The strangling remainders of the war band returned to the horses and prepared them for their brothers in arms.

"You'll need to take different paths, and, and this goes no further," Leofwine said, fixing them all with his eye for a brief moment, "you'll need to avoid any who look to the Mercian ealdorman, he's possibly implicated in this."

Horic's head bobbed with the news, and anger flashed across the other men's faces, but none spoke. They all had a shared abhorrence for the man, and it was long past time to worry about giving voice to it. Eadric was a force none of them understood or respected. That was enough.

"And when you reach Ulfcytel, the king has asked that you do all you can to protect his daughter."

As the men turned away to see to their duties, Leofric approached his father, his eyes a little angry. Leofwine more than admired his son, but at twelve, he was not yet man enough to be in a small, stealthy operation such as this. The other men would trust him implicitly, but whether he had the presence of mind was something that Leofwine had yet to be convinced off.

"And you Leofric, we'll raise the fyrd from the Hwicce and make our way to the East as well."

Mollified, Leofric turned away without speaking, but he called to those he knew, excitement high in his voice.

Behind him, Leofwine felt a soft swirl of air and turned to see the queen, her young daughter tottering on her feet behind her.

"Is it right about Eadric?" she asked quietly.

"I imagine it is, but as the king says, we must give him the benefit of the doubt."

"You're going to approach him?" she pressed.

"I might just come across him, yes my Lady. I think it's high time that I extradited my son from his greedy hands."

"I agree, now go with speed," she said, "and get rid of these bastards once and for all."

With no further words, she turned, scooped her daughter into her arms and returned inside the hall. For a moment Leofwine wondered what it would feel like to command people to face their death on your behalf. An unpleasant thought, but there all the same.

The archbishop, Wulfstan came to him then, his face concerned,

"I fear that God has abandoned us all," he began without preamble.

"No Wulfstan, he just acts in perverse ways sometimes. Surely, there must be a lesson for us all to learn here."

"Humility?" Wulfstan queried, glancing around him at the splendour of the king's hall.

"Perhaps, but I think it's more to do with righteousness."

Wulfstan smirked a grin at him,

"I like talking to you Leofwine," he said, before walking away and then turning back, "you always put a different spin on things."

# 25
# EAST ANGLIA, AD1010, NORTHMAN

He'd given up trying to untangle the web of lies and deceit that Eadric had concocted during the winter months. What had plagued him most was the knowledge that Eadric appeared content to let Thorkell raid where he wanted and not to mount any resistance.

But the king's messenger had finally tracked him down, long gone from Wantage, and it seemed as though he just couldn't get away from the king and he'd been left with no choice but to raise the fyrd and march towards East Anglia.

The news was dire. Thorkell, his fleet now swelled by so many men the messengers had trouble counting them all but imagined a fleet of over a hundred and fifty ships, manned by the warriors of Swein of Denmark, had mostly sailed to East Anglia and attacked Ipswich in a devastating raid. The fyrd of Ulfcytel had been in the process of meeting but they'd not been able to put together an effective resistance. Only after Thorkell had taken Ipswich, had the fyrd partly-assembled around it, trying to block any further incursions.

Eadric had muttered and moaned and groaned about raising the Mercian fyrd, but finally, they'd marched towards the eastern tip of East Anglia. Along the way Northman had seen other assemblies marching the same way, but Eadric made no effort to meet up with them. He was resisting but complying with the king's orders all at the same time. He was foul tempered and Northman was avoiding him at all costs.

Northman hadn't been so far east since he'd been a small boy, and the flatness of the land surprised and amazed him as they rode at a desultory pace to reach Ulfcytel. On the borders of the Mercian lands, Eadric left the majority of the fyrd to protect his own back, although he'd said it was to protect the Mercian lands, and now only a small force of a hundred rode to strengthen Ulfcytel.

The people of his land were staunch in their support of their ealdorman. Northman was relieved to see so much loyalty to their Lord and their king. They gifted what food they could to the men traversing the land, offering shelter in dry barns from the early summer rains and passing on any information they might have learnt from traders.

That none were fleeing into the Mercian heartlands showed just how confident they were in their Lord. Northman wondered if Eadric noticed the complete contrast to his Lordship.

Three days riding brought them to Thetford, a thriving community of houses and businesses, with protective walls and gates closed to all.

A small force rode out to greet Eadric and Northman ambled his horse close enough so that he could listen to the conversation.

"Eadric, your presence is welcomed," Ulfcytel spoke respectfully. He was stained and dirty, almost as if he'd been in his armour for days or weeks and had been left with no time to wash or change.

"Have you bested the Raiders yet?" Eadric asked, his tone difficult to interpret.

"We've made overtures of friendship towards them and wait to see if they will accept our truce. In the meantime, Ipswich is a burnt ruin, and they've taken to their ships again and make their way slowly along the coastline."

"They're coming here?" Eadric gulped a little at the unwelcome news.

"Oh yes, Eadric. Thorkell, Hemming and their new partner, Olaf the Stout, as he's known, have made their pretensions clear. They believe there are significant gold and treasure to be found at Thetford. My spies have heard the men of the camp discussing it at great length."

His eyes glinted with suppressed rage, and Eadric looked away from him to muse,

"I wonder where they gained that idea, my Lord."

"As do I. But now, quick, come inside. We will apprise you of our battle plans, should the truce fail, and your men will assist mine."

"How many men does Thorkell have?" Eadric asked as they rode towards the locked down village.

"Seven thousand," Ulfcytel commented drily.

"That's just an exaggeration, surely?"

"No, my spies have counted the ships and the men. There are seven thousand of them, or thereabouts. Or at least there were. Some few have perished at Ipswich, but not many. We were not able to mount an attack soon enough after the king's warning."

"The king sent a warning?" Eadric asked in shock. "He knew they were coming to the Eastern lands?"

"Oh yes, and Leofwine of the Hwicce sent word as well. We were as prepared as we could be given the short space of time."

Northman watched Eadric carefully. He looked alarmed and dismayed in equal measure. Eadric turned to meet his gaze, but Northman had already looked away. He didn't want Eadric to suspect him of working against him and he chose not to feel the sting of his stare. He could suspect all he wanted, but if he had no proof, then he couldn't act.

"And you've attempted to treat with them? Is the king aware?"

"The king sent word that we could do whatever needed to be done to keep the people safe, if that meant a truce and a geld, then that was what must be. We're much smaller than the whole kingdom, though, and we've only been able to offer the modest sum of £10000. With the number of men they have with them, I'm not at all convinced that they'll accept the geld."

"You're preparing for battle then?"

"Yes, with all haste. We want to choose the site of our next battle, gain the upper hand. Drive them from our coasts. The fyrd is amassing near Thetford. Thorkell still holds Ipswich as his new base. If he comes overland, or by sea, we should meet him. There was a great slaughter of our men at Ipswich. Many people lost their lives to allow the inhabitants to flee as best they could. Not everyone escaped. There simply wasn't time."

"It's unfortunate that they left their winter quarters so quickly and without warning," Eadric said. Northman noted that Ulfcytel's stance held no rancour. News of Eadric's treachery hadn't yet reached him so he was unaware of the terrible irony of his foster father's words.

Northman still wondered what he'd hoped to achieve by paying Thorkell to raid the eastern lands. He also harboured a secret fear that the king may have been complicit as well. There was little love between the king and his sons by marriage. It was no secret that he thought them as disappointing as his sons. The fact that he never gave any of the men the opportunity to prove their worth was not lost to most people, only to the king.

Their limited conversation over, for the time being, they rode together towards Thetford. Wooden spikes were reinforcing the defences surrounding the walls and men, and women were busy labouring under the gentle summer's sun. There was an element of fear in the movements of the workers, and yet they called to each other and laughed and joked as they worked. Northman was proud of the stoicism of the English people.

A week passed slowly for Northman. Eadric was foul tempered and fractious, unhappy that Northman was so content among the mass of warriors and the messengers that rode in and out of Thetford brought nothing but bad news. The Raiders had abandoned

Ipswich, only then they hadn't. The Raiders were travelling overland towards Thetford, and then they weren't, they were coming by ship.

Ulfcytel spent as much time as he could riding around his lands, reassuring people, asking them to seek shelter within Thetford, and most importantly, seeking out his preferred place of battle.

And then in a rush news came that Thorkell would not accept the geld and that they were both marching and travelling by ship to the coast near Thetford. At the same time, Ulfcytel sent out the word that the fyrd was to mass at Ringmere. He was content that it would be an excellent site to join the full battle and his closest friend and comrade in arms, Thurcetel agreed with him. He commanded almost an entire half of the fyrd and had a personal troop of nearly two hundred men. Northman wondered how the man could afford to keep them all.

Northman felt the faint stirrings of fear that had accompanied his first journey to Oxford as he readied himself inside Thetford. Eadric had made himself scarce by offering to fetch the Mercian fyrd, but Northman knew he wouldn't be returning, and had spoken to Horic on the matter. Horic had informed Ulfcytel as much, and although he'd been dismayed to hear that his brother in law was not to be trusted, he was too concerned with preparing for the coming battle to concern himself with the matter. He thanked Horic for his words of advice and promptly ignored any possibility of the Mercian fyrd advancing into Thetford.

Northman and Olaf had purposefully hidden from Eadric, with Horic and Oscetel, and too worried that he'd be caught up in the coming battle, Eadric had ridden out without them. The two young men were prepared to face his wrath if they must if they lived through the fight, and if Eadric was still the Ealdorman of Mercia.

More reassuringly, news reached them that his father had amassed the fyrd of the Hwicce, and was almost within the lands of East Angles. They might well arrive in time to prove useful.

Horic, as instructed by the king, was to stay within Thetford and guard his daughter. She'd refused to leave her husband, even at her king's command, and she'd won much respect for her actions. Ulfcytel had publicly thanked her, and she'd blushed prettily at the praise and then busied herself arranging provision and healing herbs for the wounded.

They left Thetford early one Thursday morning, the air chill but the sun promising warmth. Outriders had sighted Thorkell's army, but none knew how far they'd travel that day. Northman was of an uncertain mind, he wanted to engage in his first battle, but at the same time waiting another day longer would have given him the chance to get some sleep after his long night of staring at the ceiling and seeing dead men and warriors all around him.

He'd thought to leave a message with Horic for his father before he left; assuring him of his love and respect and thanking him for all that he'd done for him so far. He had few possessions, but he hoped that his father would see to sharing them amongst his brothers and sister. Horic for once had not attempted to brush the topic of death to one side, but had kissed both his son and Lord's son and wished them well. In an aside he'd reminded them both that sometimes the ancient pagan gods could be better patrons in battle, but when Olaf had looked dismayed he'd brushed his comments aside. But, Northman had learnt something vital about Horic then.

Beneath them, their horses rode well across the flat land. There was no high speed to their advance because the fyrd had amassed there the day before. Northman and the men were going as both reinforcement and the skilled warriors of Ealdorman Leofwine. They would slip into the battle where they were commanded, and throughout the journey, Oscetel gave a steady string of instructions to his young charges, so much so that Northman almost felt it would have been better if Horic had accompanied them. He'd have taken the responsibility a little less seriously, and would have known that no matter what, their Lord wouldn't blame them if the worst should happen.

Hringmara Heath, as the local inhabitants knew it, was one of a handful of places in the vicinity that boosted a small rise that

Ulfcytel had commandeered. From its peak, it was possible to see a great distance across the flat land. Even more fortuitously, behind it, there was a far larger peak, almost a mountain, by comparison, an old burial cairn from the ancient people, that Ulfcytel had decided to use to strengthen his stance and to offer a final, final last stand if they should be overwhelmed by the Raiders. From its height, it would be possible to strike them down with bows and arrows and spikes.

The sheer numbers that greeted Northman almost turned his innards to water. To hear the figures discussed near enough seven thousand men of the fyrd was nothing compared to actually seeing them all. Men and tents stretched as far as the eye could see. Olaf whistled low under his breath, and Oscetel too showed his surprise.

"I've never seen so many men," Olaf said, his voice tight with nerves.

"Nor I, not all in the same place. If Thorkell leads his men this way, this will truly be a battle to talk about. Now come, we'll find where we'll be fighting."

Dismounting from their horses, they lead them to the pens set up for their animals and then found Ulfcytel holding court from a half tent, mostly open to the elements, and from which he could keep an eye on his men and any possible advance from the enemy.

"We've official word this morning that the truce won't last. The geld has been formally rejected by the enemy. It surely can't be long now until Thorkell's attack. If not today, then tomorrow. I think he's an impetuous man who, once decided on a course of action, must follow it through as soon as possible."

The commanders of the various elements of the fyrd listened attentively to Ulfcytel as he made known his battle plans.

"We'll keep watch throughout today, this evening and tomorrow. I envisage an attack with the dawn, but I may, of course, be wrong. Warn those on the watch to be vigilant and report everything that makes their skin crawl a little. We don't want any of them circling behind us when it's dark. The rest of the men will get what rest they can in the tents provided, and will eat and drink as and when they need. At sunrise, if we've heard nothing, we will all form up in our respective positions, and we will wait, all day if necessary, although I doubt it'll take that long. And then we'll attack and drive them back to their ships, and out from our lands. We will take a few prisoners no more."

"And if they don't come tomorrow, as today, we will send so many of the men back to rest, eat and sleep and we will stand a night watch. Those men will then be excused from forming up on Saturday morning. Instead, they will rest. Is that clear?"

"My Lord Ulfcytel," one man asked, his face young and flushed at asking his Lord, a question in front of so many people. "Do you think the rumours are true that there are seven thousand men?"

Ulfcytel thought for a moment and then called another to him. He spoke to him quickly, and then answered,

"My outriders have done their best to count the ships and the men who pour forth from them. Seven thousand is a huge number but one that they all agree on."

The young lad swallowed at the huge numbers,

"Never fear Ordulf, we're just as many, and while we may not be ship-men, our men of the fyrd are strong and have one thing going for them that all these other men do not. They want to protect their land, for it's theirs. And that's more of an incentive than possible riches, and possible payment can ever be. Thorkell has promised much, but if we thwart them here, their trust in him will start to dissipate."

Northman watched with fascination the effect of Ulfcytel's words on the young lord. He stood a little straighter, held his sword more tightly, and his face lost its unhealthy flush. One day Northman hoped to instil the same amount of pride into the men who served him.

The hastily convened meeting broke up then, and Northman found himself following Oscetel to a small open area where they erected the tents they'd brought with them, and shared space at a campfire. They were, as was expected, to fight near to the edges of the battlefield, to bolster the resolve of those who might have to curve round in the shield wall if they wished to cut off the Raiders advance. They would hold the shield wall straight and steady, but if needed they could proceed at a faster pace and attempt to encircle the enemy.

No news came that day, just as Ulfcytel had predicted. When night came, Northman slid into a dark and dreamless sleep without worries. His exhaustion had been evident since he'd slid from his horse, and he'd craved sleep but denied himself it because he had to show that he was as much a man as the rest of his father's war band.

Altogether there were ten of them, the men Oscetel had led, the men Brithelm's son had brought with him, and he and Olaf. It wasn't a huge presence to represent his father, but everyone there was keen to face their enemy and if battle should be met, to show that their years of training had not been in vain.

A gentle shake on the shoulder woke Northman in the morning.

"Come, it's time," Oscetel murmured. For a brief moment, Northman struggled to remember where he was and why Oscetel was there, but then he remembered, and his limbs turned fleetingly leaden. This was it. Today he'd fight his first battle, and hopefully, live to the end of the day.

He readied himself in silence, as did Olaf, even his bluff nature dimmed by the struggles they'd face that day. A hasty breakfast of bread and cheese and they strode to where the shield wall was forming up, maybe four fields in front of them. On a whim, Northman raced up the hill the ancients of the land had built and looked all about him. What he saw had him speeding back down in no time at all.

Across the landscape, as if it came with the tendrils of morning sunshine just starting to illuminate the land, came a sea of shining irons and silvers. The enemy was coming.

Oscetel interpreted the look on his face immediately, and in no time at all, news had sped across the line of men, reinforced to the back by a further ten men each. It was impossible to see the full extent of the shield wall as Northman could only see the men to either side of him, but the rustle and clanging of iron were clear to hear.

Silence descended, broken when the enemy began to form up before them. Northman, not in the front row of the shield wall could see little, although he strained to see over the heads of the men in front.

"Northman, keep your head down," Oscetel commanded, "they'll have some bows and arrows, and they may release them if they see the odd head."

So reminded Northman crouched down low, behind the man at the front of the shield wall, and the two who held their shield ready to go above his head and their own.

Sweat beaded Northman's face, and he angrily wiped at it. He'd done nothing yet but walk to the shield line, and yet his body was shaking and shivering in equal measure, and for the first time he had to question whether he could do this. Could he fight as his father did and as all the men of the household troop did? Was he man enough to fulfil his obligations?

"Calm down Northman," Olaf muttered at him, 'it's not even started yet, and to be honest, with this many men, I almost doubt that we'll encounter any warriors. The men of the shield wall are trained for this, it's only those who come behind who're not, and they'll do all they can to protect the skilled warriors."

Northman nodded in understanding, although the words had barely registered in his fear-crazed mind. In front of him, one of the other men turned to stare at him, an older man, a little wrinkled and wizened in places but kindly for all that.

"This your first battle lad?" he asked, his voice kind and cumbersome with the local accent.

"Yes," Northman forced past his dry mouth.

"It'll be upon you soon enough, and then you'll have no time to worry about what you're doing. The waiting is always the worst part."

Angry shouts were heard from in front of the shield wall, but Northman knew nothing of what happened although those in the front line did pass back details of the conversation that occurred between Ulfcytel, Thorkell, Hemming and Olaf of Norway. None of it accomplished an extension to the truce. Instead, Ulfcytel and his three warriors raced back to their places in the shield wall. With a roar of 'attack' that echoed up and down the lines of the thousands of men, the shield wall was correctly established, the front shields locked with their two neighbours, and above those warriors heads, the shield of the man who stood behind him, and so on. The press of bodies was terrifying and calming at the same time. Northman knew a moment of complete clarity. He'd trained for this. He knew what to do.

They didn't advance, but only moments after they'd formed up, the crashes of swords on wood could be heard, alongside the intermittent whistle of arrows flying through the air.

"Raise your shield boy," the older man in front hissed, and Northman did as he was told, his arms screaming with the agony after not too long, but knowing that he couldn't lose his hold.

Thumps and angry cries echoed around him, and Oscetel ordered him to push forward. Along the line, everyone was trying to do the same. The ground was bare beneath their feet. No crops had been planted on the site, and they had a good purchase on the land. And slowly, very slowly, the line inched forwards, hoping to drive the enemy backwards.

Northman strained to hear what was happening over his ragged breathing, but only a white noise filled his ears.

What felt like the entire morning passed in that position, the thunk of swords on wood never once stopping, the cries of the angry and the wounded the only sound to be heard. Men heaved and held their position, denying themselves the comfort of resting tired arms or tired feet, refusing to eat or drink, although the sun edged higher in the sky and the clouds were small and wispy, with no hope of rain or respite if they crossed the sun's path.

"What's happening?" Northman called to Oscetel, but he received no response. Glancing to his left, he saw Oscetel in a press of bodies, one against the other, all taking small steps forward. And then his line lurched forward, and Northman moved quickly to keep his shield in place. He had no idea of who was winning.

"Bloody hell," Olaf shouted from his right, "this is hard work." He puffed with exertion, his shield above the head of the man in front, sweat dripping from his helmet down his nose, and into his half-formed beard.

Brithnoth overheard his words.

"This is a test of resolve as well as a test of strength. I don't think the enemy have started to attack yet."

A cry greeted his words, and then a great surge forward sent Northman further in front than any of the other men. Confused he glanced around, wondering what had happened. The body he stepped over was testament to what had happened. The man at the front of the shield wall was dead, a spear through his neck. Grimacing at the slight flailing of the corpse, Northman noticed the bloody grime on the spear point, and the dark red blood that pulsed from the open wound. The spear had passed right through the man's neck.

A grunt from the man in front, and they were back in line and matched up with the others to the left and right as they should be. Only it was no longer Olaf to his left and Oscetel to his right, but new men he didn't know and who didn't even notice the change, so intent were they on the task they faced.

And now the attack began in earnest. The hammering of weapons on the shields sent reverberations flowing backwards along the press of shields so that his own, already tired arms, quivered painfully, and there was no let up in the attack.

The screech of iron on wood filled his head, the cries of men in agony filled his ears and slowly but surely, he shuffled ever closer to the front of the shield wall.

To either side of him, Oscetel or Olaf would occasionally catch him, until he'd be forced to move on again without them. Somehow he just knew that of them all. He would be the one who had to take a more prominent role in the shield wall. The men in front of him seemed to be enduring a brutal attack, and Northman wondered how many men slashed and hacked at the shield that protected him.

He stepped over another body, eyes staring dully at the sky, a huge gash all down the right side of his face, still pulsing bright red blood, and Northman was pressed further forwards.

Another agony of shaking wood and howling bows and he stepped forward again. Another discarded body lay before him, this one exhibiting a fatal blow to the head. The man must have had no helm. Only this time Northman took the time to stare at the man. He was starting to see a pattern.

He was now fourth in line to the shield wall, and he tried to get the attention of the man who he'd spoken to at the beginning of the battle, but the man was infused with battle fury, insensible to anything he said, focused exclusively on his imminent attack.

Another step over a fallen body, arms dangling uselessly by the side, and Northman was pleased to note that it was the right arm. If he got to the front of the shield wall or rather, when he did, he knew he'd be facing a left-handed warrior, and unluckily for the man, Northman was capable of fighting just as well with either of his hands. He was the envy of his father and brothers for his skills, but he'd worked hard to master them.

A cry of pain cut short mid scream and Northman moved ever closer. A wound to the head again. A deep slash of purple blood and the gore of an eye half in and half out of its socket.

Northman swallowed hard trying to banish the image, but he knew it would haunt him for the rest of his life.

A heave of effort and he was third in line. The blood and sweat were more overwhelming now, the tang of blood heavy in the air, the heat and sweat of men even heavier. He could taste only his dry mouth and other men's fear.

And then there was no more time for thought. He was second to the front. The man of earlier was armed well with his shield, but he seemed fazed by the slashing of the weapon before him, not even looking over his shield to see whom he fought.

Thunderous blows landed on the shield that Northman held above his head. Northman risked a glance from below his shield and was greeted with the bloody face of a grinning Norse man. He was slippery with blood and sweat and gore, but his eyes burned bright, and Northman knew that this warrior was filled with battle rage. Clutching his sword in his left hand, his shield in his right, he attempted to shout encouragement to the man in front.

"Left hand, use your left hand," but his words were unheeded.

Beside him Olaf slipped into his line of sight, his eyes a little crazed, blood flowing freely down his right arm. Northman wondered how he'd gained such an injury but had no time to ask.

A thud, a crunch and a howl of rage, and it was Northman's turn to hold the shield wall. He stepped forward, affording his enemy a close look. He was scattered with small cuts, a nick to the face, and a gash on his right arm, a half cut where his lip was. This he licked with his tongue, and his eyes alighted with joy to see such a young adversary. Northman met his eyes, and behind him felt a shield crash into place above his head.

His shield firmly in his left hand, he took the initiative, lashing out from below his shield to strike at the man's legs. A howl of rage greeted his actions, and when he pulled his sword back, it glistened with the man's blood.

His first blood. Pride surged through him.

In response, a hail of angry hammer blows landed on his shield in front, and the shield above his head. And a voice shouted encouragement. Oscetel. It could be no other.

When his assailant paused for a moment, Northman quickly shifted his hands and lashed out with the sword on the other side of the man's legs. A grunt of pain and Northman had his sword back and swapped back to his left hand. He wanted to confuse this brute of a man who'd claimed so many lives by using his other hand for the killing stroke.

Northman felt the sting of sweat in his eyes, but could do nothing about it. He couldn't let go of his sword or his shield and so blinked repeatedly in the hope the sweat would continue to slide down his cheeks.

Oscetel was shouting at him, but he couldn't hear his words, and then he forced him to lower his shield by the expediency of forcing his own down. Northman was temporarily confused until he felt the efforts of a sword to cut at his legs. Seizing his chance, he stood abruptly, hitting his head on Oscetel's shield, but gaining the ability to move his sword more freely. Forcing it over his head, in his left hand, he struck at his attackers head, and felt the resounding crunch of bone on iron. A howl of rage was too late, Northman swung the blade again, this time slicing through the man's exposed neck. Blood sprayed free, but Northman had his shield back in place and was holding his own in the shield wall.

His first kill.

He'd done it, almost without thought, and he'd vanquished those brave warriors who'd fought in front of him.

Oscetel congratulated him, briefly, but his voice sounded worried, and Northman paused for a moment to gauge the time of day. The sun was high overhead. They'd been fighting all morning long.

But there was no time to enjoy his victory, quickly, another warrior filled the space of the fallen man, and Northman knew nothing about how this man fought. Would he, like his adversary before, be able to use his ability to fight left-handed against the man?

At his side, Olaf slid into view and Northman realised that while his line of men had fallen quickly, all along the shield wall, those in reserve were coming closer and closer to the shield wall. It wasn't a good sign.

Olaf's arm still bled, and his eyes were glazed with exhaustion and determination.

From his vantage point behind them, Oscetel spoke,

"It looks like we're beginning a retreat. We need to stay in place and walk backwards, without falling over our dead. Can you do it, lads?"

Nodding instead of speaking, Northman felt the tension in the line around him increase. It looked as though, after all, the small incline they'd found had been little use to them, and they were now to retreat to the higher burial mound.

Trying to remember exactly where the men had fallen, Northman carefully stepped backwards, his shield arm echoing with the crashes of the enemy's sword or hammer. After five steps back, Northman realised the man wasn't going to stop his attack even though he was retreating. He took a moment to look at him and realised he needed to take at least another thirty steps, and every one of them was fraught with danger. And if he fell, the enemy would surge through the hole he created and attack those who formed the shield wall from the rear.

Daunted by the task before him, he moved carefully, testing each footfall before he committed fully to it. Olaf was doing the same beside him and Oscetel stayed close, offering a steady stream of instructions.

"Step to the right, now to the left, raise your shield, now to the right, now two steps are clear."

Slowly but surely, they reached the mound, and Northman felt himself start to rise, and as he did so, he remembered to hold his shield low to the ground to protect his feet in their moment of vulnerability.

Once upon the slope, the attack lessened a little, and Northman was freer to step where he wanted and could do so even quicker. Still, the shield wall needed to move as one, and he didn't rush although he could feel the safety the top of the burial mound would afford him.

Finally, Oscetel shouted for him to stop, and Northman did just that.

Oscetel stepped up behind him.

"Move now Northman, let me take your place. The enemy has stayed at the bottom."

Every muscle and bone in his body ached, and it was all he could do to lift his shield and walk out of the shield wall. He looked urgently for Olaf but noticed that one of the other men was relieving him as Oscetel had done for him.

Exhausted, he found a space on the mound and collapsed to his knees. His breath was coming fast but slower than it had been, and he could see some way into the distance. The field before them was a sea of blood and gore. Shields lay discarded, mixed in with the broken and mangled bodies but more worryingly, archers were lining up ready to attack Northman and his fellow warriors. Hoarsely, he called a warning and lifted his shield above his head.

The thunk of the arrow warned him that he'd been correct to act as he did.

Still, he lowered his shield and looked around again. Where were all the warriors now? There seemed few people stood on the burial mound. Frantically, he looked again and further afield, dismayed to see the backs of men as they ran away from the Raiders in vast swathes, almost as if it had been planned.

Had treachery befallen Ulfcytel, even with Eadric out of the way?

Absently, he raised his shield again and another bow struck it but he barely noticed. Looking out at the horde of Raiders, fear choked him. They were a small depleted force, and the Raiders were still mostly standing. Surely they'd not survive.

Ulfcytel fought on, encouraging his men from his place among the shield wall and Northman closed his eyes for a moment. A prayer for his God at his time of need.

"Thurcetel took his men," Olaf shouted at him above the din of battle.

"What?" Northman asked, his hearing shot to pieces by the battle rage of the enemy.

"Ulfcytel's main ally, Thurcetel, he fled the battlefield. He never had any intention of fighting to the death."

"How do you know?" Northman queried, the tiredness of his exertion slowly leaving his body as he realised he still had much to accomplish.

"The news has been passed from man to man down the line. Ulfcytel is angry beyond words."

"I don't doubt it," Northman muttered, reaching for his water skin and swilling it gratefully. He also took the time to clean his face with a handful of his water. The sweat and blood slicked away freely with his actions.

"What does he have planned now? Surely we can't fight off all those attackers," he pointed out towards the scene of devastation before them.

"No, we can't. Perhaps he's hoping for reinforcements."

"They won't come from bloody Eadric," Northman commented sourly.

"No, but there are other men, and better ones at that. I would have expected Athelstan to be here. Perhaps he might come yet."

"Perhaps," Northman said, not prepared to speak the harsh truth to his friend. Not just yet.

Below, the sounds of battle faded away, and Northman watched as the other men who'd been relieved from the shield wall, began to drag wooden stakes into place. Leaping to his feet, he beckoned Olaf to aid him, and between them, they took one to where Oscetel was still in formation, although no one was currently attacking him.

"Move aside Oscetel, if it's safe to do so," Northman asked and after a moment of hesitation, Oscetel did as he commanded. He shielded the lads as they worked the spike into place, and then they ducked back inside the temporary safety of the shield wall.

"What will happen now?" Northman asked Oscetel but for once, Oscetel didn't respond.

"Get some rest boy," he growled, "it's going to be a long afternoon and night, and you'll have to stand your watch with the rest of them."

Somehow, and he was never sure how Northman managed to snatch some rest while the remaining men protected their position atop the burial mound. He woke to a strange calm and the ending of the day, the sky streaked with purples and golds. Beside him, Olaf snored contentedly away.

He tried to stand but his legs groaned in agony, and he crashed back to floor. Oscetel opened his half-closed eyes to look at him.

"Stay where you are lad. There's no need to fear. The enemy has stopped their attack for now. The draining of the light makes it impossible for them to see where we're stood. No doubt it'll be a quiet night and then tomorrow, we'll resume the battle.

"How?" Northman asked. His brief sweep of those who remained showed that their forces were badly depleted. He wondered how many had run and how many had died.

"Ulfcytel is remaining tight-lipped so I can't tell you."

"Does he still live then?" Northman queried.

"Yes, and his rage at the deceit of Thurcetel is a living force as well. That man had better have left the lands of the English. Otherwise, Ulfcytel will hunt him down, and I think strike him down without any recourse to the king's justice."

"I don't blame him," Northman uttered, and Oscetel smiled at him.

"And what of Brithelm's son, does he live?"

"Yes, he and all the others of Leofwine's men have survived. They're holding the defences for us."

"Then I should relieve one of them, for I've rested."

"You can, but later. You need to eat first. Once you get down there, you'll be staying for the night. Give yourself a little time. It's better to be thoroughly prepared than reckless." Oscetel sounded amused and resigned at the same time.

'Do you think we'll die here?" Northman finally asked the question he'd been thinking ever since they started to retreat.

"Perhaps lad, I'm not sure. I hope that some agreement can be reached, and if not, we may yet sneak away at night. But we'll have to wait and see what Ulfcytel demands of us. You fought extremely well," he added and Northman, despite their predicament, was pleased with the praise.

"That Norse man, he was a monster of a man. He hacked down all who faced him and yet somehow, you finished him. How?"

Northman smirked then with joy at his first kill,

"He was left-handed. I used the same trick on him that he was using on everyone else, only, as you know, I can fight with both hands. I think it confused him."

Oscetel laughed then, his face shining with joy and admiration,

"How did you work that out?"

"I looked at the injuries on the dead men."

"Ah Northman, you truly are your father's son. Most men see nothing but battle rage, and yet you're there, carefully watching how your opponents fight. I can't wait to tell your father, and of course Wulfstan."

The thought of seeing his father filled him with joy. Oscetel was right. Leofwine would thrill to know how well he'd fought. And when Oscetel spoke, his thoughts weren't concerned with their dire predicament. Surely that was a good sign. If he could see them meeting Leofwine again, then surely he thought they would live.

When the light fully drained from the sky, he took his place along the line of defence. Bright spots of light showed that the enemy was encamped not too far away, but they weren't pressing the defences. Clearly, they didn't want to have the corpses of the dead men as bedfellows that night.

A huge fire burnt for much of the night, the smell of burning flesh scorching his nostrils and turned his face into a grimace. Olaf joined him at some point, and they spoke quietly, reliving what they'd endured that day.

And then hasty conversations sprang up along the line of men, and Oscetel raced to the boys.

"We're to sneak away during the night. Ulfcytel has commanded it. He and some of his men will stay and ensure the defences hold. An outrider has reached Ulfcytel from the combined forces of the atheling Athelstan and your father. They're at Thetford now, and when the outrider finds them, they'll spread out and protect our retreat. Ulfcytel wants to stay and treat once more with Thorkell, do what he can to prevent any more slaughter."

"And you're coming with us?" Northman asked, worried by the look on Oscetel's face.

"Yes, I am, and my men. But Brithnoth, I think he's decided to stay, and those with him as well."

Northman glanced to where he imagined he sat.

"He wishes to avenge his father's death, no matter what."

"I know Northman, but these men, they weren't even involved in that battle. I fear he has a desire to meet his maker. But come, say your goodbyes, gather your things. Ulfcytel wants us in the first group of men to leave. He feels it would be a stain on his honour if he failed to keep you safe after all you've done, and all your father's done."

Northman knew there was no point in arguing, and so, with a final glance back towards the dark field of battle, he scrambled back up the slope, as silently as he could.

A small group of men were gathering near the back of the mound. None spoke, but their eyes were haunted. Ulfcytel himself stood there, offering words of advice and praising the men for their efforts. The men might have thought they were sneaking away, but Ulfcytel wanted them to know that they went with his blessing.

Thetford itself lay within easy reach, provided they met no enemies, and Northman felt his confidence building. This was it. He was going to survive, despite the appalling odds. His first battle, while a success for him, was catastrophic for the English forces.

A quiet word of thanks from Ulfcytel and they were out, released onto the flat lands that would take them to Thetford. The night was silent, apart from the clatter of their feet and their weapons, and Northman concentrated only on finding his way through the night, where only a handful of stars glowed through the dense clouds. A good night to escape, cloaked in darkness as they were, but it made the actual implementing of their flight fraught with danger.

Time passed slowly, each loud breath a torment of not knowing who was hidden by the blackness of the night. Slowly and surely they crept closer to Thetford, and then, when the first faint wisps of a new day were lightening the sky, outriders found them, lead by Athelstan, and joyfully they mounted on fresh horses and raced back towards the walls of Thetford.

Once there, his father greeted him with a wide embrace, pride and joy shining from his face, but Northman was too exhausted to speak.

# 26

# THETFORD, AD1010, LEOFWINE

Horic had greeted him on his arrival, the news a little grim. Outriders had sighted the commencement of the battle, and the treachery of Thurcetel was already known. It was a losing battle before it had even half started, but Horic understood the remaining force was fighting well.

Fear engulfed Leofwine, and although he wanted to do nothing more than ride out and rescue his son, he knew he could do no such thing. His son wouldn't ever forgive him if his father hauled him away from the shield wall.

Shaken by the fear that coursed through his body, he sought sanctuary in the Church, where the local priest was offering comfort to the troubled souls of his ministry.

He took no particular notice of Leofwine, but as the day turned to evening, and Leofwine didn't move, he came and sat beside him.

"My Lord," the man said, "Your son is a credit to you, he'll fare well in the battle."

"My thanks, Priest," Leofwine said, not raising his eyes from the splendour of the coloured glass window that dominated the tidy church. "As his father, I still worry, regardless."

"As you should, but a little faith, and I'm sure he'll be with you soon."

"The battle doesn't go well."

"They rarely do," the Priest commented matter-of-factly, "but there are always survivors."

"Yes, there must be," Leofwine admitted, "otherwise how would we fight another day?"

"Exactly my Lord. Now, I think our Lord has heard your prayers enough. I'd suggest you seek an update before you despair further."

Feeling suitably chastised, and a little foolish for his fears, Leofwine stood on his stiff legs, Hammer at his side obedient as ever, and together they left the Church. Horic greeted him, his face grim and Leofwine faltered in his steady steps.

"My Lord," Horic began, and Leofwine glanced at him furiously. Damn the man for turning to formality to mask the news he carried.

"Out with it Horic, quickly, tell me now."

"Apologies Leofwine. They've retreated up a steep hill and hoped to hold out there until we can relieve them, or they can attempt an escape."

"And the boys?"

"There's no news. This came from one of the outriders. They feared to go much closer."

Nodding as he absorbed just the facts, and banished his more fatherly concerns for the first time that day, he spoke.

"Has Athelstan arranged for a closer encounter?"

"Yes, on receipt of the news, Edmund and a select group of men rode out. They'll attempt to communicate with Ulfcytel and find out what we should do for the best. It's a great slaughter. And not on the side of Thorkell."

"Bloody Eadric," Leofwine cursed, "I imagine his fyrd hasn't been sighted?"

"No. No one has seen him since he left on Thursday morning."

"Damn the man and damn the king for not keeping him where we could all keep an eye on him."

"You know we all agree with you, but what will we do now?"

"We'll make ready to lead our force to relieve the embattled men of Ulfcytel. But we'll wait for Edmund to return. We won't act irrationally."

Horic stopped where he stood then and looked at Leofwine.

"The boys will be fine, Leofwine, I feel it."

"My thanks, Horic," Leofwine said, struggling to control his emotions in the face of such dire news.

"I trained them," Horic said, "since they could barely walk. They'll be well." And with that, they lapsed into silence, returning to Ulfcytel's hall. A strange hush of expectation had fallen.

Time passed slowly, and Leofwine wondered if he turned grey with worry as he waited. But then finally, Edmund arrived, his face flushed.

Athelstan and Leofwine rushed to his side, and he spoke quickly,

"He's asking for us to cover their retreat. He'll stay and attempt to make terms again."

Relieved to know that they had a role to play, Athelstan and Leofwine quickly discussed their plans and implemented them. Their aim was to retrieve all the men who still lived. And Leofwine could only hope that it included his son and his friend's son.

# 27
# THE KING'S WITAN, AD1010, NORTHMAN

TEMPERS WERE FRAYED, ACCUSATIONS FLYING FROM ONE SIDE OF THE ROOM to the other. Northman almost wanted to flinch away from the terrible repercussions of the battle at Ringmere but at the same time, he felt more outraged than any other, for he'd been there. He'd fought with his father's men in the shield wall. He'd seen men cut down before him, he'd killed to defend his land, and he'd been there when Eadric had purposefully deceived him and started the entire chain of events that had culminated at Ringmere.

It was he who'd tasked himself with keeping the king informed of what was happening at Oxford, and it was he who'd been made a fool of. His anger was boundless, and because of that, barely recovered from his ordeal, his father had allowed him to come to the Witan, to speak as a man must to his king and to face the man who'd allowed all the king's careful plans to fall to ruin. Twice.

The king was once more at Enham having moved closer to London to be as close to the East Anglian lands as possible but without imperilling himself. Rumours and counter-rumours of Thorkell's movements, and Olaf's and Hemming's, now that the vast raiding army had split into its parts, sped through the Witan and across the land. It seemed as though no one was safe. Even the greatest warriors could not single-handedly defeat so many highly skilled warriors.

Women and children fled at the faintest hint of trouble, but often they fled into greater problems, their men remaining to protect their possessions leaving them without recourse to violence when they happened upon a contingent of one of the fleets.

At Deerhurst, Northman knew his mother was locked up tight, their defences raised and their warriors ready to defend to their last breaths. But the knowledge made his father grumpy and belligerent. It was never natural for him to spend time away from his wife when such danger lurked.

Ulfcytel and those who'd survived the battle had retreated to Thetford but had soon been forced to withdraw even further, dragging the wounded with them when they had to. And then Thorkell had torched the place, his anger truly magnificent at the pitiful attempts of his enemy to stop his advance. And then from there, the army had split, part to Cambridge, part to Bedford and part to snake its way back along the Thames. Everywhere there was misery and outcry.

The fyrds had assembled, the men had formed up, but no matter where they went, the enemy was always elsewhere. The intelligence received by the local reeves and ealdormen could not keep up with the mobility of the fleets. And it all stemmed from Eadric; the man who'd paid Thorkell to attack the lands of the East Anglians.

Forced before the king, Eadric had spent yesterday protesting his innocence, while Northman had fought the bile rising in his throat. To be responsible for so much death and destruction was one thing, but to deny it with such relish was too much for Northman to endure. Yesterday he'd walked away from Eadric; turned his back on his foster-father, and made a very public display as he'd left the Witan.

Still, and even with the knowledge that Eadric's own foster son fully believed the accusations levelled against him, Æthelred was unsure in the face of such total failure.

The archbishop Wulfstan had, only just, been called upon to offer an explanation of the failure of their penance last year, but the man had turned fiery, blaming the sinful nature of the people of the English for God's failure to listen to them in their hour of need. And he'd not been alone either. The archbishop of Canterbury, Aelfheah, had raised his voice in agreement, and Æthelred had reacted with blazing eyes and an aggressive demeanour to demand the clerics devise a new way for Divine intervention.

Wulfstan had not damned him for his blasphemy, but the shocked gasps from the assembled men told the story well.

Leofwine sat with a troubled expression, Uhtred of Northumbria beside him but Ulfcytel lost somewhere between his lands and Enham. Athelstan was incensed, Edmund was nursing a wound from his attempt to assist the retreat, and a sense of fear permeated the air. It was almost tangible.

Cries for Eadric to be punished went unheeded, the king still unconvinced that Eadric had really done what he was accused of, and with each passing moment, Northman's eyes narrowed a little more. He'd kept his suspicions to himself, for surely the king could not have been complicit as well? But the king's refusal to accept the word of good and loyal men who told him it was so, was painful to watch. Either the king would accept them, or he wouldn't, and on the outcome, the future of the kingdom rested.

The ætheling Athelstan, despite his father's best efforts, had his own powerful power base that stretched from the Mercian lands down into the Wessex heartland. His men were whispering that it was the time he was king. He'd be a wiser king, a more valiant king, a warrior king, and more able to tackle Thorkell.

The queen sat white faced and agitated. Emma was aware of the threats to Æthelred's kingship, and she knew her children were too young to rule in his stead. The endurance of her marriage, the birth of her children, might all be irrelevant if these men became convinced that only a new king could fix the problem.

Northman glanced at his father. His face was angry, contorted as he stared straight ahead. Leofwine had taken him to one side last night and hadn't berated him for his actions, understanding them only too well, but he'd been at pains to make Northman understand how devastating it would be for everyone in England if the country descended into factions and power struggles. Æthelred may not be a good king, but he was *their* king. At least until his death.

Northman, incredulous at his father's words, had refused to listen. But now, as he watched the bickering and shouting, screaming and demands for action, Northman understood what his father had been trying to tell him. This was anarchy, pure and straightforward.

When news of the men who'd perished was read out, Oswy of Ipswich, his son, Wulfric and Eadwig at Ipswich, the room had fallen quiet, and there was still no official accounting of the casualties from Thetford. That Thetford had burnt, and Cambridge too had sent shockwaves through the assembled men.

The queen had held her hand to her mouth to cover her shock, and tears had filled her eyes. The people of England had been slow to accept her, but she loved them all the more for that. To hear of the pillaging and rapine that had occurred, left her almost incapable of staying sitting.

Even she turned hate filled eyes towards her husband, but Northman realised that the full blame could not be laid at Æthelred's door. This was something that he couldn't have foreseen.

There had been no word from Thorkell as to his intentions. Money hadn't swayed him in East Anglia, although, if Northman was to be believed, it had done at Oxford. Or had there been something else? Had it not been money that Eadric had gifted to Hemming?

"My Lord," his father stood, and Northman feared for him. Always he'd been conciliatory in his approach to Eadric. It had done him no good, but the belief that he worked for an overwhelming purpose had always driven him. Northman wondered how he could correct the situation now.

"Leofwine?" the king responded amongst the cries and shouting. Leofwine waited for a semi-silence to fall, still interrupted with the occasional outraged comment, but as quiet as he could hope for.

"My Lord," Leofwine said again, his voice steady, "Many wrongs have befallen our land of late, and in only a short space of time. Despite this, and despite any implied wrong-doing, we must act as one, stay together, and fight this threat as best we can."

Angry voices greeted the reasonable words, and Northman flinched for his father. Once more, he was putting himself firmly in the line of fire.

"We must work together, put aside our differences until a time presents itself that allegations of treachery can be dealt with as they should be."

"And when should that be, Ealdorman Leofwine? When Thorkell the Tall and Olaf the Stout sit in the place of our king, the path there greased by the Ealdorman of Mercia's wishes and desires, his treachery?"

Uhtred of Northumbria was candescent with rage, his voice mocking and it was he who received cheers of appropriation from the assembled body.

"No, my Lord Uhtred, it must not be then. But neither should it be when the forces of the ealdorman are already raised and answerable only to him. I would suggest, with the king's forgiveness for my outspokenness, that Eadric has his position augmented with the support of Athelstan, a man above reproach in this and every endeavour for his father and our king."

A half hush had fallen at the idea, and Leofwine took a moment to compose himself. He stood tall and straight, Hammer under his outstretched hand, but still, to stand so alone against a host of others was brave. His eyes flickered uncertainly, and Northman genuinely admired him at that moment. His words made sense, so much sense that his plans slotted into place.

Athelstan scrambled to his feet, keen to agree to this change of tactic,

"My Lord Father it would please me to act on Ealdorman Leofwine's suggestion. The Mercian lands are enormous, with far too many men for the command of just one man. It would," and here he floundered desperately for a word that would be neutral, "reduce any risk," he finished a little feebly.

Edmund too was on his feet.

"And likewise, I could offer my support to any other areas where the ealdormen could do with an extension of the king's authority."

Edmund's supporters murmured their agreement, but there were still many who were unhappy, and Uhtred gave voice to the fears of those.

"And so Eadric walks away again without punishment?"

"I don't call having to live with the knowledge of the lives not saved as going without punishment. Until this threat, this overwhelming stampede of violence against our people is contained, we can't afford the threat of an open split in the governance of the land," Leofwine spoke candidly, not disagreeing with Uhtred's words, but not condoning them either.

Eadric's eyes blazed with anger, his brothers beside him, and any moment now, Northman expected him to walk out of the king's hall, vowing never to return.

Sadly, no amount of whispering and vitriol could move Eadric. Stony-faced he waited for the king to make his judgement.

Æthelred, sunken in his wooden chair, met the eyes of no one. This was his decision to make, and he must, as always live with the consequences.

"As you will," he finally said, "Athelstan, my son, you're temporarily a fellow ealdorman of Mercia. You will govern and act in my name, and you have the power to act against Eadric if his decisions are detrimental to my reign, although, I pray God they'll not be."

Athelstan bowed at the honour his father had bestowed upon him, as Eadric opened his mouth to countermand the king's words.

"Eadric, you have this final opportunity to prove your loyalty. If not, you will lose everything, including your life. Now, we have more important things to discuss than this. We must mount a defence, curtail the actions of Thorkell. Suggestions?"

And the Witan was a hubbub of discussion again. Everyone had their ideas as to how the Raiders could be stopped.

In the suddenly relaxed atmosphere, Northman moved to his father.

"Son," Leofwine said as he sat heavily down. Exhaustion marked his body, and Northman wondered how he could still be standing after the exertions of the last few weeks.

"Father, I've come to apologise. Your words last night were justified. I must learn to listen to others with greater knowledge than I yet have."

"Should you son?" his father asked tiredly, "I may just have made a terrible decision and in doing so, put the king's son at terrible risk."

"Yes, but you might also have saved the country from a civil war."

Smiling sadly at Northman's assessment of the situation, Leofwine motioned for him to sit down beside him.

"No, I shan't."

"Why?" his father asked, but Northman had the distinct impression he already knew what he was going to say.

"I have a foster-father I must serve," and ignoring the resignation that flooded down Leofwine's face, Northman walked from his father towards the outraged Eadric and his equally vociferous brothers. This wasn't going to be a pleasant experience, but he was the only one of them who could truly get close to Eadric. He might have evaded him at Thetford, determined to be in the coming battle, but Eadric was so vain he would think Northman capable of deserting his father. And Northman could use that.

# 28

# DEERHURST, AFTER MIDWINTER, AD1010, LEOFWINE

At last, the snows had fallen, and a delightful silence enveloped the land. Thorkell and his men were locked up tight in Canterbury for the dark winter months, and so, for the first time since Easter, Leofwine felt as though he could take his ease a little.

The fyrds had done their best to evade the Raiders and dissuade them from further attacks. They'd been unsuccessful, the raiding parties reaching as far inland as Northampton. They'd attacked and burnt the place, just another name to add to those already fired and devastated.

Leofwine dreaded to think of the atrocities being committed by the Raiders and felt powerless to prevent them.

Æthelflæd fluctuated between rage and pride at her oldest son's activities and rage and anger at her husband for letting him do so. Leofwine knew that whatever he said would be ineffectual and unwelcome, and so he spoke little and pondered much.

His younger children were his comfort, although his daughter was as haughty as her mother. At ten years old, she was good company, when she forgot her anger at her father and spent much of her time speaking to Wulfstan, desperate to hear as much about her father's childhood as she could. Leofwine had wondered whether he should caution Wulfstan and his tall tale telling, but Æthelflæd had made him hold his tongue. Wulfstan enjoyed the story telling, and Ealdgyth would spend the next day pestering him to know whether the stories were true or not.

But despite the deep snow, the work of the Witan didn't stop. It simply couldn't. Some way out of the terrible predicament had to be reached, and in the depths of winter, when all was quiet, Leofwine finally made his most difficult decision to date. Come the warmer weather, he'd once more step foot inside a ship, and he'd travel to Denmark and beg if need be, king Swein to recall Thorkell and his son. And if that failed, he would ask for his assistance in having Thorkell accept their offer of payment.

The decision reached, he took Horic and Oscetel into his confidence, and they plotted and schemed as much as they could in the closed quarters of the house. Come the first warm day; they would leave. His ship would be pressed into service, and by travelling by sea, Horic would guide them to Denmark.

While preparations were made, he continued to hear intelligence from his son about Eadric's movements, and he learned of Athelstan's growing ties with the Mercian Reeves and lesser nobility. Eadric was embittered, but there was little he could do. While Athelstan spent his winter months in Lichfield, Eadric sulked in his Shropshire home, receiving messages from the king grudgingly, and offering no words of help. He was a lost cause, and even he must have seen his time running out as Ealdorman.

Finally, the day arrived when they must leave England and seek out Swein. Only the night before had Leofwine informed Æthelflæd of his plans. She had fluctuated between anger and pride in her husband's decision, and her tears surprised him when he took his leave from her. He promised to return, but they both knew he'd decided on a desperate course of action. Anything could befall them at sea, and there was no surety that he would return at all.

Oscetel didn't accompany him. In his absence he would govern in his stead, with the help of Æthelflæd, and although it wasn't necessary to keep their mission a secret from the king, it was thought best to be careful about whom they told.

Stepping into the ship, Leofwine felt a deep feeling of premonition and for a fleeting moment, he considered not going at all. Perhaps he could simply send a messenger? Maybe Finn would go in his stead, but he knew in his heart that he needed to go. No other had any tie with Swein.

His ship had been prepared and was ready, manned with a full compliment of shipmen, and he greeted his ship's captain amicably. He'd not often seen him in the intervening years since his injury, but the man had served him impeccably well. The ship was always ready for battle, always seaworthy when it needed to be.

"It'll be an exciting journey," he offered, as Leofwine scrambled abroad, Hammer with him, and Leofwine quirked a smile.

"I don't doubt it will be."

And yet, for all his fears, things seemed to go well. The ship, birthed on the small stretch of his coast, had a long journey to make, around the dragons leg of the far West, and then ever onwards. Initially, they travelled close to the coast, but when they neared the Isle of Wight, they moved further out to sea in the hope that they'd avoid the shipmen of Thorkell and his allies. No intelligence had reached them of whether the enemy was still on land or whether they'd returned to their ships, and they wanted to take no chances. If they were intercepted so far out to sea, they'd never reach Swein and Leofwine would never be able to bargain with him to arrest Thorkell's successes.

Surprisingly, and against all the odds, they made it through the seaways that Horic had thought Thorkell would be monitoring. He muttered about the arrogance of the man, and Leofwine agreed with him, only for Leofwine it showed just how fearless Thorkell was of anything the English king could throw at him.

Horic had decided that they should put ashore as soon as they were sure they were in the lands of the Danish king. As such he chose a place he called Ribe. He said from there they could find out where Swein was then residing. Unsure of the probable reception they would receive, Horic asked to be put ashore in a sheltered cove, a day's walk from Ribe. With his son, he said he'd travel to Ribe and find out what he could.

The weather was bitterly cold, the seasons a little delayed to those in England, and for two days Leofwine and his men sat and shivered within their ship, none wanting to go ashore for fear of a hostile encounter.

Only when the short day was ending on the second day did Horic arrive, and he didn't come alone. By some great chance, Swein had himself been visiting Ribe, eager to take stock before the summer trading began. As a mark of his understanding with Leofwine, he'd come in secrecy and with only a few men.

Leaping from the ship, Leofwine met the man as he slid from his horse. He was grinning a little with the absurdity of the situation.

"Leofwine, I never thought I'd see you step foot on Danish land."

"Nor I Lord Swein," Leofwine commented lightly. There was no point in being accusatory to the man. He might well have given Thorkell his leave to attack England, but he hadn't convinced the horde of people to accompany Thorkell and raid quite so aggressively.

A hastily constructed tent appeared, and Swein invited Leofwine inside as a fire was lit, and Leofwine felt warmth for the first time in two days.

"Come, sit Leofwine. We will drink and discuss your predicament as though we were in one of my great halls, and it were not passing strange to meet you in secret."

"My thanks, Lord Swein for agreeing to meet me."

"Ah, come, forget the Lord. I'm Swein and you Leofwine, and this, this is Horic and his son, a brute of a man, and a real miss from my standing army, but I can't have all the best men under my command. Now, tell me of Thorkell and his successes in England." He was intrigued, leaning forward on his campstool and Leofwine wondered just how much he knew.

"Have you not been in contact with Thorkell?"

"No, I last heard from a ship that returned to my waters early last summer. It carried the wounded from a battle in Thetford; I think they said."

"Then there is much you don't know. Thorkell, he is a mighty warrior."

Swein laughed with glee at that understated assessment of his finest commander,

"He is and a good foster-father to my son Cnut. You may remember him?"

"Yes I do Swein, and for some time he was a hostage at the king's court, and I got to know him a little better, but that was two years ago now. I'm sure you knew of that."

"I did yes, Thorkell was unhappy but Cnut insisted, as I understand it."

"Yes, that's what he told us as well."

"He's honourable and inquisitive in equal measure. I fear it's my fault, for after meeting with you I said I'd very much like to meet the king and see how his court functioned."

"Then you've had your wish. I'm sure Cnut learnt much in his time with the king."

"Ah," Swein said, dismissing that part of their conversation with a wave of his hand, "You didn't come here to tell me of Cnut. Tell me what you need me to know."

With a pause for breath and a drink of warmed mead, Leofwine began,

"Thorkell is a great warrior, but he is running rampant upon the English king's land. Initially, a truce was agreed, but the king refused to pay the geld of £30000. And then, and we're not sure of all the details, Thorkell left his winter quarters and began attacking the lands of our combined ancestors, the lands of the Five Boroughs."

Swein's face creased with puzzlement then,

"Why would he do so? We've always said that we'd not attack our people. It creates bad feeling."

"We believe, and it pains me to say it, that there may have been treachery from one of the king's Ealdormen, we fear that coin or some favour passed from one of our own to Thorkell, and that is why the lands of the settlers were attacked."

Swein looked unhappy at the news,

"I know I don't orchestra his every move, but still, this unsettles me. Is this all you came to say to me?"

"No, sadly not. Since that time, Thorkell and his allies have split their forces. They raid far and wide, and, and I wish I didn't have to share this with you, my people are unable to stop Thorkell. He sends no word of his demands, and before the winter, he fired another of our thriving markets, far into the lands of the Mercian ealdorman, and I fear that England will be unable to endure another summer of constant attacks."

Swein's eyes shone with the images of success that Thorkell was enjoying, but he also looked a little haunted.

"He's a great warrior and men flock to him."

"They do, that's for sure. Prepared to fight for any tuft of grass or sliver of silver, and England can't take the beating."

"What would you have me do? As I say, I'm not responsible for his actions."

"I appreciate that Swein. I had hopes that you could recall your warriors who fight for him and perhaps, send word that he might negotiate with the English king. If we were able to offer him a geld again, it would stop much suffering."

Swein listened with interest, as did one of the men behind him, who Swein hastily introduced.

"This is my eldest son, Harald. He has hopes to the kingdom when I'm dead. He's a real warrior, but alas, no friend of Thorkell."

Harald was almost identical to his father, even down to his eye colour and hair. Leofwine stood offered him an arm clasp of friendship, and with only slightly raised eyebrows, he accepted. The strength in his arm surprised Leofwine.

"You should recall him, father," Harald said without preamble. "You don't want him to become richer than you. The English king was a fool not to give him the geld of £30000 but, if he offers more now, he'll have far more treasure than you."

Swein laughed away his son's fears, but Leofwine could see that this father and son spoke straight to each other and that indeed, Swein may feel the first stirrings of jealousy for the other man's success.

"You make a good argument Harald, but I must remember that you and Thorkell don't think much of each other. He is, after all, your half-brother's foster-father."

"Ah, father, Thorkell is arrogant and not possessed by Odin, although he says as much to all who'll listen. He should be a Christian father, as we all are. Recall him or he'll come for your throne next."

A little shocked, Swein turned to glare at his son, and Horic laughed a little forcefully.

"Cubs are always keen to tell us what to do, aren't they, my Lord Swein?"

"Yes, they are. It's the way of the world that our sons want to replace us before our time is up." The king spoke benignly, but his face was thoughtful.

"And what will you give me if I do this?" Swein demanded.

Leofwine was uncertain what to say, but Horic stepped in,

"I'm sure my Lord Leofwine and the English king will be able to reward you handsomely once Thorkell is gone. Perhaps a small geld for your trouble, or some other priceless item you might desire."

A smile played around Swein's lips then,

"You mean I could share in the geld even though I've not lifted a hand to do anything in this raiding mission. Now that's an idea I like. I'll do as you ask. I'll send word that I want Cnut home, after all, I've not seen my son in two years, and with the messenger, I'll caution

Thorkell that he overextends himself and should return having reached an accord with the English king. More than that I can't do." Swein shrugged as he finished speaking and Leofwine had the feeling that he was enjoying this more than he should.

"My thanks, Swein," Leofwine said, "You do me a great honour in coming here to speak with me, and you do me an even bigger one in taking these actions."

"I know Leofwine, but one day I'll ask something similar of you. I can't see that our interest in your lands is yet at an end." Swein laughed as he spoke to take the sting from his words, but they both stilled in thought. There was something there, hovering on the periphery of both of their consciousnesses and neither enjoyed it.

Business done, for the time being, Swein invited Leofwine to dine with him. On that windy beach, the king of Denmark and much of Norway, and Leofwine, the half blind ealdorman of the Hwicce spoke about their one time either ally or enemy. They laughed, and they drank, and they drank a bit more, and then, with fierce winds howling outside, they both slept where they sat. And in the morning, they went their separate ways.

# 29
# THE KING'S COURT, AD1011, NORTHMAN

Northman sat beside Olaf, his leg jumping up and down with the imposed inaction. Northman elbowed him, but he didn't stop. Rolling his eyes, Northman shuffled forward on his chair and looked around the crowded room. Where was his father? He was never late, and he never failed to attend when the king demanded, but his absence was notable and amongst the other Ealdormen, Eadric smirked with pleasure.

His time back with Eadric had been passable, having the king's son nearby made Eadric behave whereas before he'd have beaten and cajoled his foster-son in equal measure. The devastation that had accompanied the enemies raids had been sobering and Northman often watched Eadric, wondering what he thought about his one time ally's inability to rein in the men he supposedly controlled.

At the front of the Witan, Æthelred had failed to bring the meeting to order. He too was looking about desperately, and Northman hoped it was for his father, although he wasn't sure.

Athelstan sat deep in conversation with Edmund. Much of the

decisions to be ratified here today had already been reached. This was just the opportunity for everyone to give his or her assent at the same time and in the same place. And that involved Leofwine.

Ulfcytel was there, having resurfaced from the battles that had ravaged his lands the previous year, but he was scared and walked with half a limp. He cast angry glances Eadric's way as his alleged treachery was just about the worst kept secret the length and breadth of England.

Just then there was a disturbance at the slowly closing doorway, and Leofwine strode through, Hammer, as always, at his side. Northman wondered why he was so late. And then, to add to everyone's consternation, he didn't immediately take his seat but approached the king instead. Intrigued, Æthelred beckoned him forward, and a quick whispered conversation ensued. When it was done, Æthelred was visibly more relaxed, and Leofwine met his son's eye steadily. Just what had his father been up to?

But he didn't get his answer anytime soon. Instead, the king launched into a lengthy description of the deprivations that had been inflicted. The enemies had left almost nowhere untouched; they'd raided deep into the Mercian heartlands, along the Thames River, and to the South, near Canterbury and Sandwich and further round, to Swein's old favourite haunt, the Isle of Wight.

The recitation was grim hearing, but aware that the king was about to present a case for the highest geld ever yet given to the Raiders, Northman knew that the king needed to do all he could to have an agreement reached.

Northman doubted that there was anyone in the room who'd been unaffected by the Raiders. Anyone.

The king hadn't even mentioned the amount of the geld to be paid when voices started to shout their acceptance to its payment. The land was tired. The people beleaguered and if they had to pay for their peace, in the face of God's evident wrath, then so be it, even if it was £46000.

And that was it. The king again called for the fyrds to be raised, until the geld could be paid in full, but he had little more to add to the assembly of men. There was no need for words when everyone within the room, apart from the king, had seen the extent of the damage done.

Northman was pleased that the Witan came to such a fortuitous ending. He was desperate to know of what his father and the king spoke about.

But he was not to get his chance, for Eadric called him to him, full of petulant demands and petty wants, and Northman wondered how long the man had worked on his list. Had he spent the journey here working out how to foil Northman's attempts to see his father, or was he just so desperate and needy that he'd not let Northman out of his sight? For all that his contempt of Eadric was well known, he was at least a known quantity for Eadric.

So resolved, Northman stood attendance upon his foster father throughout the muted feast that followed the Witan and found himself sneaking from his bed to see his father. Leofwine, apparently aware of his son's predicament, kept himself up late that night. Long after everyone else had sought their beds, he sat silently within the king's hall, with no one for company but the snores of those unlucky enough not to have their own room within the palace, and his faithful hound Hammer.

Without the need for words, Northman sat beside his father and just for a moment allowed himself to be a boy by resting his head on his father's shoulder. He was disconcerted by how far he had to bend his neck to do so and the faint twinge of pain that the movement caused. By his side, his father laughed softly,

"Too old now my lad, far too old for those sort of manoeuvres."

"I don't think I'll ever be too old father. That'll be you, one day."

Leofwine punched him lightly on the arm as they both stared at the smouldering remains of the fire. Northman felt his father push a drinking cup into his hand, and he drank deeply of the mead. It was sweet and clear, much nicer than Eadric's mead.

"Mother is well?" Northman enquired, and once more Leofwine laughed softly.

"I believe she was before I left on my journey, but it's been two weeks now, so something may have changed, although I doubt it. She would have sent word."

Still, his father didn't mention where he'd been, and sighing dramatically; Northman wondered how long his father would keep him guessing for.

"I've been across the sea, to meet with Swein," his father surprised him by saying.

"Swein!" Northman gasped loudly, forgetting for a moment, the lateness of the night.

"Yes, to prevail upon him to try and reason with Thorkell. The notion came to me in the winter months, and I couldn't forget it and so made myself go."

"And he saw you?" Northman asked, intrigued by his father's actions.

"Yes, Horic found him, and he came to meet me, all in secret of course. You must not tell anyone, and I mean anyone of this. Well, apart from Olaf, he should know for it was his father who greased the wheels of the trip, as it were."

Northman whistled softly through his teeth at the sheer audacity of his father.

"You went without the king's blessing?"

"Yes, I did. I knew that if I waited the king would contemplate for so long that the trip wouldn't be possible. As it is, Denmark seems to be still steeped in winter, or at least what I saw of it was."

"So what did he say? Will he approach Thorkell?"

"He says he will do what he can. He'll try and recall the men from his fortresses, and he will advise Thorkell to take the geld and bring his son home. That is the hook he plans to use as his bait. He's not seen Cnut for two years, and he's going to call the boy home and have him relay his words to Thorkell. But they're not commands. He can't control the man as he acts independently from him. He didn't say as much, but I think he may be a little jealous of Thorkell, and a little fearful of his growing power. His eldest son Harald said as much, very blandly."

Northman still couldn't quite process the words his father was saying. He was in awe of him. After all these years to purposefully seek out a man who'd once sworn vengeance on him was a truly honourable thing to do for the good of his people. He could only wonder that none had suggested it before.

"And mother knew you were going?" he asked as if to assure himself that his mother hadn't lost her sharp tongue and acidic tone.

"She did know, and she gave me a firm talking to, as you would expect. But I had to try Northman. Can you see that?"

"Oh yes, father. But, won't some call you a traitor for going to the Danish king after all the grief he's caused our people?"

"I imagine many will see it as such. I just hope that it works, and Thorkell leaves our shores. Swein had a covetous look in his eye when we spoke. I hope my assurance of a geld in exchange for his intervention will cure him of that."

"The king took the news well when you told him?"

"The king is desperate. He sees his hold on the land weakening, and fears for his future and that of his children. His efforts to have God intercede have so far failed. I hope a more earthy approach may help."

"Goodness me father," Northman exclaimed in a whisper, "I can't process all that you're telling me. It's amazing and scary and bloody reckless all at the same time. I think you've spent too much time with Horic and his sons. This sort of action has their name written all over it."

Leofwine giggled like a boy being scolded then,

"I can scarce believe it myself. I feel sure I'll wake tomorrow, and it'll all have been a dream."

But when they both woke the next morning, heads aching from the mead they'd consumed as they'd talked long into the night, sleeping where they sat, the king went out of his way to laud Leofwine and heap honours onto him. He didn't mention his ealdorman's meeting with Swein, for it was to remain a secret as Leofwine had said, but to all in the hall, it was clear that Leofwine had accomplished something monumental for their king.

# 30
# LATE SUMMER, AD1011, LEOFWINE

TIME PASSED SLOWLY THAT SUMMER AS THE FYRDS ASSEMBLED, THE SHIP army as well, under the control of the ealdormen, athelings and Reeves in each shire. Thorkell was approached and offered a truce and after an interminable delay, word was finally received that the Raiders would accept the geld as offered. Once more they demanded an exchange of hostages and agreed to meet later in the year when the geld was collected. Only Thorkell was not done with his raiding yet, and in the late summer, when the harvest had been gathered, and the people were busy raising the geld, he attacked Canterbury.

After a summer of inactivity, when Leofwine had risen the highest he ever had yet in the king's affections, the seizure of Canterbury was a blow that the king couldn't accept with any good grace. Called to him when the Witan met at Michaelmas, Leofwine knew his interview would be about as pleasant as when Richard of Normandy had played him for a fool.

The king, at Winchester, paced his private room fractiously.

"My Lord," Leofwine bowed when he entered his presence. And so he stayed for long moments before Æthelred even looked at him. A bad sign and the interview went from bad to worse from there.

"You told me that Thorkell wouldn't attack anyone further. You said the Danish king was going to stop him." The king hissed the words angrily, mindful that Leofwine's intervention was still a secret and one, in the light of recent developments, that he wanted to keep.

"My Lord, my apologies. I understood that Swein would act so. It appears as though his gentle persuasions were inadequate."

"Inadequate, he's damn near burnt Cambridge to the ground, well those bits that were still standing anyway. And none of his warriors has disbanded."

"No, my Lord, I'm aware of that, although the bands led by Hemming and Olaf the Stout have confined themselves to a winter barracks near London. They're taking the food we send them and waiting for their part of the geld."

"I don't want to pay them any bloody geld," Æthelred hissed again, his eyes blazing with fury and his lips trembling with his suppressed rage.

"Nobody wants to pay them the geld," Leofwine hissed back, his anger getting the better of him. "We've built our ships, and we've paid the Raiders in the past and yet somehow, and forgive me my Lord for thinking that you are more than aware of the problem if we're undermined from within there's little that I can do on my own to stop the enemy. I am one man, not seven thousand."

Shocked at the words erupting from Leofwine's mouth, Æthelred was left standing with his mouth opening and closing ineffectually.

"Apologies my Lord," Leofwine offered instantly. That the words were right made the apology burn on its way out.

"Apologies for what?" Æthelred asked, his tone dangerously low. "For what you've just said, or for Thorkell?'

"For Thorkell, my Lord," Leofwine responded. He couldn't apologise for what he'd said about Eadric.

"What of the things you imply about me?"

"I can't apologise for speaking the truth, can I my Lord?"

Leofwine was amazed at his boldness and the thrill he felt in watching the king's face turn redder and redder with anger.

"Get out Leofwine," the king roared, "and never show your face here again unless I command it."

"With pleasure my Lord. And my Lord," he paused, turning on his way out of the door, "Likewise, don't call on me unless it is to apologise for your impossible demands of me when you accept failure so readily from everyone you surround yourself with. In fact my Lord, I'd say that you expect the failure. Only never from me."

Without allowing his king and Lord to speak further, Leofwine marched from the room. Impatiently he gestured for his men to mount up, and in no time at all, they were gone from Winchester, as if they'd never been there. But the repercussions ran deep, and the king was even more unforgiving than usual.

# 31
# SHROPSHIRE, LATE AD1011/EARLY AD1012, NORTHMAN

There was an expectant buzz in the air that Northman somehow felt was directed at him. Called to Eadric, Northman found him smiling while he sat before his fire. Northman's heart sank. What new treachery was this?

"Come Northman, sit, drink and eat with me. I've news from the king. Excellent news in fact. Well apart from for Cambridge and the poor archbishop, Aelfheah, who's been taken hostage. Bloody fool agreed to go if they spared the other holy men and women of Canterbury. Idiot. He should have saved himself and left the nuns and monks to their fates."

Northman was struggling to keep up but knew that Eadric would get to the point eventually.

"The king has sent word to me of Thorkell's treachery at Cambridge. He managed to steal his way inside and burn the place down and all while we were allegedly taking part in a truce, facilitated by your father. Your father is in disgrace and has retreated to Deerhurst. The king has recalled me to him, at my earliest pleasure."

The smugness on Eadric's face was impossible to ignore and yet somehow; Northman did just that. Plastering a smile on his face, he toasted his foster-father and congratulated him as he knew he wanted him to do.

"And when will you go, Eadric?" Northman asked, not wanting to know the answer but asking the question anyway.

"As soon as I can. I think a winter with the king will strengthen our ties. You will stay here, guard my wife and sons, ensure that there are no further problems from across the border."

Knowing that Eadric thought this punishment, Northman allowed himself to look disappointed and grudgingly accept the instructions of his foster-father. Once he was gone, he'd be able to send Olaf to Deerhurst and find out the truth of the matter.

The king's daughter looked distressed to be left out of Eadric's plans once more, but she held her tongue. Eadric was not a gentle husband, and at least with him gone, she'd have the run of the house to herself. She was a good woman, capable and caring to all who had the misfortune to be slaves or servants within the household. Northman respected her but stayed away from her. He'd long since realised that any show of compassion and her calm façade would crumble. He couldn't be responsible for that.

Sadly, a storm blew up during the night, and the temperature plummeted. Northman lay awake all through the long night, listening to the wind howling and praying that it hadn't brought snow with it. When he woke in the morning, gritty-eyed and grouchy from lack of sleep, it was to see Eadric departing in all haste back to the king. Northman sighed with relief and hoped that the snows would come quickly now. He didn't want to see him again until the start of summer. Although, as he thought about it, he realised how dangerous that wish was. All that time alone with the king; Eadric could cause untold harm.

Olaf was keen to visit his father and set out when they could be sure that Eadric was well and truly gone. He went alone, confident that he could travel quicker and more stealthily if he went by himself. With misgivings, Northman agreed but warned his friend that he'd never forgive him if he didn't make it there and back in one piece.

Eadric hadn't gone alone. He'd taken his brothers along with him, but left behind his father and Northman took to spending his time avoiding the old man. He'd do anything not to have to speak to him, even to the extreme that on cold wintry days, he'd insist on riding out to check the borderlands.

He'd arrive home, frozen to the bone and he'd shrug free from his soaking wet cloak and leggings, and make himself comfortable around the fire. The first time it happened, he noticed a girl similar in age to him was watching him, and he wondered who she was. The next time, she watched him again, and yet, during the normal day-to-day running of the household he never once laid eyes on her.

Confused, he was distracted from his musings when Olaf returned four days later, bringing with him the first snows. Impatient, Northman met him in the stables, and there Olaf told him the truth of what had befallen his father. Northman smirked with wry amusement when he repeated the words that Leofwine had spoken to the king, but at the same time, he felt a stirring of fear. It wasn't good policy to cross the king. Not ever.

His father had been full of his quiet belief that the king's anger had been unfounded, and Northman knew he was right, but still, no others knew of Leofwine's journey to Swein, only that he'd helped bring about the truce. Would the king make it widely known as a way of punishing Leofwine? Northman truly wasn't sure. And he prayed earnestly that Eadric would never hear the truth of it, for he would savage his father, regardless of his own many and inexcusable acts that had damaged the king and his efforts to better the Raiders.

More than a month after Eadric had left for the king's court, Northman returned from another of his forays to the border to find the girl sitting in his place by the fire with a whimsical look on her face. He'd finally found out who she was, Mildryth, Eadric's niece, daughter of his disgraced brother Brihtric by a servant girl he'd taken a fancy to as a youth.

The girl had been accorded high status within the house as to date she was the only female in the younger generation, and usually served Edith, the king's daughter. That was why in all his years he'd never before seen her. She was secreted away, Edith having taken an instant dislike to Eadric's father, and for perhaps the first and only time in their marriage, Eadric had acted to divide the warring parties and had bowed to her wants. Edith spent most of her time within her rooms, or upon the balcony level, avoiding the old man and almost everyone else.

Northman knew she was often sad and pitied her the marriage her father had made for her. If he was aware that how Eadric treated her, Northman doubted that Eadric would have been allowed to continue. Although, if he was honest with himself, Eadric seemed to be authorised to do anything he damn well please, so maybe he would.

He walked towards her, his eyes aglow with interest, and sat beside her.

"It's cold today?" she asked quietly, her eyes downcast as she spoke.

"Bitter would be a better word," he offered in reply, pleased that she'd talked to him. On the other side of the fire, Eadric's father watched and glowered, and Northman chuckled a little at his annoyance. He'd been accorded no greater responsibility when Eadric had left, and it had turned the bitter man even more malicious. Northman did his best to avoid him and antagonise him all at the same time.

"I thought I might go out later, but if it's that cold, I think I'll stay inside," Northman noted she had her cloak on her knees, and he wondered if he should? If he could offer to walk with her?

And then Olaf slumped down beside him, unaware of anything he might have been interrupting, and simultaneously Edith had shown her face before the fire and Mildryth rushed to her side.

Northman sighed when she left in a swirl of sweet smelling air, and Olaf looked at him in confusion,

"What's the matter with you?" he said while working his jaw around a piece of bread he'd gathered from the table.

"Nothing Olaf, nothing at all," Northman said incredulously, amazed his friend could be so dense on occasion.

"Good, as long as it had nothing to do with that girl. You need to stay away from her because I think she quite likes you."

Northman glanced at Olaf in shock. Perhaps he was paying more attention than even he was.

"Why do you say that?" Northman asked, intrigued.

"She sits here every time you go out knowing full well that you're going to come in and sit there. She must be doing it on purpose. I can't think of any other reason."

"Every time?" he pressed.

"Yes, every time, but stay away from her. You know who she is?"

"Yes, I do. Eadric's niece."

"Good, then stay away from her. You don't want to be dipping anything in something that's a part of Eadric's family. Think what your father would say."

Northman sobered a little then, and the flush of excitement that had shaded his face faded instantly. Olaf was right. He shouldn't have anything to do with her. But still, she was a lovely thing and if she liked him? Well, he was sure he could speak to her without getting in trouble with his father.

The darkest time of the year came again, and Northman found himself looking for Mildryth whenever he returned from a journey outside. He also saw her watching him in the great hall. With Eadric gone and his father taken to his bed with a winter illness, Edith spent more time in the company of the others in their hall, happy to take advantage of the warmer fire and warmer company.

They never spoke again, but Northman couldn't stop from thinking about her all the time, and he grew a little less aware of everything going on around him. So much so that it took an outraged Olaf to remind him of his duties to his father, and that he should seek him out again, or at least send Olaf to do it for him.

Consenting to his friend's agitated demands, Northman watched him disappear into the low cloud on a chilly morning at the beginning of the New Year. There was a covering of snow on the land, but it had lain for more than a week and was frozen firmly in place. Provided it didn't snow again; Olaf would have a pleasant trip.

Northman watched him go and then he turned back towards the fire. He was determined that in his friend's absence he would find the will to talk to her. He wanted to speak to her, spend time with her, know what she thought and spoke. If Edith liked her, and Edith genuinely seemed to enjoy her company, then Northman realised she mustn't be at all like her father.

So resolved he wondered with intent to her place near the fire. She was busily sewing a new outfit for Eadric's growing son, and seemed to be completely absorbed in her work, or so he thought until she sat beside him.

"Your shadow is gone, I see," she stated, not looking up from her work.

"To visit relatives yes," he responded, not wanting to give away his real purpose.

She laughed softly, and not unkindly,

"It must be wonderful to have family who cares about you enough that they worry when they're not near," she said, and Northman realised that no messenger had come to them from Eadric. Whatever the king and his disloyal Ealdorman were doing, it didn't involve them or concern them. Still, he was surprised that no message had come from the king. That was most unlike him not to even enquire about his daughter.

"It is yes, and I miss them greatly."

"I don't miss my father or my uncle, and wish I had the courage to pray for the death of old Æthelric, but I don't." She grimaced as she spoke and Northman realised that her life, for all that she was an acknowledged daughter of a king's thegn, was not as perfect as it should be.

Hoping to find more neutral ground on which to speak he asked,

"The Lady Edith is well, and the boys?"

"Oh yes, they, like I, thrive in this atmosphere without her husband, my uncle. Long may it continue?"

"I agree wholeheartedly, but I worry about what the king is planning with Eadric."

Again she laughed, a little mockingly.

"You know it'll be no good, as it always is. Eadric needs to become his favourite Ealdorman again, and the only way he can do that is to trample over someone else, so I imagine that he'll be planning someone's downfall and the king will be going along with it as he always does."

"You don't have a very high opinion of the king?"

"Are you surprised? Look at his daughter. His flesh and blood and yet she's here, at the farthest reaches of our kingdom and he never sends messengers to see how she fares or to ask after his grandchildren. And that's before even considering his inability to fight off the Raiders. He has men at his command who would do good work. His sons would govern well too, but he listens to no one but himself or whoever fawns upon him."

"The king is a fool and my Uncle a sly fox. He knows how to get what he wants. He made a mistake with his haul of coins and treasure for Thorkell. He wanted the king to give him the Eastern lands as well as Mercia. He hoped to drive Ulfcytel out or have him killed, and he almost succeeded and all for his gains. He cared not at all for those who perished, and he cared not at all that he made no agreement with Thorkell for when he should stop."

"You seem to know a lot about this?" he said, surprised by her summing up of her king and her Uncle. He'd not realised that anyone else saw quite so well through the lies and the deceit.

"Eadric likes to brag of his plans to the Lady Edith. She sits and she listens, and she nods for if she doesn't, he grows angry. He doesn't beat her, nothing like that. But he castigates her with his tongue and sometimes I wonder how she can sit so still and not lash out and murder the smug bastard. I know I would."

Taken aback by the vehemence in her tone, Northman looked around to ensure that no one had heard what they spoke off.

"Don't worry Northman. Eadric is fully aware of my feelings for him. It makes him smile when he sees me so riled, and then he will hit me instead of his wife, but that is all for the better. I would rather feel his wrath than her."

Northman was shocked by what she said, and then everything fell into place at once.

"Is that why I rarely see you when he is at home? Do you hide your bruises away?"

"No, but he makes me. I wear my bruises proudly. I want him to see what he's done to me and feel some remorse, and he does. For he leaves me be afterwards until Edith offends him again or I offend him. I know when it's going to happen now, and I bait him on purpose to get it over and done with all the sooner."

She stood abruptly, and walked away from him, and he watched her go with unease. His need to protect her had just increased tenfold, as had his need to spend more time with her, but that just made his life more difficult. Eadric already tolerated him only out of a perverse need to offend Leofwine. If he returned home and found him friends with his niece, he might harm her more.

His head was pounding with his newfound information. Northman returned to his sleeping quarters to change out of his wet clothes and slump tiredly onto his bed. Closing his eyes, he saw her in his mind, laughing, smiling and joyful, as she would be if he took her away from Eadric. If only he could do so.

# 32
## AD1012, NORTHMAN

OLAF RETURNED WITH A SNOWSTORM, CURSING HIS BAD LUCK AND FOUL tempered to boot. Northman wandered to the animal barn to speak to his friend and found him filled with rage and grief combined.

"Olaf what ails you?" Northman asked fearfully.

"Nothing for you to fear Northman, and nothing for you to concern yourself with. Your family are well, your father still in good spirits and even Wulfstan seems fitter than I've seen him for some time, although that can be a bad sign," he offered as a side thought, but Northman was too caught up in getting to the bottom of the problem now.

"Then what is it?"

"My father,"

"What of him?"

"He's grumpy and foul tempered and demands that I leave here and return to the family home. He says I've been gone too long and that I should be thinking of other things than keeping you company. He would like me married, or commended to a Lord, and he thinks that your father should demand the same from you. When your father refused, my father commanded me to return home. I'm sorry Northman, but I've come only to say goodbye."

Northman's heart sank at the news. He knew he'd been with Eadric too long, but while he could remain he'd decided to. Eadric needed watching and other than Mildryth, who had no recourse to anyone, he seemed to be the only person who could do it.

"My friend," he said, standing next to him and offering him an arm clasp of friendship, "it's not your fault. Your father has been generous to allow us to remain together for so long. Don't hate him for a reasonable request."

"I will Northman. It burns inside me, the dishonour of the thing. I came with you to be your companion while you were forced to endure Eadric. It's not my fault it's been so long, and my father should see that." He grumbled as he spoke, apparently having rehearsed his arguments many times over on his return journey.

"Did my father say nothing about my leaving?"

Here Olaf looked at him slyly,

"He said it was your choice to make. You could petition the king to leave now if you so wished. Eadric clearly thinks little enough of you that he didn't even take you with him. But he knows, and I know, that you'll do no such thing."

A little dismayed to find that his father was allowing him to make his own decisions in this matter, Northman didn't know what to say or how to feel. His father was accepting he was a man now, and that was a strange thing to discover in the animal barn, knee deep in manure, in the middle of a snowstorm. The thought of going home made him happy, a crazy smile lighting his face, but then it fell again. If he left, he'd never see Mildryth again, or be able to save her from Eadric, and he'd know next to nothing about Eadric's latest plans, even if he had excluded him from a winter at the king's halls.

"It pains me Olaf, but, you're right, I feel I should stay, but that shouldn't stop you from being pleased to return home. If I didn't feel as though I had to watch Eadric, I'd go."

"And no one has considered that I've made the same commitment," Olaf roared, and Northman started to realise the root of the problem.

"Your honour won't have been impinged if you leave. Few even understood why you came with me in the first place."

"Oh stop trying to make it better," Olaf snapped, striding from the barn, "we all know it isn't and I'm not going to forgive my father for this. Never."

Into the sudden silence, a traitorous thought entered Northman's mind. With Olaf gone for good, he could continue his friendship with Mildryth. There was no reason for anyone to know. Not while the winter still raged and Eadric was absent from his home.

Two days later Olaf left again, for good this time, in a foul mood made even fouler Northman suspected because Olaf had realised that rather than ignoring Mildryth in his absence, he'd grown closer to her.

"You're a bloody idiot Northman," he whispered harshly as he mounted up, "your father will disown you and so will I. You know it, she knows it, so get it through your thick head. And to make matters worse, you'll be playing straight into Eadric's hands. Why do you think he left her here?"

Without so much as a goodbye, Olaf left then, his shoulders tense, his horse side stepping in frustration as it tried to gauge the mood of its rider.

Northman turned away, just as angry and cursed himself for not being able to see the truth in front of him. Olaf was right. It was a trap, pure and simple and one that he'd unwittingly fallen into, thigh deep. But then, he returned to the warmth of the fire and Mildryth's gentle presence. Cursing himself, he knew there was nothing for it. He was head over heels in love with the niece of his father's enemy.

He spoke with her a little, sat with her a lot and watched Edith's haunted eyes as she watched the beginning of a relationship born out of mutual affection bloom before her eyes. She never chastised either of them and Eadric's father, newly restored to health although weak and frail, seemed to view it with satisfaction now. And still, Northman couldn't keep away from her.

As the weather began to warm, Northman found himself spending more and more time outside, luxuriating in the gentle heat of the sun. He'd walk to the small river nearby and sit on the banks, or lie flat out watching the birds' overhead, listening to the delighted cries of the animals released from their winter pens. He'd still ride to the border, but it was more out of habit than anything.

It was on the bank that Mildryth came upon him one day, a huge smile on her face at finding themselves utterly alone.

"Northman," she said, sitting beside him.

"Mildryth," he responded, noting how the sun made her auburn hair shine brightly and brought a glow of deep blue to her bouncing eyes. She was truly beautiful, and he wanted to take her in his arms more than anything, but he held himself back. He didn't want to take their relationship any further but had a feeling that she perhaps did.

Un-braiding her hair, she let it fall like a curtain around her face, and he couldn't stop himself from reaching out to brush it back.

"You shouldn't hide behind your hair. You have a beautiful face," he muttered softly as he ran his hands along the curve of her chin. She felt soft under his touch, soft and warm and he closed his eyes as he wound his hand around to the back of her neck.

He wanted to kiss her, more than anything in the world. Everything else had faded away to nothing. There was no sound, no noise, and no commotion that could disturb him now.

She leant into his touch, further forward until she pressed her body against his, and there was no time for thought or to stop it.

He kissed her once, gently, her lips pliant under his own. He pulled away quickly, worried he'd caused offence, but she didn't move, her eyes meeting his own. They met again in another gentle kiss, longer this time, and far more intimate.

He pulled her to him, crushing her against him, feeling her breasts brush against his chest, and he sharply inhaled as she moaned a little in pleasure.

Their kiss deepened, as his need for her rose, and suddenly, she was lying on top of him, her slight body pressing him into the damp ground, and he was aware of her against him. Her breasts, her hips, her long legs. His arms snaked around her back, pulling her closer, needing her more.

One hand he allowed to fall, and he used it to run his hand up and down the side of her body, feeling the parts of her breasts and legs that weren't pressed tightly against him, and still they never stopped kissing.

Her hands explored his body with tantalising patches of warmth, and then she was under his tunic and running her hand up and down his flat stomach. The pleasure shot through him like a bolt of lightening and he swallowed a little nervously. She giggled into their kiss at his shock and laughed again as she slid herself sideways a little so that she could pull more of his tunic up and feel his mounting excitement.

He wanted to stop, knew in his mind that this step was irreversible, but his need was too great. He'd have given anything for a soft bed and a little privacy, but all they had was a grassy bank and the sun on their backs and faces.

Rolling her over completely, still with their lip locked together, he worked his hand under her rucked up dress and finally found her skin on her lower thigh. He groaned again knowing that he'd be unable to stop this from happening, and she stopped for a moment, pulling free from his lips, to hold his head up before her and look into his eyes.

"I love you Northman," she whispered, and he couldn't stop himself from returning the words.

"I love you too Mildryth." As he spoke, she pulled the brooches loose on her dress and wriggled a little to free herself from its confines until she lay before him, naked and pliant and welcoming.

He covered her nakedness with his body as he caressed and explored its wonders and then, a little impatiently, she tugged at his trousers, and he was as naked as she was, and what was about to happen between them would change their relationship forever.

A sharp cry of pain from Mildryth and Northman pulled back a little, but she beckoned him on with gentle moans of pleasure, and he immersed himself fully in the joys of first love, any thoughts of his father's wrath, or Eadric's happiness firmly in the back of his mind. An early summer's day, the perfect time for newfound love and pleasure.

# 33
# EARLY SUMMER AD1012, NORTHMAN

The following months passed in a riot of secrecy and pleasure, as Northman and Mildryth sought each other out whenever and wherever they could. He loved her more and more each time they met and knew that somehow, he'd need to gain his father's permission to marry her and take her away from here.

The realisation that when Eadric returned they'd not have time together again, made their actions a little fervent and their desire intense. And for the first time since he'd been fostered to Eadric he paid no attention to visitors or to any news that filtered through from the court. Not until, returning from another secret tryst, Northman encountered a messenger at the door, his horse foaming at the mouth from his fast ride.

"Northman," the messenger called, as Northman watched Mildryth slink her way back inside the hall.

"Yes," he replied, still replaying his time with Mildryth in his mind, almost able to feel her whole under his hands.

"This is for you," the messenger said, thrusting a parchment into his hand and then turning abruptly.

"Do you not need food or drink?" Northman queried, not remotely interested in the message he'd been given.

"No, I've to get a similar message to the archbishop."

Worry creased Northman's face then as he realised that this was a letter from his father, not Eadric after all.

"A fresh horse?" he asked, but the rider had gone in a hastily thrown up cloud of mud and water from the rain the night before.

Feeling unsteady, Northman looked at the parchment in his hand, his heart sinking and his stomach almost turning to water. The message must contain news of the direst nature.

He slit the seal and staggered as the words leapt from the page.

"Northman," his father wrote, "Eadric is now the king's leading ealdorman. He does everything he commands. The geld of £48000 has been paid to the Raiders, and they are in the process of dispersing from London and returning home. Sadly, during a night of celebration and when they still had the archbishop as a hostage, they murdered him in a drunken rage, and instead of punishing them further, the king has made an accord with Thorkell. His ships will remain within English waters, and the king will clothe and feed his shipmen."

Dismay swept through Northman. How had so much happened without him even being aware? And then he read the last part of the letter.

"The king has announced that Eadric can further redeem himself by marching into the lands of the king of Dyfed and seeing off the Viking Raiders who've settled there. He is coming home first to collect you, and the remainder of his household troops. Go with the blessing of your mother and myself."

Northman felt too weak to stand as he read and re-read the letter.

The geld had been paid to the Raiders, only for at least five hundred of them to remain in England and at the king's expense!

Eadric was fully restored as Ealdorman and acting in his king's name!

Eadric was to attack Dyfed and stir up trouble with the Borderlands, even though they'd been quiet for many years!

But worse, far worse, was the news that he was coming home. He'd discover what had happened between him and Mildryth. Northman felt his world fade away to a pinprick of consciousness as he staggered inside the hall. Mildryth glanced at his drunken demeanour in shock, and he handed the letter to her, which she quickly took to Edith to read.

Northman watched as all colour drained from Edith's face and Mildryth glanced to him in panic as she too heard the words.

Eadric was coming home, to take him away to war, and his woman, the girl to whom he was to all intents and purposes married to, carried the first swell of her pregnancy beneath her skirts. There was no possibility of their union going unnoticed, and Eadric would crow with delight that his plan to undermine everything that Leofwine had ever worked for had been undone by Northman's desire for a woman.

# 34
# THE BORDERLANDS, NORTHMAN

EADRIC HAD ARRIVED HOME IN A FLURRY OF DEMANDS AND GREAT CHEER, NOT letting anything disturb his pleasure. Nothing at all.

Somehow, in the short space of time he'd spent in his hall, he'd managed a heated argument with his father, a desultory kiss for his wife and sons, but he'd not noticed anything unusual between Northman and Mildryth.

Northman had ridden away heavy-hearted. He'd not wanted to leave her when he might never return, but she'd assured him she'd be well. Ideally, he'd wanted her to leave and seek shelter with his family, but she refused. When Northman returned, they'd make plans for their future. In the end, he'd entrusted Edith with a message to be conveyed to his father in the event of his death. She'd smiled at his concern for Mildryth and promised to do all she could to keep her safe. And she'd thanked him too, for restoring her faith in men. Her eyes were sad, but they'd glowed a little with delight at the happiness she saw before her.

Eadric was leading his men and some of the king's household troops that had previously looked to Athelstan as their Lord. Athelstan had not so much been removed from his position within Mercia, as been sent home, with his forces dispersed after he'd left. The men were angry and unhappy at the king's treatment of his oldest son, and Northman was aghast as well. He knew many of these men. They'd been encamped outside Oxford together, and he also knew that Athelstan had been much loved in the Mercian lands, forging links with the local nobility in the old heartlands of Mercia. He'd become particularly close to two of the local thegns, Morcar and Sigeforth and Northman had even heard rumours that he planned to marry one of their sisters. Once again, the king and Eadric were storing up trouble for themselves.

To travel to the lands around St David's, Eadric announced they'd go to Gloucester, and then take a ship from there. He wanted to avoid any further confrontation with the men who inhabited the border, a move that Northman approved of. He also had a sneaking feeling that Eadric planned on pretending to be Raiders themselves when they attacked the Vikings in Dyfed. He smirked at the idea and wondered if it would work.

Northman wondered too if he'd be given the opportunity to meet with his family, but Eadric cruelly baited him for much of the journey, and then purposefully pulled away from Deerhurst. Northman held his anger in check. Just. After all, he had some secrets of his own now and wasn't sure if he was ready to face his inquisitive mother. He felt sure that she'd work out what had happened before he'd even stepped through the door.

At Gloucester, Eadric's plan finalised when they were met by Thorkell and by twenty of his ships as well. Northman looked at the man carefully, and all the other faces but he didn't see Cnut with him. Then he remembered that Cnut had been summoned home, and doubtless, had not been allowed to return to the lands of the English.

Hastily, the force was loaded onto the Raiders ships, and Northman watched the smooth way the highly trained men guided the small fleet down the river and into the sea. They travelled within sight of the land, and only for a full day before they came ashore again.

Eadric and Thorkell were close. Their heads often bowed together and they could be heard laughing and joking as they plotted how they would join battle with the enemy. Northman wondered if Thorkell was aware that Eadric had not yet faced any enemy in battle. He doubted it but stilled his tongue. Eadric was already angry with him for something, and Northman feared that Æthelric had managed to share his secret with his son, although in their brief meeting they'd done nothing but argue and row.

Northman watched the coastline with interest, noting the steep cliffs and sandy beaches. The lands of the ancient British appeared as varied as the Mercian lands and enjoyed the advantages, or disadvantages, of a varied and beautiful coastline.

"Northman," Eadric called to him when they were making their camp above a sandy cove, "You'll lead a small reconnaissance team tomorrow. I need to know exactly where the men are hiding."

At his side, Thorkell stiffened at the command that had apparently not been discussed with him,

"And some of my men will come with you," he said, looking at Eadric as if daring him to argue.

"Of course Thorkell, I'm sure they'll have more experience of hunting for Raiders than young Northman here. But then, he's expendable and the rest of my men are not."

"Expendable, why do you say so?"

"The king is most displeased with his father, and if his son should die, I think the king will not care either way."

"But his father is Leofwine?" Thorkell queried, his face furrowed in confusion. "He's a great warrior and now an ally of Swein of Denmark, as I once was. Surely your king wouldn't want to force a rift with such a talented man?"

Eadric hid his annoyance poorly, as Northman listened impassively to his commands.

"I have seen this boy before, at Oxford. He is loyal and a friend of the king's sons. I wouldn't treat him so lightly."

"No but then you've not had the disappointment of being his foster-father."

"Disappointment!" Thorkell exclaimed, completely unaware that he was making things worse for Northman. "Why I hear he fought against us at Ringmere and proved himself well in battle. Cnut marked him as we fought and said he fought with genuine battle rage. That can be a rare thing."

Northman couldn't keep the shock from his face at the unlooked-for praise, and the knowledge that it came from Cnut doubly surprised him.

"And, he looks to me as though he's grown even stronger and more confident since then. And enjoyed his first woman."

Thorkell laughed at his words and walked away, oblivious to the rage burning on Eadric's face.

"Enjoyed your first woman have you boy," Eadric spat, "if I find it was my niece you'll marry her before I can make any more difficulties for your father, and then you'll have your snake living within your household."

Eadric bristled with anger and walked away without issuing any further commands.

Northman stood for a few moments longer, and then recalled himself to his task. It would not do to dwell on the future now. If, or when he returned to Shropshire he'd deal with the almighty mess he'd made for himself.

In all, ten of them set off to track down the Viking Raiders campsite. It didn't take them long either, as they tripped carefully along the jagged cliff tops, being careful not to fall into the crashing waves below.

Men he knew accompanied Northman, but still, he missed Olaf's good cheer now that he was away from Mildryth. Thorkell's men were a sullen bunch, evidently unhappy at their allying with the English. They spoke amongst themselves but made no effort to talk to Northman and his comrades. Northman listened to their desultory comments about the English but didn't show that he understood nearly all they said. One thing was sure though. Thorkell might well have defected to the English king, but his men were unhappy with that decision.

The smell of burning and the raucous noise of laughter directed them to the Raiders encamped close to a river but far enough inland that they'd not be caught out by sudden high tides. In the flickering flames and the dull moonlight, Northman peered at the encampment before them. Whatever he'd been expecting, this wasn't it.

The Raiders had evidently been encamped for a long time, making Northman wonder what the urgency had been. They'd built houses out of wood and had constructed defences around them. It didn't look at all like it would be an easy battle to drive the men out. They were sheltered on a small raised platform that looked out to the river and the distant sea.

Confused Northman looked at his fellow warriors with concern.

"I thought it was a temporary camp we were attacking?" he whispered. The other English men nodded to show they'd thought as much as well, and then, finally, one of Thorkell's men spoke to them.

"No, they've overwintered here. Thorkell knew of them and told the king of them. Eadric pounced on the opportunity to attack them. He wants a victory against my people so that he can count himself as proficient in battle as Uhtred and Ulfcytel and your father. He's an idiot. Attacking my people isn't easy."

Northman held the man's gaze for a moment longer and thought himself an idiot to be duped by Eadric again. No doubt he'd brought him out here so that he could lose his life in some half-hearted attack against a far superior force. Not for the first time, he wished he'd had the courage to go home, with Mildryth and his, as yet, unborn child.

'The king wants the Raiders moving on as well. They've been

attacking shipping in and out of Bristol and the traders are becoming concerned."

Northman sighed audibly, this time, his thoughts angry. To die in battle was one thing, but to die because the king was worried about his tax was quite enough.

On the return walk to where they'd left the ships, he consoled himself with the knowledge that he was a mean warrior. He'd live through this, and he'd go home to Mildryth, his mother and his father.

# 35
# NEAR ST DAVID'S, AD1012, NORTHMAN

Deciding that it was imperative to attack as quickly as possible, Eadric and Thorkell decided that they'd confront the Raiders immediately. Uncaring of the few who'd been up all night looking for the enemy campsite, they were all ordered back to the ships, fully armoured, and told that they'd be attacking without delay.

Thorkell laughed at the challenge, enjoying the thrill of the battle to come. Eadric looked a little less happy, and Northman felt his anger flare at him. In a small party such as this, he had no choice but to be involved. Untested as he was in battle, he clearly intended to lead them, or at least direct their every move. Northman fancied it would be a disaster and resolved to listen to Thorkell's commands over Eadric's. That man knew how to fight and more importantly, how to win.

In the end, it was no great battle at all. They directed their ships up the river and beached them on the shore before the small settlement. All was quiet there, and Northman had an inkling that they'd witnessed a feast last night and that all slept, safe in the knowledge that no one was going to come and rouse them from their beds and force them to fight.

Thorkell chuckled at the lack of defence, and indicated that only half of the ships should disembark, the others could stay where they were. For all that there were a number of wooden houses, the force looked to be slight, and it was the frightened face of a sleepy faced youth who became the first victim, cut down where he stood, by Thorkell.

They moved quietly through the still streets, and at Thorkell's command, as Eadric somehow appeared to have stayed on board one of the ships, simultaneously entered both the front and the back door on the main wooden hall.

A fire smouldered in the grate, and a shrill scream from a woman met their appearance, but before any of the men could rouse themselves, a warrior was at their throats and slashed them where they lay. A pool of blood formed under Northman's hand and he felt sickened by the carnage. There was no honour in this killing. None at all.

The woman's cry brought no one rushing to her aid, not even other women. Instead, Thorkell and his men moved stealthily through the settlement of twenty houses, murdering every man they found, but keeping the few woman. A permanent camp it may well have been, but not yet secure enough for the Raiders to have collected their families and settled them there as well.

And all Thorkell's men could concern themselves with was finding any goods of value. They rifled the dead men's clothes, taking armbands where they found them, and golden trinkets and any weapons that they fancied.

It was almost over before it had begun and the houses were fired, and the twenty or so women lead onto Thorkell's ship. He'd clearly claimed them for himself. Eadric didn't step foot on shore, not once, leaving the work to Thorkell and his own men.

Northman watched him angrily, his mouth twitching as he fought his resolve to just tell him what he thought of him, once and for all. Annoyed, he stomped onto his own ship, his sleeves stained with the blood of a man who'd put up absolutely no resistance when his life had been taken. Northman decided he wouldn't be that passive again. Never.

# 36
# DEERHURST, AD1012, LEOFWINE

His anger was palpable, vibrating in the air around him and sending all that knew him scurrying from his rage. Well all apart from Æthelflæd. She stayed in the room, a faint smile on her face as she watched him. He knew exactly what she was thinking, and it exasperated him to know how well she knew him.

He let her have her way. Eventually, he'd calm down, and she'd chide him, and he'd feel a fool but for now, his anger was a burning brand lacing his back.

How dare he? How dare his good for nothing oldest son come within spitting distance of home and not call upon his mother, who he'd not seen now for years, not just a few seasons.

In his heart, he knew it wasn't his son's fault that he'd not come, but he needed to vent, and it was easier to direct it at his missing son than at any other.

He'd more than half hoped when he'd given Olaf his cryptic message about it being Northman's choice whether he returned home or stayed, that Northman would finally lay aside the mantle of responsibility he'd assumed and come home to his family. He missed him, and he wanted to spend time with him before he married and left the family home with more permanence than a foster arrangement.

He should have known better, and he blamed bloody Wulfstan for it all. If he'd not instilled such honour within the boy, he'd have come home years ago.

Ah, whom was he trying to fool? He knew it was his honour that the lad had inherited. And he was aware that it had done him little good, and was doing Northman even less. He needed to be away from the poisonous atmosphere that Eadric had created and colluded with the king upon. He needed to be home with his family, in disgrace, but together, so who cared what the king was about.

And to come so close to home, without so much a hello or goodbye, without making the effort to push Eadric towards his home was a sign of how great that honour ran. Eadric and his mother loathed each other, and Wulfstan had never had a good word to say about Eadric. That coupled with the knowledge that he'd gone to fight on behalf of Eadric and the turncoat Thorkell, riled all the more.

"You know you're only angry at yourself," his wife said testily after he'd nearly worn a hole in the floor. Initially, his ageing dog had kept pace with him, but the beast now slept beside Æthelflæd, warming her feet with his exposed belly. Leofwine envied the dog.

"That doesn't make it any better," he snapped at her, and her eyes flashed briefly with anger. And now he was thinking the same about her that she was about him. She was beautiful when she was angry, her cheeks flushing and her mouth set in an angry line.

Against all the odds, she smiled at him then.

"Come Leofwine, take your ease beside me, and if I can, I'll let you forget your troubles for a few moments." Her eyebrows were raised suggestively at him, and he'd have liked nothing better to do than to bury his problems within her. But, and he knew for a fact he'd done it, he'd shouted at everyone within his household, and he needed to make amends to both Wulfstan and his son, Leofric, who'd brought the news to him in the first place. It was neither of theirs fault that Northman had been so tantalisingly close and yet so far away at the same time.

"He better come home in one piece," he eventually relented, trying to avoid the gentle tug on her lips from her suppressed smile, "or I'll kill Eadric once and for all."

"Come on you know you don't mean that," she said, surprised by his continuing vehemence.

"You just watch if you don't think I do," he countered, pleased he'd shocked her.

"Northman will be well. Not because he's with Eadric but because he is, as you have told me, an excellent warrior and he has the most successful Viking leader with him that this land has ever known, Thorkell. The man knows tactics and how to win. He'll not let Eadric sway him. He won't harm his men. He's not a reckless man. Everything he's done in the last three years shows he's devious and quick-witted."

Leofwine stopped mid-step then. He'd truly not considered that. His son had been gone for too long. He still visualised the slight youth who'd left four years before, forgetting that in the intervening years he'd faced death and battle and become a man.

Smiling he turned to Æthelflæd,

"You're right. Thank you. I sometimes forget that he's a man grown and no longer a boy."

"You forget that you're getting old and fussy like an old woman," she countered, enjoying the outrage on his face. "Now, go and apologise to your son and your old friend. I don't want to see you in here until you've performed your duties."

A little sulkily still, for all that she'd been right to confront him, he marched through their wooden doorway and strode into the hall. It fell strangely quiet as he did so, and realising how his rage had affected everyone, he stood for a moment, until the eyes of all were upon him.

"My apologies for my wrath," he said loudly so that all could hear. "It was none of your faults, and I acted irrationally. I hope you'll accept my apology."

Hooded eyes glanced at him, from his youngest son to his oldest friend, but then Wulfstan called out,

"You always were a petulant boy," and a whisper of laughter ran through the room, that intensified when they saw Leofwine's smirk for Wulfstan. He was forgiven in a heartbeat, and he walked towards Wulfstan and Leofric. Clearly, the older man had been consoling, the younger lad.

"Leofric, I was wrong to berate you for something you couldn't stop, and Wulfstan, I was wrong to attack you for backing the boy up. Will you both forgive me?"

Wulfstan smiled widely at the apology, but Leofric still looked haughty with annoyance. Wulfstan slapped the unresponsive boy on the arm, and Leofric looked at him a little angrily, before softening his face.

"Alright, I forgive you, but Father, you need to hold your tongue far better. The things you said were truly shocking, and I'm sure word will get back to the king. There were traders and farmers aplenty within the hall when you lashed out at him."

Leofwine grimaced a little, but then smiled,

"He'll only have himself to blame if he has something reported back to him that he doesn't like. He should learn to bloody well trust me, especially after all these years."

Shrugging Leofric turned back to the game of boards he and Wulfstan had been playing but not before Leofwine heard him whisper,

"And you better remember that when he punishes you further."

Leofwine ignored the comment. He'd just about had enough of the king and hadn't forgiven him for his behaviour last year, or for his purposeful exclusion of him at the meeting in London with Thorkell. The news of the archbishop of Canterbury's death had shocked Leofwine, coming as it did at the hands of the Raiders after the geld had been paid. To know that the king had now made terms with Thorkell chaffed even more. Could the king not work out for himself who to trust and who to disregard? Clearly not.

# 37
# SHROPSHIRE, AD1012, NORTHMAN

THE COLONY OF RAIDERS NEAR ST DAVID'S SUCCESSFULLY ANNIHILATED, they were not long in returning to Gloucester, and from there to Eadric's home. Each jangle of the horse's tack frayed Northman's nerves. He wanted to get home to see Mildryth, assure himself that she was well, but on the other hand, Eadric would immediately suspect and guess and then he'd make Northman's life untenable.

He'd spent his few nights away from home berating himself for his inability to stay away from the girl, but he knew that he'd fall willingly into her arms when he returned. He wanted to feel her hot breath on his cheek as they joined, and hear her small gasps of pleasure from his touch. And now that she suspected she carried their child, he felt even more protective of her. He must devise a way to marry her and get her away from Eadric. And it needed to be soon.

The early summer was well on its way when they pulled their horses to a stop outside the hall. Boys and slaves ran to take the animals away from those Eadric had allowed within his courtyard, the majority of the men he'd instructed to erect camps away from his home. Thorkell, he'd left at Gloucester. The raider had promised to return to Sandwich with his half of the fleet and Northman had watched him leave with some regret. No matter the damage done to England at his hands, he was a competent commander, open and honest with his men and respected all the more for that.

At the doorway, he caught a fleeting glimpse of Mildryth's flushed and excited face, but she must have disappeared by the time he strode into the hall, Eadric already yelling commands and demands to his wife and servants.

His oldest son, a sturdy lad of three, toddled to his father and Eadric lifted him high in the air with a wide grin, but the little boy only burst into tears unsure who the stranger was. Annoyed, Eadric dropped him to the ground, and he ran towards Mildryth his hands outstretched towards her.

She clasped him to her chest, and as she did so, Eadric's eyes narrowed, and a smirk of pleasure lit his face.

"I see you had her boy, and now you will take her as your wife. I'll inform your father at once."

Instantly alarmed, Northman wondered how he should proceed for the best.

"I have every intention of making her my wife, my Lord, and with your consent, and I'll happily contact my family about it. I'll not stint her at all."

"I know you'll not boy," Eadric spoke quietly and with deadly seriousness, "but boy, you can only have her if ... certain conditions are met."

Northman's heart sank, and he turned to look at Mildryth's suddenly white face.

"You need not concern yourself with the details. I'll send a messenger to your father immediately. You've taken advantage of my family's hospitality towards you, and you've bedded my niece. I'll have to seek reparation for your soiling of her, and the fact that I'll have to take you as my nephew by marriage. Your father will understand that my demands are reasonable. Now Mildryth," and he turned to her then, "get out of my sight and don't let me see you again unless it is to say goodbye to me when you leave for your new home." His tone was icy cold, and pity for Mildryth almost forced Northman to speak in her defence. But he knew better. Instead, when Eadric turned away he mouthed a sorry to her, and she replied by shrugging and mouthing that she loved him. And really, that was all that mattered.

# 38

## SUMMER, AD1012, LEOFWINE

Once more rage engulfed him. Of all the stupid things to do, he couldn't quite believe that his honourable and staid older son had managed to get himself involved with his enemy's niece. It was beyond comprehension, and he was not so much a fool as to deny it, entirely in keeping with Eadric's scheming ways. He could only be grateful that it hadn't happened sooner, but still, as before when he'd not visited his family, his anger was a physical force.

Eadric had sent his messenger to Leofwine, a haughty faced individual with acquisitive eyes, and a pinched face. Leofwine had hated him on sight, a rarity for him, and had hated even more the demands he'd made.

In exchange for his niece, Eadric demanded land that he'd long coveted but which had long been a part of the inheritance of Leofwine's family. No amount of cajoling or pouting before the king had allowed him to claim the land, but now he did, and more besides. He wanted the land near his home in Shropshire, and he also wanted an obscene amount of coinage as well, not to mention an assurance that from henceforth, Leofwine would stop using the term

Ealdorman of Mercia. That riled because Leofwine never used the word about himself, and it wasn't his fault if others still regarded him as their Lord. Eadric should have worked harder to ensure their loyalty.

He also wanted a public apology from the boy, before the king, and an assurance that his niece would be handsomely provided with another plot of land, near to the one he wanted, and which would remain hers no matter what. Leofwine was candescent with rage, Æthelflæd at his side white with the shock and knowledge that she'd soon be a grandmother.

A grandmother. That thought chilled him. Æthelflæd was little aged in their long years together, and he thought it outrageous that his son should have prematurely aged her by being reckless with his wants and needs.

He turned to tell her as such, but she was sat with a faint smile on her face, and he wondered if perhaps, just perhaps she was pleased with the news.

"It'll be a blessing for this house, no matter that Eadric is involved. Give him what he wants, make him believe he's won, but let the boy come home and bring his wife with him."

Leofwine felt his jaw drop open in shock as she spoke, and he tried to reorder his thoughts. Could he do that? Could he just let Eadric get away with the manipulation of his son? With the possible ruin of his future happiness?

Old, frail Wulfstan looked across the hall at him, shaking his head softly from side to side in an apparent 'no' gesture, and Leofwine realised he'd be alone in this. None of the others would want to make so much of it as if the imminent birth of a child made it allowable to forget all past indiscretions. Leofwine wasn't at all convinced but realised that once more he'd have to try and take the upper hand, work this to his advantage in the long term.

Shaking his head, he curled himself back into his seat, signalling to the messenger that he agreed to the demands and bidding him be on his way as soon as he'd eaten and drunk. He'd take back little gossip with him. Leofwine glowered into the fire.

Men and boys.

Women and girls.

Babies and grandparents.

None of it thrilled him, but it was life, and he'd accept it.

# 39
# DEERHURST, LATE AD1012, NORTHMAN

FINALLY, AND ONLY AFTER MORE HAGGLING THAN WAS NECESSARY, EADRIC had consented to the wedding and he and Mildryth had been married only the day before in his father's local church, the abbot pleased to act for his lord, although Leofwine was ill-humoured about it all. To those who didn't know him well, they'd have thought him overjoyed, but Northman knew his father and knew that internally he was seething.

Northman felt anger, hurt and grief overwhelm him. He'd wanted his father to be happy for him, but he feared he was too angry with his son and Eadric's demands to make the best of the situation.

The marriage had been performed not a day too soon for in the night, Mildryth had woken, in pain. The child was keen to make its presence felt.

Pleased that they were staying with his parents, regardless of his father's rancour, Northman had felt confident in alerting his mother to his wife's need, and the house had burst into activity on the chilly Winter day. Fires burned and water boiled, and Mildryth cried in pain and grunted in agony and Northman didn't know what to do with himself.

He was terrified of this new responsibility about to be presented to him, and he was worried for his wife. She'd reassured him that she would birth the babe well, but doubt clouded his judgement and he moodily pondered the fire.

Wulfstan joined him, his movements were slow and ponderous, his eyes a little cloudy and his hands shaky.

"It'll go well lad, don't worry."

Northman offered a genuine smile of thanks for his assurance.

"So everyone tells me."

"Well if everyone tells you then it must be the truth," Wulfstan coughed a little wetly.

"Are you ill Wulfstan?" Northman asked, concern making him dance a little around Wulfstan as he made himself comfortable in a beautiful wood chair.

"Yes, ill and old and buggered," Wulfstan coughed again. "But I don't fear death so don't fear it for me. I've lived well past any use I could offer your father."

Northman swallowed his grief, his throat aching with tears he couldn't shed.

"But I'll miss you," he offered sadly, and Wulfstan reached for his hand and held it within his bone dry one.

"And I'll miss you too. You've been like a grandson to me, and I'm proud of all you've done, and your father will be one day as well."

"I hope so," Northman sighed. "I didn't mean to disappoint him."

"It's not you who's disappointed him. It's the king and Eadric, but worse than that, he's disappointed himself. So busy trying to play politics with the king, he's missed you growing into the man you are, and sadly, there's nothing that can bring back those lost years."

"But he allowed me to go to Eadric."

"He consented, it's not the same thing. He didn't want to, and your absence has caused him distress."

"And I've missed him too," Northman said, glancing at the door behind which his father still slept. He'd have quite liked him to wait with him.

"Promise me you'll reconcile with him," Wulfstan suddenly said meaningfully, "sometimes the son must act more the adult than the father, and this is one of those rare occasions."

"You mean I should attempt to win his forgiveness?" Northman queried, feeling his rage mount.

"Yes, for father's can lack vision where their enemies are concerned."

"I don't think I can do that Wulfstan," Northman said feeling genuinely sorry to upset the old man.

"I didn't mean this very moment. But think about it, for my sake. I'll be gone soon, and I'd like to know that you'll be allies again. One day."

"I'll think about it, but nothing more," Northman said after a long silence, during which he thought of almost anything but asking his father for forgiveness.

"You're a good man Northman. Quick witted and gentle but strong and fierce when you need to be. They're good qualities to have."

And between one word and the next, Wulfstan slept and Northman felt his loneliness engulf him once more. He prayed for the sunrise and for Mildryth to deliver their child without any problems. Slumped forwards, with his elbows on his knees, he had an inkling that being thought a man would perhaps not be the great achievement he'd always thought it'd be. Already responsibility weighed him down.

# 40

## AD1012, LEOFWINE

Fuzzy headed, it took him an age to recognise the cry of a newborn baby echoing around his hall.

He'd drunk too much the night before, Horic plying him with cup after cup of mead in the hope of making him relent in his anger against his son. It hadn't worked, and now Leofwine grimaced. It seemed he had to face the embodiment of his son's bad decision making, and with a pounding head as well.

At the foot of his bed, Hammer looked at him with accusing eyes, and Leofwine rolled over in frustration. Even the bloody dog didn't approve of his anger. But, he couldn't make it go away. He couldn't just accept what had happened, no matter how much he wanted to.

The door to their room opened, and Æthelflæd entered with a delighted grin on her face.

"A boy, Leofwine, you have a grandson."

He groaned, and she started to giggle with delight, running her hands over her slim waist. He knew she longed for another child, but he thought it unlikely that she'd have another now. It had been too many years since Eadwine's birth and she'd not shown any signs since. He knew she'd dote upon this new baby, regardless of its heritage.

"Is it hale?" he queried, knowing that his petulance shouldn't detract from that important fact.

"Yes, lusty and big. Just like his father before him. Will you come and see him?"

"No, not now, my head pounds too much, and it's crying."

Again a smirk of pleasure,

"Newborn babies always cry and old men always drink too much mead, but that's the way of the world." It was clear that her good cheer was beyond dimming.

Momentarily he considered forgetting his ill humour and greeting his son with the pride and joy he deserved but then, between one breath and the next, his world fell apart.

A loud knocking at the door and Leofric burst, not ungently, through the doorway, his face bleached with shock.

"What is it Leofric?" his mother asked, turning to hasten out of the door. "Is it the baby?"

"No mother, the baby is fine. Listen you can hear him?"

"Then what?" she asked.

But Leofwine was out of bed, his stomach in his shoes. He knew what that look portended.

Staggering from his bed, relieved to find himself dressed, Hammer preceded him into the silent hall. Few were actually out of their beds, most recovering from the excesses of the wedding feast last night. But of those, there was one face missing, and it would always be missing from now on.

On leaden legs, Leofwine walked towards the fire and the wooden chair that Wulfstan had long occupied. Leofwine had insisted on its construction when his back started to ache and sleep became almost impossible.

Now the small form within the confines of the chair covered with blankets, was still and quiet, almost as though he slept, only his eyes were open, and a small smile covered his face.

Bereft, Leofwine struggled to stand. Hammer immediately at his one side, and his wife at the other. Still, his knees buckled and he tripped over his own feet in his desire to get both close to his friend and stay as far away as possible from the truth of what had happened.

Leofric had returned to Wulfstan's side, reaching out once more to test that no breath came through the still form, but Leofwine knew in his heart that his oldest friend, mentor and dearest father figure had breathed his last.

Hastily, Ealdgyth pushed a stall under his wavering body, and gently he placed himself on the stool beside Wulfstan so that he could take his friend's hand in his own, and hold it just one last time.

The hands were devoid of their strength that had guided him throughout the last twenty years of his life and grief overwhelmed him. No, not Wulfstan.

He was unaware of the activity going on around him, as Æthelflæd commanded the servants to make ready a place in the outer barn to lie Wulfstan out before his burial, and also called for the local priest to come and sit with him. Neither was he aware of Horic standing beside him, and squeezing his shoulder, or of the sadness on Oscetel's face.

He sat, as candles burned low and the wind and rain lashed his home, and he did not move. Not once.

He dropped his head to the arm of the chair beside Wulfstan's hand, and he looked at his friend and took in all that he could. Someone had seen to his eyes, and they were now closed so that he looked as though he slept, and his body had not cooled because it sat before the fire and Leofwine hoped that at any moment his friend would open his eyes and all would be well. But it was a futile hope. Wulfstan was gone.

Soft words were spoken to him, words of condolence and sympathy but nothing permeated his sadness. Nothing could break through the horror he felt engulfed by.

He knew Wulfstan had wanted this. He'd been ill all summer

long, and Leofwine had suspected that he'd fought to stay alive, to see his son reconciled with his father, and to see the birth of the new baby, but to know that the birth had caused the loss of his friend caused his blood to boil with rage. And then bitterness consumed him.

How dare the baby be born so soon? He'd not had the time to say his goodbyes, to thank his friend, to tell him how much he loved him and respected him.

How dare Northman be the cause of all this upset?

Before him his son materialised, his eyes shining with joy, his child cradled in his arms as he held him out for his father and Wulfstan to inspect.

Leofwine reacted angrily, not even looking at the child, or meeting his son's eyes, but striding out of the door into a maelstrom of wind and rain.

He didn't notice the confusion on Northman's face or the grief as it crumbled as he realised that no one had told him of his father's loss. But by then, it was all too late.

# 41
# DEERHURST, AD1012, NORTHMAN

ANGER INFUSED HIS EVERY STEP, THOUGHT AND WORD. NO MATTER HOW much his mother tried to smooth the waters it was too little too late, and he couldn't, just couldn't forgive his father for his dismissal of his newborn son. Regardless of Wulfstan's sudden loss, his father should have shared his joy. Wulfstan would have wanted that, demanded it in fact.

He'd been forced to return to Mildryth, a smile of joy plastered on his face, telling her of how pleased everyone was with their joyful news. He knew she'd not commented on just how little time he'd been within the hall or the outpouring of grief she'd heard, too tired to note anything.

As sleep had claimed her, he'd slumped to the bed beside her, clutching his son, and holding his wife's hand as tears pooled down his face. Not Wulfstan, not now!

His mother had found him there, her grief enveloping her, slowing her actions and clouding her face. She'd held her son and wept with him, and finally, their tears had turned to joy at the tiny bundle he held in his arms, protectively.

She'd spoken of her joy and her love for his new son, but when she'd tried to apologise for his father's actions his heart had hardened, and his anger had resurfaced. And all credit to her, she'd realised and quickly changed the conversation. Her eyes worried and hooded at this devastating occurrence.

Later than night, when he'd been sat by the fire, nodding himself to sleep, his father had come to him, face all apologetic, his grief weighing him down so that his footsteps were uneven although tired old Hammer kept pace with his master. Northman had heard his words of regret and apology, but he couldn't forget what had happened. Ignoring his father had been one of the hardest things he'd ever done, but he'd made his decision as to his next actions, and they didn't involve his father. No, he was going back to Eadric, to demand to become his commended man, to swear his oath and live on his lands. At least with Eadric, he knew to expect disappointment.

The next month had passed painfully slowly while Mildryth recovered from the birth. With no word to anyone he'd hustled his son and his wife from his father's hall in the chill early morning without forewarning anyone, not even Mildryth.

She'd been confused and concerned as she'd held her son close to her chest, but it was Leofric who'd spoken, his brother coming upon him in the animal barn as he made his horse ready for their journey.

"What are you doing brother?" he asked.

"Leaving. I think it's pretty obvious."

"So why sneak away like this?"

Northman didn't answer his question,

"What are you doing here Leofric?" he asked instead.

"I've been watching you, and mother's been watching you. We both knew that you were planning something, but this, I would have expected more from you."

"And I would have expected more from my father, but then, it looks like we've both been disappointed." His words were angry, rage flooding through his body at the reminder of what drove his actions.

Atop her horse, Mildryth looked confused and concerned in equal measure.

"Your father?" she queried. "What's he done?"

"It doesn't matter. All that matters is that we leave here. Now."

"You've not even told her then?" Leofric pressed, and Northman felt his anger surfacing at his brother.

"There was no need," he replied in a quietly raging voice, his eyes boring into his brother's in the hope that he'd not speak further. He couldn't, just couldn't tell his wife the truth of what had happened.

Shrugging Leofric looked at him but held his tongue,

"As you will brother, but remember, he's just a man and men make mistakes. All the time. And brother," he'd been in the process of turning around but looked back to meet his eyes once more, "remember that your mother loves you, as do I and your other brothers and sister. We'll assist in any way we can. And so will father."

And without so much as a backwards glance, Leofric was gone, and Northman felt his resolve crumble, but then his son cried out, and he looked at his innocent face, and his anger returned full force. No, he'd not ignore what his father had done.

The journey to Shropshire had been hazardous and slow going. Mildryth, still weak and sore from her birth, had grumbled not once, but he'd been aware of her slow movements and gasps of pain. The short winter's day had afforded them little time to make headway in the weak sun, but somehow they'd made it to Eadric's hall.

Swallowing his fear at coming back to this place, he'd walked calmly into Eadric's hall, Mildryth carrying her son with pride and at last, and quite unexpectedly, he'd received the welcome he'd been hoping to receive from his father.

Eadric had spoken not one single derisive word, instead of saying he'd arrange for them to have a home to call their own shortly and that in the meantime they were welcome within the hall. Mildryth, worried to be back with her Uncle and Father, had been greeted with delight by Edith who'd secreted her away so that they could discuss babies and children and motherhood away from the men. Brihtric had handed Northman a mead cup full to the top and together he'd toasted his son's birth and spoken of the future.

Late into the night, they'd drunk and spoken of trifling matters, no mention of Leofwine or the king or the Raiders and Northman had reached the drunken decision that he'd acted as he should have done. In this house of his father's enemy, he would always be welcome, and now, finally acknowledged as a man by all, he hoped he'd be gifted with land and his household troops. He'd work for the benefit of Eadric in everything he did, hoped he'd forget all about his father. He'd abandoned him long ago, and now Northman felt that he could abandon him back. No more would he look to be recognised as the son of the Ealdorman of the Hwicce. No more.

# 42

# AD1013, NORTHMAN

Northman and Mildryth had pondered long and hard about what to name their son before his birth, but the death of Wulfstan had made them change their mind so that despite his rift with his father, he decided that he needed to honour his grandfather in all but name. So little Wulfstan grew well and strong within the household of Eadric, the idea that Northman should have his own home somehow forgotten in the rush of everyday activities, as was his demand to become his commended man. Eadric was not often at home, called to serve the king often. Without him, it was almost as if they didn't dwell within Eadric's home.

Mildryth, pleased to have Edith as her companion, never complained and Northman, happy to be back amongst the household troops, training daily, was pleased not to shoulder the burdens of fatherhood all on his own. If any had dared to comment that he had the responsibilities of a man and yet seemed to be sidestepping them all, he'd not have reacted well, but while he lived a little in denial, he was content.

Eadric had found him a willing accomplice in his efforts to further undermine Leofwine and any initial unease at what he was doing, soon evaporated when the king presented him with his first grant of land within the Mercian lands. Eadric assured him that it had been his work that had ensured his favour with the king, and at the Witan to confirm the grant, Northman studiously ignored any overtures from his father to reach an accord. He didn't care that even the king commented on his father's virtues. He'd made his decision, and he would stick with it.

Leofric congratulated him heartily, as did Oscetel when they chanced upon each other, and neither mentioned his father. Northman was grateful and relieved all at the same time. Even Eadric rarely mentioned his father and somehow, the year turned slowly towards the summer with Northman thinking that his life was complete and fulfilled. Gifts came from his mother for the baby, and Mildryth crowed with delight over them all and gently pressed her husband to arrange for them to meet again. Northman agreed happily, content in the knowledge that his father would be busy about his duties. And so, with the summer sun high overhead, a stark contrast to the wintry night he'd left his home on, he returned to his childhood home to reunite with his mother and allow her time with her grandchild.

It was on that journey, on a pleasant patch of meadowland bordered by a gently gurgling stream where Northman received devastating news. Leofric, apparently looking for him, came upon them in a shower of churned mud and foaming horse, his eyes haunted and relieved to have found his quarry all at the same time.

"Leofric," Northman gasped, "what brings you here?"

Instantly, and traitorously, his thoughts had turned to his father. Had something befallen him?

"Northman come, you must get to Deerhurst immediately. A calamity has befallen us again. Swein, Swein of Denmark has attacked Sandwich."

Shock and horror and a screech of terror from Mildryth had Northman moving without thinking. Swein? What the hell was Swein doing attacking England?

"Where did you hear the news," he asked, roughly helping Mildryth to mount her horse. He passed Wulfstan to her, and then mounted his horse, his hound lagging at his feet. The old beast was too old to have made such a long journey, and he more than anything, was the reason they'd stopped. Looking from his wife to his brother, to his son and his hound, he hauled the dog up beside himself on his saddle. The old dog looked relieved and embarrassed all at the same time.

"Father has sent news from the Witan. The king has received messengers, at least five of them from the eastern coast, and they all confirm the details. It's a massive fleet, Northman, even surpassing Thorkell's."

"And there was no warning?"

"None, not even Thorkell knew of what was to come. His fleet was at London undergoing repairs, but they've sailed out to try to counter Swein, but I fear it's too late. He already has a foothold on English land."

There was no chance for talk to continue then as they all turned their horses towards Deerhurst. What had started as a pleasant summer's journey suddenly taking on a whole new impetus. Northman felt a cold certainty take root within his body. Somehow, and he didn't know how he knew this, this new invasion signalled something far more concerning than anything that had gone before. Olaf, who'd murdered his grandfather, Swein in the past and Thorkell more recently, they'd come only for easy money and easy plunder. Swein, now the very well respected and revered king of Denmark and part of Norway, able to snap his fingers and have four thousand specially trained troops do his work, was a whole new challenge.

The land, so tired of the constant attacks of the recent years, had thought itself free from the depravations the Raiders inflicted, and an almost fair-like spirit had infected everyone. No one was ready for another attack. The ships from the ship army were still in good repair, but they were beached high above the water lines at Sandwich and London, the king content to let the effective command of Thorkell keep his lands safe. Once more, it appeared he'd put his trust in the wrong man.

His mother greeted them at Deerhurst, her face both concerned and joyful at the same time. His father's household troops had been busy amassing and in a conflicted moment Northman didn't know what to do. Should he rush home to his men, or stay here and travel with Leofric and the men to where Leofwine was awaiting them?

It was Horic who made the decision for him, with Olaf at his side,

"Well don't stand there looking like a useless mule, get your things together. Take what you don't have from the extras in the storage shed."

His tone was abrupt but kindly, and Northman noticed that his mother had already taken command of Mildryth and Wulfstan. Still, he couldn't just leave. Not like this. Running to his slight wife, he grabbed her around the waist and turned her towards him.

Running his hands through her unbound hair, he met her fear filled eyes and held them.

"Be safe, my love," he said, kissing her tenderly.

She grabbed him, holding him close, her soft arms suddenly empowered with a strength he'd not realised.

"And you come home, safe and well," she murmured after their kiss. "Come back to your son and make amends with your father. Mistakes can be forgiven."

Shrugging aside her comment about his father as unimportant, he planted a kiss on his protesting son's face,

"Keep the boy safe for me."

"I will," she whispered.

"And mother, keep everyone safe. And mother, please keep my hound for me, he's old, and this'll kill him."

A kindly look clouded his mother's face as she watched the animal being lifted down from the saddle. Grateful to be on the ground, it walked softly to Northman, and he cupped its muzzle in his hand, and then he walked away as if he knew what was to happen. He swallowed and his mother shook her head in exasperation at the emotion for the animal,

“You men and your bloody hounds,” she muttered with rancour and turned away from her son. Mildryth too shook her head at him and reached for his hand one more time,

“Be safe my love,” she uttered, and then she was gone. None of the women wanting to see their sons, fathers and lovers ride out to war once more.

# 43
# WINCHESTER/LONDON, LATE SUMMER, AD1013, NORTHMAN

By the time he'd reached the king at Winchester, the news flooding in from the entire eastern coast was devastating. The king ensconced in his high chair on the raised dais, could barely process one messenger's words, before another fell over themselves to report to the king of the calamities befalling his people.

No sooner had Swein overrun Sandwich, then he moved to London, and then along the eastern coastline, towards the mouth of the river Humber. The raids were lightning quick, his intentions a little unclear as he reached accords with the men in the specific places, taking their money, their hostages and moving on to the next place.

Northman, as with everyone within the great hall, watched the king keenly. How would he cope with this threat?

Northman had immediately sought out Eadric once he'd arrived at Winchester, but as ever, he found Eadric too concerned with himself and not the good of the country. Still, he'd thought enough to bring Northman's men with him, and he'd greeted the small fighting force of ten with delight. With these men at his back, he knew that he'd be able to assist in the defence of the land, wherever the king chose for him to make his stand.

The king was surrounded by his advisors, Thorkell chief among them, his own eyes haunted by the news that became more and more dire with each passing day. Finally, and when news reached them that Uhtred of Northumbria had reached an accord with Swein, giving hostages, his geld and his oath to Swein, a crushing realisation became apparent to all and not just Northman. Swein was after more than just geld. He'd come for the crown.

Thinking quickly, Thorkell had instructed the king to remove himself to London, where his fleet was currently stationed. The first lightning fast raid there had done little harm. It was well defended, and Thorkell was adamant that from there they'd be able to mount an effective counter-attack.

Flailing for some way to counter Swein's aggressive stance, Æthelred had readily agreed. His wife he left behind at Winchester, far from the ravages of the Raiders reach and surrounded by a full half of the king's own household troops, the queen placed as their commander. Everyone else marched towards London.

A sense of expectation infected everyone, from the horses to the mightiest warriors. Somehow London would be decisive. One way or another, Swein and Æthelred would resolve this dispute.

At no time did Northman move to make amends with his father. Leofric he spoke to daily, but his father, no matter the efforts he took to resolve their falling out, Northman steadfastly refused to accommodate his apology. No matter how many times Olaf twittered in his ears, he'd not make amends with the man. And he'd damn well dare him to die in the coming battle!

THE COUNTRYSIDE WAS UNNATURALLY CALM AS THEY RODE TO LONDON. THE smell of smoke often drifted in the breeze, but the fires stayed tantalisingly out of sight. Outriders scouted far ahead, and Athelstan, at his father's command, took control of his household troops and those of the king's who remained. Edmund and Eadwig also rode to battle with their father.

London appeared on the evening of the second day of travel, appearing serenely before them as though the rest of England wasn't under attack.

On the advice of archbishop Wulfstan and Eadric, the king had sent a message of peace to Swein, but as he entered London, he received a rebuff. The Danish king informed the English that he'd established his power base at Gainsborough, that Uhtred of Northumbria had submitted to him and that he'd be in London as soon as possible, to face the English king and resolve the conflict once and for all.

Eadric took the news badly, and Northman felt embarrassed for the man. His own father had apparently been expecting the rebuff, his troops ready and waiting as he deployed them along the exposed walls of London. A grudging admiration for his father had Northman seek out Leofric and ask where his men could best be sited. Leofric, without a further word, informed Northman that he and his men could stand a watch over the bridge. They feared that Swein would attempt to enter via the river, using his ships or the bridge.

Northman accepted his deployment in silence but took a moment to grab his brother in a fierce hug. He wished he knew him better, but that was, after all, another grudge to hold against his father. Although, Leofric's knowledge of where he'd take his troops reeked of his father pre-empting his decision. That annoyed him. He wished his father knew him a little less well.

The battle came only the next morning. Further messengers had ridden in to inform the king that Swein had entrusted his hostages and his ships to his son, Cnut, and now travelled overland to meet the king in London.

A quick scramble, and the host of troops, both household and the fyrd, were arranged against Swein's approach. There was no mystery as to where they'd come from. Æthelred had made his position well known, and Swein, in his arrogance, came to meet it, head on. News reached them that while Æthelred had made his journey to London, Swein had circled him and set fire to both Winchester and Oxford. Horror at the news had swept through the camp at London, but then the next messenger confirmed that the queen had sought shelter closer to London and would soon join the king.

With the lightening of the day, Northman saw the combined host of the Danish king. Its sheer size took his breath away; its organisation astoundingly efficient. No dishevelled shield wall linked loosely, but instead, warriors, tightly packed together, their heads covered by helms, their shields painted a devilish red and their war axes, spears or swords, ready in their hands.

Unable to see their faces from such a distance, Northman felt a moment of fear, as though he was gearing himself to mount an attack against faceless foes from an ancient legend.

Around him, he could hear the men of the fyrd moving into position. The Danish king, coming as he did from the south-west had perhaps not fully considered the placement of his troops, for before them all stretched the expanse of the great river. Northman wondered if the river would be their major defence and quickly banished the thought. Whether it would be or not, he had bigger things to consider. The high wooden bridge, with its stone standings, was his to protect, and he mustn't let the Danish take it. With their ships effectively excluded from entering London by Thorkell's ships, this, for the time being, was their only way into London itself.

On the far side of the river, the English king's troops were lined up and ready, Northman marking the spot where, if the Danish broke through, the English would be able to make a final stand against them. If the Danish broke through the English shield wall, they'd yet have Northman and his men, and the reserve warriors to defeat.

As in the Battle of Ringmere, a final attempt was made to make peace, Leofwine taking it up himself to approach Swein. Even from this great distance, Northman could tell that the exchange was friendly, Swein greeting Leofwine expansively. A murmur of disgust swept through the men that Northman didn't decry. He too felt a little sickened to see his father with their sworn enemy.

The meeting was over quickly, Leofwine returning to the shield wall, his stance clear to read. No agreement had been reached.

Swein and the men who'd accompanied him to the brief meeting, stayed where he was, looking at the English and their war leaders, eyeing London with what Northman could only assume to be acquisitive eyes. Everywhere else had fallen before Swein, and he expected the same here.

A shout from his shield wall and Swein was racing back to his men and calling for order. The English stood silent, waiting to see what would happen. Northman knew a moment of complete calm and acceptance of what was to come. Rage did not fuel him this time, not like at Ringmere. Instead he felt a resolve to defeat these men, these upstarts, these warriors who fancied that they could just take England.

A further cry, and another and another, and the Danish were advancing slowly and in tight formation, Swein proudly flying his flag so that all knew where he stood and fought, staking his claim to London.

Northman watched in satisfaction as the English archers loosed their arrows, falling amongst the enemy, but as he knew would happen, they had little effect. Swein's men were too battle seasoned, too well trained to let possible death falling from the sky distract them.

A sudden burst of speed and the men met in a howling screech of rage from the English, professionalism from the Danish. Northman felt himself stir in admiration for the Danish king's troops. They were truly terrifying to behold. Disciplined and precise, they did their best to strike directly through the English. Only the English, with far more at stake than the Danish, fought with passion and desire. And for the time being, that was the winning force.

A concerted effort was made to slice through the defence

guarding the bridge to London itself, and Northman called his men to attention. It was their opportunity to fight the attackers.

Already moving into position, Northman directed the men to line the bridge crossing. Other household warriors also stood there, the shield wall still at least five men deep, but the crushing force of the attack was being directed here, the remainder of the Danish men seeming to work to distract the English from their real intent. Immediately he saw that in giving him this command, his father had done him a great honour. To him would fall the ultimate task of repelling the Raiders.

His men stood firm around him, still and resolved so that when the first Danish warrior somehow fought his way through the tight shield wall, they were ready for him. Covered in blood and grime, the warrior had a crazed look in his eyes, his professionalism long fled. In the centre of the shield wall guarding the bridge, Northman met the eyes of the man. This was his kill, pure and simple.

The rest of the battle faded from his consciousness as he stepped forward, the shield wall immediately closing behind him.

The warrior grinned with delight, taking a moment to wipe the blood that marred his eyes from his face. In doing so, he left streaks of bright red blood running from his forehead to his chin, a chilling sight.

Northman smiled at the warrior tauntingly, and he took the bait. A screech of rage and he was moving towards Northman, his shield ready, his war axe held firm in his hand. Northman had, by contrast, chosen his sword for this encounter and he hefted it from hand to hand as he looked at the warrior.

Were all of the Norse men left handed?

The warrior grinned once more, raising his war axe, and Northman quickly switched his hands, the shield in his right, and the sword in his left. The warrior furrowed his brow in consternation, and at that moment, Northman stepped in. A swipe of his blade to the unprotected left-hand side of the man's body, a howl of outrage and a brutal pounding on his now raised shield.

Northman grinned with delight. The easiest way to excite a Dane was to defeat them at their own game. He'd learnt that at Ringmere.

Once more, he swapped his shield and his sword arm, while crouching behind his shield. When the ferocious attack lessened, he lashed out with his sword, slicing the other side of the man's unprotected neck, and then lightening quick, he slashed at the man's feet, his blade encountering little resistance as it wiped through his right ankle. The warrior howled once more in outrage, but Northman had heard enough, stepping forward, he dug his sword through the man's protective tunic and straight through his flesh, feeling the grate of his sword on the man's ribs. The warrior's eyes closed in pain, and Northman leant forward and held the man's discarded war axe out to him. The man grasped it, his death coming, and a faint smile upon his lips.

These bloody Danish, Northman thought with admiration, and their love of a good death.

A moment to assess the situation and he was back within the shield wall. No others had yet made it through. But they would. He knew it.

His sword was slick with blood, and he wiped it absentmindedly on his trousers as he watched the shield wall in front of him. It was holding firm, but bodies were being dragged backwards by those not yet actively engaged in the battle. He approved of the move. It would have made the retreat at Ringmere so much easier if the bodies of his fallen comrades had been removed.

At his side, Olaf was speaking to him and belatedly he listened,

"You fought well Northman. He was a big man, but you downed him quickly enough."

Olaf's was clearly impressed by his friend, and Northman grinned with delight.

"The big ones always think they can win because they're so powerful. Like everyone else, they have their weak points."

Suddenly a roar from in front and Northman felt rather than saw, the shield wall collapse at a juncture in front of him. Other warriors rushed to fill the gap, but before they could, a contingent of men rushed through, shields protectively in front of them, their heads protected by warriors from behind.

Northman called his men to order, not that they weren't already prepared. Within moments, the first clash of war axe on shield set the shield wall reverberating and Northman grinned a little manically. Now he'd learn just how good his abilities were.

Head down, he was unable to see what happened on the battlefront at the further shield wall, but he hoped that the gaping hole there would soon be filled, effectively trapping this small horde of men between the two English sides.

He heard the cries of the warriors as their leader beckoned them on, promising glory and golden riches when they entered London. The roar his words received shook the shield wall as surely as the impact of the war axes.

"Hold men," Northman bellowed to those around him. The shuffle of feet behind him alerted him to reinforcement coming hastily to his aid, and he once more praised his father's forethought, for it was he and Thorkell who'd devised the battle strategy.

A crack on his shield, a volley of spears above his head, he ignored, pressing against the combined mass of the men of the other side of his shield.

His arms, once so weak that they trembled all through the battle at Ringmere, held firm and he delighted in his greater strength. A few years older and a lot of practice later.

Beside him, Olaf grunted and ducked all at the same time as a sword attempted to wind its way between the two shields protecting him. A quick glance to his right, and his sword was burying itself in the exposed underarm of the warrior there. A cry of shock and the man gaped at him I surprise. The man fell to his knees, slipping from the glistening blade as he did so, and Northman was once more behind his shield.

"My thanks, Northman," Olaf breathed, but Northman didn't reply, his attention on the next attacker.

This time, the sword came under his shield, trying to play the same trick on him that had downed the first warrior, but Northman was ready. He ducked his shield, trapping the sword where it was and adding his foot to it when he could. Annoyed grunts greeted his efforts, but Olaf had seen the opportunity and acted, sticking his sword through the man's side as he laboured to free his sword. Suddenly, the sword stopped moving, and the man slumped to his knees, death quickly taking him.

"Well done Olaf," Northman crowed with delight, his voice ringing loudly in a strange silence that had descended upon the bridge. Dismayed, Northman lowered his shield and looked in front of him, but there was little to see.

The attacking force had been decimated. All lay dead, and at the original shield wall, the defenders had ceased their efforts. Swein and his men had retreated, running as far and as fast as they could.

Grinning wildly with delight, Northman turned to Olaf to share their success, but he was too slow. Olaf grabbed him in a joyful embrace, banging him on the back and exclaiming,

"We did it. We beat the bastards."

Northman couldn't have phrased it better if he'd tried.

# 44

# LONDON, AD1013, NORTHMAN

He woke abruptly, having managed to sleep, somehow. Around him, there was a swirl of conversation, urgent and none too quiet.

Sitting, he blearily rubbed at his sleep encrusted eyes and looked at those who surrounded him; the king, his foster-father, the tall Dane, Thorkell, the king's older sons, Athelstan and Edmund and of course, his father, Leofwine.

He wondered if any of them had slept and decided that they hadn't. They all looked weary with defiance, hemmed into London, the only place to still hold true to their anointed king, Æthelred. Nowhere else had held out against the ravaging of King Swein of Denmark and his well-disciplined and ruthless household troops.

The other ealdormen, Uhtred and Ulfcytel, had wasted no time in declaring their allegiance to Swein. Not that Northman blamed them. Swein's combined force was almost too vast to comprehend, and every single man amongst them was a fully trained warrior. Not for any of them would the tricks work that could sometimes be played against the less well-trained fyrd, or the men from above the old wall. And it wasn't as if Æthelred had worked to endear himself to his sons by marriage. Eadric had put into motion Thorkell's earlier attacks upon the lands of the East Anglians, and then, to salt the wound, Æthelred had allied with Thorkell. And Uhtred was no happier with the king either.

They had of course known of Swein's vast recruitment campaign, and the building of his four military bases to house those men and their families who he'd decided to train as elite warriors. Thorkell had brought some of them with him when he'd first attacked four years ago, but never in their wildest dreams could they have imagined that Swein would unleash the entire brutal strength of them against England, not when he'd worked to save England from Thorkell's depravations. Although, as Northman had to keep reminding himself, that was not common knowledge.

He'd seen and been a part of many battles and skirmishes this year. Since the summer when the first attack had landed at Sandwich, Swein had swept through the East Anglian lands and as far as the River Humber. On land and sea, he'd shown his prowess as a warrior and Northman had seen at first hand just how ruthless the Danish king and his well trained, and well-armed men could be. And now he held Gainsborough as his own, and much else of England besides.

Thorkell was the only one of them all who'd truly appreciated the implied threat behind Swein's actions when he'd landed at Sandwich in August. He'd realised that he was just as much a target as the English king, a threat to Swein's command now that he was so closely allied with the English king. Without Thorkell's quick actions the king could have been chased from his land in Swein's first attack. It was a war for survival now, pure and simple, and Northman, as the other men did, knew that they'd lost it long ago.

Now they spoke of the best course of actions, and the king, looking frail beyond his forty-five years, still unbelieving of the change that had come upon him unbidden and unlooked for, seemed unable to comprehend what had happened and what must happen.

"My Lord, if we fight again, it'll be a bloody battle, our small force against the might of Swein's specially trained household troops and his vicious ship-men. Or you can leave quietly, now when you have the chance, taking your wife and your children with you, and you can seek shelter with your brother-in-law and hopefully, regroup. Rumour has it that Swein has been wounded, some say mortally. Perhaps, after all, our God may intercede for us." Eadric's tone was cajoling, almost pleading for his king to do this thing for him. Eadric had no taste for battle and blood, once more leaving that to the other men of the land, Leofwine, Uhtred and Ulfcytel, at least until the last two defected to the opposition.

Beside him, Northman watched his father's face collapse at the bold statements. He didn't deny them, they all knew them to be true, and he also knew that of them all in that room, there was only him who had nothing to fear. Yes, he'd fought for his king against Swein, had sent members of his household troops to try and stay Swein's hand, and yet somehow, Swein held faithful to his words of many years ago when he'd promised friendship. Whether Leofwine chose Æthelred now, or Swein, he was assured of his position, not one of the others could say the same.

Not that Eadric hadn't tried to double bluff the two competing king's, it was just that he'd tried to bribe the Danish king for his loyalty and the Danish king had not appreciated that. Out of them all, he was the man who seemed most scared now. He looked set to lose everything. The Five Boroughs had submitted, Northumbria had submitted, and now the north-western thegns were close to submitting. Eadric would be left with no land if Swein won, and he'd be left without his life if Æthelred didn't slink away with his tail between his legs. For Eadric, a battle now would be catastrophic. He had no ability in combat, his failure to engage against the Raiders in the lands of Dyfed last year had made that clear for all to see.

Northman watched him carefully. His plans lay in disarray and for once, Northman felt a faint stirring of sympathy for him. Like the king, he couldn't have predicted what was to happen. There'd been no portents of the disaster threatening them all. Not even Thorkell, the man who'd once been a confidant of the Danish king, could have predicted such swift and total success.

Northman glanced at the man. He was battle scarred but that just added to his imposing nature. He wondered if the rumours were true, that it was sheer jealousy that drove Swein to attack England, and not jealousy of Æthelred, but rather his one-time ally, Thorkell.

Last night he'd decided they must be, after all, his father had received his life-changing wound when Swein had lashed out at his one-time ally, Olaf. The unfairness of the situation was difficult for Northman to reconcile. His land was under ferocious attack because Thorkell had been so successful at raiding and being bought off and Swein now saw him as a threat to the security of his lands. Why couldn't Swein have attacked Thorkell on Thorkell's land? Why desolate England if revenge was the motive? Or even jealously?

He hadn't heard Æthelred's reply to Eadric's words, too caught up in his thoughts, but then Olaf nudged him. He'd stayed awake throughout the discussion and now nodded his head to where his father was pointedly looking at him.

Northman looked away. He didn't want to meet the gaze of his father, or his younger brother Leofric, also grown to manhood while they'd been separated. He knew it was foolish to continue with their argument, but he couldn't bring himself to either make an apology or accept one. His father had abandoned him a long time ago, into the clutches of Eadric, and now he struggled to look to his father as his father.

He felt his father's eyes on him, and his face flushed angrily. What had he expected when he'd sent him away, that he'd not learn to become a part of Eadric's family?

The oath he'd sworn as a young boy to his father hung like a heavy chain around his neck. He wished he'd never spoken it. His honour, such a unique thing to him when he'd been younger, was now more elastic. He didn't think he shared his father's special dispensation, being classified as one of Eadric's adherents, one of those who'd held London against Swein's initial attack and who sheltered there now. If he had to he'd go into exile with Eadric and the king; he'd never see his father again, or his mother.

Eadric called his name, and he stood on his tired legs and slumped towards where his lord, uncle by marriage and foster-father sat on a hard wooden bench surrounding the remnants of a once strong wooden table. Before them was a piece of a script with a diagram etched onto it clearly showing the defences of London and where they'd been breached and damaged. It didn't look at all hopeless. He imagined they could hold out here for months if not years, but without the support of the rest of the English lands it was difficult to know if it was a worthwhile endeavour.

Eadric's face was twisted as he glanced at Northman, now a man for all that he didn't regard him as one in any way apart from in matters of warcraft. He'd had the king reward him for his prowess in battle earlier in the year but still treated him as little more than a servant. Northman held his words. For now.

"Here," he pointed on the script, "take your men and watch this part of the defences. Don't let anyone out, and don't speak to any messengers that Swein might send."

Bowing he accepted his orders and turned away from the table, anything to avoid his father's eye. Outside, he breathed deeply of the bitterly chilly air and coughed as a waft of wet smoke covered him. Between the persistent drizzle and the bitter cold, the walkways were slippery and difficult to manoeuvre and littered with puddles and mud. It had been a miserable few weeks, and it didn't look as though it was going to get any better.

The hall they'd been within was magnificent and well-maintained, the smaller buildings around it just as well cared for. Indeed, until Northman found his way to the place that Eadric had commanded him to, he could see little damage to the structure of the houses and businesses that made up London. Swein and his horde of men had not managed to get amongst the houses that littered the town in a tidy sprawl. To all intents and purposes, life continued as normal. It was the rest of the lands of the English that existed in a crazed state of preparedness or attack or submission.

"Northman, you must make amends to your father," Olaf began his familiar call for reunification. Annoyed, as he always was when Olaf spoke to him of a matter he thought was bitterly personal, he stopped abruptly, and Olaf slammed into his back.

"Apologies Northman," he muttered softly, more than aware that his desire for peace between his friend and his father was rupturing his friendship.

"What would you do if your father died in battle, today or tomorrow?"

"He won't though will he," Northman responded, his anger infusing his words as he spoke through gritted teeth. "He's the only one of us who has nothing to lose here. Nothing at all."

'Northman, you know it's hardly his fault if Swein is so accommodating."

"Well, I say it is his fault. He should never have become friends with the bastard. It wasn't his place to do so."

"He did have to be part blinded, and endure years of threats before he got to that position," Olaf recited his time-worn argument, and Northman felt his temper flare, and then die, for once actually listening to the words. His father had endured more than most. Perhaps he was harsh to blame him for his misfortunes and then good fortunes. Indeed, it couldn't ever have been predicted.

Still, it riled. Eadric was facing ruin just for not being injured and being partly blinded. He'd worked wonders for the king, pulling together as many followers as he could, serving his king, providing him with grandchildren to carry on his line, and yet he was going to lose everything.

And then he shook his head at his pitiful attempts at resurrecting the terrible image of Eadric. He was only here with the king now because no one else would have him. He'd stolen from monasteries. He'd taken a cut from the taxes collected by the king and used them to enrich himself, and he'd used the king's daughter as little more than a birthing cow. He had no affection for her and never said a kind word to her. Or at least he hadn't, not until a few days ago when the king had himself seen his daughter for the first time in many, many years.

The king had been dismayed to see his once beautiful daughter looking so worn down by years of constant childbearing. If Eadric hadn't been one of his few allies still standing, he knew that Æthelred would have banished him for the cruel way he'd treated his daughter.

And yet for all that Northman knew that his loyalty was split between his father and foster-father. His oath tied him to his father, but he'd spent too much time with Eadric not to feel something for him. Even if he couldn't put a name to what it was. It had been hate for many years, and it certainly wasn't respect, but it was something.

"My father shouldn't have reacted as he did," Northman answered, and not for the first time.

Northman knew he sounded petulant even to his ears, but he couldn't stop himself. What did it matter if his wife was a niece of Eadric, daughter of the long disgraced Brihtric? All that mattered to him was that he loved her and wanted to be with her. It wasn't as if the marriage brought the two families into any closer alliance than they already were. That had been sealed when Leofwine had agreed to his son being fostered by Eadric.

He knew the thing that angered him most was his father's rejection of his grandson. If only he'd smiled, or willingly taken the small bundle into his arms, Northman felt he could have forgiven him anything. His mother had done just that, her joy at seeing her firstborn with his own firstborn too great to be contained. She'd taken to his wife with good humour as well. But his father, he'd taken some time to come around to the whole thing already being accomplished.

Northman had been shocked and surprised, so used to relying on his father for always accepting his decisions. It had been disappointing, and even the knowledge that Leofwine had been mourning the death of his father figure, Wulfstan, had not made Northman think any more kindly towards his father. If anything his anger had increased. Why had his father not informed him that Wulfstan was so dreadfully frail?

His men followed him quietly as he strode to the place Eadric had deemed he should guard. Olaf had lapsed into silence. He was a faithful hound, occasionally a little snappy but quick to subside into his expected subservience if he was unsuccessful in his attempts to garner a reaction. He'd happily returned to Northman when he'd been given his war band, and served him faithfully, if without his father's flair for the unexpected.

At the lookout, he found another of the king's sons, Eadwig, with his household troop. He greeted Northman sombrely, pleased that someone had remembered he couldn't stand on guard all day long, but reluctant to leave all the same.

"Any decisions yet?" he asked with a little enthusiasm as he gathered his small force of twenty men together, while Northman's deployed into the positions they'd been guarding.

"No, but Eadric is trying to convince your father again."

Nodding in understanding, Eadwig walked away with his men without speaking again. Northman watched him go with interest. The king had been blessed with many sons, but slowly over the passing years, the number had dwindled. He was now short of two of them, Edgar and Ecgberht had succumbed to the regular infections and maladies that often swept the land. A strange premonition swept over Northman whenever he saw Eadwig, but he was young and healthy, not that Edgar and Ecgberht hadn't been. He shook it away in annoyance blaming the darkness for his flights of fancy.

His father had been far luckier in continuing his lineage. None of his brothers or sister had failed to make it out of childhood. No, now all he had to worry about was one of them dying in battle.

Defeated by his thoughts, Northman realised that he had no choice. He'd have to make amends to his father. He couldn't imagine dying here without seeing his son again, and he knew he couldn't inflict the same on his father.

So resolved, Northman took his post, watching the land keenly towards the south-west. It was from there that word was expected to come from Swein, perhaps with his demands or possibly with his army. Northman didn't know, and neither did the king.

Later that night, back in the hall where they were all sheltering together, Northman was dismayed to find that although he'd been absent the entire time the sun had shone on the short dreary day, no decision had been made. The king still hoped that some other resolution could be reached. Not even the words of the archbishop Wulfstan had swayed him. Not even the thought of salvation for his people. No, in a moment of stubbornness, Æthelred had decided that as small as his troops were, they must fight for his kingdom, or at least, that was how his silence had been interpreted. The king hadn't spoken throughout the short day. Not once.

Northman admired the resolve of the old man, and the haggard countenances of the others, apart from Eadric, showed that they too admired their king. So many years he'd seen them through one strife or another, it seemed ludicrous to think that this time, some intervention would not arrive. What form it would take, no one knew, but in his heart, Northman prayed that the rumours of Swein's injuries were right and that soon, he'd be dead and life could return to normal.

Thorkell had sought the company of his father, and although Northman had fully intended to speak with his father as soon as he returned, he found himself hesitating. His brother Leofric saw him, however, and beckoned him over. Their friendship hadn't been affected by their time apart, or by his rift with his father. In fact, if anything, they'd grown a little closer.

"Brother, what brings you here?"

"I wanted to speak to father."

"Well don't let me stop you. In fact, come, he and Thorkell are reminiscing about old Olaf, join them. Father will take that as all the apology needed."

Northman knew it to be true, but hesitated again, until Olaf quietly walked behind him, and forced him to take the few steps required to sit at the table and benches his father had commandeered.

Leofwine immediately noticed his oldest son's presence but didn't speak. Never a man for making a scene, he only waited to make eye contact before turning his full attention to Thorkell.

"See, I told you," Leofric whispered, not quietly, and for the first time since the high summer, Northman felt the tension in his shoulders relax. His father, after all, was as little to blame as the rest of them for the events now unfolding.

The evening passed calmly enough, the fire burning bright and pure as it warded off the chill outside air. The food was, for now at least, readily available, and for a disconcerting moment, Northman could imagine himself at the king's Witan, not holed up in London waiting to see what Swein would do next.

"Mother, she is well?" he asked his brother as they shared a drinking horn.

"Yes, everyone is well brother, including your son and wife. As you would imagine father left many of his household troops to guard them, but unless one of Swein's minions get loose, she's in no danger. In fact, I wouldn't be surprised to find that Swein has intentionally visited her to show that he has peaceful intentions to those who look to father and mother as their Lord."

"And Horic, what of him?" Olaf asked. Northman wondered how many times Olaf had almost asked Leofric the question before he'd remembered that it'd be disloyal to seek out the brother of his Lord.

"He is, as you would expect, with mother, but Olaf, he's suffering from the cold and the chill. They infect his old injuries and make him even more grumpy than normal. If it came to a fight, I think it'd be far safer to sit him in the corner than give him a sword or shield."

Olaf smirked at the idea of his father doing that,

"I wouldn't think you'd have much chance. The old fool would far rather meet his new God or his old ones, with a sword in his hand."

"He would. That's a certainty."

Northman let the conversation flow around him. It felt good to be amongst friends and family. If only for a brief moment in time.

# 45
## LONDON, AD1013, LEOFWINE

His years weighed him down; responsibility, decisions, broken promises and a fickle Lord. He'd had so much joy in his life, and he thanked the Lord daily for his good fortune, but sometimes a niggle, and a doubt infected his mind. And sometimes he knew full well that he was a fool and that tricks were being played on him.

At the fire, he chatted with Thorkell, tales of Olaf that made him smile sadly with joy and remorse. He still wished he'd known him better, even now. He'd clearly been a mighty man, a great warrior. A bastard as well, but who wasn't when you got to know them?

On this night of quiet conversation, he felt as though his world was changing, irrevocably. Something was coming soon, he knew it, and it would permanently scare him. Again.

He didn't feel as though he'd recovered from losing Wulfstan yet.

He also knew that he'd survive it, but at what cost?

Northman entered his firelight, and Leofwine felt a weight lift from his chest. The boy was back. No longer a boy, a man now, fully-grown, strong, well mannered, well spoken and a father to boot. He'd been a fool to let his anger and frustrations with Eadric boil over so that they affected his relationship with his son.

Ideally, the arrival of his grandson and son should have elicited joy, but coupled with Eadric's machinations and the death of Wulfstan, reason had been driven from his head. He'd felt driven mad with grief and anger, two emotions that sat as comfortably on him as bee stings. A niggle here and there following a moment of intense pain.

And his son had been the object he'd vented his frustration, anger and grief on, all these years of being balanced, all gone to waste in an ill-conceived moment.

But at least he'd been forgiven now. He'd made many overtures to Northman in attempts to reconcile, but none had been successful. He wondered what had brought about his change of heart now?

Walking past his oldest son, he reached out and touched him on his shoulder with a squeeze of welcome, love and thanks. Northman didn't react in any way other than to crush his father's hand within his own. The strength of the lad never failed to amaze him. Far stronger than he'd ever been, the very ripple of his muscles against the cloth of his tunic showing his strength. He loved just as fiercely, and Leofwine had been a fool to forget that.

Now, hopefully, they could forgive and forget. Now, when the kingdom was in such peril, it was vital that Northman be seen as a member of his father's family. That way he would be covered by the accommodation that Swein had already presented Leofwine with. When the messenger from Swein had reached Leofwine on his way to London, he'd been unsure how to react. The injustice of it all had burnt too brightly, and yet, at the same time, the knowledge that his wife and sons, daughter and grandchild were safe had eased the ache of fear in his heart.

He was growing too old for the constant threats to have no impact on his wellbeing.

Æthelred sat slumped at the same table as earlier. Leofwine didn't think he'd moved all day. He made a pitiful figure, a man more out of depth than Leofwine was and for all different reasons.

The firelight spluttered and sent ghostly shadows up and down the wooden walls of the hall. The light was unkind to the king's haggard face, and Leofwine detoured, even if it was against his will.

"My king," he began, sliding onto the wooden bench beside him.

"Leofwine," the king said tiredly as if the word was an effort almost beyond him.

"The decision weighs too heavily on you," Leofwine began, and then stopped, he felt as though his words were inadequate to voice the turmoil that the king was in.

"No, not really," Æthelred surprised him by saying. "The decision has been made, in fact, it was made as soon as the conundrum presented itself. It's the speaking of it that gives me pause for thought."

Leofwine looked to the men who still supported their true king, noting the drained faces of all. It was inhuman to make battle during the winter season, but all had been happy to, in the name of their king. He wondered how many of them knew that the king had already decided to abdicate and gift the throne to Swein.

"Would you have me speak it for you? My Lord," Leofwine asked, hating himself for saying the words but accepting that he would act for his king if he needed to.

"Leofwine, as ever, you're too free to offer yourself for the unpleasant tasks. But my thanks all the same. I will do as I must, but perhaps tomorrow. Athelstan has ridden to find the queen at Winchester. He'll bring her here as soon as he can, and then we'll leave for her brother's lands. You met him didn't you?"

"Yes," Leofwine said with consideration, it hadn't been the most pleasant of experiences and on that day, Duke Richard, the second of that name, had made a fool of Leofwine and his king. Leofwine didn't like to be reminded of that event, preparing to see the good that had come from the marriage of Æthelred to the young Emma. "He was a man sure of himself."

A hearty chuckle escaped Æthelred's mouth then,

"You always were excellent with words Leofwine, but again, my thanks for trying to make the situation as rosy as possible for me."

"I hope that the rumours of Swein's wound prove to be correct, and then in your absence, I can work for your reappointment."

Now Æthelred fixed him with a firm stare, and Leofwine didn't flinch from his probing gaze.

"Really, Leofwine. You would have me back, after the disasters the country has faced under my kingship?"

"It's hardly your fault if Swein and Thorkell and Olaf and all the other Norsemen who've plagued our land have come under your reign. You've been my king all my life. I know of no other, and nor do I want to. You were anointed as my king and so, yes, I would have you back if I could. As would the country. I'm unsure of the magical powers that Swein has exerted over everyone else within your lands, but I can assure you, if any English man had a choice, they'd have their true king, not a usurper."

Æthelred's gaze finally shifted from Leofwine's face. He reached out and grasped a wooden cup and drank his fill before he spoke again.

"If we should never meet again Leofwine, you have my thanks for all you've done during my reign. I know you worked for the good of your people and the good of the land, but your loyalty has been unswerving. Not many can say that. None other than my sons."

"Then you must tell them that my Lord. You should thank your sons. They'd have governed your lands more wisely than your sons by marriage. They would have fought harder and for longer, even if faced with Swein and his son." Leofwine spoke urgently, overjoyed finally to hear Æthelred speak so of his sons.

Æthelred slumped on his folded arms at those words.

"Hindsight is a wonderful attribute but one that gives me sleepless nights. My older sons, Athelstan and Edmund and Eadwig, they're all good warriors, good with men. Perhaps too good. Maybe I've always been a little jealous of them. And held them back. As you say, they deserved better. I can't help feeling that I've only myself to blame. I rely too much on men who say what I want to hear."

"Your sons have been æthelings since their birth, but not king's since they were eight. You should give yourself more credit, as you should your sons. Although, I won't deny that you're correct in your assessment of yourself. Some dissent makes a man stronger."

"Is that what you tell yourself about your oldest son?" the king asked, anger in his voice.

"Yes, I do. I'm just as much a fool when it comes to my son as you are with your own, but I'm not saying any different."

The king laughed then, as Leofwine felt his anger rising.

"Men and their sons. Idiots, one and all," Æthelred qualified his humour and his rancour, and went on,

"and daughters my Lord Leofwine. Daughters are somehow less trouble and more all at the same time. Daughters do things to your heart that sons do not do. Sons should be active in battle and strong against their enemies. Daughters should be comforting and soft and pliable. And well looked after by their husbands." He finished on a snarl, his eyes looking at Eadric's back where he sat with his men around the fire.

Leofwine had heard enough about Eadric's treatment of the king's daughter to sicken him, and he understood the king's rage, but equally wondered how he'd let it happen in the first place. Daughters, should, he thought silently, be used for more than just political gain. Some measure of their happiness should always be guaranteed.

"But go now, be with your son. Enjoy your time together, and know this Leofwine, I do not envy you or feel jealous of you and your accord with Swein. More than anyone in this room, you've earned your right to govern your lands, and Swein, when he becomes king, will have a loyal follower in you. I command you to be loyal," the king growled, his grief at what was to happen easy to hear.

"And when I return, whenever that may be, I'll expect you to be waiting for me."

With that the king stood, took a last lingering look at the men who'd stayed loyal to him, and retreated out the closed door, a flurry of chill wind coming with him. Leofwine imagined he knew where the king was going.

# 46
# LONDON, DECEMBER AD1013, NORTHMAN

AGAIN, HE'D BEEN SENT AS SENTRY TO RELIEVE EADWIG FROM HIS NIGHT TIME position. The morning was colder than the day before, and he pulled his cloak tighter to ward off the chill. It'd be a long day on duty, but he thought that it'd be his last.

The king had made his announcement in the early morning gloom, that he'd be seeking to renounce his claim to the throne and would be leaving the country. Swein was not welcome to it, but for the benefit of his people, he'd let the Danish king hold it.

He'd wished his men well, pointedly ignored the frustrated cry of Eadric, and the looks of dismay on his oldest son's face, and announced that if Swein didn't send a messenger to him today, that he'd begin sending messengers out the next day. Other than the knowledge that Swein was in the Southwest of the country, none knew where he was precisely. None within London, that was.

Eadwig was grim when Northman informed him of the king's decision, his cold and tired face looking even less lifelike as the implications of his actions sank in. Northman pitted him and respected him at the same time. All of the king's sons were honourable. For all that Eadric had been desperate to associate himself as closely as possible with the king and his family, Northman was pleased to be distant. Any loyalty he had to give to the king was his to acknowledge as he wanted. No ties of family and blood forced him to accept the king.

When Eadwig had done, Olaf began to speak,

"I don't much envy him anymore. To be the son of a deposed king can't be any life. Not when the new king has his family and sons aplenty."

"Yes, he's gone from being a man with a chance at the throne to a man who's simply a threat to the new king. I can't imagine Swein going out of his way to ensure that Æthelred's sons survive."

"They'll lose their lands?" Olaf asked.

"If they want to keep their lives they'll have to lose everything, as will the king, the queen and anyone else too closely associated with the old regime."

"What about you then? What will you do?"

"My wife and son are with my mother. I'll bow my knee where I have to to keep them safe."

"I knew you'd say that. Will you abandon Eadric then?"

"I doubt Eadric will slink away from this without a final play for power. It'll be intriguing to watch him try and infiltrate the Danish king's inner circle of advisors and friends."

"And Thorkell, what of him?"

"He says he'll go with Æthelred. He and the Danish king have become ardent enemies of late, and Thorkell doesn't wish to go against him. After all, he is Cnut's foster father."

"Never stopped Eadric."

"No, it didn't but then, the Norsemen hold honour in different ways to some of the English men," Northman commented drily, accepting Olaf's assessment of the relationship between his foster father and his father. If only Eadric had been an honourable man, or the king less keen to please his favourite ealdorman. If only...

The day, as predicted was cold and slow and tiring. The men standing guard began the day full of gossip about the future, but as the day wore on with a light covering of snow falling, their interest waned, and as the afternoon sun slunk away, almost in embarrassment, Northman found his thoughts almost as frozen as the ground. There were too many variations that needed to be thought about, and he lacked the energy to follow them all through to their logical conclusion.

Finally, one of the men spotted a rider on the horizon, and the frigid men jumped to attention, mindful that hopefully, this was what they'd been waiting for.

One rider, covered in a deep fur cloak, finally came into view, and Northman stepped through the broken down wall to stand between the rider and London. Before the hood was thrown back, he knew whom he faced. Cnut, the Danish king's son.

He'd not seen him since Oxford, but he recognised the bright blond hair and piercing eyes, now looking a little crueller than before, but then, Cnut had spent the intervening years with his foster father, Thorkell, raiding and slaughtering those of the English who came between them and their treasure. His part in the murder of the old archbishop was much talked about, but little proved, many saying that he'd still been in Denmark with his father. At that moment, though, Northman knew that Cnut must have been involved.

Cnut clearly recognised Northman, and he smiled in welcome, although it never quite reached his eyes.

"Are you the welcoming party?" he asked, condescendingly.

"Yes, if you need welcoming. Do you come with good news? Has your father seen sense and retreated?"

Cnut grinned a little manically then,

"No, but I hope that your king has. Now, if you would be so kind as to escort me to him."

Cnut slid from his horse then, expecting Northman to do as he'd instructed, and it was at that moment that Northman recognised how truly difficult it was going to be to accept this youth's father as king. What right did he have to the lands of the English? The right of conquest? That didn't seem like the correct term to use. No bitter pitched battles to the death had taken place. Perhaps he'd be able to call it the harrying of England? That would belittle the achievement of the Danish king.

Shaking the thoughts aside, Northman stepped towards Cnut.

"Come, I'll take your horse for you. Have you come alone?" he queried, peering into the deepening sunset.

"No, but only I've come this far. I knew I had nothing to fear."

The men stirred at the casually flung words, and Olaf shushed them as Northman led Cnut through the men proudly standing to attention.

"Rumour has it that all the king's warriors are now my father's warriors, and that only fools and the blind stay with the king."

Northman stopped abruptly then, and Cnut walked into him in the gloom where the reach of the fire and the brands did not reach.

"Cnut, I would suggest you step a little more carefully. Sadly, your informants have missed out a good number of warriors who even now surround the king."

"If you're talking about yourself Northman, I'd play yourself down a bit more. Great warriors must prove themselves before they can be proclaimed as heroes."

"And king's son's should realise that killing old and defenceless men doesn't make them heroes either."

In the darkness, Northman could see Cnut's blazing eyes, and he enjoyed the thrill of upsetting the cocky upstart. He might well regret it in the future, but for now, the little moment of triumph needed savouring.

"I suggest you ask those who were there for the correct details before you say things such as that," Cnut blazed, his hand hovering over his sword.

"I have, Thorkell has told me the story."

"Thorkell?" Cnut queried, clearly wrong-footed to hear the name, "Thorkell is here, with your king?" he could barely suppress his incredulity at the news.

"Yes, he is, with his ships and all bursting with men. He has been for more than a year."

They'd begun walking again by now, but Cnut had lapsed into silence at the news.

"You were unaware of his allying himself with Æthelred?"

"No, but, well yes, completely unaware. My father is even now waiting for him on the Southern Coast."

"He'll be waiting a long time then."

"Perhaps," was all the reply he got, and then they arrived at the king's Hall.

Northman made a note to himself that he must inform his father that Thorkell had not been as ignorant of the Danish king's movements as he'd led them to believe.

News of Cnut's arrival had preceded him, and as Northman pushed open the door, silence greeted him, apart from the crackle of the fire and a sharp blast of warm air. A squire ran hastily to him, and he handed the reins of Cnut's horse to the boy and asked him to see to the beast with all care.

Inside the hall, Northman directed Cnut to walk behind him towards where the king had set himself up in as much royal grandeur as he could find within London. He sat on an elegant wooden chair, in beautifully decorated clothing that showed only at the cuffs of his deep fur cloak. Surrounding him were his two remaining ealdormen and his two second oldest sons. All that was missing was his wife and younger sons but they were with Athelstan; the king, in his greatest moment of need, finally trusting his son with something vitally important to him.

"My Lord, I present Cnut, son of the Danish king Swein," Northman spoke by way of an introduction before stepping aside. Northman had not forgotten that Cnut had once been a hostage at the king's home, he merely wanted to proceed in the correct manner.

A squire hastily appeared and presented Cnut with a warmed spiced mead that he took in his hands after he'd painstakingly removed his gloves. He was clearly a man of much show and knew how to hold his audience.

When he'd drunk his fill, he strode towards Æthelred and spoke openly.

"My father sends his greetings and hopes that you're well."

Æthelred inclined his head at the formal reception but didn't speak. In the silence, Cnut took a moment to survey his surroundings with acquisitive eyes.

"This is an elegant hall Æthelred. I may claim it as my own."

Æthelred still didn't rise to the bait, waiting to see, as everyone else would, just what Swein's demand was.

"Ah, Thorkell, I see the rumours are correct, that you've chosen to ally yourself with the weak English king," Cnut now side-tracked as his eyes alighted on his foster father. There was little warmth in his words, and Northman was pleased not to have them directed at him.

"Cnut, son, you have finally finished growing," the massive warrior countered, not answering the allegations of disloyalty.

Cnut flushed a little at the personal reminder of the time they'd spent together when he was just a boy.

'King Æthelred, as you would expect, I've come here with news of the terms my father will accept your surrender on and let you leave this country without further loss of life. However, I would rather have the discussion in more private surroundings."

A rush of voices greeted the words, and Northman looked to where every warrior and household troop member was quickly conversing with their closest neighbour. He wished that Cnut's words had been greeted with a little less relief, but he was not one to chastise the men.

The king looked around at the faces and gestured for Leofwine and Eadric to step a little closer towards him. A brief conversation ensued and then Eadric walked away towards where the cook pot was being stirred, and two huge pigs were being roasted. The smell was appetising after the cold and slow day Northman had endured.

Leofwine gestured for Northman to come towards him, and then he imparted his instructions. The king wished to speak to Cnut closer to the fire but in an area that was devoid of others. They'd share a meal together.

Æthelred stood and walked towards Thorkell, his eyes never leaving Cnut's face as he asked or had a previous question answered. Northman wasn't too sure.

Cnut remained where he was, comfortable as the object of everyone's attention.

Quickly, the table the king had been sat at the day before was brought before the fire and laid out with food. At the same time many of the household men were filing out of the doorway, disgruntled voices unhappy at being forced into the snowstorm now raging outside. For their sakes, Northman hoped the king and Cnut would talk quickly.

Along with his father, he stood to one side as the king and Cnut ate and discussed their terms. Northman watched carefully, waiting for the king to show some tell-tale body language as to how well the talks were going but nothing happened. Instead, Cnut ate and spoke much, while Æthelred ate and talked little. Only when Cnut stood abruptly did Northman even realise that any agreement had been reached.

Hastily, he stepped back beside Cnut, wondering if he was needed to escort him back outside into the fully dark night, lit only by the moon, stars and the whiteness of the freshly fallen snow.

"My thanks, Northman," Cnut thundered, his voice carrying to the far reaches of the hall where those lucky enough to have been allowed to stay inside had been quietly watching the king.

"I'll return to my father now and let him know of developments here. And Æthelred, may we never meet again," Cnut said, turning his back on the man with disdain, and stepping briskly forward. Northman snapped to attention and walked promptly to open the door for the Danish prince. It was evident that he was going to offer no word of explanation but was going to leave that to Æthelred, and that meant that Northman would have to wait until he returned from escorting Cnut away to discover what had been agreed.

Cnut's horse was ready and waiting outside. The squire must have run to retrieve the beast, and Northman thanked him loudly for his timely actions.

Cnut offered no words, so Northman only turned and began retracing his steps of earlier. The air was bitterly chill, especially after having been inside for so long next to the roaring fire. He tugged his cloak tightly around his face and watched the figure of Cnut where he strode purposefully in front of him.

Snow had been falling the entire time that Cnut had been speaking to Æthelred, and there were no footprints in the snow. Still, Cnut apparently knew the way and Northman wondered if he'd been in London before. Then he remembered he had, with Thorkell a year earlier, when the archbishop had met his unfortunate death.

At the wall, Cnut turned towards Northman and held out his hands for his horse's reins. Only once mounted did he speak,

"Be thankful that my father is such a sentimental old fool. Your entire family will be safe when he's king. But, I've allied myself with another Mercian family, enemies of your foster-father. I suggest you switch your allegiance, and quickly at that. I'd not want to give an open invitation to your father, and have to temper it with the provision that it not include you."

With no further words, Cnut mounted his horse, and extending his hand impatiently for a lit brand; he rode off into the dark night, a speck of light in one of the darkest nights Northman had ever known

Northman watched him go with dread. No, surely not. He tried to deny those final words but knew there and then that he and Cnut would never be allies, and that his foster father would never reconcile with their new king, Swein.

# 47
# LONDON, NORTHMAN

ÆTHELRED HAD GONE TO THE ISLE OF WIGHT WITH THORKELL AND HIS MEN. His wife was gone to her brother in Normandy, but he'd lingered a few days longer and then the winter storms had come. Aware that he must leave England, as agreed with Cnut, Æthelred had taken the only option he could, he'd retreated away from the mainland and would remain on the Isle of Wight until he was able to make a safe crossing.

All in all, it had been a little anticlimactic.

And now they waited for Swein to come to London for his coronation. Throughout the last week, the other Ealdormen had slunk their way into London without apology on their faces, but a little quieter than normal. The land was still in shock at the rapid change of events. No matter how many times anyone tried to put the rapid sequence of events into order, they still didn't add up to a change in kingship. Not at all.

Æthelred had made a departing speech to his men, thanking them all for their efforts and wishing them well. He'd made it clear he blamed no one but himself for what had happened. But the meaningful look he'd shot Eadric had not gone unnoticed. And the king had left with Thorkell, not Eadric. Eadric he'd left behind, not entirely abandoned to his fate, but Northman knew he was unhappy, especially as the king had taken Edith and his grandsons with him.

The coronation would take place the next day. A hastily arranged affair but well attended for all that. Swein had won support because men liked him more than they ever had Æthelred and it wasn't hard to see why.

Swein rewarded those who endeavoured on his behalf. When he'd come through the gateway yesterday afternoon, he'd slipped armbands on to Northman's hand, and liberally distributed coinage that showed Æthelred's face. Swein may have merely been ridding himself of anything with the former king's image on, but at the same time, he was showing his generosity to all and sundry, and it was appreciated by every warrior, trader and farmer.

His father had been called immediately to Swein's presence, joined there by Ulfcytel, Uhtred and Æthelmær of the Western Provinces, the man who'd taken control of the Western lands and treated with Swein to ensure that battle did not rage there. Only Eadric had been left out, and that had been purposefully done.

Cnut had arrived before his father, issuing instructions and taking charge of the forces left behind by Æthelred, few as they'd been, and bringing with him members of the Mercian family he'd allied himself with. Like Northman, Cnut had married young and hopefully, to good effect. The family he's chosen had been that of the disgraced Ealdorman of Northumbria when Northman had been a boy, Ælfhelm. There was no hope of a reconciliation taking place anytime soon between Eadric and the new king for Eadric had murdered Ælfhelm, at the bequest of Æthelred or not as the case may be, it didn't matter to his young daughter, who was now the consort of Swein's probable heir.

It was a pretty mess and one that Northman didn't wish to become embroiled in any further. Neither had his honour allowed him to abandon his wife's family altogether. He'd do what he could for Eadric, but Ælfhelm's daughter wasn't the only one out for his blood.

Godwine, the son of the Wulfnoth that Eadric's brother had risen against during the disastrous campaign of 1009 before Thorkell had arrived in England, had made a reappearance alongside Cnut. The rumours were rife that Eadric's downfall would not be long in coming, and Northman couldn't deny that Cnut appeared keen to surround himself with the enemies of Eadric.

Whatever had happened during the winter of 1009 when Cnut and Thorkell had been in secret communication with Eadric, it had apparently soured Cnut's opinion of the man. Thorkell had been more magnanimous, but then, he was a warrior, not a king in waiting.

Northman sighed deeply and beside him, Olaf laughed.

"It won't be too much longer now. Get the coronation over and done with and hopefully we'll be allowed to disperse back to our lands, and you'll see your son again."

"I hope so, Olaf. I've barely been home since he began to sit and gurgle, and I miss him, and Mildryth of course."

"I think maybe you just miss the warm bed, but I'm too much a courtly man to mention that," Olaf chuckled, and Northman cast him a thinly veiled look of annoyance.

"You're just envious," he retorted and saw Olaf flush a little at the truth of the matter.

A disturbance at the wall and Northman and the men were instantly alert and ready to face what was coming their way, only, it came from within London.

A scrabble of hooves on the icy ground, and Eadric erupted from the nearest street, barrelling his way towards Northman. His heart sank. The bloody idiot was trying to leave.

Quickly he called his men to him and had them stand across the small gateway.

"Move aside Northman," Eadric demanded angrily.

"You know I can't. The new king has made his instructions clear. You're not to leave. None of us is. Not until after the Coronation."

"Move aside; I'm leaving."

"No, you're not Eadric, get back to the hall and stop this nonsense."

His eyes blazing Eadric jumped from his horse and strode towards him. Reaching out he grabbed Northman around the collar of his cloak and brought their faces level,

"Let me pass or your wife will be punished."

"My wife is with my mother, protected by our household troops and king Swein's writ allowing my family to retain its position."

"I'll still get to her," Eadric glowered, and Northman looked at him carefully. He was sweating and shaking all at the same time.

"What has Cnut done now?" he asked softly, according to his foster father some respect for all that he was sorely testing him.

"Nothing, and everything. It matters not. Let me pass."

"If I let you pass, I imperil my family," Northman retorted angrily, surprised that Eadric could still act in unpredictable ways.

"If you don't, you'll imperil them all the more," he snarled.

Annoyed Northman worked Eadric's hand loose from around his neck.

"I'll take my chances, now go back to your lodgings. Don't think that just because we're family; I'll let you run free. We all know the damage you've caused over the years. If it weren't for you, Thorkell would never have attacked East Anglia and set the chain of events that lead us to today."

Eadric's face turned whiter,

"What do you know of East Anglia and Thorkell?"

"Everything you fool. Why do you persist in thinking you can do whatever you want Eadric and no one will ever know."

"Does the king know?"

"Which one?" Northman countered angrily.

"Æthelred of course, the rightful king."

"Of course he knew. Why did he never mention it to you? I'm surprised. He was angry beyond words."

"And how did you know?"

"You were being watched by Athelstan's men. They waited all winter long and saw everything you did."

Eadric pulled away from Æthelred then and looked about in panic.

"Then all is lost. Æthelred will not want me and nor will his daughter, and Cnut has made no bones of his intention to drive me from England. What am I to do?"

"I would suggest you bow your knee to the new king and make the best of it," Northman offered softly, "like the rest of us."

Eadric barked with laughter at his words,

"You are your father's son that's for sure. So easy for you to see the good in people and accept that they will act in your best interest at heart. Cnut hates me. He longs for my death."

"He's not the only one either is he, Eadric? You've survived this long by the excess use of your glib tongue. I'm sure you'll do the same again."

"Am I to get no pity from you, my nephew by marriage?" he implored.

"No, get from here and return to your lodgings, and let's hope that Swein and Cnut have not heard of your attempt to escape. Neither of them appreciates disloyalty. You'd do well to remember that and then you might keep breathing a little longer."

So defeated Eadric remounted his horse, with his select band of five followers and turned his horse back towards his lodgings. Northman sighed with relief when he watched him go.

Behind him, Olaf spoke angrily,

"Why did you do that? You should have just let him go."

"I know Olaf, it would be far easier to rid ourselves of him, and I believe that Cnut will do so quite happily, but, he is our foster father."

"He's an arse, just as Oscetel once said, and the sooner he's dead, the better."

And so said, Olaf turned away from Northman, anger evident in his stance and Northman watched him with interest. He wished he could see the world in such shades of black and white. It was, after all, the greys that undid him.

# 48

# LONDON, CHRISTMAS DAY, AD1013, NORTHMAN

Considering the bitter weather, the attendance at Swein's coronation was high, and not just with the warriors who'd escorted him from Denmark. As many of the English thegns and ealdormen had come as were welcome.

Swein was magnificently dressed in a warm fur cloak, and fine trousers, his boots brightly polished, and hung with jewels, as was the rest of him. At his side, Cnut was equally resplendent, and Northman traitorously thought that they did both look the part of king and king in waiting.

For all that rumours of Swein's ill health were circulating violently and he didn't look quite as vibrant as when Northman had met him as a child. He imagined that the years would have worked their worst on him, but still, he wasn't convinced that he was in good health. Not at all.

Regardless, though, he was determined to wear the English crown, and so he'd endured the long ceremony of coronation. The new archbishop of Canterbury, Lyfing, had carried out the coronation. Swein had been anointed, given a massive golden ring, had a sword placed into his open hands, and also given a golden sceptre. And so he'd pledged himself to protect the English people and to do so with God's assistance and acceptance.

Northman watched with tired eyes. He was unsure how far any of them could trust Swein and his son, and for how long Swein would even be their king but at least he would be called upon to pledge his oath as Swein's commanded men. That was more than Eadric understood he was to do. Sullen eyed and casting baleful looks towards Northman; he was fidgeting his way through the ceremony and all the time Cnut watched him with contempt.

Leofwine as ever appeared calm amidst the upheavals taking place, and Northman didn't think it was because he'd been offered neutrality from Swein. No, it ran deeper than that and Northman anticipated that it had far more to do with a discussion he'd watched his father have with the king than anything else. He wanted to query his father about it, but for all that their relationship was outwardly healed, asking for his father's confidence was pushing things a little too far. In time, maybe, in time.

Before him, Swein was proclaimed king to rousing cheers from all assembled, and Swein, in a most un-kinglike move, grinned wickedly from ear to ear. How long he'd been planning on securing England's crown for himself, Northman didn't know, but rumour had it that he'd made his eldest son Harald regent in his place when he'd set out for England. That forethought made all his actions appear preconceived.

Northman had a worry of fear that it had been his father's attempts to involve Swein in recalling Thorkell that had given him the idea of not just attacking but taking the crown. He shared those thoughts with no one. Especially not his father.

Northman grinned along with this new king, Swein of England, his good cheer too infectious to rebuff even at such a distance, and when it was his turn to kneel before his king and offer his pledge, he did so willingly. The congregation of the Church seemed invigorated with their new king, a feeling of hope sweeping through those assembled. It might not be ideal to have the Danish king now as the English king, but one thing was determined. It would, once and for all, put an end to the devastating and cataclysmic raiding parties that had decimated the land for so many long years, almost without let up.

# 49
# LONDON, CHRISTMAS DAY, AD1013, LEOFWINE

THE CORONATION WAS ACCOMPLISHED, THE FEAST IN FULL SWING, AND Leofwine was more than a little giddy with the excellent wine his new king was serving to him.

Just as inebriated as Leofwine, Swein and he were roaring with laughter and chuckling loudly at the conversation flowing between them, as if they'd been boyhood friends, and not at all violent enemies and then grudging acquaintances and then, perhaps, almost friends.

Cnut stonily watched as they imbibed and Leofwine wondered why he didn't relax his guard at all. He abstained from the mead and the wine, preferring instead, plain water, boiled to purify it.

"You know Leofwine," Swein swigged drunkenly from his beautiful golden cup, slopping his wine down his well-made tunic and being oblivious of it all at the same time.

"Yes, my Lord Swein," Leofwine slurred happily, his eye almost entirely closed in sleep, so much alcohol sloshed around his body.

"It was you who gave me the idea to invade England you know, and that is why I've spared you any retributions."

Leofwine's eye shot open at that admission, looking around desperately to ensure that no one else heard it.

"If you hadn't come to me and asked for my help, I'd never have had the thought."

"I don't quite follow," Leofwine breathed out, relieved that it didn't seem to be his fault as such, just that he'd somehow sparked the idea.

"Forty-eight thousand pounds in weight," Swein slurred, as Leofwine watched him carefully, "is a bloody huge amount of money to pay a little runt like Thorkell. You only gave me £30000, and I'm an ordained king."

Leofwine could hazard a guess where this way going,

"And then you only paid me a further £5000 even though I recalled my son and my men. Honestly Leofwine, I was a little angry at being treated so poorly."

"My apologies my Lord," Leofwine uttered, trying and failing to get the cheer back into his voice.

"Ah, it's not your fault. It's your tight-fisted king. If he's sent me £15000 I might have stayed at home, but no. A measly £5000 and I felt I should come and see for myself the great riches that England had to offer, and while doing so, I thought, why not take the crown as well. That way, I can have as much money as I want." The king swallowed another mouthful of wine and looked out at those before him, his head swaying from side to side.

"Look at them all, desperate to have a king with some backbone and one who doesn't let that weasel Eadric do as he pleases."

"Perhaps if you'd asked for more, I could have arranged for a bigger geld as a thank you for your actions," Leofwine suggested, but Swein waved his words aside.

"It's no matter now. I got my £5000, and now I'll have much more, and as I say, I'll get more as and when I need it."

Leofwine paused for a moment but realised there was little else he could say.

"Then I'm pleased I was of assistance to you."

"As am I," Swein quipped back, his eyes now thoroughly glassed over, slumped in his regal chair. Leofwine wanted to laugh at his strange position but realised that he looked little different.

Figures materialised around them, and Leofwine understood that Swein was being removed from the front of the royal hall, where he soundly slept, so confident in his new kingship that he could sleep in front of all those assembled, even when he suspected there were traitors amongst them.

Leofwine watched the activity without concern or interest. He'd seen enough men in this predicament to give it no thought.

The king was picked up and carried away by four huge shipmen, who lay him flat between their outstretched arms. As they did so, Leofwine saw a flash of red and his heart sank while he leapt to his feet and covered the telltale weeping wound that streaked the king's stomach. The rumours appeared to be correct. Their new king carried a stomach wound of the worst kind. It was a wonder he'd lived this long to have himself declared king.

Suddenly sober, Leofwine walked away with the men, his mind in turmoil.

# 50
## DEERHURST, FEBRUARY AD1014, NORTHMAN

ALTHOUGH THE WORK OF THE KING AND HIS COURT CONTINUED APACE IN London, Northman had been allowed to return home to see his wife and son. He rode in anticipation of a night in his wife's arms and a bouncing baby boy in his arms, and he wasn't to be disappointed.

Although the day was grey and grim, they made fast progress on the hard packed ground, the horses as keen to be away from the confines of London as the riders.

He and Olaf laughed and joked throughout the journey. The land seemed to be at peace. No one met them with angry faces or any weapon they could hold, wondering whether they were Viking Raiders or Englishmen. No, the few faces they encountered were open and smiled, happy even though the winter was persisting in its length and coldness. The sun was a shadow of its summer self, there but barely.

Leofwine hadn't left the king's side, and Northman knew his mother would be disappointed that he'd not come. His excuse had been ethereal and insubstantial, but Northman hadn't been concerned or listening. He just wanted to be home, and now.

Riding into his father's forecourt, he was greeted by the most welcome sight a man could wish to see, Mildryth stood in the doorway, his son upon her hips, but more importantly, apparently very close to birthing another child for him.

His face sparkling with joy, he swept them both into his arms, his joy complete and his annoyance that his wife, brother and father had kept the news from him for so long, completely forgotten. What did it matter?

His son was a huge weight in his arms now, as he pulled at his father's hair and beard and grabbed his nose with a chubby hand. Northman smiled and laughed, overjoyed to see everyone within his family's home. His mother was sat before the fire, she and his sister working together on some intricate embroidery. His younger brothers, apart from Leofric who'd remained with his father, deep in conversation with the men of the household troop, and the assortment of dogs in various stages of rest and play about the fire.

He breathed deeply of the earthy smells of home, and he breathed deeply of Mildryth, safe in his arms, unlike her uncle, who still fought for his place at Swein's court.

And yet with all that joy, he felt the absence of Wulfstan and much later, when most were ensconced in their beds, he found himself sat on a stool before Wulfstan's chair. He'd not noticed anyone sitting within it all day and wondered if it was there as a reminder of Wulfstan only. Was it still referred to as his chair? Was it waiting for him in vain to return? Northman didn't know, but he hazarded a guess that he might be right to assume so.

It comforted him anyway, making it feel as though Wulfstan still sat and watched the household at work, offering words of encouragement or censure as he thought best. His father had, now that they'd reconciled, broken down in distress at the events of the day of Wulfstan's death and Northman had finally realised how totally bewildered he'd been by it all. It made him wonder how he'd feel on the day that his father died, an unpleasant thought and yet it had made him realise that he and his father shared a special bond, no matter their years apart. In a complicated way, it had brought them closer together.

With his mead cup in his hand, he stroked the side of the chair, enjoying the peace and quiet, aware he couldn't have quite the reunion with his wife he'd hoped for, and so doing his best to stay away from her bedside. The temptation would prove too much for him.

The silence made him a little whimsical, a little sad, lulling him to close his eyes and sleep as he was. It would be nice to sleep and wake in his childhood home. He'd hoped to leave Deerhurst and travel to his new lands, gifted by the previous king, but in light of the new king and his wife's pregnancy, he was reconsidering his decision. Perhaps he could stay here a little longer, let his mother pamper his wife and the new baby. Stay as far away from any of Eadric's adherents or Cnut's new ones in the former Mercian lands.

A smile graced his face. The thought of a little bit of peace cheered him.

A loud commotion outside startled him awake, his head bouncing on the arm of Wulfstan's chair with a great force that sent a shock of pain reverberating down the left side of his face.

Rising he started towards the door but was met half way by a flurry of chill air, blowing wind, and his brother Leofric.

He gasped out loud, his head throbbing painfully, his hand gingerly probing it for signs of injury.

He glanced at his brother in shock as his vision cleared.

"Swein's dead," Leofric announced.

# CAST OF CHARACTERS

## LEOFWINE'S FAMILY

Leofwine, Ealdorman of the Hwicce

Æthelflæd, his wife

Northman, his oldest son born 996

Leofric, his son born 998

Ealdgyth, his daughter born 1000

Godwine, his son born 1002

Eadwine, his son born 1006

## MISC

Burghed (Athelstan's warrior)

Thurcetel (Ulfcytel's ally)

Ordulf (East Anglian thegn)

Morcar (Mercian thegn)

Sigeforth (Mercian thegn)

## KING

Æthelred II

## THE ROYAL COURT

Athelstan (the king's son with his first wife)

Edmund (the king's son with his first wife)

Eadwig (the king's son with his first wife)

Emma (the king's second wife – renamed from Ælfgifu – mother of Edward and Alfred)

Wulfhilda – king's daughter – marries Ulfcytel of East Anglia in AD1004

## EALDORMAN EADRIC'S HOUSEHOLD

Edith, his wife. The king's daughter by his first wife

Æthelric (his father)

Brihtric (his brother)

Ælfric (his brother)

Goda (his brother)

Æthelwine, Æthelweard and Æthelmær (his brothers)

Mildryth (his niece)

## EALDORMEN

Ælfric of Hampshire (Kent, Sussex, Surrey and Berkshire and Wiltshire)

Leofwine (of the Hwicce)

Eadric (of the Mercians) (marries Edith in AD1007 – the king's daughter)

Ulfcytel of the East Angles (from 1004 marries Wulfhilda – the king's daughter)

Uhtred of Northumbria (marries Ælfgifu – the king's daughter)

## LEOFWINE'S HOUSEHOLD

Wulfstan (commended man and war leader)

Horic (commended man and second in command) his wife, Agata

Oscetel (part of the warband/household troop)

Lyfing (part of the warband/household troop)

Brithnoth (part of the warband/household troop)

Hammer (Leofwine's hound)

## RAIDERS AND KINGS

Thorkell the Tall, King Swein's commander

Hemming, Thorkell's brother

Cnut, King Swein's son

Olaf Tryggvason (King of Norway dies c.1000)

Swein (King of Denmark and Norway)

Harald his son and regent in Denmark

Duke Richard II of Normandy (Emma's brother)

# HISTORICAL INFORMATION

Slowly, but surely, the Earl of Mercia is stepping from almost total obscurity to some 'historically' attested facts. That these relate more to the other characters than Northman and Leofwine makes weaving their narrative both more intriguing and more difficult.

The Anglo Saxon Chronicle appears almost full for some of the years from AD1007-1013, well that is until you look for the detail needed to create a complete story.

So for instance in AD1007, £30000 was paid to the Raiders, and Eadric made ealdorman of Mercia.

In AD1008 the king decided to build his ships, one warship from every 310 hides and a helmet and mailcoat from every 8.

In AD1009 we are told of the ships being built and brought together at Sandwich and we're also told of the argument between Eadric's brother and Wulfnoth and of the total disarray that resulted. We're then told of Thorkell's arrival and the places they raided and the king's efforts to banish the Raiders.

In AD1010 we're told of Thorkell's attack on Ipswich and many other places.

In AD1011 we're told of the arrangement to pay the geld and the continuing raiding and of the archbishop's murder.

In AD1012 we're told of the archbishop's martyrdom and of the 45 ships switching their allegiance to Æthelred.

In AD1013 we're told of Swein's crowning and subsequent death.

The bias of the Anglo-Saxon Chronicle and its later compilation does mean that events that might have been of little significance are accorded greater merit than they might deserve. It's a fantastically intriguing puzzle to unravel.

To augment that knowledge, there's also the details of who was signing charters and when. This isn't a complete source as there are a few years when no charters are signed and there aren't actually all that many, only eight charters remain in total from 1007, 1009, 1012 and 1013. Once more, a tantalising glimpse, nothing more.

One of the greatest historians of the Anglo-Saxon period has commented that Eadric gets blamed for everything, almost regardless of whether it was his fault or not, and yet, Æthelred still has the name, the Unready, a play on his name Æthelred which means 'wise counsel' while 'Unraed' means 'no counsel' but has come down to us as Unready. Were both men incompetent? It's not that easy to decide, and one thing's for sure, they both ruled during years when the English were almost beleaguered by the Raiders.

As to how many ships might have been raised if one was paid for by every three hundred and ten hides, well, it's actually not that easy to work out, and I hope that someone can give me an answer. As famous as Domesday Book is, I can't yet find the details of how many hides were assessed in total (I think mainly because no historian will fully commit). The earlier source, the Tribal Hideage, again not an easy source, seems to imply there were 244000 hides which would have made over 800 ships possible. I think a slightly fuzzier interpretation is better!

# ABOUT THE AUTHOR

I'm an author of historical fiction (Early English, Vikings and the British Isles as a whole before the Norman Conquest) and fantasy (Viking age/dragon-themed), born in the old Mercian kingdom at some point since AD1066. I like to write. You've been warned! Find me at mjporterauthor.com. mjporterauthor.blog and @coloursofunison on twitter. I have a monthly newsletter, which can be joined via my website. Once signed up, readers can opt into a weekly email reminder containing special offers.

facebook.com/mjporter
twitter.com/coloursofunison
instagram.com/m_j_porter
bookbub.com/authors/mj-porter
patreon.com/MJPorter
tiktok.com/@mjporterauthor
amazon.com/MJ-Porter/e/B006N8K6X4

# BOOKS BY M J PORTER (IN SERIES READING ORDER)

<u>Gods and Kings Series (seventh century Britain)</u>

Pagan Warrior

Pagan King

Warrior King

<u>The Eagle of Mercia Chronicles</u>

Son of Mercia

Wolf of Mercia

Warrior of Mercia

Enemy of Mercia

Protector of Mercia

<u>The Ninth Century</u>

Coelwulf's Company, Tales from Before The Last King

The Last King

The Last Warrior

The Last Horse

The Last Enemy

The Last Sword

The Last Shield

The Last Seven

<u>The Tenth Century</u>

The Lady of Mercia's Daughter

A Conspiracy of Kings

Kingmaker

The King's Daughters

The Brunanburh Series

King of Kings

Kings of War

The Mercian Brexit (can be read as a prequel to The First Queen of England)

The First Queen of England (can be read as a prequel to The Earls of Mercia)

The First Queen of England Part 2

The First Queen of England Part 3

The King's Mother (can be read as a sequel to The First Queen, or a prequel to The Earls of Mercia)

The Queen Dowager

Once A Queen

The Earls of Mercia

The Earl of Mercia's Father

The Danish King's Enemy

Swein: The Danish King

Northman Part 1

Northman Part 2

Cnut: The Conqueror

Wulfstan: An Anglo-Saxon Thegn

The King's Earl

The Earl of Mercia

The English Earl

The Earl's King

Viking King

The English King

The King's Brother

Lady Estrid: A novel of Eleventh-Century Denmark (related to the Earls of Mercia series)

**Fantasy**

The Dragon of Unison (fantasy based on Viking Age Iceland)

Hidden Dragon

Dragon Gone

Dragon Alone

Dragon Ally

Dragon Lost

Dragon Bond

As JE Porter

The Innkeeper

**20th Century murder-mystery**

Cragside – a 1930s mystery

The Erdington Mysteries

The Custard Corpses

The Automobile Assassination

Made in United States
North Haven, CT
23 August 2023

40673434R00202